# LynDee Walker

# THE
# PASTOR'S
# WIFE

bookouture

Published by Bookouture in 2025

An imprint of Storyfire Ltd.
Carmelite House
50 Victoria Embankment
London EC4Y 0DZ

www.bookouture.com

The authorised representative in the EEA is Hachette Ireland
8 Castlecourt Centre
Dublin 15 D15 XTP3
Ireland
(email: info@hbgi.ie)

Copyright © LynDee Walker, 2025

LynDee Walker has asserted her right to be identified as the author of this work.

All rights reserved. No part of this publication may be reproduced, stored in any retrieval system, or transmitted, in any form or by any means, electronic, mechanical, photocopying, recording or otherwise, without the prior written permission of the publishers.

ISBN: 978-1-83618-909-1
eBook ISBN: 978-1-83618-906-0

This book is a work of fiction. Names, characters, businesses, organizations, places and events other than those clearly in the public domain, are either the product of the author's imagination or are used fictitiously. Any resemblance to actual persons, living or dead, events or locales is entirely coincidental.

# THE PASTOR'S WIFE

*For my incredible family, with all my love. Thanks for believing in me when I don't, and for making my life such a wonderful one to live.*

# PROLOGUE

*November*

I never meant for anybody to get hurt.

Not that my intention when I walked into this fleabag motel room matters one diddly damn. Nobody is going to believe me. Standing here looking around at the evidence, I'm not even sure I believe myself.

Any sane person would call the police right this second. But I don't reach for the phone. I am perfectly sane, but I'm not stupid. I've worked hard to build this life—tucked away in this postcard-perfect town so far from the mess that sent me running here I generally pretend everything before was a bad dream. Looking around, I realize how foolish that was. The past always has legs that can chase you. Mine has teeth that could eat me alive.

Has it finally caught up with me?

I check the room again. It's dark—musty orange drapes drawn tight—and bare aside from the standard motel furniture that seems to populate places like this one, no matter where they are or how long they've been there.

It could be anywhere, a thing I loved about this place. Anywhere is closer to nowhere than people like to think, which works for people who need to disappear.

I hadn't been sure what I was looking for when I walked in here, but I'd found trouble—and a large body that looked smaller crumpled on the mottled brown carpet.

I kneel and check carefully. No blood.

I hadn't touched anything. No prints.

The girl won't be a problem, if I can even find her. The question is, did anyone see me?

I know the hills outside have eyes.

Sunday morning, though... might just be my saving grace. I have no idea if it's been ten minutes or a week since I came in here, but the low light wrestling its way around the edges of the ratty orange drapes says it's still early. This entire town sleeps until it's time to get ready for church on Sundays—country folks take that whole "day of rest" business to heart.

All that matters is what they can prove—that might be the one useful thing my daddy taught me. And I can maybe keep anyone from proving I was ever even here. Stay settled in the quiet, easy life I found for myself when I came to this no name, nowhere mountain town.

Where I'd started over. Where I fit in. Where, by the grace of God, I had finally made a true friend.

The thought of everything I have to lose now makes my stomach seize up with dread, the panic trying to overwhelm me again. I take another deep breath, drawing resolve in with the air. I just have to get this perfectly, exactly right, then. There's no other option.

*She* cannot ever know I was here. None of this is my fault.

Eyes on the heap in the floor, I step carefully backward, flipping up the hood on my new First Baptist Fall Festival sweatshirt before I open the door. We handed out enough to outfit the whole town Friday night, so as long as my face is hidden, I could be anyone.

Outside, I suck fresh, cool air into my lungs as the high edges of the Ozarks to the east go crimson, the sun blazing up over the jewel-toned treetops like fire is consuming the mountain, rustling leaves the only thing breaking the silence. Every room is dark, the parking lot nearly empty, even the highway quiet.

Pulling my sleeves down far enough to cover my orange and white Fall Festival manicure, I lock the door, wiping the knob and sliding the key back into my pocket.

I've melted into the trees behind the building in less than a minute, using their cover to hurry all the way back to my car. I whisper a prayer, and the car starts on the first try.

Thank you, Jesus.

I drive through silent, sleepy streets, looking for any sign of life or movement and working out a plan in my head.

I can find the truth.

I might even end up the damn heroine of this story. Wouldn't that be something?

Back in my room, I nod at my reflection in the mirror: my bleary eyes are hollow from lack of sleep, my high cheekbones flushed from stress—but I'm focused on my blonde hair, smoothed into a tight ponytail, which makes it less likely any was left behind.

As I strip off my sweater and my faded jeans and stuff them into the wood stove, a certainty settles heavy in my chest that I've only ever felt one other time—a month before I came here.

Whatever happened back there, it was evil. And I'm not about to let evil take anything else from me.

# PART ONE
NEW GIRLS IN TOWN

# ONE

## MARTHA

*March—Eight Months Earlier*

"Not here. Please, Jesus, not now." I yanked frantically back on the gearshift of my ancient Civic, my left foot pressing the clutch down so hard I was afraid it might bust right through the rusty spot in the floorboard.

In the middle of a picturesque early spring afternoon on Elias Lane, I was supposed to fade into the background. Be silent. Go unnoticed.

Not have my rotting old dragon of a car split the lilting silence with a metal-on-metal shriek of protest that probably rattled windows in the stately homes on either side of me before it slipped into second gear.

I mean, I guess at least she didn't stall, though right then I wasn't sure which was worse. I wanted to wriggle under the seat and stay there, but I sighed instead, giving her just enough gas to get up the hill.

To my left, two women from the First Baptist Ladies' Auxiliary frowned from the sidewalk and whispered to each other, quickening their pace as they herded their children past me like being poor—or maybe just being nobody—was catching.

I barely noticed it anymore, not that it ever bothered me much in the first place. Being nobody from nowhere was kind of why I came here. And if I had to disappear, I'd stumbled on a lovely place to do it.

Whitney Falls was almost too pretty to be real, like a fairy waved a magic wand over one of them Norman Rockwell paintings and nestled it in a valley surrounded by the prettiest country God ever created. In mid-March, the trees downright glowed with neon green baby leaves, while bright, ragged new petal edges peeped out of fat, round buds on crepe myrtles and the tulips lining every mulched bed on Elias Lane showed their soft colors through green tips, ready to explode into a ground-dwelling rainbow any minute.

I'd come across the village entirely by accident, following a road so narrow I never found a place to turn around after I misread a snow-covered sign on my way to Malvern. Seeing the town for the first time from the mountain, Christmas lights shining bright colors through the snow, I couldn't resist driving in. And once I'd found my way to Elias Lane that night, I'd just stopped to stare, pressing my nose against the cold glass of the car windows and spinning fantasies about the last-minute gift wrapping and cookie baking that must be happening in such beautiful homes. In about five minutes, I'd decided the Good Lord led me here, and so here I was, fighting with my stick shift on a gray March afternoon.

Ignoring the sidewalk moms, I watched the massive houses roll by, their manicured winter fescue lawns ready for spring to arrive. I didn't need to peer at the numbers on the mailboxes to know which one I was looking for: number eighteen sat directly across from the First Baptist Church, which cast a long shadow from the corner of Elias and Maple in the late afternoon sunlight. The silhouette of the steeple's point skewered the wide front porch and stabbed straight into the Easter wreath on the door like a sword to the throat of the grand Victorian.

I shook my head at the thought—as if even a hint of darkness would dare to disturb life on Elias Lane. The wide, tree-lined boulevard was the beating heart of Whitney Falls, its towering homes as perfect and pretty as the folks who lived in them.

Or so I thought.

I was just turning into the driveway when an angry scream completely trashed my afternoon.

At first I assumed it came from the car—I jammed the clutch in and knocked the shift stick into neutral to shut it up, but the howl dragged on. A flicker in the mirror caught my eye, and I spotted Ruthie Tomlinson charging in my direction, mouth wide and hands balled into fists at her sides.

Nobody in Whitney Falls liked me much, really, but most folks just ignored me, which was fine by me. Ruthie—well, she'd made it her mission in life to make sure I knew how unwelcome I was here. The last thing I wanted was drama with her in the pastor's front yard.

I was so busy trying to get myself out of her line of fire that I didn't realize my foot was on the gas—not the brake—until it was too late.

Like in one of them slow motion scenes in movies, I watched helplessly as my battered old Civic rammed right into the back end of a shiny black and chrome Grand Wagoneer with woodgrain running up the sides of the doors. I closed my eyes when the massive Jeep's front end jumped forward into the closed garage door, just as my head bounced off the steering wheel.

I didn't pass out or anything, but the skin at my hairline burned as it busted open, and the warm pitter-pat of droplets landing on my hand told me the cut wasn't a small one.

I should've parked on the street. Any street but this one would've done, really. But I didn't have time for hindsight or self-pity—Ruthie tapped on the window with a glare on her face that could've wilted a cactus, and I had to figure out how to get out of here and never be seen again, since I'd just wrecked a very fancy car and done damage to a beautiful historic home, all in less than a minute.

To think, I went there trying to be helpful.

You might say I've always had a gift for finding trouble. I've just never been able to figure out how to send that sort of gift back.

I took two deep breaths and waited for my eyes to stop looking like I was seeing everything through swirling water before I opened the car door. I couldn't think about my car or the Jeep or the garage door right then—the panic rising in my chest would flat suffocate my ability to think, and I still had a job to do. The cars would still be in the same shape in a few minutes when the groceries had been delivered, and at least the pastor's beloved rum raisin ice cream wouldn't melt.

Ruthie would gloat all the way to the door no doubt, but I wasn't afraid of Ruthie Tomlinson. She just thought I was.

"Excuse me," I muttered when she wouldn't move to let me out of the car.

She folded her arms across her nearly flat chest and slowly stepped back over the trailing roots of a massive oak that was just starting to sprout copper-colored baby leaves.

I felt the burn of Ruthie's gaze nearly as acutely as the sting of the bleeding cut on my head, but I refused to meet her eyes, keeping my head down as I hurried to the back of the car to get the grocery bags.

Balancing the rear hatchback on my right shoulder blade because the hydraulic lift hinges had failed long before my time, I scooped a paper grocery sack into each arm, closing my hands around a third bag before I started to back up. I had everything balanced pretty good and was trying to duck out from under the hatch door when Ruthie's voice startled me again.

"You really think you're special, don't you?" she barked.

I would've laughed, because if anybody walking God's Earth ever knew just how unimportant they were, it was me.

The problem was, I jumped when she spoke, and the liftgate's latch slammed down into my head, warm liquid trickling fast through my hair and down my neck this time. I also only managed to hang onto one bag of groceries, gasping as the other two thudded to the driveway in a spectacular crash of breaking glass and cracking eggs.

Well, sure. Ruthie's bad timing rivaled my bad luck. Combined, they left me too busy bleeding to pay her much mind.

Not that she let my indifference deter her. As I stared at the ruined bags of groceries, their total cost flashing in my head like a neon sign, I had to count my breaths to keep panic at bay. I could never replace all that and be able to eat myself next week on what I made at the Pick and Go. Before I could figure out what to do, Ruthie sidled up so close I could feel her breath on my ear.

"What business do you think you've got letting that rust bucket spew oil all over my road?" she hissed. Blinking back tears, I followed her gaze in a hopscotch over fresh fluid spots all the way back down Elias Lane. I couldn't even pretend to be surprised. Eighty-seven dollars' worth of ruined groceries, and now the dragon was going to need another quart of oil, too. All because Ruthie couldn't pass up an opportunity to remind me that she'd stepped in more valuable things than me.

"I'm sorry," I muttered, a tear slipping through my lashes as my head began to throb.

Ruthie didn't like me because her husband Sam, who happened to be my boss, seemed to like me a little too much. Not that I invited the attention—I didn't have money for luxures like makeup, and every piece of clothing I owned was baggy and dated. But I had the benefit of youth where hers was fading: it didn't take makeup for people to notice my high cheekbones, full lips, and wide eyes, and my boobs stayed big no matter how much weight the rest of me lost, giving me the kind of top-heavy figure you usually only see on Barbie dolls.

"My momma always said trash brings trash along with it. Not that anybody's going to care a lick about oil when they see the damage you've caused with your reckless operation of this sorry excuse for a vehicle." She looked pointedly toward the pastor's house. I'd never wished so hard that the ground would open up and swallow me whole—and that's saying something.

"Yes, ma'am," I said through gritted teeth. I was not giving Ruthie the satisfaction of bawling, no matter how much my head felt like it was on fire or how humiliated I was.

I went to the passenger side of the car, pulling a small canvas bag from behind the seat to gather what could be salvaged from the bags I'd dropped. Ruthie drew back one foot and drove her beige and navy duck boot into my hip, sending me sprawling, a broken chunk of pasta jar eating into my knee.

I swallowed hard, gazing up at Ruthie. Her face, usually decently pretty for her age, twisted into a scathing glare, the gleam in her hazel eyes daring me to stand up for myself.

You know the type. Ruthie Tomlinson was nothing but a grown-up mean girl, a bully who'd found an easy target in an outsider.

A bully who had no idea who she was picking on.

I pulled in a slow breath, because that was the whole point, of course: she didn't know me as anything but a mousy grocery cashier who wasn't from here. And she never could.

"You lost your balance," she sneered when I dropped my defeated gaze back to the mess.

"Don't you have something better to do?" I muttered,

picking up a green paper crate of strawberries that was still covered with plastic wrap.

"I know you can't possibly be talking to me," Ruthie said, squatting next to me and leaning in but not bothering to lower her volume. "You are nothing but trash, plain and simple. Your whole life is about as worthless as yesterday's dog shit, Martha, no matter how some of the men around here look a—"

"That will be enough out of you, Mrs. Tomlinson." Another voice, melodic as wind chimes with an icy edge that could've cut glass, smothered the last of Ruthie's bile. "And you can replace these groceries tomorrow, just leave them on the porch."

Ruthie shot straight up and sucked in a gasp so fast she choked on her own spit, staggering backward as she coughed. I barely felt the burning gashes on my scalp as I turned my head to watch her retreat—five yards away, she barked a gurgling sound like the chilly words had punched her clean in the throat before she turned and took off into the red brick Georgian house that sat four lots up from the church.

There was only one woman in Whitney Falls who could put the fear of God into Ruthie Tomlinson. I turned back just as she spoke again.

"My stars, honey, you're bleeding!" Mary McClatchy's pretty brown leather flats skittered softly on the blacktop as she hurried toward me. I looked up at the pastor's wife and felt my eyes fill again as I pointed at the crunched cars, then waved my hands over her destroyed groceries.

"I can't believe I've caused so much trouble. I'm so sorry, ma'am." I forced the words out around the dread curdling in my throat. Mrs. McClatchy hadn't much noticed me before, but I had sure noticed her: with her collarbone-length blonde curls and eyes so blue they bordered on violet, Mrs. McClatchy was the closest thing I'd ever seen to an angel. Or maybe even a beauty queen. The thought of having her move from the group of townsfolk who ignored me to the ones who hated me made me sadder than I would've thought possible just a half hour earlier when I was packing her grocery order for delivery.

Not that the Whitney Falls Pick and Go delivers, mind you. This was a special favor for the pastor that wasn't usually my job, but I'd jumped at the chance to help out when asked. I loved Elias Lane, I just never had a reason to be there except on Sunday mornings.

Before I could get my mouth open to say anything else, Mrs. McClatchy had cast an unworried glance at the damage to her Grand Wagoneer, shrugged, and scooped the ruined grocery bags and their contents into the canvas sack and hefted it, closing cool, pale fingers lightly around my arm to help me stand before she grabbed the unharmed paper bag and shoved it into my arms.

"I'm not at all sure what you think you're apologizing for, but I'd like you to explain it to me over a glass of iced tea after I look at those lacerations on your head." Her smile was bright and curious, the words dripping with warmth nobody had directed my way in longer than I cared to admit. "You're okay to bring that bag, aren't you?"

She set off across the yard and was nearly to the steps before I could process what she'd said. Mary McClatchy, wife of Pastor Tim McClatchy, first lady of the First Baptist Church and President of the First Baptist Ladies' Auxiliary... was inviting me into her house?

I didn't know much that didn't have to do with numbers or bad memories, but I knew this in my bones: I had no business in a palace like the McClatchy home. I stood there clutching the brown paper grocery bag, grateful she'd given me a useful chore, but also wishing she'd just taken it herself so I could leave.

Mrs. McClatchy paused on the wide porch and looked back, smiling and shaking her head as she waved. "Come on, hon. I don't bite."

It wasn't her I was worried about. I wasn't the sort of person

Mary McClatchy could keep company with, and even if she was too perfect and too new here to know that, I knew it. I opened my mouth to explain, but the words wouldn't come out.

My feet, though—they didn't have any trouble with being stuck right then. They hurried up the sidewalk no matter how hard I tried to turn around, beckoned by the promise of belonging, even if only for a few minutes.

# TWO

## MARTHA

*March*

Mary McClatchy was a bonafide angel.

I decided that about forty seconds after she waved me inside the fancy front hall of her home, the crown jewel of Elias Lane. She set my canvas bag on a round marble table in the center of the space, ignoring the liquid seeping out thanks to the shattered jars, and held up one finger as she hurried to a closet and returned with peroxide and ointment.

Looking up at me, she laughed and gestured to the height difference. "This is probably going to make it challenging for me to patch up your head."

I put the sack of unspoiled groceries on the table next to the mixed bag she had carried in and reached behind my head, afraid I was about to drip blood all over her shiny white marble floor after I had just wrecked her car and dented her house. "I'm sorry, ma'am," I stammered. "I'm really okay, I can go, and if you'll let them know what was broken I can pay to replace the groceries and your regular person will bring them. About the car—"

Mrs. McClatchy's pretty rose lips twisted into a scowl. "First of all, you are bleeding. In this house, bleeding does not equate to 'fine.' Second, why in the name of all that is holy would you ask if you can pay for a ruined bag of groceries that someone else ruined? Or damage to my car that someone else caused?"

I found out the hard way that scrunching up my forehead in confusion hurt the cut at my hairline, starting up the bleeding again. "Ma'am, I was driving my car when it hit yours. I pressed the wrong pedal on accident." I stared at my stained white sneakers, my pinky toe peeking out of a small hole in the left one. The shoes looked twice as dirty against her gleaming marble as they did on the concrete floor at the Pick and Go.

Why didn't she see that I wasn't supposed to be here?

"Well now, that's like saying God was responsible for the destruction of Eden because he put the apple tree there in the first place." The scowl dissolved into a smile as I pondered that. "I saw—and heard—everything from that window before I went outside. Ruthie Tomlinson was at fault, not you." She laid her hands on my shoulders and stared into my eyes. "Now, come right into the kitchen and sit on a stool so I can reach to see what happened to you." She picked up the oozing canvas bag and left again, either not noticing or not caring that Prego/egg/pickle juice goo dripped onto the floor in her wake.

"It's my own dumb bad luck," I said as I followed her with the paper grocery bag, my feet moving more according to her instruction than mine. "I smashed my forehead into the steering wheel when I hit your car, and then I jumped when Mrs. Tomlinson spoke to me while the hatch was open and it slammed down and caught me somehow. Maybe in my hair? I'm not sure."

Mrs. McClatchy pointed to a sleek gray velvet upholstered barstool at the high counter that separated the kitchen from the dining nook in the nearby bay window. "Sit," she commanded, putting the leaky canvas grocery bag in the sink and gathering a bowl of water, three clean white kitchen towels, and a... was that a shot of bourbon?

Hurrying around the end of the island, she handed me the shot glass and dipped one of the towels into the water, scooting behind me and moving my hair gently. I heard her breath go in sharply and closed my eyes. "Drink that, all at once," she said.

I hadn't had a drink in months. I didn't want the bourbon that was burning my nose hairs from half a foot away. But I couldn't make the word "no" come out of my face directed at the pastor's wife, either, so I downed the whiskey, familiar warmth ebbing outward from my throat and belly until I was a little floaty and a lot cozy. I frowned. I didn't want to feel cozy, not like this. I wanted my 120-day chip. Which I reckoned I ought to get, still. I mean, I didn't go looking for the whiskey—it came looking for me.

"Your house looks like a magazine," I blurted as Mrs. McClatchy started poking at the back of my head with a towel.

"Thank you," she said, tension in the words that made me worry if she was queasy by nature. If she wasn't, I didn't want to know what my head looked like. "I think this is my favorite place we've ever lived."

I winced as she hit a particularly sensitive spot, and she dipped the towel—no longer gleaming white—into the water again. Blood seeped out, curling into red strings in the clear water against the blue ceramic bowl.

I watched it stretch and roll like it came from someone else as the water sloshed gently. She went back to work on the cut, muttering a couple of things I was pretty sure the bourbon made me hear wrong, because Mary McClatchy probably didn't even know any vulgar words.

Minutes ticked by, and the water in the blue bowl went from pink to red as she worked. I've never minded silence, so I just let it stretch as long as it could.

"I think this is clean now, but I need to let it dry a little," she said, stepping in front of me and tipping my chin up so she could see the cut on my forehead. She smiled when her impossibly blue eyes met mine. "This one won't hurt nearly as much. You doing okay?"

I nodded and she patted my shoulder and picked up the last towel.

Mrs. McClatchy patched the cut on my forehead with butterfly tape and crouched to clean up the gash on my knee from the broken glass, fitting a large Band-Aid over it as she shook her head. "I am so sorry this happened to you."

I snorted, then clapped one hand over my mouth. That bourbon was making me entirely too comfortable here. I cleared my throat. "I've had worse. Thank you again for your help, you're very kind."

She smiled, standing and moving behind me again to look at the cut on the back of my head. "I really don't want to have to cut your hair away from this, it'll never grow back right," she fretted. "But I can't stick a bandage to this gorgeous thick hair of yours, either."

"Is it that bad?" I asked, my eyes popping wide and my hands trying reflexively to go to the back of my head.

Mrs. McClatchy pushed them away. "Don't touch, I've just gotten it clean." She stepped back into my line of sight to get the peroxide. "I think it will be okay if we can disinfect it good and keep some antibiotics on it. Is there anyone at home who can help you with applying the ointment?"

I started to shake my head and stopped for fear I'd make my hair move. "No, ma'am."

"Well then I'll just have to do it." She flashed a grin as bright as the white stone counters. "Might as well use my training for something."

"Training?" The bourbon had my head feeling fuzzy. It didn't help that I hadn't eaten anything all day—tomorrow was payday and there was only enough peanut butter and bread left for one sandwich, so I was saving it for supper.

"I went to nursing school." Mrs. McClatchy waved one hand like that was something everyone did. "A hundred years ago."

"Everywhere could use more nurses," I said. "I saw something about that on TV. And around here especially—you practically have to be dying to get in to see the doctor without waiting a week. I heard someone say that just the other day."

"Oh, I couldn't," she said. "I've never worked, I met Tim right before I graduated and fell in love, and most folks look down on the pastor's wife having a job outside the church and home. But I stay plenty busy, and I always have time to help out a friend." She followed that last part with the kindest smile I've ever seen.

Friend. I blinked, fear sweeping some of the whiskey fuzz from my brain.

"Mrs. McClatchy, you are the nicest person I've met in... maybe my whole life," I said, turning the stool so I could stand. "But I can't take up any more of your day. I wouldn't want to bother you."

She put one hand on my shoulder before I could get up, her grip stronger than I would've thought for a lady her size. "That will be enough of that 'Mrs. McClatchy' nonsense," she said. "Tim's mother is Mrs. McClatchy, and she is... well. I try to be a good Christian every day, so perhaps I won't say. But I'm Mary. Just Mary. And I still need to disinfect this and put some medicine on it, if you'll sit still for just a couple more minutes." She picked up the peroxide and frowned. "This will probably sting. But I can't give you more Bourbon and let you drive home."

I nodded, hoping I didn't jostle my hair and not sure what to do with this situation. She'd asked me to call her Mary and sort of roundaboutly called me her friend in the span of a few seconds. Part of me wanted to bask in the glow of that, but the bigger, more practical part knew I needed to hightail it back to the shadows where I belonged.

I didn't move.

She was right—the peroxide stung like a whole nest of mad yellowjackets, but I was so busy trying to devise an exit strategy for the nicest house I'd ever been invited into that I barely noticed.

"Oh, I'm so glad that wasn't as bad as I thought." Mary—no, Mrs. McClatchy—patted my shoulder and traded the peroxide bottle for the ointment tube.

A few more dabs later, she put both back on the counter and washed her hands before she pulled a pitcher of iced tea from the fridge and filled two glasses. "You shouldn't wash your hair for a couple of days, and try to sleep on your side or your stomach tonight since I can't really cover that because of your hair." She waved for me to follow her out to the porch and pointed me to a rocker as she put the tea glasses on the low table and plugged in a string of warm white fairy lights.

"I love this porch," she said as she sat down on a wide wood swing that overflowed with bright pillows in pinks and yellows. "The swing and the twinkle lights and the sunsets make it feel like my own little slice of heaven."

I nodded, my eyes on my car. You couldn't even tell I had hit Mary's SUV because my front end had already been so scratched and dinged up. It didn't belong on Elias Lane, though, any more than I belonged on this porch—but there it sat, right in the pastor's driveway for everyone to see, probably still dripping the oil that Ruthie had been so mad about. I should go.

"Now, then. You'll come back tomorrow about this time and I'll check that and reapply the medicine," Mary said, not as a question but an order.

"Yes, ma'am." I blurted, before I shook my head. "Mrs. Mc—"

"Mary." Her voice was firm as she reached over and

squeezed my hand. "I'm Mary. And you're Martha, right?" She read it off my Pick and Go name tag.

I was, thanks to her husband. The McClatchys' very first Sunday in Whitney Falls had been my third, and there'd been a welcome potluck for them at the church. I'd made my granny's burrito casserole and joined, though I was never entirely sure why I felt so compelled to go. Some days I thought it'd be better if I hadn't, but regrets are like gut worms—they'll eat you from the inside out if you let them grow big enough. Best I could tell, I was just supposed to be there. Baking a burrito casserole on the half-rusted charcoal grill out behind the motel on Route 5 that I called home hadn't been easy, but I'd managed.

The Pick and Go manager hadn't bothered to ask my name those first couple of weeks—I didn't even have to fill out an application there. He'd stared at my chest for a five-sentence conversation, then asked me some second-grade math questions and held my hand too long when he shook it, and I had a job—one that paid me every Friday in cash because the couple who owned the store didn't believe in taxes. So that Sunday when I slid into the church potluck, I didn't know a soul, and Pastor Tim took one bite of granny's casserole and grinned at me and said, "Well, you're just a regular Martha now, aren't you?" on account of that pretty blonde lady on TV who does the cooking and the crafts. I'd laughed and said it was my name, really, because it was as good as any, and I thought cooking and making things and ringing up people's groceries sounded like a nice life.

Sitting on Pastor Tim's porch four months later, I just nodded at his beautiful wife, stricken by the kindness shining in her blue eyes. I couldn't remember the last time anyone was kind to me.

"I'm Martha," I confirmed.

She squeezed my hand again. "Martha and Mary." She nodded like she liked the sound of it. "We're going to be good friends, I can tell."

I nodded again, unable to recall why that wasn't a good idea while Mary held onto my hand, her fingertips pressing into mine as her smile drooped into a small frown for a flash so fleeting I wasn't sure I hadn't imagined it. "I haven't made many friends here yet."

She'd barely been here three months, but I was kind of shocked, anyway. Who in their right mind wouldn't want to be instant friends with an angel like Mary McClatchy?

"Me, either," I said before I could stop myself.

"See, I told you." Mary clapped her hands, delight plain on her pretty face. "I'm a master at reading people." She folded her legs under her and tucked her bare toes under a pink pillow shaped like a tulip. "I like you, Martha. And I'm having the hardest time figuring out why Ruthie Tomlinson doesn't. Can you tell me what happened there?"

"I guess so," I said, fidgeting with my glass.

Mary sipped her tea and settled back into the cushions. "Don't leave anything out."

# THREE

## MARY

*January—Two months earlier*
*The McClatchys' first Sunday in Whitney Falls*

"Why do you always do this, Mary?" Tim straightened his tie and flashed his best toothpaste-commercial smile—that's not a figure of speech, he really was in a toothpaste commercial once—in the mirror hanging over his bathroom sink. "They're going to love you. You're the pastor's wife. You're beautiful, you're well spoken and well dressed. They always love you."

No, they love you. They tolerate me. I didn't bother to say the words, rooting around in a cardboard box I hadn't had time to empty in the three days we'd lived here until I found a clean washcloth. We'd had that same argument in the last four new bathrooms in new towns before the first Sunday service at a new church. Not that Pastor Tim McClatchy and his perfect wife argued—no, if you asked Tim, we'd had the same "discussion" four times already. And I could tell by the slight edge to his tone and the way he leaned close to the mirror to fuss with his thick, just-unruly-enough-to-be-handsome chestnut hair that he had no interest in a fifth.

"You're right," I put one hand on his shoulder and peered around an impressive bicep, encased in a freshly pressed Oxford shirt, to meet his eyes in the rimless oval mirror hanging from brass attachments on a white tile wall. "As usual."

He laughed the big laugh that had drawn my eyes to him that very first day at the music festival. A decade and a half later, that laugh was still one of my favorite things about Tim. He didn't chuckle or guffaw—when Tim laughed, it was a whole body event: his head back, eyes closed, Adam's apple bobbing, shoulders and belly shaking. Sometimes he even slapped a thigh or stomped a foot. Not that morning, but I wasn't any less thrilled to be the cause of his delight.

My mother had told me the night before our wedding that someday, I'd stop feeling sparks skate up my arm when Tim touched me, or butterflies batting around my middle when he laughed.

I didn't know when that day would come, but we weren't there yet. He might not touch me as often these days, but when he did there was no shortage of sparks. The only problem we had in the bedroom was that sometimes those sparks didn't exactly start a fire for Tim, and he refused to ask a doctor for the little blue pills I'd heard other ladies whisper about. He said he was too young and it was humiliating. I couldn't get past the idea that he was lying because he knew it wouldn't matter if he took them—that somehow what he called his "little problem" was my fault, and he didn't want to tell me. I leaned into the mirror, scrutinizing my face for signs of crow's feet or frown lines. None. Maybe it wasn't my face, though—it wasn't like it happened every time.

Tim bumped my shoulder with his elbow and winked, drawing my attention back to the here and now. Whitney Falls. New church. First sermon. My job this morning was to pump up his ego, which meant he wasn't wrong about anything. Just like I'd said a second ago.

"Can I get that in a signed statement?" he teased. "We'll ask if anyone in the congregation is a notary." He shrugged into his jacket and spun on the heel of one perfectly polished wingtip, catching me around the waist and pulling me into a hug before I could pretend to be indignant. I almost never told my husband he was wrong about anything—I might not be the badass ER nurse I'd wanted to be when I met him, but I had given everything I had to being a darned good pastor's wife.

While the women at the other churches we'd led might have disagreed, I knew Tim thought I'd succeeded. And he was all that mattered to me. He was enough.

I told myself that a lot as the years—and the new towns and new faces—blurred by.

As I buried my face in the lapel of his favorite Armani suit jacket and breathed in the comfort of his smell—Dior cologne mixed with amber and leather Dove deodorant and that magical hint of spice that didn't come from either, but somehow was always there, making him smell like home—I felt my shoulders relax under his touch.

"There now." He pushed me back slightly and used two fingers to raise my chin, closing his lips over mine in a kiss that made my knees wobble while somehow not smudging my lipstick a bit. He called it his Sunday morning special.

Opening the aquamarine eyes that had stolen my heart by the time the second band took the stage at that long-ago music festival, he touched the tip of my nose.

"You are always too hard on yourself, and too slow to trust people, love. Nobody but the good Lord is always right. Not even me." He winked, drawing a small smile from me. "But I know this will go better if you give them a chance to love you instead of just assuming they won't."

He still had it: the same charm that had pulled me to him that first evening, rolling off him in waves until it seemed like we were the only two people in the world, let alone in that dinky little amphitheater; the charisma that made him the instant darling of every church, every town, every room he ever walked into. I couldn't tell you the name of a single act that played at the concert where we'd met, but I remembered swaying to decent attempts at covers of popular songs as electricity crackled in the warm summer night air between me and the tall, dark-haired guy in the khaki shorts and blue polo. We never agreed on who saw who first, but I could close my eyes—or look into his—and still feel like the luckiest girl in the world when Tim McClatchy flirted with me. The first night, I'd seen a glint of determination and a whole lot of mischief in those striking eyes after each trip he'd made to the ice cream truck parked up at the road after he'd sworn he could guess my favorite treat and wouldn't allow any hints. It took him five times up the hill and back to pick the pink screwball, and he'd pumped one fist in the air like he'd just won a trophy when I'd told him he was right that time as I opened my ice cream.

"What even is that stuff?" he'd asked, clearly delighted as he watched me eat it with the little wood tongue depressor masquerading as a spoon that always came with them. "Is it strawberry?"

"Nope. It's..." I'd shrugged. "It's pink. If that can be considered a flavor. It tastes good."

He'd leaned in close. "I believe that. Your lips are pink and I bet I've never tasted anything better."

That whispered line, his breath warm on my cheek—that was it for me, right there in front of God and everybody. My knees turned to water, and Tim McClatchy had owned me body and soul every day since. Which was why I had to make things work here. I had to. I owed him that.

The thought pulled me from warm, electric summer memories back to the cold reality of our first Sunday morning in Whitney Falls, where fear and what-ifs made panic well in my chest.

"But Carol and Debbie—" I began, and he put one finger over my lips, laughing again when I pulled my head back and pretended to bite it.

"Carol and Debbie and all the rest are the past. They aren't Whitney Falls. The Lord brought us here, and he will provide. Maybe not everything we want, but certainly what we need. We just have to believe."

I nodded.

I just had to believe. Harder. Better. I was good at that after so many years with Tim.

And maybe he was right. Just because we'd found despair and disaster before didn't mean that would happen here.

I moved him gently aside and turned back to the mirror as the alarm on his watch that meant it was time to walk across the street to the First Baptist Church sounded. I smoothed my cream wool slacks and checked my hair and lipstick.

"Still as beautiful as the girl who sang along to those awful Springsteen covers," Tim said, resting his chin on top of my head.

"Love truly is blind. Or maybe it just has a good filter." I pulled in a deep breath. "Okay, Pastor. Let's go meet the congregation."

"The town, you mean?" He started for the staircase.

"It is odd that it's called 'First Baptist' when it's the only church around here," I agreed.

"This place isn't big enough for more than one church. Or much of anything else," he said, the colored light from the high stained-glass windows throwing rainbows across his white shirt. The stunning old Victorian house on the town's most beautiful street came with the job—another sign God meant this place to be our home, Tim had said when I'd squealed at the sight of the house. "Which is exactly why it's so perfect for us."

I followed him out the front door into blinding sunshine and bitter cold, not wanting to wrinkle my outfit with a coat for such a short walk.

Perfect for us.

I really wanted him to be right about that.

# FOUR
## MARTHA

*March*

There had never been a place less deserving of its name than the Dreamscape Motel on the eastern edge of Whitney Falls, Arkansas. From the asbestos-riddled ceilings and peeling paint to the rickety doors and beaten-down customers, decrepit desperation was the overwhelming vibe. Even the outside air smelled of off-brand cigarettes and Keystone Light beer laced with despair, and you could almost see shards of shattered dreams littering the gravel parking lot if you squinted and the light was just right. But the rooms were cheap, somehow the roaches were minimal, and the manager didn't even blink when I told him I didn't have an ID. So it was home.

By the time I finished telling Mary the story about Ruthie and made it back there, it was dark out. I rolled the last half mile on fumes and a prayer that my burned-out headlight wouldn't attract the wrong kind of attention.

Parked in front of my room with the engine off, I sent Jesus a quick thank you—even with the side trip to Elias Lane, I'd made that tank of gas stretch all week, and I'd have money for more tomorrow.

I let myself in, clicking on the light and the boxy, brown-cased TV that only got four channels. One of them showed old sitcoms at night, and the noise made me feel less lonely. It also drowned out most of the sounds you might expect to come from some of the other rooms after dark at a place like the Dreamscape.

On the TV, a pretty teenage girl who had been costumed to look frumpy so it could seem like a plot twist when the football star who wanted to take her out agonized over the upcoming date while she baked cookies with her mom. I watched them work in a big, bright kitchen not unlike Mary's. I bet Mary baked fantastic cookies. The mom on the TV burned the first tray trying to explain sex to her daughter without actually saying the word. That last part was believable after having been inside Mary's house—I couldn't imagine Mary McClatchy even knowing much about something so... common. And icky. Let alone talking about it.

I went to the bathroom to take off my blood-spattered clothes and try to get the stains out, if it wasn't already too late.

Turning the hot water in the sink on full, I stuffed the drain with a dirty sock and filled the small basin, shucking my plaid button down and submerging the top half in the water, watching it turn pink as the blood steeped out of the cotton fabric like tea. Good. I couldn't afford a new shirt. I nodded at myself in the mirror.

My reflection—with end-of-the-day plus scalp-repair-messy dishwater blonde hair capping a face devoid of makeup, but still notable enough with its high, defined cheekbones, petite nose, and wide green eyes to ensure that women like Ruthie Tomlinson didn't like me—offered a smile.

I pulled on a cotton sleep shirt, leaving the button down to soak while I walked barefoot to the nightstand drawer where I kept food. I bent over, plunging my hand into the dark recess of the drawer hopefully, but came up empty. I had one piece of bread and whatever peanut butter I could scrape from the sides of an empty jar.

Not exactly what most folks would call dinner. On the TV, the girl was coming in from her date, a dreamy smile on her face, her parents sitting together on a beautiful flowered sofa, both pretending to read magazines.

That was what being a teenager was supposed to be like. School and boys and giggling with friends on the phone—that was what my sister should've been doing as spring crept up on us. Heck, it wasn't too far removed from what I ought to be doing, if you asked TV writers. But that wasn't our story. Wasn't my story. Unless maybe I could rewrite my life.

I found a plastic knife and opened the peanut butter, but for the first time in a long time, not having enough to eat wasn't the thing I was most worried about.

Because I was definitely going back to see Mary.

I shouldn't go anywhere near the McClatchy house. Or even Elias Lane, for that matter—I had no business there. If there was an option I would say I should've changed churches, but First Baptist is the only one in town. And besides—more than a solid hour of Mary's kind attention turned out to be more warming and craveable than the bourbon shot: I was hooked. As much as I knew it was a bad idea, I couldn't wait to see her the next day.

She'd told me to come by after my shift at the Pick and Go and her refusal to take no for an answer coupled with my apparent starvation for human contact and a little kindness meant I never really had a choice.

Maybe I had moved to Whitney Falls looking to disappear, but what if there turned out to be more here for me than just that? I didn't want to let myself hope. Life had long since taught me that hope is a dangerous gamble, inviting destruction and sorrow when it's crushed by reality. But I felt the bubbles of hope in my gut more acutely than the hunger right then.

Or maybe... Maybe it was just a different kind of hunger. Friendship had always been an elusive fantasy for me. Something I read about in books and watched on TV, but seldom—maybe even never—really experienced. But I had seen and read enough to know I had to be careful. There's bare-your-soul friends, and then there's just-right-gossip-about-other-folks-over-iced-tea-once-or-twice-a-week friends. As long as Mary and I stayed in the iced tea zone, I would be okay. Better than okay—maybe I could really live here, instead of just existing in a world away from the one I'd escaped.

All I had to do was not blow it.

The closing credits rolled on the TV, and I scraped the sides and bottom of the peanut butter jar and smeared the remnants on a slice of wonder bread. I knew better than to gobble my food—when there's never enough, you learn how to make it last. I chewed each bite twenty times, giving my belly time to adjust. By the time I was done, I wasn't hungry anymore—not for food, anyway. The physical effects of the bourbon Mary had made me drink were long since worn off, but the promise of a retreat into the comfort it provided danced around the edges of my brain, whispering temptations that made me thankful I didn't have the money to buy booze. Like Pastor Tim had said just this past Sunday: "Even through deprivation, the Lord provides what we need."

I checked on my shirt, using a little soap to get the last of the noticeable blood out of the cotton. When it was dripping dry over the tub, I cleaned the sink, brushed my teeth, and crawled under the worn coverlet that had faded from blue to gray in most places, stretching out on my stomach and turning the right side of my face as far into the pillow as I dared to save my cuts from touching the scratchy motel pillowcase.

Tomorrow, I would work my shift, get my paycheck, eat a real turkey sandwich for lunch, and go see my new friend Mary.

It was enough to make me look forward to Friday for the first time in months. Even knowing it was Ruthie Tomlinson's regular grocery shopping day couldn't snatch the hope from my chest.

Turns out hope, not Ruthie, was the monster I should've feared.

# FIVE
## MARTHA

*March*

"Those grapes were not six dollars and seven cents." Ruthie Tomlinson's green eyes flashed as she leaned over the end of the counter and pointed one pink-gloved finger at her receipt, ignoring the customer I was helping. "They're on sale."

"I know that." I kept my voice calm, punching in the first deacon's weekly value pack of Keystone Light. He had become very interested in the brown tile floor when Ruthie stomped back into the store, and kept his gaze there and his mouth shut as she ranted. "I actually didn't even charge you the sale price, Mrs. Tomlinson. Two and a quarter pounds of grapes at two dollars and eighty-five cents a pound is six dollars and forty-one cents." I rang in a can of cheddar Pringles and put them in a bag.

"Where in blazes do you get off charging nearly three dollars a pound for some grapes? Do they have diamonds inside?" Ruthie tapped one foot as I weighed apples. "I'd sure appreciate the courtesy of you looking at me when I'm speaking to you. Or maybe I should take this up with Sam."

Sam Tomlinson, Ruthie's husband, was the store manager here at the Pick and Go. He'd hired me "on a trial basis" because he liked the way I looked, but he kept me around after he figured out I'm real good with numbers, because the old couple who owned the place never had wanted to spend the money to install any computer equipment or scanners and the cash register was older than my granny, Lord rest her.

Sam didn't seem to like the way I always managed to fix things so I wasn't ever alone in close quarters with him no matter how hard he tried. I figured he was why Ruthie didn't seem to like the way I kept doing little things like breathing and showing up for work no matter how hard she tried.

"I don't set the prices, ma'am," I said like Ruthie didn't know that already. "But I know grapes aren't in season around here yet, it's still early spring. Perhaps Sam would be a good person for you to ask about the cost."

She wouldn't do that, because her problem wasn't with the grapes—it wasn't even really with me. Her problem was her husband's wandering eye. I had watched the two of them have a gesture and scowl-filled conversation two Fridays ago, after she'd fussed at me about the quality of the bologna she'd picked up. Afterward, Sam had not apologized so much as told me he'd ordered her to leave me alone.

But Sam was fishing today.

I could feel Ruthie's gaze as I weighed the first deacon's T-bone steak and punched in the $4.85 charge, sliding it into its own bag because he didn't like his meat to touch anything else. "That'll be thirty-three oh six, sir."

Not that I planned to let on that Ruthie was bothering me. Indifference is often the most effective weapon against a bully—though Ruthie was a particularly stubborn one.

The deacon counted out the money down to six pennies and passed it to me.

"Check your receipt for overcharges," Ruthie told him, stepping into the space he vacated in front of my antique register as I laid the bills in the drawer and dropped the pennies into their section.

Shaking his head as he collected bags, he said nothing. I expected no more—I was an outsider, so folks here who weren't hateful were indifferent.

"It's freakish the way you figure the charges in your head," Ruthie snapped as the deacon left the store. "I know you must be doing some of them wrong." Her mouth stretched into a triumphant grin as I raised my gaze to meet hers, the raisin lipstick garish against her pale skin. "You admitted it, even. You said you didn't charge me right for the grapes."

First you were snapping my head off about overcharging you, and now you're mad because I took a few cents off the grapes you bought? I wanted to say it. I knew Sam had told her he didn't have a choice, he had to keep me on because I was good at math, and figured she thought if she could prove I wasn't, she could get me fired.

But I was far more confident her plan would fail than I was that Sam would overlook me being rude to his wife. Especially after she'd scampered off like a scalded cat when Mary told her off for harassing me not even twenty-four hours ago. So I swallowed the words because I needed this job. No place else I'd applied in three towns would hire me when I couldn't produce identification. People on TV get fake IDs like they come in cereal boxes, but in the real world, good ones are made by the sort of people I couldn't have knowing where to find me, and cost prohibitive when you're barely keeping peanut butter and bread on the table. Here in Whitney Falls at the Pick and Go, Sam had been too busy leering to ever even ask.

So I ducked my head and held my tongue with his wife. "I will always make sure your groceries are properly rung up, Mrs. Tomlinson," I murmured. "I was trying to be courteous with the charge for the grapes, because just about everyone else samples them in the store, so their bags weigh slightly less when I ring them up. You never eat them until after you can wash them."

My eyes flicked to the gloves she wore every time she went out of her house and she shoved her hands into the pockets on her cardigan.

"I didn't know you noticed that," she muttered, backing up a step. "Just make sure you ring up people's orders right. Overcharging costs the store customers."

She said that with a straight face and everything. Before I could reply, Mary's voice came from my right. "Where exactly are those customers going to shop if it's not here?" Mary sounded polite and conversational as she put a bag of apples, a bag of grapes, a carton of eggs, two jars of pasta sauce, and one of pickles on the counter. "There isn't another grocery store for twenty miles."

She smiled at me before she turned a less friendly gaze on Ruthie. "I'm so blessed to find you here, Mrs. Tomlinson. I wonder if you remember what we discussed about these groceries yesterday? I wanted to go out this afternoon anyway and thought I would save you a trip, but here you are."

Ruthie nodded and fumbled with her wallet, her gloves making it hard to unzip it. I rang up Mary's small grocery order. "That's $24.37."

Ruthie put the money on the counter.

"Thank you so much, Mrs. Tomlinson," Mary said in a fake syrupy voice that sounded just different enough from the way she'd spoken to me that I could tell it wasn't sincere.

"You're welcome." Ruthie managed to get the words out without choking on them before she hurried out the door.

Mary leaned across the counter and patted my hand. "You really are welcome." She winked. "How's that head today?"

"Sam isn't here so I didn't get in trouble for not wearing my hat," I glanced up at her. "It's very sore, but I don't think it's worse today. Thank you so much for your help." I bagged up the eggs and the Prego, then added the huge bag of grapes.

She handed me a twenty and waved one hand when I raised my eyebrows and pushed it back across the counter. "Keep it—consider it a tip for your delivery yesterday."

"Oh no, ma'am, I couldn't." I shook my head and pushed the bill again. "Mrs. Tomlinson paid for your groceries, and this money isn't mine."

"Then put it in the offering plate on Sunday and give it to Jesus, because I won't take it." Mary's tone was still kind, but her face was serious.

I gave it a beat and then put the cash in my official Pick and Go apron pocket. "Thank you, Mrs.—"

"Who?" her left eyebrow scooted up.

"Thank you, Mary." I glanced around to make sure nobody heard me call the pastor's wife by her Christian name.

"Happy to help." She took the bag of groceries from the counter and turned with a wave. "I'll see you this evening, Martha. I'm looking forward to it."

So was I.

I watched her all the way out the door, a black pickup backed into the corner of the parking lot catching my eye. Half of Whitney Falls drove pickups, but I didn't remember seeing that one before. The windows were tinted so dark all I could see was the reflection of the budding trees in them, the glare on the windshield making it impossible to tell if anyone was inside. No plate on the front, and I couldn't see the back, but something about it made my skin crawl right up my arms—a visceral, "stay away" reaction my granny would've told me to trust.

Mary McClatchy loaded her bags into the back of her Grand Wagoneer and left the lot. I turned a smile on a teenage girl whose name I didn't know as she handed me a pack of gum to ring up, tires screeching out of our lot as she handed me two crumpled dollar bills.

When I turned back to the window, the black pickup was gone.

# SIX

## MARY

*January—Two months earlier*
*The McClatchys' first Sunday in Whitney Falls*

Ruthie Tomlinson was the reigning queen bee of Whitney Falls.

I spotted her holding court on the steps of the church before I even knew her name, her dark hair perfectly curled around her shoulders, the front of it pinned back from her porcelain face under a knit beret that was more chic than it could've been warm. Even in the biting cold with two-day-old snowdrifts piled all around, Ruthie wore an amethyst-toned suit, her legs bare save for thin, pale stockings, a cream wool coat hanging from her shoulders and lace-trimmed gloves the same shade of purple as the suit completing the look.

"That's Ruthie Tomlinson," Tim whispered as if on cue. His observational skills were almost spooky—when folks didn't know him well, it came off like he could read minds, almost. But I'd asked about that years ago and he swore he was just "very good at paying attention."

I'd had enough uncharitable thoughts about him in more

than a decade to believe he couldn't actually read them. I was pretty sure.

"Her husband runs the only grocery store in town, the Pick and Go on Main Street, though they don't own it, from what I gathered. She seems to volunteer almost constantly with the church and the community—she's been head of the First Baptist Ladies' Auxiliary for the past five years, since the old pastor's wife passed on."

Oh boy. So this Ruthie woman was going to love me. I had ridden the power struggle horse a couple of times already—he was a mean beast, as likely to throw you off and stomp on you as he was to bite.

But there was nothing for it—if I tried to abdicate the responsibility of chairing the ladies' auxiliary, other women would see that as either weak or lazy, and southern mommas don't abide weak or lazy.

Rock, meet hard place. Seemed like that was where I lived a lot of the time, supporting my husband the best I could.

I sucked in a deep breath of freezing air and started up the steps next to Tim, smiling at everyone who shook my husband's hand as we made our way to the door. The church was lovely, like it had been lifted from an old painting of a small southern town—orange-red brick with white accents that gleamed bright in the brilliant January sun, the steeple piercing the blue sky above all the other buildings in Whitney Falls. "Church is our real 'true north' around these parts," the former pastor had said when we came to visit. "You can see the steeple from most anywhere in town."

Two dozen handshakes—and just as many "God bless you both"s—later, we stopped in front of Ruthie and her husband, a tall, lanky man with a bit of a beak nose and a receding hairline. Sam Tomlinson had an intense gaze, and I could see remnants of handsome around the edges—he was fit and clean-shaven, with a smile that seemed to come easily, even if his looks hadn't aged as well as Tim's.

"Ruthie, Sam, this is Pastor Tim McClatchy and his wife Mary." The first deacon waved his hand between us like a knight presenting two royal families to one another. Sam and Tim shook hands, and I put mine out to Ruthie, who looked down at the small pocketbook she clutched in both of her gloved hands and shrugged as though she couldn't easily tuck the bag under her arm to free them, her lips barely tipping up in the smallest smile I'd ever seen.

The men walked inside, ignoring Ruthie's slight as men always seemed to do. I stepped smoothly to one side as a trio of towheaded boys in adorable little suits ran past, charging into the church and disappearing down a staircase just off the lobby.

I felt my lips turn up in a reflexive smile as I watched them go, my eyes staying on the open church doors for a few beats after the boys were out of sight. I turned back to Ruthie, whose sharp eyes scanned the crowd.

"Where are your children, Mrs. McClatchy?"

I swallowed hard as I looked her directly in the eye. "The Lord hasn't blessed us with a baby yet, but we remain ever prayerful." I recited the same line I'd said a hundred times at a dozen churches in the fourteen years Tim and I had been married.

"I'm sorry to hear that." Ruthie's face softened slightly. "I do understand the longing. I help my brother and his wife care for their children to help fill that gap in my own life."

Wait.

Ruthie Tomlinson wasn't a mother, either?

For the first time since at least before we'd left Broux Parish —that was six churches ago—I felt a flicker of hope.

The unfulfilled need to be a mother was a powerful emotion. Perhaps even more powerful than jealousy.

Maybe, just maybe, Ruthie Tomlinson and I could be friends.

Maybe Tim was right and God had brought us to Whitney Falls to settle down. To find real friends and build some kind of family the best way he would allow.

As the bells above us began to peal the signal that it was time for service, I smiled at Ruthie one more time. "I'm so glad you have the blessing of being an involved aunt. Tim and I are both only children."

It was true enough, and far easier, I'd learned.

Ruthie nodded. "I'll look forward to knowing you better, Mary."

Something about the way she said it made me think I shouldn't get too excited just yet.

# SEVEN
## MARTHA

*March*

Lazy droplets splatted on the windshield as I coaxed my Civic up Elias Lane for the second day in a row, the rain just heavy and cool enough to keep everyone inside. At least I didn't have an audience for the car's belching and squalling today.

I parked in front of the McClatchys' house just as the bigger part of the storm soared over the mountains to the west, dumping water outside the shelter of my car.

The dark clouds stretched as far back as I could see, so I'd have to run for it, open head wound and all.

I turned in the seat and put one hand on the door handle, shoving with both feet and hitting the ground running, my tired feet aching with every step. Despite being pretty fast, I was sopping wet by the time I raced up onto the McClatchys' front porch. I pulled my plain black T-shirt up slightly and wrung water from it, leaning forward so it wouldn't flood my shoes.

That was about all I could do. The idea of water dripping from my clothes onto that white marble floor made my heart race, my feet backing away from the door automatically. But.

She was expecting me. I would hurt her feelings if I didn't show up, and she had looked bothered, even if only for a second, telling me she didn't have many friends here. We did have at least that in common.

I lunged forward, stabbing one finger at the bell before I could decide it was better to run.

Soft footsteps came toward the door almost immediately.

"Martha!" The smile on Mary's face and the light in her eyes were the kind you can't fake—she was glad to see me. I almost didn't know what to do with that. "Matthew, Mark, Luke, and John, but you are soaked! Come in, let me find you some clothes to change into."

I opened my mouth to protest as she grabbed my arm, pulling me to one of those funny rich people bathrooms that didn't have a tub and handing me a towel she pulled from a cabinet. "Get out of those wet things and dry off, I'll be right back."

I didn't have a chance to say anything before she hurried off. I looked around the room, a faint, sweetly perfumed scent hanging in the air that reminded me of the one time I'd been in a department store as a child. I'd wanted to bottle the air and take it home so I could continue to smell that scent, and I didn't remember noticing it the day before, though surely it had never smelled anything but clean and pleasant in Mary's house.

Pulling off my heavy, wet shirt, I shivered, blotting my skin with the towel before I shimmied out of my jeans. Twisting my arms back to unhook my bra, I caught sight of myself in the mirror, the words "drowned rat" springing instantly to mind. Even Sam Tomlinson wouldn't leer at me if he saw me looking like this: my hair was plastered to my head and cheeks, too-thin shoulders hunched over breasts that were far bigger than they should've been for my waifish figure. My hipbones jutted out too far, a sharp frame for my sunken belly. The only good thing about any of it was that I looked so different than I had six months ago. If I were braver, I might say I could go home and nobody would notice me.

Sometimes the line between brave and stupid is thin and blurry.

I did miss having plenty to eat. But not much else back home was worth remembering, let alone missing. Nobody there —especially me—would've thought I'd ever stand in one of these weird, tiny rich people bathrooms staring into a gilt-edged mirror trying to decide what to do about my rain-soaked panties. I mean, I dropped the bra on top of the pile of wet clothes, but... was I supposed to go commando in clothes Mary was about to loan me? That didn't seem proper.

I had good and worked myself into a near panic when she tapped on the door. "Wardrobe service," she called.

I giggled, wrapping up in the towel and cracking the door. She passed me a stack of garments, topped by a pair of pink undies and a cotton sports bra.

"Those are from packages I bought on clearance in Malvern last week for the donation bin at the church," she winked. "Just so you know they're new."

"You really are an angel." I couldn't help myself from blurting it out, and I pinched my lips together and felt my cheeks burn when she laughed.

"Aren't you just the sweetest thing?" She patted my hand and backed out of the room. "I'll get our tea while you get dressed."

I waited until the door was closed and then used the towel to blot my hair dry before I kicked my panties into the wet pile and finished drying off. The undergarments fit well enough and felt so soft against my skin I kind of hoped she'd let me keep them. I only had two of each item, which I rotated washing in the rickety sink at the Dreamscape and hanging to dry in the bathroom since any quarters that went to the laundry machines would be quarters that couldn't buy food. The bar soap in the motel wasn't great at cleaning clothes, but I had made it work so far.

The fuzzy gray sweatpants were a kind of silky-soft I didn't know fabric could even be, like sliding down feathers over my legs.

I pulled on the plain blue T-shirt and some thick socks with rubber grips on the bottoms and washed my hands in the sink, the sharp, orange-sage smell of the soap so delightful I cupped my clean hands over my face and breathed deep before I opened the door.

"Better?" Mary smiled from her seat in the corner of a cushy white couch that faced the ornate fireplace in the living room.

"Yes, thank you so much. Do you happen to have a plastic bag I can put my clothes in? I want to clean up your floor."

"I can do better than that." She hopped to her feet before I could object, hurrying into the bathroom and coming out with her sweater sleeves pushed up and an armful of my drenched, dirty work clothes.

"Oh no, Mary!" I rushed forward, horrified. "I didn't mean—"

"Why do you seem to feel like you're bothering other folks just by existing?" She quirked that left eyebrow up again and shook her head, but she didn't stop moving. "I'll put these in to wash. Your tea is on the island by the first aid kit—grab a seat at the counter and I'll take care of your head when I come back down."

I went to the same barstool I'd occupied the day before, sipping my tea and looking around her huge, spotless kitchen. I'd never seen a kitchen with room for knickknacks, but Mary had three sets of salt and pepper shakers—plain white cylinders made of some sort of stone sitting with napkins on the island, a cat and dog next to the stove, and a Snoopy and Woodstock next to her mahogany and stainless-steel knife block. Just behind Snoopy was a little framed sign that read,

*"Other things may come and go, but we start and end with family."*

It was a real nice idea for people who had families that didn't try to kill them.

Not that I was getting bogged down in bad memories sitting in Mary McClatchy's kitchen.

I kept looking, focusing on the fluttering flame of the candle burning in a thick, amber glass jar shaped like a star at the end of the island. That right there was why it smelled so amazing in this house. I hopped off the stool and walked over for a closer look. Whatever it was, I'd never be able to afford it, but I wanted to know anyway. Standing right over the candle, I breathed in deep—vanilla, but with hints of a flower. Honeysuckle, I thought. And cinnamon. The jar was beautiful, too, bubbles of air trapped in the glass glowing like tiny lanterns in the dancing candlelight.

"Doesn't that smell good?" Mary's voice came from just behind me. "It's my favorite, but I have to order them by the case from New Orleans. A family company that started fifty years ago with an old woman local folks there said had magical powers with herbs and flowers."

"What kind of magic?" I asked, thinking I'd never be able to buy a whole case of something as unnecessary as candles, even if I got Sam Tomlinson's job someday. I went back to my barstool as Mary talked.

"According to the stories, she could heal serious diseases, make love potions, bring dead plants back to life. If there was something a plant could accomplish, Mama Felice could make it happen."

I nodded as Mary began gently moving my hair away from the cuts. "What kind of magic does that candle have?" I asked.

She laughed. "You can't tell I burned the prosciutto for dinner, can you?"

I shook my head, just a little. "It smells like heaven in here."

"I hope Tim will be okay with a vegetarian dinner tonight." I couldn't see Mary's face because she was behind me, but her tone got an apprehensive edge. "I didn't want to go to the store and risk missing you."

Missing me... instead of laughing, I said, "You know if that happens again you could just call the store. I'm happy to bring you something by if it will help out."

"That's very kind of you," she said. "I'll remember that, though I am forever trying to be a better cook. Do you like to cook? You make that casserole everyone at the church likes so much, don't you?"

"My granny's recipe," I said. "I don't know if I'd say I've ever enjoyed cooking, but I learned from my granny when I was little and I'm pretty good at it, I guess. Though I can't say I know what prosciutto is or what you'd do with it."

Talking kept my mind off her poking and prodding at my sore scalp.

"This looks a whole lot better today," she said. "Head wounds bleed a lot, but they also heal quickly. A little more antibiotic, and you'll be good as new in a few days. I think even if the hair doesn't grow back in these spots, yours is certainly thick enough to cover them."

I had survived head wounds before. My hair always grew back. But I didn't need to say that out loud, so I just murmured agreement.

"Gosh, I wish I had half the volume you do, even when your hair is wet—you certainly have been blessed, between that gorgeous face and this thick, lovely head of hair," Mary continued. "What kind of shampoo do you use?"

I felt my eyes pop wide. I didn't think it was a great idea to tell her I used the bar soap at the motel to wash every part of me including my hair. "Just regular old Suave." I blurted out the name of the last shampoo I remembered ringing up at the Pick and Go.

"So you're saying my problem is I'm paying too much for shampoo?" she asked, her eyes shining and her lips fighting a smile.

"Oh no, ma'am!" I clapped one hand over my mouth. "You don't have a problem at all, you couldn't... you're... well. Perfect."

"I assure you I'm not," she said, dabbing ointment on my forehead and tapping the end of my nose with a wink. "There was only one perfect person to ever walk the Earth, and they crucified him."

"Of course," I mumbled. Could I say anything right today? At least she wouldn't invite me back.

Mary finished what she was doing and rounded the end of the island, waving for me to join her. "Let's take our tea to the sofa. The fire is so nice and it'll be summer before we know it."

I picked up my glass and followed her, the sweet smell of the candle and softness of the clothes—and kindness of my hostess, of course—making me forget all the reasons being friends with me could put Mary in danger. They'd been lurking around the edges of my thoughts all day, but I kept beating them back. Nobody south of Malvern or north of Little Rock had ever heard of Whitney Falls. I was safe.

And if I was safe, so was my new friend Mary.

I set my glass on a coaster and pointed to a book that looked older than the house, a slightly tattered leather cover that used to be white folded around a thick stack of blue-edged pages. "Are you reading that?" I asked.

"I've read it," she said.

"Was it good? I would love to have more books. I miss reading and my TV only gets four channels."

"It's long. Has a lot of different narrators. Violence. Sex. But a lot of people say it's the greatest story ever told." Her lips tipped up into a smile as my eyes widened.

"That's a Bible? The only ones I've ever seen are the tiny ones in motels and the plain little black ones in church pews."

"My husband collects antique Bibles," Mary said. "This one is too pretty to keep on a shelf."

I leaned forward and reached one hand toward the center of the table.

"No!" Mary barked, her face twisting in... that wasn't anger. Panic? I froze, staring at her.

What in the actual name of all that was holy?

# EIGHT
## MARTHA

*March*

The storm crossed Mary's face and disappeared as quick as it had come.

I pulled my hand back slowly, avoiding any possibility of a quick reflex that might knock my tea glass over. "I'm sorry."

"No. I'm sorry." She put one hand on my arm and sighed. "I didn't mean to startle you. It's just that this one is very old and fragile, and Tim is particular about the handling of his collectibles. He was looking through it and left it there last night, but I don't want him to be upset. He's already going to be mad about dinner."

Didn't she just say it was there because it was too pretty to be on a shelf? I didn't ask out loud, because her wide blue eyes were locked on me, concern gushing out of them like water from a hydrant. "Please forgive me," she said.

I would've given her the moon right then if I'd had a way to.

"Of course." I nodded. "Nothing to forgive. I know better than to touch things that aren't mine without asking." I sipped my tea and then moved the coaster and glass to the side table. Just in case.

"You really are one of the nicest people I've ever met," Mary said, staring at me over the rim of her glass.

I laughed right out loud. "What?"

"It's true," she said. "I noticed it yesterday but then today—you were so kind to Ruthie at the store even after she was horrible to you for the second time in two days."

"She wasn't entirely wrong about the price being off." Why on Earth did it sound like I was defending that woman? "I did take a little discount because everyone else samples the grapes, but she's afraid of germs, so she won't eat them until she's washed them herself."

Mary's eyebrow went up again. "Afraid of germs? How do you know that?"

I looked down at my hands. "I don't mean to gossip." Well, I did, only because talking about Ruthie meant we weren't talking about me, but she didn't need to know that. "I've just noticed things. She always wears gloves. She jumps out of her skin if anybody sneezes or coughs within thirty feet of her. And she's the only person in town who has never once sampled produce in the store before buying it."

Mary's eyes were round and wide when I looked back up, her red lips tipped up just a bit at the corners. "She's afraid of germs," she said.

"I believe so."

"I wonder..." Mary trailed off. I let the silence stretch, not wanting to seem nosy even though I was fascinated by what she might say next.

She waved one hand. "I don't know."

I slumped forward, resting my elbows on my knees. Mary tapped one fingernail on her tea glass, the soft chiming sound complimenting the pops from the fireplace.

"It's just... do you think that's why she doesn't have any children?" Mary mused. I couldn't tell from the faraway look on her face if she was talking to me or herself. "I thought when we first moved here that she and I could be friends, because we had that struggle in common, but this makes me think maybe it's not me she doesn't like after all."

Did she mean because kids are sort of inherently germy little creatures? Because that wasn't where my brain went once Mary asked that question.

"It's giving her husband's behavior a whole different feel, too." I didn't really mean to say that out loud.

I've wondered a hundred times what might be different if I'd kept those ten words to myself that first Friday night at Mary's house.

Mary gasped. "Is Sam Tomlinson being inappropriate with you?" Her blue eyes flashed like they were about to spit fire as she looked in the general direction of the Tomlinson house. "Because my husband always says judgement is not for mortal men and the Good Lord punishes the wicked, but my daddy taught me that sometimes Jesus needs a little help."

The outburst seemed so unlike the kind, quiet pastor's wife I'd seen for the past two months that I almost laughed. Then I tried to stifle it and it came out as a snort. Embarrassed, I clapped one hand over my mouth. "I'm sorry."

"You're sorry for thinking I'm funny?" Mary shook her head. "Though my aim was more righteous than comical, I'm glad you think I'm funny. You tell me the truth now, Martha, because we're friends, and friends have to trust each other, don't they?" She unfolded her legs from beneath her and leaned toward me, putting both her hands over mine.

I nodded, hairs pricking up on the back of my neck though I couldn't pinpoint a reason.

"Is Sam Tomlinson taking liberties he doesn't deserve with you?" She held my gaze without blinking. "I try hard to be a good Christian every day, but the good Lord will just have to look away from a conversation or two."

I wouldn't let Mary impugn her faith on my account.

"No, ma'am," I said, stammering when she wrinkled her brow and squeezed my hands. "I mean, I think maybe he might if he thought he could get away with it, but I'm real good at making sure we're not alone in tight spaces, and I never do anything that might encourage him. I was just thinking—"

The soft chime of the doorbell interrupted me, and Mary's forehead bunched up as she stood. "Hold that thought."

I've never been sure why I stood and followed her to the door. Maybe because it was dark and raining buckets. Maybe because I was nosy. Maybe because I was vain and wanted someone to see me in these soft clothes in the pastor's house on a Friday night. Maybe because Mary's face said she wasn't expecting anyone.

My breath came faster as she opened the door and turned on the light, and I followed her out into the cool, damp air on the porch, shivering as I peered into thick, watery darkness.

The wind howled around the corners of the massive old house, rain loud as it lashed at the porch roof.

Somewhere in the direction of the church a tree branch snapped with a crack that made us both jump.

But there was nobody there.

# NINE

## MARTHA

*March*

"Children getting up to mischief." Mary's voice shook as she locked both the deadbolt and the chain on the front door before she hurried back through the house to the kitchen porch door and the back door to check the locks.

Because she thought a child was playing ding dong ditch? Who would even do that in the chilly, dumping-down rain?

It wasn't my place to argue, though, so I wandered to the kitchen, where she'd stopped to pull a glass casserole dish from the oven.

"That smells wonderful," I said of the waft of creamy, cheesy goodness as she lifted one corner of the foil and peeked under it. I loved cheese growing up, but these days it was a luxury I had no way to keep cold.

"Thank you. Tim prefers meat for dinner, but I messed that up today." She stuck the foil back down and shut off the oven before she put the dish back in it, a heavy, jerky quality to her movements that hadn't been there before. Whether it was because of the doorbell or thoughts of upsetting her husband, I

THE PASTOR'S WIFE 57

couldn't tell. I hoped it wasn't Pastor Tim. He seemed nice, and I liked thinking of him that way.

"Oh my stars!" Turning away from the stove, Mary put one hand over her mouth, shaking her head. "Please forgive my incredible rudeness."

I blinked, genuinely flabbergasted as to what she could possibly mean. "I... your what?"

Mary opened a high cabinet and reached for three thick, light blue stoneware plates. "You must stay for dinner, of course." She spoke like she hadn't heard me, putting the plates on the counter and laying out napkins next to them. "It was so rude of me to wait so long to invite you, when I know you've been working all day, same as Tim, and we have plenty." She covered her face with both hands and spoke through them. "My heavens, I even talked to you about the meal twice. My daddy would take a switch to my hide over my lack of manners."

This couldn't be real life, Mary McClatchy inviting me for dinner and apologizing to me for forgetting to do it sooner. Things like this definitely did not happen to me.

I pulled in a deep breath, plucking at the inside of my left wrist with my right thumb and index finger. My cousin told me once that where you can see the veins on your wrist is a painful place to get a tattoo because there are a lot of nerves near the surface. So I clenched my eyes shut and pinched for all I was worth.

I held it until tears sprang to my eyes, opening them slowly, a bruise blooming on my skin already.

I was still in Mary's kitchen, so I wasn't dreaming. But she had disappeared.

"Mary?"

I heard dishes sliding across the table and went to the dining room through a butler's pantry with stained glass in the upper cabinets, a big, boxy coffee machine with *De'Longhi* in gold letters on one counter, and under the other one, a pretty fridge with a glass door that just held wine bottles.

"I'm setting the table. I won't take no for an answer, you don't need to go home and cook after a long week on your feet."

And maybe if I was here, her husband wouldn't be mad about the meatless meal? Whatever. I didn't care why she'd invited me, I was happy to run interference if the reward was a plate of that cheesy pasta. She'd been ready to take Sam Tomlinson straight to the woodshed for me twenty minutes ago, and I was starving—literally. Her casserole smelled fantastic and there was more than enough for three people.

"I wouldn't dream of saying no." I picked up napkins and folded them into swans the way my granny had taught me before she died and everything in my world went to hell, putting one beside each plate. "Though for the record, I didn't expect you to ask, and I would never have thought you were being rude."

Mary turned to the tall sideboard and pulled out a wood box that held a silver service, setting each place with two forks, a spoon, and a butter knife. Why was all that necessary for some cheesy pasta?

"Anything else I can help with?" I asked brightly.

"I think we're all se—"

A knock at the kitchen porch door cut off the end of her sentence.

Mary pulled in a deep breath, fluffing her halo of blonde hair and smoothing her cream wool slacks before she hurried to the door.

"Why in the world is this locked?" Pastor Tim's voice almost had an edge to it as it came through the thick, solid wood door. Or maybe I was projecting—every man I'd ever known yelled more than they'd talked.

Mary pulled the door open and stepped to one side. "Silly of me, I must have turned the lock without thinking." She tipped her face up and he kissed her—for longer than most people would consider polite in front of company, but he didn't know I was there and for some ridiculous reason I couldn't manage to look at anything else.

Mary finally backed away—or maybe she just needed to come up for air—and I snapped my head around and pretended to rub at a spot that didn't exist on the white-painted doorjamb.

"Hello to you too," she giggled. "We have a guest for dinner. You remember Martha, don't you? She made that—"

"The burrito casserole!" Pastor Tim stepped toward me with one hand out to shake. I took it automatically and shook firmly, then let go as fast as I could. His brown eyes lit up. "Are we having that for supper?"

I laughed. "I'm afraid not," I said. "But I'm glad you enjoyed it. I can make you another one tomorrow if you'd like."

"On your day off?" That came from Mary, her lips pursed and a slightly sour look on her entire face. "I wouldn't ask you to spend it slaving over a hot stove! And we have plans tomorrow night, anyway." Her face relaxed back to its polished, happy beauty as she took Tim's jacket out of the room and reappeared with a pair of the same socks she and I wore, except these were navy blue. He winked at me and pulled his shoes and socks off, stashing the black wingtips in a basket beneath a cabinet before he put the fluffy socks on.

"Now I'm ready for the evening," he said. "Mr. Rogers had his cardigan, I've got my sticky socks."

"And I've got clean floors with no scuff marks." Mary laughed. "Everyone's happy."

She pointed to the dining room. "Sit, both of you. I'll be right in with dinner."

I waited for Pastor Tim to walk into the butler's pantry first, but he didn't, staring expectantly at me for a few seconds before he murmured, "Ladies first."

"Thank you." I hurried to a chair before I could mess

anything else up, fussing with my napkin as he took his seat. Mary came in carrying a tray with the casserole dish on one side and a large bone-colored salad bowl on the other.

Pastor Tim rolled up his shirtsleeves, clapping his hands once when he saw the food. "You picked a good day to visit, Martha. Mary's tortellini alfredo is just as good as your burrito casserole."

He studied the ladle as Mary scooped a generous portion onto his plate, frowning. "No prosciutto?"

I held my breath, my eyes glued to Pastor Tim and Mary, waiting for the explosion.

# TEN
## MARY

*January—Two months earlier*
*The McClatchys' first Sunday in Whitney Falls*

Tim's sermon for the first Sunday in a new church was always well received. He had refined it over years of reuse, focusing on the first words Jesus said to various important people in his life, and the ones others had said to him, as well as the words the disciples used to open different books and chapters of the Bible that struck his fancy.

Watching from my seat in the front pew of the beautiful old church, it was easy to see why crowds fell for Tim's charisma. Every eye in the packed sanctuary was on my husband as he talked about Jesus's welcome of strangers throughout his life. Even the choir members watched from their spot behind Tim, instead of studying their music for the end of the service.

I kept my spine straight, my shoulders square, my knees together and my legs crossed at the ankle, various muscles knotting with the effort. But when I'd been called up for my introduction to the congregation after the choir sang "Worthy Is the Lamb", I'd noticed Ruthie sitting with the same posture as she whispered with two other women one row behind me, and I didn't want to risk looking dumpy or lazy, and making a bad impression.

The longer the sermon stretched, the more uncomfortable I got. Staring unblinking at my husband, I had never prayed so hard for him to have actual psychic ability.

*Shut up shut up shut up*, I chanted in my head, feeling more frustrated with church than I had since I was a child swinging my Mary Janes over the red carpet in our home church, waiting for the singing to start again. Goodness—maybe the Lord hadn't blessed me with a baby because even if Tim didn't know how hateful my thoughts could turn, God did.

Almost like God was agreeing with me, Tim's voice was drowned out by the sudden high-pitched squall of an angry infant. Every head in the sanctuary swiveled toward the sound, mine included. Mortified, a young woman with disheveled red hair shushed and patted the baby as she tried to climb past the other folks in her pew, none of whom stood to help her get by. I watched her hurry out after she finally made it to the aisle, my heart aching with how badly I wanted to be that kind of embarrassed. I knew at once exactly how bothersome she felt, and exactly how much I wouldn't care about who any baby of mine bothered by crying.

A master of commanding any room, Tim drew everyone's attention back to the pulpit with a booming laugh and a "Jesus loved the little children—even the ones who had a temper." Giggles and murmurs swept the congregation, and he resumed his sermon.

The young mother never came back, and what felt like hours passed before Tim asked everyone to join him in prayer. I breathed a huge sigh in and out as I bent my head and relaxed my posture, pretty sure Ruthie and her friends wouldn't dare peek even one eye open during the closing prayer on the pastor's first day.

Because I knew what was coming next, I rose for the closing hymns before Tim said, "... and all God's people said together," which was followed by the requisite chorus of "Amen."

I picked up my purse as the first deacon stepped up to the altar and invited everyone to the fellowship hall to welcome us to the church. Tim glanced at me and I just smiled, tired and sore from stress and social anxiety, but knowing there was no option but to go.

A long two hours of smiling, shaking hands, and hearing dozens of names it would take weeks for me to actually learn later, I walked through the heavy wood and stained-glass front door of our new home and kicked my high-heeled shoes off tired feet.

Boxes. I'd done nothing but unpack for the two whole days that we'd been here, and there were still so many boxes. Tim had been busy, meeting people in town and preparing his sermon, and while I had no idea how we'd accumulated so many things, I had worked myself ragged trying to make this big old house the home we deserved.

I knew Tim would be a while, getting to know the deacons and maybe even watching the football game at someone's house if he was invited, and I was starving. He had eaten three full plates of food at the welcome potluck, and while it had looked and smelled like the ladies of First Baptist could cook, I was too busy smiling and making small talk to taste anything.

I shuffled to the kitchen, which had been redone by the former pastor and his wife: the room was cut off from the rest of the house, but three walls were lined with bright, modern white and gray cabinets and white marble counters, a huge island with plenty of bar seating dominated the center of the space, and the fourth wall held floor-to-ceiling pantry cabinets, several outfitted with drawers and pull-out shelves of various sizes to hold everything from appliances to granola bars. So far they were mostly empty—my cookware was still packed, since the moving truck had just arrived on Friday and I hadn't been to the local grocery store yet. We had a box of Life cereal, a bag of bagels, and a jar of pickles. The pickles had come with us from Mississippi, a local barbecue restaurant's special sweet and spicy recipe. I stared at the bag of Tim's bagels until my mouth actually watered, picturing toasting one and eating it so intensely I could've sworn I smelled the warm yeast.

"Mary doesn't eat bread," I heard Tim's voice in my head like he was standing there—which he had been when he'd said those words to Ruthie Tomlinson after she'd offered me a dinner roll two hours ago. I'd never wanted so badly to make the ground swallow up a person just by thinking it, though I wasn't sure which of us would deserve it more.

Not that Tim was wrong. I didn't eat bread, and I had told Ruthie I had a gluten allergy. It was the way Tim seemed to take joy in reminding me that I shouldn't eat something I'd once enjoyed, something he kept in the house and stuffed himself with almost daily—that was the issue. But all sacrifice is rewarded by God, I reminded myself.

Swallowing hard, I shut the pantry door and got an apple and a bottle of water from the fridge. I ate slowly, alternating bites of the apple with big swallows of water, until my stomach was full on only sixty-seven calories. Twelve other small-town congregations in fourteen years had taught me that there were different rules for me. While southern mothers are forgiven for extra padding in their figures because they have carried and birthed children, a pastor's wife who has not is expected to remain trim and fit. Southern church ladies are unmatched in their ability to point out a handful of extra pounds while disguising the insult as concern. But even if I could stop caring what they thought and whether they liked me, I knew how Tim felt—having the most desirable wife in town helped establish him as a leader, he insisted. And the idea that everyone else wanted me made him want me, too. Sometimes.

I put the apple core and the water bottle in the trash and went upstairs to make our bed, which I had run out of time to do as I tried on seven outfits before church. Stripping off the comforter, I shook out the sheets and folded them into the apple pie corners Tim liked, tucking everything back together and arranging the throw pillows. I wiped down the bathroom sink and counter and ran the toilet brush around the bowl before I went back downstairs and tackled a box in the living room.

Shelving books and unwrapping tchotchkes left my mind free to wander back over the morning.

It hadn't gone badly. Could have been better.

The former pastor hadn't been exaggerating when he'd told Tim most Sundays the congregation topped a thousand people —I'd been shocked at how many folks crammed into the pews for the service, even if only half of them had stayed to eat afterward.

Tim's sermon had stuck the landing—though it was largely the same from place to place, he always tweaked it to try to fit each town and he'd done that well here. The people of Whitney Falls seemed pretty simple: a hard-working, God-fearing bunch who loved hunting and fishing and relished the remote location that kept them largely cut off from the rest of the world—and the twenty-first century, in a lot of ways.

I'd made an error with my outfit when I chose pants in the cold, because most of the other women wore dresses or skirts, but it hadn't seemed to be an unforgivable sin.

Ruthie put on a great church potluck, though I hadn't seen her eat a bite or even remove her purple gloves. She might still forgive me for my gluten allergy if I worked fast enough.

Tim's favorite dish of the afternoon was a simple burrito casserole made by a young woman he'd greeted more enthusiastically than I would've liked, but she was quiet and timid—I couldn't even remember her name, and Tim didn't care for wallflowers. But I should get her recipe, he'd really had a fit over the dish and it was the first to disappear, despite being in the middle of a buffet that could've fed half of Little Rock.

I emptied one box and broke it down flat, randomly picking another to start on and finding craft supplies. I turned a circle in the center of the room, weighing a place for that kind of stuff to live. The built-ins flanking the fireplace had cabinets with doors for the lower half. I adore a good cabinet—they're an excellent way to hide clutter, and Tim loves an orderly house.

I knelt and unloaded the box into one before I stood, wondering if my husband would mind pizza for dinner again. Sergio's on Main made an excellent cheesy cauliflower with sausage and peppers, which I had eaten every night since we got to town. I might not eat Italian again until Labor Day, but the food was good and delivery was free for the pastor.

He hadn't come home yet, so maybe he was watching the game with a deacon or two. I went to tackle the kitchen, promising myself I'd venture into the small, dimly lit grocery called the Pick and Go the next morning. Maybe I could even track down the burrito casserole recipe if he'd deal with one more pizza tonight.

Not that I didn't have enough recipes. What I really needed was friends in Whitney Falls.

And I needed them quick.

I knew staying holed up in this house fussing with moving boxes wasn't a way to find them. So I would go out and try, one more time. For Tim.

Maybe for myself too.

# ELEVEN
## MARTHA

*March*

Maybe Mary was too worried. Maybe she was smart to ask me to stay for dinner.

Whatever the reason, gnats have sneezed bigger disturbances than the lack of meat in Pastor Tim's dinner caused.

Mary bit her lip, casting her eyes down at the table. "I'm so sorry. I let it burn by accident and there wasn't time to get more. But the tortellini is good without it."

Tim's eyes slid my way. He nodded. "So it is. But perhaps not quite as good as Martha's burrito casserole now."

And that was it.

I let my breath out and turned to Mary, who was rounding the table with the ladle. "I am sure this is way better than anything I've ever made. Especially on that old charcoal grill at the Dreamscape." I tried to laugh, but all I managed was a nervous smile.

"The Dreamscape?" Mary dropped the ladle and I jumped in my seat at the loud clatter of silver on glass. "Sorry, I just... are you staying in that... " she swallowed hard, "place?"

"It's not as bad as it looks." It kind of was, but that seemed like the right answer for the worry dripping from Mary's words.

"I think it might be worse." Pastor Tim put his napkin in his lap. "But we trust the Lord to look after our needs. I must admit, Martha, I'm very interested in how you made that casserole on a motel charcoal grill?"

Pastor Tim folded his hands on the edge of the table as Mary filled my plate with pasta and creamy sauce before she returned to the seat across from me and passed her husband the salad bowl.

"Martha?" the pastor prompted.

"Oh. Well, I just lit the grill and put the pan on it, and then covered the whole thing with foil to help trap the heat. Same as making biscuits on a camp stove."

Tim nodded as he used tongs to put salad on his plate and then passed me the bowl.

I watched Mary, sitting across from me with her hands on the edge of the table, her plate still empty.

"Don't you want some?" I nodded to the casserole dish.

"She's waiting for salad," Pastor Tim said. "She doesn't eat carbs."

"I don't eat gluten," Mary murmured. "I have celiac disease."

Tim shrugged. "Same difference."

I dropped a few leaves of salad on my plate and passed her the bowl quickly. "I'm sorry, I can't imagine that's fun."

Why had she made pasta for dinner if she couldn't eat it? The obvious answer—that her husband liked this dish—was probably the right one. On the face of it, there was nothing wrong, exactly, with her making his favorite dish and having a salad for dinner, but the vibe I was getting from the two of them was odd—and mixed. She'd seemed so worried about how he'd react to a couple of things before he even made it home—timid, even—that I'd been a tiny bit concerned Pastor Tim wasn't near as nice as everyone thought he was. But the kiss he'd planted on her when he came in the door wasn't the way abusive men treated their wives. Trust me. Just don't ask me how I know.

"I don't even miss it anymore." Mary smiled and passed the dressing around. Tim took half of what was in the little oblong china pitcher before he handed it to me. I knew they were being polite, but it felt so weird to sit at Mary's table and take food for my plate before Mary got hers.

I passed the dressing quickly to her and reached for my fork, the smells coming from my plate making my stomach pinch painfully with hunger. Across the table, Mary finished pouring dressing and put the funny pitcher down. She looked pointedly at my fork and shook her head ever so slightly, looking down at her hands, empty and folded at the edge of the table. Almost like an altar.

Grace.

Of course the pastor didn't eat without saying grace. I'd never felt more like an idiot.

I laid the fork on my plate and bowed my head as Pastor Tim began to pray.

"Heavenly father, we thank you for this day, for our health and our community, and for this meal," he said solemnly. "Thank you for the fellowship shared by Mary and Martha, and we ask you keep Martha safe as she sleeps at the motel and works at the Pick and Go. Bless our home, our congregation, and our town, and always help us to do your will, Lord. Please bless this food to the nourishment of our bodies. In Jesus's holy name, Amen."

"Amen," Mary and I said in unison.

I waited for them to reach for their silverware, but they both stared at me.

"Is there anything else I forgot?" Panic burned in my chest as I swiped what I hoped was discreetly at my nose and laid my napkin in my lap.

"You're our guest," Mary said gently. "Please." She waved her hand toward my plate.

Didn't need to tell me twice. I dove into the plate like a person who'd eaten a whole lot of dry ramen and peanut butter and wonder bread sandwiches lately.

The sauce was thick and creamy, and somehow light at the same time. That blonde Martha on the TV would have something to say about this—the cheese flavors, and balance of hearty and tart. I didn't know a thing about food critique, but I knew Mary's tortellini was the very best thing I'd ever put in my mouth, and that was a tall order since my granny was the best cook in five counties.

My plate was clean before Mary got three bites of her salad. Tim looked up from his half-eaten meal and grinned. "I guess you liked it just fine without the meat," he said.

"It's incredible," I gushed, Mary's face lighting up as she chewed. "Probably the best thing I've ever eaten."

"Goodness now, Martha," Mary said. "Careful or you'll have to eat here every night. You're good for my ego."

I didn't know how to say that wouldn't be an imposition without sounding like I was fishing for an invitation, which seemed rude, so I giggled and sipped my iced tea, watching Pastor Tim eat his last few bites.

"I still say the prosciutto makes this dish," he said finally, pushing his plate away. "But that was a valiant effort, my love."

Watching the smile on Mary's face as she finished her salad and put her napkin on the table, I felt a little tug of jealousy. How nice would it be to have someone direct those two words— my love—my way? I knew it couldn't happen, but that didn't mean I didn't wish it could. Of course, Pastor Tim was the sort of almost movie-star handsome that probably had half the women in town wishing he'd call them by a pet name. It felt disloyal to Mary to so much as think that sitting here at her dinner table, though. She was so kind and trusting—I knew that was true even if I was getting a sort of unshakeable feeling that everything in the McClatchy house wasn't as it seemed to the rest of the town.

Or was that just my past trying to wrestle its way into my new life? Aside from the occasional flash of anxiety or loneliness, Mary seemed happier than anyone I'd ever known on a first-name basis. As well she should be.

"I'll do better next time." Mary stood and reached for his plate.

I jumped to my feet. "Please let me clear the dishes. You cooked such a great meal and were kind enough to ask me to stay, it's the least I can do."

Mary hesitated, Tim's plate in her hand and her eyes on his face, before she handed it to me. "That's kind of you, Martha, thank you."

I scooped all the plates and the empty salad serving bowl from the table and carried them carefully to the kitchen, turning the water on in the sink and letting it run into the bowl while I went back for the casserole dish and the glasses.

Mary perched on the arm of Pastor Tim's chair, their faces close together as they talked over each other in low tones. "I was just thinking we have—" she began as he said, "Don't be ridiculous, she'll never—"

They both stopped talking when they saw me. I smiled like I hadn't noticed, gathering the rest of the dishes and turning back for the kitchen.

I wasn't sure how to work her dishwasher, but I found a sponge under the sink and some soap in the dispenser sticking up out of the polished white stone counter. Those, I knew how to clean a mess with.

As bits of food and soap bubbles washed down the sink, I piled the clean dishes in the other side of the sink since I was sure Mary didn't own anything as simple as a dish drying rack. I wouldn't want to clutter up this gorgeous counter with one if I were her, either.

My worries wandered to the sentence she'd cut off when I walked back into the dining room. While I hadn't invited myself to dinner by a far stretch of a wild imagination, I didn't want to think Pastor Tim was upset that I was there.

But he probably was. In just a few months here, Pastor Tim had come to run things in Whitney Falls. Small southern towns are famous for valuing faith above everything, and even the mayor had nothing on Pastor Tim in the eyes of the congregation. Why on earth would the most important man in town want me at his dinner table on Friday night? Or in his home at all, for that matter?

Tears welled in my eyes as I rinsed my plate and laid it on the pile, sure this would be the last time I was invited here.

"Thank you for helping clean up." Pastor Tim's voice came from behind me and made me flinch. I dropped a fork. "Sorry, I wasn't trying to startle you."

"I startle easily these days." Now why in Jesus's name did I say that? I closed my eyes and pinched my lips together.

"I imagine a young woman staying alone at a place like the Dreamscape Motel would be on edge," he agreed.

"No one there has bothered me." I shut the water off and reached for a towel. "I wish I could afford something better, but it keeps me out of the rain." Every word was true, though damned if I could tell why I felt the need to defend an obviously seedy motel to a man who probably hadn't ever known what it was like to want something he couldn't have.

"I meant no offense." He raised both hands and flashed the smile I'd only really seen from a back pew on Sunday mornings. Up close it was easy to see why a woman as angelic as Mary ate salad for dinner after she cooked for him all afternoon. He was what my granny would've called a dandy—good looking and charming. And he knew it.

I stepped backward, the edge of the counter hitting my lower back. "I'm not offended. Just didn't want you to think something that wasn't true."

He nodded. "I'm glad to know you're safe there. Mary will be, as well." Reaching past me, he put his glass in the sink before he turned toward the living room. "Forgive me, I've had a long week and need some rest." He paused in the doorway, his eyes on the white and blue Bible. "I must have left that out last night." He rounded the sofa and plucked the book from the table with bare hands. I watched, my jaw loose after Mary had flipped out when I started to touch it earlier. He slid it onto a shelf. "That's a Cambridge Bible, one of only a few hundred that's survived this long."

"Cambridge? I'm not sure I've heard of that one. Is it like Methodist?"

Pastor Tim laughed, and a fluttery sensation erupted in my middle. I'd never met anyone too good looking and charming for their own good before. I looked around for my friend Mary and swallowed the laugh that was trying to bubble out of my throat in reply to his. I better make darn sure Pastor Tim didn't turn out to be too good looking and charming for my own good. "It's just the oldest Bible publisher in the world. They are exceptionally made, collector's items. This one," he tapped the spine, "was printed in the 1660s. It belonged to my great-great-grandfather. It's why I started collecting them."

I blinked. "That book is older than America?" I wasn't sure why I almost whispered it, just that the book suddenly required reverence because of its age.

"I suppose it is." He laughed again and said goodnight just as Mary came into the kitchen.

"You did not have to do the dishes, Martha," she said in a tone that told me she appreciated it more than I would've thought.

"It was so little trouble. I wish I could do more for you, you've been so kind to me."

Mary put one hand on my arm and then threw her thin arms around me. She was strong for such a tiny person. "You have no idea how happy I am to show you kindness," she whispered. "I have wanted a friend so much, for what seems like a very long time."

Stunned, I returned the hug. I wanted to say "me, too." Instead my lips blurted, "You're the pastor's wife. You have a hundred friends."

Mary laughed as she stepped back. "There's a difference between knowing people and having friends, Martha. And we are really going to be real friends." She grabbed my hands in both of hers and swung our arms back and forth like children on a playground. "Promise?"

"Of course." I had never meant anything more, or understood less why something was happening.

Mary clapped her hands, then wiped down the counters before she stretched and yawned.

I got the hint.

"I really should be getting home," I said.

She smiled again, and I wondered if I'd ever get tired of having her smile at me. I'd only known her two days, and her approval already mattered to me far more than anyone's had since Granny died. "It was so lovely of you to come keep me company today. I hope we can do this again soon, even though your head is healing just fine."

Was that uncertainty creasing her forehead as she said the last words? Before I could think about that, she turned and pulled a pen and paper from a drawer.

"Can I get your phone number before you go?" She held them out for me to take.

"I didn't come over just so you'd take care of my head," I

said. "And I don't have a cell phone, but there's a phone in my room at the motel." I took the paper and wrote the number on it.

"Why don't you have a cell phone?" Mary's brow creased. "I'm not sure if I've met anyone who didn't have a phone in... I can't even remember the last time."

I stared at my fluffy socks. "They cost too much," I said. Plus, I'd seen something on TV about people's whereabouts being tracked with their cell phones. I couldn't tell Mary that was why I'd never have one, but even if I could afford it, it wasn't worth the risk.

I looked up and smiled when she squeezed my hand. Her eyes were sad. "Besides, I almost never do anything but work and church, and I couldn't talk on the phone there anyhow."

"Well, then I know where to find you." Mary beamed as she walked me to the door.

"Your clothes," I said, looking down.

"They're yours now," she said. "And I'll dry and fold your others. You'll just have to come see me and pick them up." She winked.

I practically floated across the street, not even noticing the still-steady rain soaking my T-shirt.

But I sure noticed the black pickup sitting in front of the Tomlinson house when I turned on my headlights. It was the same one I'd seen in the parking lot at the Pick and Go earlier. The driver put their brights on before I could get a look through the windshield and sped off, careening right at the corner past Mary's house.

I didn't see much, but the Virginia plate under the smoky plastic cover beneath the tailgate set off a round of shivers so violent I was sure I'd chip a tooth before I got it under control.

Someone was here in Whitney Falls.

Someone who knew where I was from.

And maybe even what I'd done.

# TWELVE
## MARY

*January—Two months earlier*

By the end of January, I was sure Ruthie Tomlinson had no interest in being my friend.

Not that I could tell anyone that.

Ruthie was crafty—far more insidious in her distaste than all the rest had ever been. In front of most everyone in town, she behaved like she wanted me to be her new very best buddy.

But three "goodness, I guess I got the day wrong"s when I missed auxiliary meetings because she told me the wrong day or time, two canceled coffee dates, and five lame excuses when I asked her to lunch told me the truth well enough.

Once upon a time, I'd have retreated to my church duties like a wounded dog, defeated and sad—and alone.

But not here. This church, this town—we had to make this one stick, even though neither of us ever said it straight out.

So I took a deep breath, tried to grow a thicker skin, and rushed back into the battle for the soul of First Baptist—that's what I called it in my head, anyway. My momma always said I was dramatic.

Instead of wasting time with Ruthie, I collected her minions one by one, starting with the church secretary.

It is an almost universal truth that the quickest way to a mother's heart is to help her child. And it just so happened that Tim's secretary, Lisa, had lost her husband the year before, in an accident nobody talked about. I felt sorry for her, but I always worried when single women spent time alone with my husband —it made me do things like drop by to bring him a home-cooked lunch in the middle of the day.

Lisa was always polite, but the kind of polite that stopped short of being nice. Forced and guarded, yes. But not nice.

I popped in on a sunny Thursday in late January with a steaming plate of meatloaf and mashed potatoes with a side of bacon green beans to find Lisa on the phone, her head in her hand and the kind of defeat in her voice that could flat shrivel your soul faster than a flame to a piece of tissue paper.

"Yes, ma'am, I understand. I'll talk to her. Again."

I pointed to Tim's door and hurried past Lisa's desk. I'm not sure she knew I was there.

"Is that your grandmomma's famous meatloaf?" Tim looked up from his notepad with a grin.

"There might be more for dinner tonight," I said, putting the plate and some silverware on his desk and taking the chair opposite his.

He dug into the plate like I hadn't cooked him four eggs and three slices of bacon just a few hours ago. I waited until his food was half gone before I spoke.

"Is Lisa okay?" I asked.

Tim swallowed a big bite of green beans and blotted his mouth with a napkin. "I guess so? Her kid is having trouble in school."

I leaned forward. "With what?"

"Everything, I think," he said. "But science in particular, she said."

He took a bite of potatoes and then snapped his fingers when he saw me still watching him. "Hey now—do you think you could give the kid a hand?"

"I'd be happy to try." I grinned. I knew Lisa and Ruthie were close, and it would be a victory for me to win Lisa's loyalty away.

Tim called Lisa in from the intercom on his desk.

Watching her when she walked in, I could see her eyes were red-rimmed from crying.

Perfect. Poor thing. I pointed to the chair next to mine, and she sat, glancing nervously between Tim and me. "Have I done something wrong?"

"Mary asked after you when she came in and I told her about your situation with the school," Tim said.

"It's not distracting me, Pastor," Lisa said. "I'm sorry I had to take that call during business hours, but the bulletin is done early and—"

"No, no," Tim held up one hand, shaking his head. "Mary was a nurse. She studied biology and chemistry in college."

"I'd like to help," I said, turning to her with a smile.

She burst into tears. "Thank you." She repeated it at least half a dozen times before I left.

Her loyalty to Ruthie was strong, but her love for her daughter and appreciation of my help would win her over. I just had to give it time.

The more I thought about it, the more excited I got. The very best church secretaries have two primary skills: they know everyone and everything that relates to the congregation, and they know when to keep quiet and when to talk. Almost anyone can keep the books and make the bulletins—it takes someone special to know which secrets to keep and which ones to share.

After four weeks in Whitney Falls, I knew Lisa was a good church secretary. That was why I tried to ignore the way she looked at Tim—and the way he looked at her. New town, new Mary—accepting the things I cannot change, and all that.

I set up a time to meet her daughter and let myself out, thankful for the opportunity that had just landed in my lap.

Just have to keep believing. Like Tim said.

Maybe Whitney Falls would be different than other places. I knew it was wrong to pass judgement without giving the town and its people a chance. Ruthie Tomlinson wasn't everyone. Though she was remarkably similar to other women in other towns, I felt good about this thing with Lisa—she was Ruthie's right-hand woman, but if I could kill that with enough kindness, she'd be a good ally, even if we didn't actually become friends.

My momma used to say men could come and go, but a good female friend is worth her weight in gold.

The church ladies in every town we'd called home, however briefly, were almost always civil: they complimented my sewing skills and my cooking and my ideas for auxiliary fundraisers... but that was usually where it stopped. Maybe the real thing I should pray for was a way to make peace with that. As long as I could fit in well enough to keep the congregation happy, I certainly had other things to worry about.

Maybe things in Whitney Falls were looking up.

Just maybe.

# THIRTEEN
## MARTHA

*March*

*'Amazing grace, how sweet the sound,*
 *That saved a wretch like me!'*

I sang the words with an urgency I wasn't sure music had ever moved me to feel on Sunday morning, watching Mary sing in the choir and wondering how fast she'd come to despise me if whoever was in that black pickup decided to ring her doorbell.

I'd been too stunned to get the plate number Friday night and hadn't left the motel all day Saturday, but Mary had called my room this morning to invite me to a luncheon she was hosting for the ladies' auxiliary and she refused to take no for an answer.

"I need a real friend there, Martha," she'd said briskly. "And you're my only real friend here, aren't you? You have to come. It will be good for both of us, you'll see."

I'd twirled the phone cord around my index finger, biting my lip even as I knew I was going to the blasted luncheon.

Her only real friend.

To someone who'd only ever had one real friend—if you

count blood kin—those words in Mary's wind chime voice could've gotten me to do a whole lot more than go to a luncheon.

I was wearing my only dress, a pink shift with tiny white flowers I found at the Goodwill for two dollars with the original Calvin Klein tag still hanging from it, and a cream-colored cardigan no one had ever claimed from the lost and found at the Pick and Go. My head was still a little too raw for shampoo, though, so my hair was slicked back and tied loosely at the base of my neck.

I could do this. For just an hour or two, I could blend in enough to be there—for my friend.

Besides, if I went to the luncheon I could watch Ruthie and make sure she didn't tell Mary lies about me. Not that I was sure Mary would believe them, but it would make me feel better all the same.

Pastor Tim gave a short, powerful sermon on God's ability to forgive, and I prayed the entire time he talked that he really believed what he was saying. And more importantly, that Mary believed it enough to practice it, should the need arise.

"Understanding and forgiveness are two different things to men," Pastor Tim said in closing, raising his hands in the air. "You can understand why someone has wronged you, but not forgive them, can't you? Think of a time when you did that."

Murmured agreement rippled through the congregation, quite a few people bowing their heads.

"But the Lord our God does not differentiate," Pastor Tim's voice soared. "He sees all, he knows all. He understands us like no one else can, and he forgives us our failings every day. Y'all stand with me please."

Everyone obliged, and Pastor Tim offered a prayer for the town for the coming week. "And all God's people said together," he said.

"Amen," the whole building chorused. Pastor Tim opened

his eyes and smiled. "And now, my brothers and sisters, I challenge you to be more Christlike in your travels and work this week. Strive to understand your neighbors, and remember that understanding and forgiveness go hand in hand in the eyes of our Lord."

I couldn't help but glance at Ruthie Tomlinson when I opened my eyes. Not that she noticed. She had a gaze so sharp and cold pointed at Mary I could practically see a blade of pure ice aimed at my friend's throat.

I rushed toward Mary, aiming to protect her though I didn't really know how I'd go about it, so focused on getting to her that I didn't see Sam Tomlinson coming until he grabbed my arm.

I froze, looking first at his hand on my sleeve, then at his face, which was pinched and frustrated—nothing new—and last at his wife, smirking at me over his shoulder.

"Martha, we need to talk," Sam said, his eyes bouncing around the room looking at everything except me.

"It can't wait until tomorrow at work?" I asked. The Pick and Go, like most everything else in Whitney Falls, was closed on Sundays.

"Well see, that's the thing," he said, glancing at Ruthie over his shoulder. Her eyes narrowed and he sighed. "See, I heard that you took a delivery out on Thursday without my permission—"

"I only did that as a favor, you know, because you weren't there and it's a service the store usually provides for the pastor," I cut in. "I wanted to be helpful, to you and to the pastor and his wife."

"Be that as it may, you caused major property damage while you were making this delivery, and the store can't be on the hook for paying insurance claims from it. I'm afraid I'm going to have to—"

"What's this?" Pastor Tim interrupted, slinging one arm around Sam's shoulders. "Grocery shop talk and you haven't even made it out of the chapel—what ever happened to Sunday being a day of rest?"

Mary walked down from the choir loft to join us, the two of them shuttling Sam a few steps away from Ruthie, who stayed so still you'd have thought her brown pumps were putting roots down in the red carpet. I followed them, trying to smile.

"Yes sir, Pastor, you're right of course," Sam was saying. "I just saw Martha and needed to speak to her about the unfortunate situation with your car, so I thought I would save her some trouble tomorrow, is all."

"What situation with our car?" Mary widened her eyes and smiled at Sam.

He shuffled his feet. I glanced at Ruthie, who hadn't so much as blinked, near as I could tell, her eyes narrowed and fixed on her husband.

"Well, you know... " Sam tried to shrug, and Pastor Tim squeezed his shoulders tighter. "When she hit your car the other day. When she was dropping off your groceries."

"Hit my car?" Mary let out a peal of laughter so pure and light it floated right up into the rafters. "Whatever would make you go and say a thing like that?"

Sam's face turned red as the carpet, and he tugged on his tie. "I mean, I just..." he stammered. "I heard she hit your car and messed up the back end."

"Well, I'm afraid you heard wrong," Mary said firmly, keeping her smile fixed on Sam.

I opened my mouth and Mary poked me with her elbow, not taking her eyes off Sam. "Martha's car broke down in our driveway, but Tim was able to get it running well enough, hopefully, until she can afford to get it properly fixed," Mary said. "Maybe whoever you heard the story from was confused."

Sam glanced at me. I nodded before Mary had to poke me again.

"I'm sure everyone has heard my transmission grinding

gears," I said, drawing a nod from Sam. "I fear the pastor is right and it needs to be replaced. Hopefully it will hang on just a little longer for me."

Mary patted Sam's arm, never breaking eye contact. "See? Just a misunderstanding is all."

He about melted right into a puddle under her gaze. I knew from the way he was always staring at my chest that Sam was a sucker for a decent rack, but apparently, dazzling beauty really did him in.

"Thank you, Mrs. McClatchy, Pastor Tim," Sam stammered. "Good sermon as always."

Pastor Tim let go of Sam's shoulders. "Thank you for following the Lord's way, Sam." He clapped Sam on the back.

Mary cleared her throat. "Do you have anything else to say to Martha?"

"I don't suppose I do." Sam shuffled his feet as he dropped his gaze to them.

I took a step back, just in case Ruthie's glare actually lasered holes through his skull.

"You should apologize for scaring her," Mary chastised gently.

"Sorry, Martha," Sam muttered. He still didn't look at me.

He clearly didn't want to look at his wife, either.

"I'll see you at work in the morning?" I tried not to make it a question, but failed.

"You will."

"Wait just a blasted minute here," Ruthie's screech froze half the congregation in its tracks, and I swear for just a second when I turned I thought there was steam coming out of her ears. I'd never seen anyone's face get so red it looked purple, but hers was the color of watery grape Kool-Aid.

She wasn't going down without a fight.

"Ruthie—" Sam began.

"You shut up," she snarled, low enough that only those of us standing right there could hear her, striding past him and squaring off with Mary and me. "You two are bald-faced lying, and in the house of God. I will not have it! Martha did hit that monstrosity you drive, she pushed it into your garage door, I saw it with my own eyes. I've been telling Sam for months she's nothing but a liability to his store, and this proves it!" She stomped her foot, though it didn't really make any noise thanks to the carpet. "Sam Tomlinson, you get right back here and do as you said you would! Fire her, now, today!"

Sam looked from me to the McClatchys to his wife, shook his head, and hightailed it out the door.

Mary's perfect blonde eyebrows furrowed with just the right mix of confusion and concern, her hand going to her lips as she looked up at Pastor Tim and then back at Ruthie.

Low murmurs started in small groups all around us.

"Ruthie, I am concerned for your mental health." Mary reached for Ruthie's blue-gloved hand and Ruthie jerked away like Mary had soaked her fingers in battery acid. "I'm not sure why you believe this, but it didn't happen."

"I saw it!" Ruthie insisted, drops of spit flying from her lips, her eyes wild.

Pastor Tim bowed his head and began to pray softly. Someone choked back a laugh. Someone else snorted.

Mary sighed, the way a mother does when her child has woken her again in the dead of night to check a closet for monsters that aren't there. "Y'all come with me," she said, to everyone in the room and no one in particular.

We trooped dutifully out into the crisp March sunshine, warm with spring's promise of lazy summer days ahead, but laced with just the barest edge of lingering winter chill.

A determined set to her narrow shoulders and small, sad slope to her neck, Mary led us across the street to the McClatchy house. My throat tried to close clean up as we walked. What was she doing? I had hit the car, which had then hit the garage—her dismissing my insane mistake didn't actually unmake it. Should I worry about Mary's mental health?

Ruthie's long legs ate up the pavement, her face stretched into a grin and her arms pumping at her sides as she passed Mary, half-running up the driveway to the back of the Grand Wagoneer. "See? I told—"

She stopped, laying one hand on the perfect, polished taillight and chrome trim before she bent to inspect the bumper.

It wasn't so much as scratched.

Ruthie glared at Mary before she darted around the front of the car to the garage door. Mary caught my eye and flashed a small smile, the kind that used to mean other girls knew secrets I didn't know when I was in school. I'd never once been included in the people who knew what others didn't—not when it wasn't a terrible thing about my family.

I followed Ruthie to a flawless cream garage door, not a dent or scratch to be found. Turning to follow her gaze, I saw the front bumper of Mary's SUV had also been buffed and polished to a shine.

"Why are you lying?" Ruthie shrieked.

"I really am worried about you, Ruthie." Mary turned a confused gaze on the crowd trailing us, nodding to Pastor Tim. "You should see someone if you keep imagining things. Tim could help you if you want."

Ruthie's face turned the Kool-Aid color again, her hands going to her head as she looked from me to Mary to Pastor Tim and back again.

She let out one more shriek and took off for her house, breaking the heel on her left shoe about halfway there.

Mary met the gaze of each member of the ladies' auxiliary, starting with Lisa, the pastor's secretary. "Does anyone want to skip the luncheon to go to her?" she asked.

Heads quickly shook, murmurs of platitudes rising from the group as the men scattered, sensing the show was over.

"She needs some rest, the best thing we can do for her is leave her be," Lisa said.

Mary nodded, turning to me. "Are you okay?" She winked, but I was the only person who could see because her back was to the crowd.

I nodded. "I hope she is, too," I lied.

"We'll all pray for her, won't we, ladies?" Mary asked, turning back.

The group nodded.

Mary leaned her head on Tim's shoulder, and Tim dropped a kiss on her temple. "Well then. I hope you ladies enjoy your luncheon as much as I'm going to enjoy watching basketball."

"Come on, ladies, let's get on with our day." Lisa marshaled the other women back across the street.

Mary linked her arm through mine and followed them, leading me through the chapel and out a door into a hallway I'd never noticed behind the altar. "We can cut through here to the fellowship hall—this goes past Tim's office so we can get my cooler."

When we were alone in Pastor Tim's office, I twisted my fingers together. "Thank you."

"For what?" She winked, and pursed her lips into the we-know-something-they-don't-know smile again.

"Sam was going to fire me." My voice shook. "I don't know what I'd do without that job."

"Well, we can't have that, now can we?" Mary said. "And now you don't have to worry."

"How did you get everything fixed so fast?" I whispered, afraid someone would overhear but also suddenly wondering if I was losing my mind, too. Ruthie was right, wasn't she? I had hit Mary's car. Hadn't I? I shook my head, one hand going to the cut on my forehead. It had just been three days, for crying out loud. I cut my head on the steering wheel. I had to be remembering it right.

"I couldn't let her foolishness bring you any trouble, could I? What kind of friend would I be if I sat by and allowed that?" Mary put one hand over her heart. "I know you were driving, but that entire mess was her fault. We've been blessed to meet some skilled folks around here. The kind who understand the importance of discretion."

She put one hand on my arm when she saw my forehead scrunch at the school word. "They know how to keep secrets," she said. "And bless her heart, Ruthie Tomlinson has been due to come down a few pegs for a while now. Truth is, I ought to be thanking you. Now, help me carry this down to the fellowship hall, and let's enjoy a quiet lunch with the ladies."

I hefted one end of an Igloo cooler nearly the size of a dinner table, backing out of the room and down the hall at Mary's direction, nothing but gratitude in my full heart.

I still had a job. I had a beautiful, smart new friend.

And Mary and me—we had a secret.

# FOURTEEN
## MARTHA

*March*

Christian Southern women can throw together a Sunday luncheon with Friday notice that rivals the best restaurants big cities have to offer.

In twenty minutes, two long tables were full of Crockpots in assorted sizes and finishes interspersed with foil serving trays, all filled to the brim with concoctions that would've made my mouth water even if I hadn't eaten a handful of dry ramen noodles for breakfast.

Barbecue ribs, chicken in spicy cream sauce, three kinds of macaroni and cheese, green beans, squash casserole, asparagus with cream sauce, and of course, Lisa's famous fried chicken. She pulled a small Pyrex bowl out of her bag once everyone had chosen their seats and brought it to Mary.

"Pastor Tim said you don't do carbs, and to my taste, it didn't lose much of nothing, being made with almond flour," Lisa whispered with a wink. "I cooked these first so there wasn't even regular flour in the hot oil."

Mary gripped the bowl so tightly her fingers lost all color, then put it on the table and jumped to her feet to hug Lisa. "That is the sweetest thing. Thank you so much, I can't wait to get to try your fried chicken."

Lisa grinned. "I do know my way around a chicken. And I appreciate your tutoring my baby girl more than I can say, Mary —she got a B-plus on her science test Friday, and she hasn't been excited about anything school related in a good while. This is the least I could do."

"It means a lot to me, and I'm so happy to hear about her test." Mary pointed to the chair on her left. "Would you sit here with me if you haven't chosen a seat already?"

From Mary's right, I watched. A smile stretched my face appropriately, but worry landed like a stone in my gut. What if Mary and Lisa became better friends than Mary and I were? Lisa was Pastor Tim's secretary, after all, and she lived just one block south of Elias Lane.

I swallowed hard. Mary wanted friends. She could have more than one. I could be happy for her.

"I'd love to." Lisa beamed, putting her blue cooler bag under the chair. I didn't want to size her up as competition, but my brain was already after it, anyhow. She was older than me —probably older than Mary, too—but still pretty, with crow's feet starting to show cracks in makeup that was two shades too dark for her face. Her dark brown hair just brushed her shoulders, curled toward her face at the ends. She wore bright pink lipstick, her nails painted to match, and a navy tank dress with tiny spring flowers printed all over it, a lace border around the collar that matched the lace on the front of her peach sweater, which matched the flowers on her dress. The entire look was the definition of a proper church lady, at least where I grew up.

Certainly, I was not good enough to sit at the same luncheon table as a proper church lady, yet here I was. So I had to act like I belonged.

Mary stayed standing, tapping her fork against the side of her tea glass until the conversation quieted.

"Thank you all so much for being here with us today to celebrate the beginning of the resurrection season," she said. "I know everyone is hungry, so let's have the blessing and get to all that wonderful food. We'll have plenty of time for fellowship after we eat."

Everyone bowed their heads as Mary blessed the food and the ladies of the auxiliary. And then she went and shocked the hell out of me with the last line: "Lord, please watch over my dear friend Martha, keep her safe and comfortable, and let our friendship be the kind that endures."

Whispers started immediately after the chorus of "Amen," several women blinking and staring like they were seeing me for the first time.

"That is the cashier from the Pick and Go, isn't it?" one of the Elias Lane moms whispered.

"I believe so. Ruthie sure seems to despise her, but if Mary considers her a friend..." Her friend let the sentence trail off, like she didn't know any better where it was going than I did.

Mary patted my hand under the table and beamed at the crowd. "Let's eat, ladies," she said.

I tried not to heap too much food on my plate as I went through the line, but everything looked and smelled so delicious, I wound up with a small mountain anyway.

I sat down and watched everyone else. When Mary picked up her fork and dug into the special fried chicken breast Lisa had made her, I dove into my plate.

"I wish I could still eat like that and have your figure," Lisa said, smiling at me around Mary. "Shoot, I wish I'd ever been able to have your figure, eating or no."

I wiped cheese off my chin with a napkin and swallowed. "Thank you, ma'am." I didn't see the point in telling her I had literally been starving for months. People think what they think.

Mary swallowed a bite of the fried chicken and put her fork down. "Now this is a miracle—the crust is so crispy! Almond flour never cooks like that for me!"

Lisa leaned close to Mary. "I'm trusting you with a big secret."

Mary tipped her head closer and I pretended to be more interested in my plate than I suddenly was.

"The secret ingredient in my fried chicken has always been finely processed potato chips. I just dropped the flour-to-chips ratio in favor of the chips here. That's what kept it from getting gummy. So you know if you want to try it in your own kitchen—but don't you go sharing my secret recipe." Lisa winked and Mary clapped her hands together and nodded.

"I won't tell a soul."

I had three plates of food, the last one all sweets: cheesecake, chocolate caramel cookies, and a strawberry trifle. Mary barely got to eat because the other women kept coming by the table to talk to her. She put down her fork, smiled, and gave each one her full attention. The first few commented on her outdoor Easter decor or the squash casserole she'd made for the potluck, but by dessert, the comments about Ruthie and her outburst had started, with several of the ladies directing sympathetic looks at me, even if they didn't speak to me.

I excused myself to the restroom—turns out when your stomach isn't used to much, overloading it with butter and cheese and sugar will do a number on it. I paused outside the door to the ladies' room—I would flush myself right down the toilet on account of embarrassment if anyone walked in while I was using the facility the way my middle was burbling. And I knew good and well my lousy luck meant half the auxiliary would come and go in the time it took me to relieve myself.

I glanced behind me at the men's room.

There were no men left in the building. It would be clean, and quiet, and empty.

Grabbing the door handle, I shoved—and stopped cold when I heard a voice.

"No, I understand completely. You don't understand." That was definitely a woman, and not a happy one, though I couldn't pin the tone down as exactly fearful or exactly angry. "No, she doesn't know a thing, why would she?" She paused, but I didn't hear anyone answer, which meant she was on the phone. "Yes, I'm sure. We do a very good job of keeping church business to the church staff here in Whitney Falls."

Was that Lisa? I'd been so busy listening to people bad-mouth Ruthie in hushed tones that I hadn't seen her leave the table. I stepped back from the door and glanced around the alcove. I was alone, so I hurried into the ladies' room and flipped the deadbolt lock on the inside of the main door once I checked to make sure both stalls were empty. What was Lisa talking about? Still puzzled several minutes later, I washed my hands with the door unbolted, thankful nobody tried to come in while it was locked. Who didn't know? Mary? And what didn't she know?

The church staff here was just the pastor and his secretary—we were so small everyone else was a volunteer, even the choir director.

If Pastor Tim and Lisa had a secret from Mary, I wanted to know what it was. I was Mary's new best friend, and no fried chicken or secret recipe was about to take that from me. Here was a way for me to prove it, to do something to protect my friend. If it was something silly, nobody had to know. But Lisa's tone had sounded serious, not silly. And if it was bad, I could help soften the blow. Or even keep Mary from finding out at all, if that was better. I learned a long time ago that with some things, you're better off just not knowing.

But how would someone like me go about digging up the church's secrets?

# FIFTEEN

## MARY

*February*

I've wanted to be a mother since I held my first baby doll. She had blonde hair like mine, and green eyes that closed when you laid her down, and a pink dress and a bottle. I always called her Gibby—mother said it was the closest I could get to "give me" when she was getting her out of the box.

I rocked her in my little red rocking chair, fed her every time I ate myself, and insisted on carting her everywhere. She was made of hard plastic, but I exiled my teddy bear to sleep with her every night anyway. When Tim and I got married, I put her on my dresser in our room until he complained that certain activities were creepy with the doll watching, and she was relocated to a bookcase in the study.

Standing in the shower the morning of Valentine's Day, I watched red drops trail down my leg, watered down until they washed away pink into the drain, tears falling from my eyes as a sob escaped my throat. Another cycle, another failure. It seemed especially cruel that I should start today, when Tim would come home with flowers like he always did and take me out to the nicest restaurant in town. I didn't want to tell him.

Maybe it was wrong to feel this way, but why should we both spend the evening disappointed?

I nodded at my reflection in the mirror as I toweled off, mourning the fact that my flat belly wouldn't grow bigger this month. I could just keep it to myself.

I dressed in a tailored red suit that felt festive enough, and put on makeup, opting for my true red lipstick to match the suit and the day. I'd meant to get Tim some chocolates at the store the day before, and had walked clean out without them, but the nicest things about Whitney Falls so far were the proximity to everything and the lack of traffic—running back out to the Pick and Go today would be quick and easy, and I knew Tim would appreciate the gesture whether he decided his "new year, new church" diet was over and ate the candy or not.

Walking through the house to look for things that might be out of place, I stopped in the study to touch the end of Gibby's pert little plastic nose and say another prayer for a real baby of my own before I went to the kitchen to retrieve my keys.

They weren't on the hook.

"I know I left them there yesterday." I threw my hands up and spun in a circle, checking the countertops to no avail. "Tim McClatchy, will you ever learn to put things where they go?"

I went back to the study and checked Tim's desk, then to his nightstand, his dresser, the bathroom... no keys.

Shrugging into my coat in the foyer, I opened the door to go over to the church and ask him to check his pockets, and stopped cold with one foot on the welcome mat.

My husband was in the street, sitting behind the wheel of the most gorgeous black, chrome trimmed, wood-look-door-paneled SUV I'd ever set eyes on.

And the whole getup had a huge red ribbon around it, tied in a frothy bow over the sunroof.

"I thought you were going to leave me waiting out here till dinner," he called, putting the passenger window down.

I shrieked so loud they probably heard me on the other side of town, almost slipping on a stray patch of ice in my haste to get out to the street.

"Tim McClatchy, what have you done?" I laughed as he hopped down from the driver's seat and picked me up, swinging me around in a circle twice before he put me back on my feet and planted a long kiss on my lips that nearly made me forget about the car. If I lived to be three hundred and twelve I'd never understand how Tim's mouth on mine could make me go so empty-headed I could hardly tell you my own birthday.

"I figure she needs a proper name," he said, handing me a fat rectangular plastic key. "Any ideas, my love?"

"I like... Gina."

"After your granny." He nodded approval.

"She always kept me safe." I turned the key over in my fingers. "How did you do this?"

"It was a good month, and it's Valentine's Day," he said. "We've always gone big for Valentine's Day. Besides, I have a feeling you're going to need room for a car seat soon, and it'll be so much easier to maneuver in a big old honker like this."

I turned my head and dove into the backseat, exclaiming over all the cupholders and seat hooks so he wouldn't see the tears that sprang to my eyes when he mentioned car seats.

"Is that a footrest?" I gasped, pressing the button to lean the rear seat back.

"I think we could actually live in this thing if it had a toilet," Tim said, waving me toward the driver's seat. "You want to take it for a spin?"

"I was about to go run an errand," I hugged him again before I climbed up behind the wheel using the step that popped out of the side of the car when I opened the door.

Tim shut the door and I adjusted the seat and pushed the

start button. The engine purred to life and three screens lit up with about a hundred pieces of information as a voice on the speakers said "Hello, Mary."

"It even talks to you." Tim folded his arms and gave me a smug grin. I leaned through the open window and kissed him again, pulling back a little dizzy and waiting a few beats before I put the car in gear and moved away from the curb.

On the four-minute ride to the Pick and Go, I discovered that he'd thought of everything right down to preprogramming my favorite stations into the sound system.

I parked in front of the store, the big stupid grin starting to make my face ache, looking in the mirror at my hair and checking out what the rest of the buttons did before I got out of the car. It was a Mom car in every sense of the term—there was even a camera pointed at the back of my head so I could watch a baby in a rear-facing seat on the screen as I drove.

I went into the store and perused the chocolates that were left, which took all of twelve seconds: the selection was sparse and dismal, and I almost laughed at myself and left. My husband put a bow around my dream car, and I was going to give him a box of candy?

But, it wasn't like he needed anything in particular, and he did like chocolates. Just not the ones I had to choose from at the Pick and Go on the afternoon of February 14th.

"Would these be better?" A voice so soft I nearly didn't hear it over the low background music came from behind my left shoulder. I turned to see the checkout girl standing there with a box of Pangburn's Millionaires in her hands.

"They're his very favorite," I gushed, reaching for the box. "You're saving my life. Or at the very least, my evening."

"Glad to help." She turned to go back to the counter and I followed, handing her the candy to ring up.

"Oh no, they're not store inventory," she said. "You take them."

"Where did they come from?" I asked.

"I won them, in a contest we had here to see who could guess the closest at inventory counts. I'm good with numbers. The people who own the store gave me the candy as a prize. But you looked disappointed in what was left, and I think the pastor ought to have a nice gift today."

"Oh, I couldn't take them." I put the box down and stepped back. "I didn't realize they were special."

"If they're your husband's favorites, I really do insist," the girl said, pushing enviably thick hair out of her face. "I've never even had one, I won't know what I'm missing."

My eyes jumped from her to the candy and back again. Nothing they had in the store would do, and Tim adored Millionaires. I hadn't seen a box since we left Texas five years ago.

"I insist on paying you for them," I said, pulling a twenty out of my bag and pressing it into her hand.

"It's just a box of candy," she said. "This is way too much money."

"Call it a convenience fee," I said. "I hope you use it to pick out something you'll enjoy as much as I'll enjoy giving my husband these."

She put the cash in her pocket and smiled, ducking her head. "Thank you, ma'am."

"No, honey, thank you. You saved the day here, and I don't forget a kindness."

I fiddled with settings in my new land yacht, as my grandfather would've called it, for a good fifteen minutes before I put the car in gear. It was such an extravagant gift—had January really been that good for us? I shook my head. Tim wasn't always completely truthful about everything, but I had never known him to lie about money.

I looked back through the plate glass window at the cashier

from the driver's seat of my new car, watching her count change as Ruthie Tomlinson tapped her foot.

I was pretty sure I'd seen the girl at church, though everything about her made me think she tried her hardest to avoid being noticed. Whatever her story, I was sure thankful Jesus put her in my path that afternoon.

Maybe we'd even get to stay in Whitney Falls long enough for me to learn her name.

# SIXTEEN
## MARTHA

*April*

Pastor Tim's secretary Lisa bought the same grocery order every week from just after Christmas until right before Easter: two whole chickens, one pound of ground beef, two packets of Ranch seasoning, a head of lettuce, five apples, a half-gallon of milk, a quart of apple juice, and a box of cherry pop tarts.

The week after the ladies' auxiliary luncheon she added two bottles of red wine and a package of the fanciest cheese we had at the Pick and Go.

I noticed the wine was the same kind Mary bought for her husband, though to be fair, we only sold three kinds of red wine, and this one was the middle-priced one.

I started watching Pastor Tim and his secretary closer when I had the chance. Maybe it was my imagination, but did he stand closer to Lisa and her daughter on Sunday morning than he did to Mary?

I lost more than a little sleep the next week, with Mary's comment that first Friday night about moving so much running through my head on a loop. Did they move to get away from

Pastor Tim's girlfriends, only for him to find a new one in a new town? I knew a bit about men who behaved like tomcats, and I didn't want to think that of Pastor Tim. But he certainly had the looks to get away with it just about anywhere—if Mary wasn't my true friend, I would've had some daydreams of my own about a man like Tim McClatchy. You couldn't hardly be in a room with him and not have your ovaries ache just a little. But real friends don't look at friends' husbands like that, so I did my best to ignore it. I was pretty well alone in that camp among the women of Whitney Falls, though, married or not.

Thursday morning before Easter, I untwisted sheets that had slowly strangled my legs as I flipped about in the bed like a rotisserie chicken, then opened the shade to let some light in, hoping it would wake me up. I yanked it down right quick when I spotted the black pickup with the pitch-dark windows in the Dreamscape's parking lot.

I had almost chalked the truck up to coincidence, because I hadn't seen it in nearly three weeks, and Whitney Falls wasn't exactly the sort of place anyone could hide anything. I mean, the pastor and his secretary couldn't even keep their affair—if they were having one, I still had some hope that I was wrong—from being noticed.

I sat down on the edge of the bed, biting my lip. Now what? It wasn't like this place had a back door. I had to go outside to get to work.

What if the driver just needed a place to stay? A small, politely optimistic part of me that anybody who knew the real me would assume had been squashed into silence long ago asked in my head.

Where has the driver been all this time then? My practical side was much louder.

Fair point.

I double checked the lock on the door and showered, then dressed in my faded jeans and a black pullover, tying on my official Pick and Go apron. I carefully brushed my wet hair, still excited to have it clean nearly two weeks after my scalp had healed enough that I could wash it.

Time to go. I took a deep breath, set on my plan to get the plate number of the truck and try to see if anything else about it might identify the driver—assuming they weren't in it, of course.

I cracked the door and peeked out.

My car, an old Bronco with equal parts rust and paint for an exterior, the manager's small Toyota sedan, and two eighteen wheelers.

The truck was gone.

I wasn't sure if I was relieved or disappointed by that.

Before I could decide, the door two down from mine opened and a girl stepped out, looking around with a slow blink like it was her first day on Mars.

She flinched when she saw me, putting up a hand in a half-wave before she ducked her head and turned back for her door, probably cold in the spaghetti-strap tank top and short shorts she had on.

I opened my mouth to ask her if she'd seen the truck or knew its driver, but she disappeared inside her room before I could get any words out. Probably for the best. What if she said yes, and then told whoever it was I'd been asking about them? I didn't need anybody noticing me if they hadn't already.

It was for that same reason that I didn't go to the office and ask the desk clerk about the truck, or any new check ins the night before—folks who stayed at the Dreamscape were either passing through, just shy of homeless, or up to some variety of no good. I kept to myself. Not only because I didn't want to be noticed, but because in a place like this, it's just safer that way.

I hopped in my car and put the windows down, smiling when the engine turned over on the second try. For today, I had a ride to work. And that was something to be thankful for, my granny would say.

The cool morning air gave me energy, though by the time I got to the store my rumbling stomach had made me regret skipping breakfast because I was worried about the black pickup. I was the first one there, which was weird for a Thursday—right around Valentine's Day Sam had started getting there before dawn on Thursday mornings so he could stock shelves himself ahead of the weekend because he didn't trust the regular stock boy for some reason no one ever told me. I unlocked the doors and flipped on lights, looking around before I took the brownest banana out of the free fruit basket in the produce section and gobbled it down before anyone came in.

I went to get the cash till from Sam's office and found a note on the coffee-stained desk calendar with my name on it. Setting the register drawer to the side, I opened the envelope.

*Martha,*

*I have to go away. Something came up. I know you will keep the store running.*

*Sam*

I read it four times, not that the message was complex: there were no fancy metaphors or hidden symbolism in Sam's letter. He was leaving. Maybe for a day or two, maybe for a year or two, from the information I had. It made sense that he'd left the note for me—I was the only person capable of running the store, we both knew that. And surely if Sam had to go away, Ruthie had gone with him, which would make my week brighter all around. Just as I started to smile about that, the back door rattled in its frame—someone was banging on it. Hard. I stared for a second, not sure I wanted to open it but not seeing a way around it, either.

That black pickup truck swirling in my thoughts, I unlocked the door and cracked it, keeping a firm grip on the handle. The thing was old as these hills, solid metal and heavy, and my arm was tensed to jerk it shut or fling it into whoever was on the other side if need be.

"You ain't Sam." A stocky guy with shaggy blond hair poking out from his trucker cap at odd angles and too many pimples to be much older than me took a step backward, bonking his head on the edge of the open door of a Mack truck, the rig taking up the whole alley.

"He's not here today," I said, still holding the door but cracking it wider. "I'm in charge for today. You have a delivery?"

"I ain't talking to anybody but Sam." He shoved his hands in the pockets of his faded jeans.

"Then you'll have to come back another day, because he's not here." I pulled the door back a bit.

"What am I supposed to do now?" he asked, tipping his head toward the sky so I wasn't sure if he was talking to me or not.

"If you really don't want me to help you, I guess you go on to your next stop."

"It doesn't—" he paused, nodding his head as he looked at me again. "It doesn't matter that much I guess. You have a nice day, miss." He tipped the cap and climbed back into the truck, backing out like he was driving my Honda.

I shut and locked the door and set about getting the store open, wondering if Sam was buying some contraband beef or produce, or if maybe the delivery guy was just weird.

As I counted the till and set up my register, I realized I hadn't paid much attention at all to the way Sam ran the store. He was quiet, and I was content with silence usually.

I was sure I could handle whatever might come up, but delivery guys refusing to deal with me might cause trouble. For the first time since I saw his note, I wondered if the old folks who owned the Pick and Go knew that Sam had taken off—and if it would make them ask questions about me that they hadn't before.

———

By four o'clock on Good Friday, I had about decided Sam wasn't necessary, or maybe even helpful, to the operation of the Pick and Go.

I had gone to work an hour early to place an order based on hand counts of inventory we were low on, balanced the register from the day before, and opened the store five minutes early when there was a four-person line outside thanks to the approaching holiday weekend.

The day sped by in a blur of hams, potatoes, and green beans coming across my counter with various other fixings for Easter dinner—the hams were selling almost as fast as the stock boy could replenish them from the back.

When the first whole chicken of the day came through the line, I looked up.

Pastor Tim's secretary Lisa had her regular order all set up on the counter—except this time, there were three bottles of that red wine I knew the pastor liked.

I bit down on the end of my tongue to keep it still, giving her the total with what I hoped passed for a smile.

"Happy Easter," I said, handing her the receipt.

"Thank you." She smiled back, picking up the bag with the wine. "I have some special plans. I hope you have a nice weekend, too."

I kept my face flat as I nodded and thanked her for her business, but my brain was running ten miles a minute. Mary had invited me over to play cards because Pastor Tim was headed out to his annual Good Friday wilderness retreat. "He goes every year, wanders in the nearest woods for the night. Says it helps him feel closer to the Lord," she'd said.

I wondered if his definition of the wilderness this year included his secretary's house.

I closed the store at six and parked in Mary's driveway at 6:08, thankful it was staying light a bit longer in the evenings as time marched toward summer.

She rushed out onto the front porch wearing sweats with her hair twisted up into a bun—but somehow still looking impressively perfect and put together—before I made it onto the bottom step, her face stretched into a smile so wide it took my breath right away. What I wouldn't give to look in the mirror and see what Mary saw, just for a day.

"Did I ever tell you Good Friday is my favorite day of the year?" She grabbed my hand and pulled until she'd turned me around, guiding me back down the walk toward the driveway.

"I don't think you did," I said slowly, wondering if maybe she'd been into some wine already tonight. "This is... the day Jesus died. Right?" I was pretty sure that was it, though my Bible stories were fuzzy at best before I came to Whitney Falls and started going to First Baptist. In my family, folks used Jesus as a reason to complain about other folks more than they actually read the Bible or talked about his life.

"It was the greatest gift anyone ever gave mankind," Mary said. "Jesus gave us his life. What more could anyone sacrifice for people they love?"

I tipped my head to one side and walked faster to keep up with her. I could see that. I guess.

Mary walked across the driveway and headed up the staircase that ran alongside the garage, talking as she towed me along. "I know most folks see Christmas as the big gift giving holiday, but I've thought for as long as I can remember almost that Good Friday is a day to give something to people you love that will really make a difference for them. Following the example Jesus set when he gave up his life to pay for our sins."

"That's a really nice way to look at something most people probably see as a sad day," I said, squeezing her hand.

"I'm glad you get it." She pulled a key from her pocket and put it in my hand. "Welcome home."

I blinked, the words refusing to register.

I stared at the little silver key, warm in my palm from being concealed in Mary's pocket.

"I—but—what?" I shook my head. She threw hers back and laughed, delight dancing in her eyes when she looked back at me. Grabbing both my hands in hers, she took the key back and unlocked the door, pushing it open wide. "Come on, I've been so excited to show you all week."

She flipped on the light switch and pulled me inside the coziest little apartment anybody ever saw. Gray wood plank floors were soft under my feet when I slipped off my shoes, a cheerful pink and blue rug under a round oak coffee table centered in front of a deep, plush navy loveseat that faced one of them fireplaces in a shiny wood box that you turn on with a switch, and a fancy flat screen TV she'd hung on the wall over it.

"Mary, you can't—" I began, and she raised one hand.

"You cannot say no to a Good Friday gift. It's a rule."

"Whose rule?" I couldn't stop my eyes from skipping from one wonder to the next, from details like a photo of the two of us I'd never seen from the ladies' auxiliary luncheon framed on the mantel to the warm, peachy-beige walls, an antique wood stove, and... sweet cartwheeling Jesus, was that a stacked washer and dryer in the closet next to the bathroom?

I needed to sit down.

"Mine, silly." Mary spread her hands, turning in a slow circle. "Do you like it? I got all the furniture donated from the church or at a thrift sale, I painted the place myself this week, and we weren't using this space for anything at all. I know it's nicer than that godforsaken motel you've been living at, and it's closer to your work. And to me." She ducked her head and smiled, almost shyly. "I mean, we could hang out and catch up more. If you wanted. But you don't have to or anything."

She couldn't be serious. While I knew in my bones I shouldn't spend more time at Mary's house—let alone move into this lovely apartment—I knew just as deep that there was no stopping it now. Acceptance and belonging, it turned out, were every bit as addictive as whiskey, and I was so far off the wagon I couldn't even see the wagon anymore.

Warmth flowed from my face to my toes as I returned Mary's smile. Why in the world Mary McClatchy would think for half a second that I might not want to spend time with her was outside my realm of understanding, but it was a whole different kind of intoxicating to feel like the person in the room who was bestowing the kindness instead of always being the one receiving it.

"Of course I would love nothing more," I said, my voice catching on the last word. "I just can't—this is just flat the very nicest thing anyone has ever done for me, except maybe that time you invited me inside your house after I wrecked your car."

She laughed. "What wreck?" She winked and flashed the we've-got-a-secret smile before she turned to the corner where there was a little table and two chairs set up next to a rolling cart that held a small microwave oven, a toaster, and a hot plate. "It doesn't have a kitchen, but I thought this would surely be at least as good as what you have at the motel. She pointed to a white cabinet on the wall over the cart. "I hung that so you'd have a place to put dishes and some groceries."

"This is incredible," I half-whispered, wandering over to look in the bathroom, tucked in the far corner of the space past a silk screen with a sunrise on it. It was small, but had all the necessities—a stand-up shower with a pretty flowered curtain, a toilet, and a white porcelain sink with a dark wood cabinet underneath.

I caught sight of my face in the mirror and flinched because the smile stretching it into odd angles was so jarring. That girl in the mirror looked safe. She looked happy.

She couldn't possibly be me. But she sure looked an awful lot like me.

Not only was I Mary's friend—her real, true friend—I was going to get to live here? This room was a thousand times nicer than anyplace I'd ever slept in my life.

"Since it's all one big room, I put the bed over here behind the screen." She waved for me to follow her. "It's just a twin-sized one, but it fits in here nicely."

I peeked behind the screen to see a white, rail-framed twin bed with a pretty floral quilt and purple pillow cases, plus a round nightstand with a lamp and a red-leather-covered Bible on it, and a metal rail holding hanging clothes on the wall next to a tall white dresser.

Pretty far cry from a stained feather tick mattress on the floor of the back end of a trailer.

"It's really incredible," I said, my voice soft and reverent, like Granny's used to get when she talked about Elvis or Granddaddy. "I don't think I've ever seen a room so beautiful."

She threw her arms around me. "I'm so happy you love it!"

I let myself hug her back for just a couple of beats. I was getting sucked in too deep. Being loved is all sunshine and wonder, but loving people gives away too much power—anyone can just walk up and take them from you, and a piece of your heart dies with them.

I wasn't looking to lose any more pieces of mine. The black pickup lurked around the edges of my thoughts even as I tried to just let myself be happy in the moment. Backing away from Mary, I perched on the edge of the sofa.

"How much will it be?"

"How much what?"

"Rent." I frowned when her forehead creased.

"You heard me say it was a gift."

"The opportunity is the gift, isn't it?" I couldn't just move up here and not pay any kind of rent. It wouldn't feel right.

"Opportunity?" Mary shook her head. "The room is the gift. It is yours to use as long as you'd like, and you can't pay rent on a gift, that's not how it works."

"Another rule?" I felt my lips curve into a smile despite my best effort at remaining somber.

"It's a good rule, I think." She sat next to me. "I hate thinking about you being out there at the motel surrounded by heaven only knows what," she said. "This is much safer, and it will make me feel more at ease to know that. You're really just doing me a favor by staying here."

Doing her a favor. Okay now, come on. I met her gaze with a raised eyebrow. I'd spent more than enough of my life being gaslighted to recognize what it should sound like, but that life had also made me pretty good at reading people. Mary's sweet face was nothing but earnest. Jesus. My heart stuttered as I blinked and shook my head.

"I thought the first time I met you that you were a real-life angel, and dang if I wasn't right." My voice thickened as I looked around the space again. Mary had such a wonderful life, and was kind enough to want to share her good fortune with someone like me—who'd spent a lifetime trying my hardest to avoid being noticed, because nobody hurts people they don't see.

It might be the dumbest thing I'd ever done, but there was no way I could walk away. She'd be hurt. After all Mary had done for me, I couldn't be responsible for hurting her feelings.

"I have to pay my own way," I said. "You want a family, it's not right for you to let me live here for free. I know how much diapers cost."

She pulled in a deep breath. "Tim said you'd insist on that. How much are you paying at the motel?"

"A hundred and twenty every Friday."

"So you'll pay us eighty," she said, raising one hand when I started to protest. "It's more than enough for the electricity and water you'll use, and we weren't using the room anyway. Save the rest of your money."

I thought that over for a minute. "I really would like to be able to get my car fixed up before it gets cold outside again. The transmission doesn't like the cold," I said. "If you're sure that will cover the extra expenses..."

"It will more than cover them." She nodded for emphasis.

"Okay then."

She grinned as she took my hand and shook it like a politician on the TV. "Welcome home, Martha." Pursing her lips, she let go of my hand and tipped her head to one side. "Is this not the best time to tell you that I asked our friend about your car and he said your transmission would probably be a simple repair?"

"Mary!" Both hands flew to my face.

"I will take you to work tomorrow and he'll fix it when he comes by to change Tim's oil. He won't take money from me, so I can't take money from you."

It was too much. I burst into tears. She put one hand on my back and pulled me into a hug. "This is what friends are for," she said. "We help each other out, even when it's hard or impractical. And I am so glad the Lord sent you to me as a friend, Martha."

Sniffling, I sat up and wiped at my face. "Not half as glad as I am. I haven't had a real friend in... well. It's been a while. Saying thank you feels like far too little, but I can't think of anything else."

"Thank you is just exactly right." She patted my hand. "I'm going to run into my room and get a shower before dinner, since I've been moving things out here all day and I'm a mess. You settle in, then come up to the house and we'll go get your things and then stop and get a pizza on the way back. A real, official girls' night."

"That sounds wonderful," I said.

She disappeared, and I flipped on the TV and found a country music channel, cranking the volume while I poked around. Blue-and-white-flowered plates and bowls rested alongside a skillet and a saucepan in one side of the wall cabinet, while the other was stocked with peanut butter, bread, crackers, and canned soups. The drawer in the cart had a collection of mismatched silverware, and the lower cabinets held dish soap, pine sol and Windex.

Tears flooded my eyes again when I opened the dresser drawers—neat rows of new underwear and socks were stacked in the top one, and I found sweats and pajama pants in the middle drawer and three new pair of jeans and two bras in the bottom. She'd thought of everything.

I grabbed a pair of jeans, a bra, panties and a soft hooded sweatshirt with a First Baptist logo that had the steeple on the church shooting out of the top of the "a" in Baptist, and hurried to the bathroom.

In the shower I found shampoo and soap that both smelled like flowers, and a new razor, too. I didn't want to keep Mary waiting, but the truly hot water felt so delightful—the boilers at the Dreamscape were as old as everything else, so showers there ran from lukewarm to icy depending on the hour.

Rinsing my hair for the second time because extra shampoo here and there would be affordable with a spare forty dollars a week, I imagined the searing needles pouring from the shower head were washing away not only the dirt and grime of the week and the smell of the Dreamscape Motel, but my past, too.

What if it could all just be washed clean as easily as standing there with the water pouring over me, if I could be born anew stepping out onto the soft pink bath rug—safe and kind and at least a little deserving of this life I seemed to have stumbled into?

Wiping the steam from the oval mirror on the wall, I stared at my reflection. A new me. Martha. I'd lost so much weight in the past few months that my face actually looked different. Maybe it was different enough, especially now that I'd be able to buy myself a box of hair color.

If whoever was driving that black pickup came at me, or went to Mary, it would be their word against mine.

And Mary believed in me.

The girl in the mirror nodded. I could still see the fear on her face, but it was mixed with a new determination.

If it came down to it, I wouldn't give up this new life without a fight.

# SEVENTEEN
## MARTHA

*April*

There was never anything good about Friday night at the Dreamscape Motel.

I was embarrassed—and almost afraid—to take Mary to the motel on a Friday night, but she had the idea of getting my things and checking me out before they charged me for the coming week in her head like a dog with a fresh hambone, and she wasn't about to let it go.

"I'm not sure you can really imagine what goes on at a place like the Dreamscape," I said carefully, watching Mary arrange logs in her family room fireplace so we could have a fire when we got back.

"You think because I married Tim I don't know there are terrible things that happen in the world?" Her laugh echoed in the fireplace, bouncing back on itself and sounding startlingly harsh. Brushing her hands off, she stood up. "There's nothing going on there I haven't heard of. And I don't expect we'll be there long anyhow."

"But..." I stopped and sighed. I wasn't going to win this.

"What?" Mary asked.

"I just... hearing or reading about bad things and seeing them up close are two different things. And I don't want you to think..." The frown on Mary's face crept all the way up to her eyebrows, stopping me before I could finish that thought.

"Think less of you?" She shook her head as she talked, grabbing my hands. "Never."

The doubt and fear must've been plain on my face, because she pulled me to the white sofa and sat, keeping ahold of my hands. "Let me ask you something, Martha: do you like me?"

I laughed right out loud at the absurdity of such a question. "You know I do." Didn't she?

"And do you trust me?" If her wide violet-blue eyes had shone with any more earnestness, I would've melted right into a puddle on the couch.

"With my life." I wasn't sure where that came from, exactly, except that it sounded better to my brain than a plain old "yes." I wasn't alone there, judging by how Mary's whole face lit up like a Christmas tree.

"Is there anything that would make you think less of me?" she asked.

I started shaking my head before she stopped talking. "Never."

"Okay then." She squeezed my hands. "Same goes. I can guess that the folks who stay out at that motel aren't our usual First Baptist crowd, which could be good or bad, I guess, depending on who you're talking about. I mean truthfully, if Jesus himself were here in Whitney Falls, that motel is probably where he'd spend a lot of his time if you go by his history. You know, according to the gospels, he cautioned against judgement more than he did against murder?"

"Really?"

"Really. And I certainly am not going to judge you, my dearest friend, by anything I might see or hear there."

The "thank you" stuck under the lump in my throat, so I nodded and returned the pressure on her fingers, standing to follow her outside. I simply had to be wrong about Pastor Tim and his secretary. Surely, no man could want for anything if he was married to Mary.

"Let's give that old transmission of yours a last ride." Mary tossed me the keys to my Honda.

I drove the familiar route to the motel for the last time as she talked about how much she was enjoying her tutoring sessions with Lisa's daughter, Charlotte, which led to talking about the church and the ladies' auxiliary and how much she wanted to make me an official member, and how backward it was that the bylaws still required that a woman be married or widowed to join.

"I bet that nonsense is still just there from when the town was founded and the church first opened," she said. "I mean, honestly. In the twenty-first century, what do they think you might overhear that you don't already know?"

I blinked. "Is that why they didn't let unmarried women into the auxiliary? Of all the things I would've thought, that would not be one of them. I assure you, there's nothing those women could say that would shock me."

"Exactly. We're just going to have to change this rule, is all." She leaned forward as I turned into the lot at the Dreamscape and pulled up in front of the door to my room.

"I won't be but a minute," I said, grabbing the canvas bags out of the backseat.

"I'll help." She opened her door and unbuckled her seatbelt as a man who could've qualified for his own zip code based on sheer size came stumbling out of the room two doors down, making it about three steps off the porch before he let out a shuddering moan and dropped face first into the gravel, the ground trembling under my feet. I jumped backward more out of instinct than actual danger, looking at Mary. She just stared, her eyes wide.

"He's—I don't think he's breathing, is he?" she stammered.

Any other day in any other company I'd have shouted a string of swearwords that would make a seasoned sailor blush, but not that day. Not in front of Mary.

She was right. He wasn't breathing.

"Can you call for an ambulance?" I asked.

"I think the volunteer fire department is having a Good Friday potluck tonight," she said. "But I'll call the chief's wife and see if we can get someone out here."

The nearest hospital was more than an hour away. I stared uncertainly between the big guy—I didn't recognize him, and I knew pretty much everyone in Whitney Falls on sight since I worked the checkout at the only grocery store—and the door he'd stumbled out of.

Mary hung up her call. "They're sending some guys."

"Thank you." I moved toward my own room. Drug overdoses weren't uncommon at the Dreamscape—truth be told, they might have been the most palatable illegal activity that went on there.

Mary followed me as the freckle-faced Friday night desk clerk wandered out to the lot.

"What happened?" he called, leaning forward and peering at us in the fading twilight.

I shrugged, pointing to the open door to the room the guy came from before dragging Mary into my room and shutting the door. Whoever Mr. Mountain out there was, the odds said he wasn't up to anything good. We'd made sure he might not die, which was all I thought anyone could reasonably expect of us given the situation.

"Does that happen often?" Mary asked, her eyes skipping around the room.

"I try not to pay enough attention to notice." I stayed in front of her, hurrying to the bedside and snatching up a cheap dime store plastic picture frame, a homemade slingshot, and a pebble, shoving them into the bottom of a canvas bag before I opened the dresser and covered everything with my black sweatshirt and my old, ratty spare underwear. I'd been washing the new ones Mary'd given me every night so I could wear them every day. With the new panties I'd found in my apartment and my very own washing machine, I could get rid of these gross old ones for good. Maybe I'd even burn them in my woodstove, leaving my tattered old life behind for something new and soft and whole.

"This room is bigger than I would've thought," Mary said. "Is that a king-sized bed?" She did a good job of avoiding letting what I'm sure she was feeling show on her face. I kept grabbing things and shoving them into the canvas bag until it was stuffed to the brim, the photo safe and secret in the bottom.

"I think so," I called, retrieving my razor and toothbrush from the bathroom. "I only sleep on about a quarter of it—the mattress is lumpy everywhere but the right side near the edge."

I stepped out of the bathroom to find Mary inspecting the post on the headboard. She looked up at me with sad eyes. "I'm so sorry anyone has to spend much time in a place like this."

"I won't be sorry to see the last of it," I agreed, pointing to the door. "Thanks to my guardian angel."

She laughed and waved one hand as I straightened the brown polyester blanket on the bed, checked the drawers for show since I knew there was nothing in them, and shut off the bedside lamp.

"Ready?" I asked Mary, who had crossed the room to peek into the bathroom as the sirens stopped in the parking lot.

She looked over her shoulder at the bags and her eyebrows went up. "Is that... everything?"

"Yep."

The corners of her lips tipped down, but she didn't say anything.

I could ask her to wait in the car with the bags while I checked out and turned in my key. Right then, it hit me that I never had to see this place—or anyone in it—again. I let out a long breath I didn't realize I'd been holding and pulled the door open just as the medics loaded the big guy into the back of their ancient ambulance, an oxygen mask strapped to his face.

For a second I worried they'd have questions I didn't want to answer, but they didn't even wave as they pulled the doors shut and drove off, siren blaring.

"Amen," Mary said behind me, getting to her feet.

"I hope he's okay," I said, figuring that's what she'd been praying for.

"It's in God's hands now," she said, stepping outside and glancing around. "But a prayer never hurt anyone."

I figured a prayer from Mary McClatchy was probably the closest a person could get to an urgent email popping into the Good Lord's inbox, so if anyone could get that guy some divine intervention, it was her.

I put the bags in the backseat of the car and pointed to her door. "Can I talk you into staying here while I turn in my key and check out?"

Mary reached for the car door handle, then shook her head. "I can't let you go in there alone."

I smiled. "You are a very good friend, Mary, but I have seen my share of ODs," I said. "I'm sure that's all this was, no one is going to get hurt. Turn up the radio and lock the doors, I'll be right back."

She straightened her spine and shook her head. "I won't leave you alone."

I glanced around. I didn't see another soul, and the black pickup was nowhere in sight.

"Fine," I waved for her to follow me.

She charged back to the walkway, grabbing my hand and hanging on tight.

In the office, I looked for the freckled kid, but he wasn't there.

I marched to the only other place he would be, Mary's hurried feet and grip on my fingers telling me asking her again to stay in the car would be a waste of breath.

The door to room sixteen was still open.

"Aren't the police on their way?" Mary whispered.

I shook my head. Whitney Falls only had two police officers, and if they came running to the Dreamscape every time someone OD'd, the town would have to pay rent here. These matters—like nearly everything else that happened at the motel—were left to management.

I had never bothered to ask Freckles his name, so I stepped into the room and called "Hello?" like some idiot girl from a slasher movie. If I hadn't both wanted desperately to put this place in my rearview mirror for good and needed the money they'd expect at midnight for the upcoming week, we'd have turned around and left right then.

Not a sound.

It wasn't like there were a lot of places to hide. Maybe the desk kid went to the bathroom.

I had one foot out the door when a thump from said bathroom stopped me cold.

Mary tugged on my arm when I started to turn back, her eyes so big I could see white all the way around the blue. "We shouldn't be in here," she said. "What if that man wasn't alone?"

I realized two things in the exact same second: if Mary was right, someone else might need help—be it a second OD or the desk kid if he'd walked in on someone who didn't want to be seen at the local no-tell motel. And, maybe terribly, that I didn't really want to help and I definitely didn't want to know any more about what had happened. I just wanted to turn in my dang key and go back to Elias Lane.

I was going to live on Elias Lane. It really occurred to me for the first time and I wanted to cry.

But first I had to not die in this motel room.

"Hey there, everyone okay?" I called, picking up a big, heavy ashtray from the dresser.

The bathroom door opened and Freckles came out, his face falling flat when he saw us. He slammed the bathroom door behind him and shook his head, managing a half smile. "That bathroom is disgusting. Are you ladies looking for someone?"

His eyes skipped over me and widened when they landed on Mary.

"You," I said, setting the ashtray down over a piece of paper on the table. "I need to give you my key and check out of room fourteen."

"Sure thing."

Another thump came from the bathroom.

"Everything okay?" Mary asked, her voice barely shaking at all. She was so kind. Too kind for her own good in a place like this.

"Shampoo bottle probably fell in the shower. I moved it when I opened the curtain." His eyes darted between me and Mary and the door behind us, his tongue poking out to wet seriously chapped lips.

I stepped in front of Mary and smiled at him. "I don't think the big guy was from around here. I hope they can track down his next of kin. Can you come to the office and write me a receipt?"

There's an unspoken code in places like the Dreamscape—don't mind anyone else's business, and you probably won't get hurt. I was trying my hardest to be uninterested in anything but getting out.

The desk kid let go of the door and pointed us outside. "Sure thing."

He knew the code. I just needed Mary to keep her very well-meaning mouth shut for five more minutes.

I turned to follow him, my eye falling on the paper under the ashtray. It was a computer-printed receipt, for a shirt, it looked like, with a size and some abbreviations about color and fit. I left it, and the room, trying to pretend I didn't hear another thump as I pulled the door closed.

Maybe that one was from a different room. It was hard to be sure with such thin walls.

Three minutes later, the Honda's tires kicked up gravel as Mary and I sped out of the parking lot. Her eyes closed, she clasped her hands over her purse on her lap and didn't say a word the whole way back to her house.

When we parked in her driveway, she didn't move at first, shaking her head after a moment like she'd been deep in thought.

Please, God, don't let it be thoughts that she made a mistake asking me to stay here.

"Stay here," I said out loud to Mary, an idea occurring to me. "I'll be right back."

She didn't move—or acknowledge that I'd spoken to her.

I dashed up to the front porch and plugged in the fairy lights, pausing to fluff up the pillows on the swing. It wasn't too chilly to sit outside for a moment and being on her porch might help Mary relax and feel safe.

Nothing bad could happen on Elias Lane.

I turned, in such a hurry to get back to the car and bring her to the porch that I almost missed it. A piece of paper someone had folded up and stuck in the hinge crease of the front door. Probably a menu for the pizza place. I'd seen people leave them like that on TV. Mary didn't like anything to be out of place, so the paper would irritate her.

I tugged it free and started to stick it in my pocket, but I spotted the ink bleeding through before I could.

My heart crawled up into my throat and made it hard to breathe as I made my fingers unfold the paper.

*I know where you come from. I know what you did.*

*I'm not going away, so you should.*

# EIGHTEEN
## MARY

*February*

Was I getting fat?

I stared critically at my body in my full-length mirror. My stomach was flat as a still pond, my waist nipped in like it had been carved by a fashion designer. My boobs could be bigger, but they were fine. The scale didn't think I was letting things go, and my clothes all fit just right.

So it couldn't be that.

Maybe my hair wasn't bouncy enough—winter in the Ozarks isn't exactly a forgiving season for humidity—the air was bone-ash dry and had been for weeks.

Poking my nose nearly to the glass, I studied my eyes. Still the same striking blue, so deep they often looked almost purple. They'd always been my best feature. But there were more lines around them these days—not deep, but unmistakably the beginnings of crow's feet.

Is thirty-one really that old?

Tim was thirty-four, but he'd always been partial to youth. That had to be it, simply by process of elimination. Aging wasn't attractive to him. I would look for a new eye cream the next time I went to Malvern, and see someone about a younger haircut.

I had to do something—we hadn't been in Whitney Falls two months, I still wasn't pregnant, and my husband's eye had wandered.

Again.

What I wasn't exactly sure of, yet, was just where it had wandered.

He'd sworn to me that last time was really the last time. He'd cried, burying his face in my belly and praying the most anguished prayer you've ever heard for a little boy he could toss a baseball with and take fishing. Every word had sunk like a dagger into my empty abdomen, tears dripping down my cheeks as I rubbed Tim's head and told him I understood.

I did. Understand, that is. He tried to follow God's commandments, but he was a mortal man who fell short of perfection. Tim was steadfast in his conviction that he would have no trouble being completely faithful to his family, even if there'd been the occasional lapse in his faithfulness to his wife.

So I prayed. I tracked basal body temperatures, became an expert in ovulation kits, and invested in frothy lingerie that made me blush to try to get him as excited as possible.

But I'd ridden this merry-go-round enough times to know the signs.

Late nights "at work," which was pretty dimwitted on his part when his work was right across the street and I could see that his office light wasn't on from my dining room while dinner grew cold on the table.

Then there was the sudden secretive aura: seven times in the past two weeks, I'd walked into a room to find his thumbs flying over his phone screen typing a text, a grin on his face. Every time, he'd locked the screen and slipped the phone in his pocket before I got near him. Every time, my heart stuttered in my chest, my stomach twisting into a bit of a tighter knot and bile burning the back of my throat as I swallowed hard and arranged my face into a loving smile, pretending I didn't notice.

Sometimes I almost wondered if he wanted me to notice. Either that or he must've thought he was just the most clever man who'd ever lived.

Valentine's Day dinner and date night had been lovely, but ever since, I couldn't do anything right no matter how hard I tried. Dinner was either cold because he came home late, dry because I'd left it warming in the oven, or late because I hadn't wanted either of the other two mistakes to repeat. Twice he'd told me his meals weren't up to my usual standards, complaining of bland sauce or tough meat. And just last night he'd shattered my blue gravy boat on the hardwood floor, sending salad dressing everywhere, because he found a wilted leaf of lettuce on his plate.

But the critiques of the house—that was how I knew real trouble was brewing. The house was never clean enough. He kept white gloves in the drawer in the foyer table, randomly pulling them out to check for dust in different rooms because, he said, he was allergic to it and couldn't have it in the house. He hadn't had them out once the first six weeks we were in this house, but in the past ten days he'd come to me waving some offensive smudge on a fingertip four times. Because he knew nothing would keep me busy like thinking that my husband thought I was falling down on a job I took very seriously: making this grand, rambling old Victorian an elegant, yet comfortable, home. I scrubbed floors on my hands and knees, singing as I went, because I refused to be anything other than thankful for the life I'd been blessed with. And I wasn't about to lose it to whoever he was infatuated with this time. We had built far too much together to let it crumble because he liked variety.

Worrying around my dreams with Tim's faceless floozy was

a black pickup, with the kind of mirror-black tinted windows that were impossible to even see a silhouette through. I'd seen it twice in real life, idling on our street, or driving slowly down the block and around the corner past the church. Whitney Falls was a tiny town and we'd lived here nearly two months—that truck didn't belong to anyone on Elias Lane.

I checked out the front windows every time I passed one, now, because the second time I saw the truck I'd promised myself I'd walk out and stop it next time to see who was inside.

I loved this house and I was trying to love this town, and I would not live in fear of anything or anyone.

Peering through a slit in the dining room blinds, I scanned the quiet street that was going to be our home. Where we would raise our family. I would see to that. And I would keep my child safe at any and all costs.

I stopped in the kitchen to grab my keys and went out to the driveway, looking entirely differently at my extravagant Valentine's Day gift. Had guilt, and not love or hope for a family, been the motivating factor when Tim bought this thing?

I was really beginning to wonder.

I knew better than to confront him, especially before I had proof.

What I really needed was to know who was on the other end of his affections. And in a place the size of Whitney Falls, it shouldn't be too hard to find out.

# NINETEEN
## MARTHA

*April*

Swallowing a whimper, I stuffed the threatening note into my pocket just as I heard the car door close. It seemed Mary got tired of waiting.

Breathing slowly, I tried to squash the panic that was squeezing my chest like some kind of dungeon torture contraption.

I'd figure out who was hateful enough to leave such a note, and I would handle it. Whatever it took. The people in this town who saw a mousy cashier at the Pick and Go, who might have thought they could bully that girl—they had no idea who they were messing with.

But first, I needed to rescue Mary's evening so I would get to stay. I said a silent prayer of thanks that I'd gotten to the porch first and pasted a smile on for my friend as she started up the steps, pausing to press her fingers to her lips when she saw that I'd turned on the fairy lights and fluffed the pillows.

"Martha, this is lovely!" She smiled. "Thank you so much for your kindness."

"I'm sorry about... all that back there," I said, waving her toward her swing. "I know you love your porch and I thought this might help you forget about it."

She settled into the cushions and tucked her feet under her, pointing for me to sit on the other end of the swing. "You thought right. Please join me, and let's start our first of what I pray will be many girls' nights, now that that horrible place and the people in it are all behind you."

I perched on the edge of the swing, keeping my feet on the floor, and Mary laughed. "Martha, honey, you've got to lighten up. This is practically your home now. Please, really sit on the swing with me. I'm worried about you."

What?

"Why?" I tried to keep the alarm out of my voice.

"I had imagined things about that motel, but that man... the things we saw." Mary shook her head, tears making her eyes shine. "I was only there for a few minutes. You've been living there for months. Are you okay?"

It took everything in me to keep from busting up laughing. She was so sweet, and I couldn't help wondering what it must be like, to come from people and places that weren't comfortable in sketchy motels riddled with prostitutes and addicts.

Places where your past couldn't pop into the seam of the door on a note scrawled in thick black ink and make you feel like you might throw up even though you hadn't had time to eat today.

"I'm okay," I said. "I learned fast that if you mind your business, you can mostly avoid trouble." It was entirely true. I just left out the part where I'd learned that particular truth before I'd learned to read. "I guess I just have faith that things will work out."

She smiled and squeezed my hand. "What a perfect testament to the power of the Lord. Would you mind if I—"

Mary's phone rang, stopping her from finishing that thought.

Her forehead scrunched up as she looked at the screen, and she held up one finger and answered the call.

"Hel—"

Mary stood up. "Sweetie, I need you to slow down. What did your mom do?"

Every drop of color drained from Mary's face as she listened to whoever was on the phone, her hand flying to her mouth.

"No, calm down now, I'm sure everything is okay." Her voice shook, but not badly. She glanced at me. "You just need to have faith that things will work out. You sit tight, I will be right there to pick you up. You can stay here with my friend and me until we sort this out."

She ended the call and turned wide eyes on me. "Lisa's daughter Charlotte is beside herself. Lisa hasn't been home tonight—or even called—which is completely unlike her."

Lisa, Pastor Tim's secretary, who'd bought three bottles of his favorite wine on a day when he was off on a retreat overnight? That Lisa hadn't been home? I knew Mary had been tutoring Lisa's daughter, a sweet girl who was probably twelve or thirteen, and they lived nearby. It made sense that the child called Mary—but I couldn't help wishing she had picked any other adult in Whitney Falls.

I pulled in a deep breath, my face creasing with concern that had nothing to do with the secretary's safety.

I certainly couldn't say anything to Mary based on my suspicions and some extra bottles of wine coming across my checkout counter. But I did send up a quick silent prayer that I was wrong and Pastor Tim was an honorable man. Maybe Lisa got a flat tire.

I ignored the voice that whispered that every place in Whitney Falls was walkable from every place else and followed Mary to her Grand Wagoneer.

# TWENTY
## MARTHA

*April*

Lisa's home didn't compare to the stately beauties of Elias Lane, but counting Mary's it was the second-nicest house I'd ever been allowed inside, a neat little cottage with blue siding, dandelion yellow shutters, and a wide front porch complete with inviting white rocking chairs.

"Charlotte, it's Mary," Mary called as she knocked on the door a second time. "It's okay, sweetie. Everything will be okay. Just open the door."

I stood behind Mary, watching her shoulders relax as soft steps approached the door from the other side. A chain lock scratched faintly as it slid, followed by the *click* of a deadbolt unlatching before a front door painted the same shade of yellow as the shutters swung inward to reveal a thin girl with her mother's wide green eyes and a smattering of freckles, who somehow looked smaller to me than she had last Sunday morning at church.

Maybe it was the way her shoulders hunched as she

wrapped her arms around herself. Like she was holding herself together. I knew a thing or two about the posture.

A single tear escaped Charlotte's right eye, and Mary swooped forward before anyone spoke, gathering the child into her arms and smoothing her long, shiny hair. Charlotte sobbed into Mary's shoulder.

"Something is wrong, it's like I can feel it." She shuddered so hard Mary's frame shook, too. "I'm so cold. It's like there's a slimy, icy cape all around me and I can't get it off."

I knew that feeling—my granny said when bad things happen to a person enough, the body has a way of figuring out a warning. Like a physical storm siren for tragedy or danger. My skin crawled right up my arms in the cool night air as Mary rubbed both her hands briskly up and down Charlotte's like she was trying to scrub off the slimy cloak.

"There now, sweet girl, your momma will be back soon." Putting both hands on Charlotte's shoulders, Mary took half a step back and bent her head to look into the girl's eyes. "God has a plan for all of us, Charlotte. You remember that and you'll never be afraid."

Red light bathed the porch as an engine shut off behind us on Mary's last word, the local law's arrival announced by way of two car doors slamming. Mary had insisted on calling them on our way over, she said it would help Charlotte feel better. I had doubts about their ability to help a stray kitten, but I kept them to myself.

Charlotte sniffled as both members of the Whitney Falls police department—one in uniform and one in pajamas—mounted the steps. Mary wrapped one arm around the girl and waved everyone inside.

The entry hall was small but tidy, with the child's coat on a hook by the door and the SpongeBob SquarePants theme blaring from a TV deeper inside the house.

"It feels less lonely with the TV on," Charlotte mumbled, scurrying around a corner a second before the noise vanished.

I knew a few things about that, too.

Following her, we found a cluttered living room, where overstuffed mismatched chairs flanked a glass end table topped with a lamp and piled with papers and envelopes. A large red pillow-back sofa was shoved up against the windows, and the TV sat on a stand on one side of the small brick fireplace. Charlotte scuttled a nearly empty cereal bowl and a plastic cup to the kitchen and Mary turned a slow circle, her eyes stopping first on the stacks of papers on the small table, and then on the half-finished jigsaw puzzle on the round wood coffee table in front of the sofa.

I saw a hint of disapproval flash across her face before she took the blue chair closest to the window and pulled Charlotte onto her lap, waving me into the beige armchair. The officers took the sofa.

"Hey there, Charlotte," the one with the bushy Magnum PI mustache said. "Can you tell me when you last talked to your momma?"

"She dropped me off at school this morning." Charlotte's voice was barely above a whisper.

"Is she usually here when you get home?"

"Not lately. She's been working later. At the church." The child's eyes skipped between the police officers. "But I just fix myself a snack and do homework, it's okay."

The shorter cop, who was in uniform, smiled. "Sure it is, honey. Take it easy, we're not here to get anybody in trouble."

I had a feeling people poking around in Lisa's whereabouts might cause trouble for more than one body, but I couldn't say so.

Mary whispered something to Charlotte, who smiled and nodded. "My mom always calls me in the afternoons, though.

She knows I worry. I tried her cell phone, lots of times, when she didn't call me today and it just goes to voicemail."

"Well now, I'm sure there's a good reason for all this, so don't you be too mad at her. Who is her closest friend, would you say?"

Charlotte bit her lip, glancing toward Mary. "Well, I guess I would say it's still Miss Ruthie. But I haven't seen her in a while."

I sat up a little straighter. Ruthie. I had forgotten they were friends. And Sam had just up and taken off.

Guilt over thinking Pastor Tim could betray Mary practically seeped from my pores as I realized Lisa might be over at Ruthie's house helping her old friend.

"Did you call Ruthie?" Mustache asked.

"Of course I did." Charlotte didn't roll her eyes, but it sure looked like she wanted to. "I'm almost thirteen, I'm not stupid. Nobody answered the first time, and the second time someone picked up and hung up right away."

I clenched my fists so tight my nails dug into my palms.

"Any other friends?" The uniformed officer, a bachelor who went through two twenty-four-can cases of Keystone Light every week according to his grocery cart, rubbed red eyes with his knuckles. "Maybe a man friend?"

Charlotte's eyes narrowed. "No," was all she said.

Uniform looked pleased with the answer.

Mustache tapped his fingers on the table and stood, nodding to each of us in turn. "Appreciate your time, ladies. I'm sure Lisa just got hung up somewhere and she'll be home soon, but we'll ride by Ruthie Tomlinson's house to check in and keep an eye out. Let us know if she's not back by noon tomorrow."

That was it? Mary set Charlotte on her feet and stood, walking the men out. She returned with a smile that would've dazzled half of Hollywood and pointed it straight at Charlotte.

"Tell you what, sweet girl—why don't we get you a bag and you can have a sleepover with me tonight?"

Charlotte tipped her head to one side, biting her lip. "What if my mom needs me?"

Mary pointed to the papers on the table. "We can leave her a note so she won't worry, and I'll send her a text, too. I'll bring you straight home tomorrow when she's back."

Charlotte nodded, a shy half smile flashing as she went back to the kitchen and returned with a purple Crayola marker. Mary plucked an envelope from the stack and scrawled a note to Lisa before she turned back to Charlotte. "May I see your room?"

That got a real smile. Charlotte led Mary down a short hallway with Mary asking about school and the girl's voice losing the quiet tremor from earlier as she talked about friends and teachers.

I waited until the bedroom door closed before I ventured to the kitchen, poking around the refrigerator and cupboards. I found both chickens and the apples in the fridge, and most of the rest of Lisa's grocery order in the cupboards. So she had come home after I saw her at the Pick and Go.

Frowning when I opened the freezer, I surveyed a stack of TV dinners we didn't carry at the Pick and Go—with kid-friendly entrees like spaghetti and meatballs and chicken nuggets—next to a big bottle of vodka. I shut the freezer, looking around. The counters were spotless, the sink empty save for the bowl and cup Charlotte had just put there.

Lisa's kitchen was clean and tidy, but not big.

And what I didn't see anywhere was the fancy cheese, or even a single bottle of wine.

"The bathroom is right outside the door in that hallway." Mary finished putting Charlotte's change of clothes in the huge old antique wardrobe and shut the doors as I watched from the doorway.

Charlotte had fallen quiet again as she stared out the car window on the short ride back. For a girl who'd brimmed with bubbly energy every time I'd ever seen her, the petite brunette looked small and lost in the king-sized four-poster bed in the McClatchys' guest bedroom. Watching Mary over the top edge of the comforter, she nodded.

"I'll be right downstairs for a while, and then next door if you need anything," Mary said.

The girl fixed her gaze on the wood-paneled ceiling, her hair fanned out like a dark crown on the pillow, her face the kind of somber and sad that comes with decades of hard knocks —or one exceptionally traumatic twist in an average childhood. I knew her father had died suddenly, though no one ever said how, which made it seem especially thoughtless that her mother would just disappear on her. Losing one parent has a way of making a child paranoid about the other's safety. After hearing Charlotte's story about calling Ruthie, I had a good guess that the wine and cheese were with Lisa, and so was Mary's husband, so while I wanted to tell Charlotte her mother was okay, I couldn't bring myself to say the words. Who was I to reassure anyone here?

Nobody. And that note on Mary's front door said I wasn't the only person who knew it.

Mary turned out the light and shut the door, crooking one finger for me to follow her downstairs.

Curling into her favorite end of the sofa, she looked at the fresh wood she'd laid out in the fireplace, shaking her head. "I can't believe her mother is just missing. Who goes missing in a town like this? The sheriff told me they haven't had a criminal case involving a person since the eighties."

"I can believe that." I could also believe the local police force of two barely had any business running a dishwasher, never mind a missing persons investigation. The questions they'd asked had been straight out of a TV detective show. And not even a good one. I'd been in the house fifteen minutes and noticed three important things: there was a stack of TV dinners that would be easy for a child to prepare in the freezer, the girl's coat hung neatly on the rack inside the front door, but the hook next to it was empty though it had been warm that day—so Lisa had known she'd be out late enough to need her coat, and only some of the groceries Lisa had bought that afternoon had made it home.

Words wrestled around my brain, trying to fight their way out of my mouth as I took the seat Mary pointed me to on the other end of the sofa. I should say something about the fact that I'd seen Lisa at the Pick and Go that afternoon—it seemed like it might have been close to the last place she stopped before she disappeared. But I had worked hard for months here to fade into the background.

If we'd been talking about anyone else, I would've asked Mary's advice because besides being as beautiful and kind as any angel had a right to be, my friend Mary McClatchy was the smartest person I'd ever met. But how in the world could I even so much as crack that can of worms? What if the wrong one wriggled free, dropping the knowledge that Lisa bought three bottles of the pastor's favorite wine and disappeared when he was gone right into the middle of Mary's perfect life on Elias Lane?

I learned early that men were not to be trusted. Primitive and greedy, they were led by their wants more than by duty, honor, or loyalty, and should always be treated as such. In spite of that, I liked Pastor Tim as much as I'd ever liked any man. He had welcomed me into his home when he didn't hardly know me, and the way he kissed his wife even with company present was the one doubt whispering around my belief that he was catting around with his secretary. Why would a man that in love with a woman as perfect as Mary want to dally?

"That poor little girl," Mary said, her gentle voice taking on an uncharacteristically fierce note. "Nothing bad will ever happen to her again, if I have anything to say about it."

I nodded, keeping my mouth shut so the wrong words didn't sneak out despite me knowing better. I believed that Mary would keep that child safe tonight and do her best to help her sleep with every tiny part of my being, and I decided to focus my thoughts on what I could do to help with that—people on TV talk all the time about "closure" when bad things happen, which is just a fancy way of saying most folks can't move on until they know what happened or have had a chance to say their piece about it.

I not only had an idea of where Lisa might be, I knew how to blend in, how to notice things, and how to hunt. By the fifth grade—which I remembered well because it was almost the last one I got to go to—I could track anything from a cougar to a badger through the woods for miles. I would never tell anyone in Whitney Falls, but that was the secret ingredient in the burrito casserole they all loved so much: whatever meat I'd been able to track and kill. Beef was out of my price range.

If I could hunt an animal, why not a woman? It had taken me about seven and a half seconds to figure out that if Lisa wasn't in town, assuming she hadn't just flat abandoned her kid, she had to be in the woods up the mountain—where it was probably chilly enough for a coat tonight. And where Pastor Tim had told Mary he was going.

So I'd sit here with Mary for as long as she needed me, and then I'd go see what I could find out about where Lisa went after she left the Pick and Go. Once I knew, I could better decide who else needed to know.

I'd never seen myself as the detective type, but right then, it was the only way I could think of to guard both my secret and my friend.

I reached to pat Mary's hand, holding her gaze. "Charlotte's really lucky to have someone like you to step up for her," I said, finally finding words I could mean with as much fervor as I wanted to direct at the unfairness of this whole situation.

Mary squeezed my fingers and tipped her lips up in the barest hint of a smile. "That's kind of you to say. I've always wondered if God won't give me a baby because I wouldn't be a good mother, and I guess at least for tonight, I have a chance to find out. And what am I doing?" She shook her head. "Carrying on with my evening like nothing has changed."

She rose and I followed her to the kitchen, sitting at the bar as she put together a silver serving tray of warm milk, toast, and a couple of chocolates. "Do you mind if I excuse myself to take care of her?" she asked as she picked up the tray.

"Not a bit. I'll get on to bed."

Letting myself out through the back door, I locked it with the key Mary had given me, darting up to the darling apartment that it seemed I had first seen about two hundred years ago to flip on a light before I crept to the driveway and put the Honda in neutral, pushing it clear past the Tomlinson house before I hopped in and cranked the engine, letting it roll down the hill and off Elias Lane out of gear. I slid it into first toward the edge of town, and kept it there all the way to the mountain. I didn't pass a single car, police or otherwise.

Pulling a large flashlight from under my front seat, I parked the car just inside the tree line and set out for the only place I could think of for Pastor Tim to go on a spiritual retreat—a cave I'd come upon looking for mushrooms in the woods in December, before I'd learned to eat less. It wouldn't be easy to find in the dark, but I could manage. And if Lisa was there with Pastor Tim... well, I would just have to figure that out when I got there.

# TWENTY-ONE
## MARY

*February*

If there's an advantage to living in a tiny, insular mountain town while suspecting your husband of straying, it's that the pool of potential temptation is manageable and finite.

By the last Sunday in February, I surveyed the congregation from my perch in the choir loft after days of thought and observation at half a dozen places and events around town. Tim had a definite type: he liked blondes, he didn't care for wallflowers, and youth was always more desirable. Above all, he couldn't risk getting in the middle of anyone else's marriage, because an angry husband telling tales would cause too much trouble.

Whitney Falls was only home to three single young blonde women.

The most pressing problem right then was that I didn't really know any of them. But they were all at church every Sunday without fail. So I watched, trying to pick out which was more interested in the pastor than the sermon.

Hitting every note in "How Great Thou Art" was so automatic my brain had plenty of time to work on that problem in the background.

The secondary school science teacher was the eager to please sort—I had emailed her about my tutoring work with Charlotte and she'd written back an effusive thank you, offering to help if I wanted to start up a tutoring business. Apparently the secondary school ranged from seventh to twelfth grades, and several of the children in her classes were behind. While I wasn't sure she understood that sharing that might not be the best reflection on her own skills, it gave me a reason to chat with her after service was over.

The postmistress was on the verge of too old for Tim to notice, but she had taken exceptional care of herself, so I couldn't dismiss her out of hand. I could, however, come up with a question about shipping packages with Easter approaching quickly. All I really needed was a decent reason to strike up a conversation and few minutes with her, because besides having at least five years on me, she wasn't the brightest bulb on the string. While I couldn't ask anyone outright if they were seeing my husband, I knew I could get that woman to admit it in less time than it took to get a good manicure once I got her talking.

Then there was the checkout girl, the one who'd made the burrito casserole that first Sunday: she was trouble, I could feel it. I still didn't know her name, and while I hadn't thought much of that before the past couple of days, I wondered now if it wasn't by design. She seemed to try to fade into the background, but her figure would be enough to draw any man's eyes no matter how well she stayed under the women's radar. She was what some people would call too thin, though I knew Tim didn't think there was any such thing, but somehow she still had breasts so large and gravity defying they refused to be ignored. She did her best to downplay them when she was at work, but Sunday mornings she always wore either a form-fitting blue sweater with black pants, or a pink dress that fit her waist and arms, but strained the darts in the bodice across her bust.

She was young—too young for me to be able to pinpoint how young, exactly. With good genes, she might have been as old as twenty-eight, without she could've been barely old enough to buy a drink.

She stared at Tim during the sermon with the sort of rapt attention most women reserve for their favorite singer or movie star, not missing a single word. Just a few weeks ago, I would've thought that was sweet, a young girl with no friends finding joy and solace in the Lord. Now I wondered if it was the word of God or the person of my husband she was more interested in.

But the thing that stuck out the most, ironically since I'd been so grateful for it at the time, was her quiet insistence that I give Tim those Millionaires on Valentine's Day. Had she really won them, as she'd said? Did she buy them for my husband because he'd confided in her that he loved them and then broken their plans for a romantic evening? Or worse, had she *taken pity* on me? Watching her sing, I could hear her words in my head: "The pastor should have something special on such a special day." Had she handed them over wishing that she could give them to him herself?

Had he been picturing her while he was with me that night?

Was that why he'd been so different? More excited—no pharmaceutical assistance necessary—more playful, and... heaven help me... more rough? My cheeks burned and I raised my hymnal slightly to cover them. I was halfway to the point where I could test, and I knew it was unlikely that I'd have conceived on a blood cycle day, but I had tried all the days the ovulation predictors recommended for actual years and gotten nothing but disappointment, so I couldn't help but hope. Everything had been different that night. Maybe the results would be, too. I'd prayed for nothing else since.

Wondering if he'd been fully there with me made my whole

body go haywire—my face could've been on fire, but the rest of me was suddenly so cold I trembled from head to toe, my muscles jerking so violently I dropped my hymnal on Sam Tomlinson's balding head. He jumped almost out of his skin and whirled, glaring.

Get it together, Mary. Honestly.

"I'm so sorry," I whispered, clapping a shaking hand over my blistering hot mouth and taking the book back from him.

He nodded in the smallest, angriest sense of the word and turned back to the congregation.

Holding the hymnal at my side, I sang "Great Redeemer" and "Amazing Grace" from memory because I was still trembling so violently I didn't trust myself to hold the book up. It was one thing, at least for me, to think Tim might be wandering —and entirely another to wonder if the passion I'd seen from him on Valentine's night had been because he wished he was with someone else.

I watched the checkout girl, careful to keep my face neutral.

It could be the teacher. It might be the postmistress, though she was the odds-off dark horse, especially when the checkout girl's chest factored into the equation. Watching her sing with soft eyes that never left my husband, conviction settled into my belly, deep and sure, that she was my new competition.

I don't like to lose.

I looked around the congregation for anything else to focus on before the girl noticed me watching her. I found that I wasn't the only one watching her.

Except Ruthie Tomlinson was outright glaring.

That was interesting. Potentially helpful.

But fascinating, any way I looked at it.

# TWENTY-TWO

## MARTHA

*April*

The local police ruled Lisa's death a tragic accident after an investigation that took a whole two days.

"I still don't understand what she could have possibly been doing out at Devil's Point alone in the dark. It wouldn't be hard to fall into the ravine, Tim said the cliff edge isn't stable at all," Mary said, sitting in Pastor Tim's office picking out flowers for the funeral service the day after Easter. Speckled light filtered in the window through the new baby-green leaves on the trees outside, a testament that May was fast approaching, summer's long hot days and humid nights not far away.

Mary pointed to a photo of a large spray arrangement with a ribbon that read "Rest with angels."

"Charlotte says Lisa loved tiger lilies and daisies. Her favorite colors were purple and yellow. Work whatever magic you can with that." She handed the catalog back to the florist and smiled when the woman rose to leave.

Once the door was shut, Mary looked at me, raising her hands palms up, and bowing her head.

I almost didn't realize we were praying before she began.

"Lord, we ask that you be with our congregation and community as we mourn this tragic loss, and especially with Charlotte as she grieves the unimaginable and begins a new chapter with her new family. This we ask in the name of Jesus Christ our Lord and Savior."

As she spoke, memories of the past couple of days played on the backs of my eyelids: Mary with her arm wrapped tight around Charlotte's thin torso, half-carrying the sobbing child up the front steps and into the house after the girl insisted on seeing her mother's body at the morgue an hour away. Mary running up and down the stairs with full food trays, trying to convince Charlotte to eat something and failing. An almost ghostly waif nearly swallowed by a black sweater at the Easter dinner table last night.

The poor child hadn't eaten a bite or said a word, not that any of us could blame her.

"Amen," I said, catching Mary's eye when she looked up. "Was she any better this morning?"

"She didn't feel like going to school. She just wants to lay in bed in her mother's sweaters and stare out the window." Mary sighed. "I'll keep on until I get through to her. She's grieving. I've prayed a thousand times in the past couple of days that the social services people will leave her with us. Tim and I moved all her things yesterday after the egg hunt, and she wouldn't have to change schools or anything." Mary's voice faded out, a lone tear dripping down her cheek. "I will do whatever I have to do to help that girl find a purpose."

I couldn't help but think it was good timing for Mary that Sam Tomlinson was still gone—I had a history with social services, and they'd nearly always choose a home with two parents, especially for a kid who'd lost as much as Charlotte had. Somehow I felt better knowing Ruthie probably couldn't get the kid if she tried, though that was probably a little mean on my part.

"Do you know what happened to her father?"

"Lisa's husband died a little over a year ago," Mary half-whispered, the way some people do when they're sharing bad news. Like saying it softly lessens the impact. "She was in the middle of trying to divorce him. Drugs or something. She never liked to talk about it—or him."

I nodded. I knew a thing or twenty about relatives nobody wanted to talk about or remember.

"I mean, I know she's not a baby, so it's not exactly what you prayed for," I said, not really sure I should finish that thought, but also not sure how to stop in the middle now that my mouth had run off without waiting for my brain to pump the brakes. "But, um, well..."

Merciful angel that she was, Mary rescued me with a pat on the knee. "I'll never replace Lisa, but I'll look after Charlotte like I would my own flesh and blood." Her words dripped with so much gratitude I felt an immediate need to thank someone for something.

"How was Pastor Tim's retreat?" I asked. "With everything else this weekend, I didn't have a chance to ask."

Mary flipped open a casket catalog, then closed it. "Do you think you would want to be cremated or buried?" she asked, almost like she hadn't heard me.

Not that I could blame her. I'd bet her mind had been running ninety miles a minute since she'd heard about Lisa, found broken and bruised at the bottom of a ravine near an obscure cave in the mountains outside town on Saturday. The coroner hadn't gotten to the autopsy yet, but the cop who liked his Keystone Light seemed convinced by *Law and Order* reruns that she'd died of internal bleeding. Or maybe a punctured lung. Either was possible really—the drop out there was a good twenty-five feet. In the two days since, Mary had broken the terrible news to Charlotte, run a flawless ladies' auxiliary breakfast and helped her husband pull himself together to deliver a positively inspiring Easter Sunday sermon on the healing power of the Lord and the promise of the kingdom of Heaven.

I would never be able to understand how Pastor Tim wrote that sermon between when he got home Saturday and when he preached it Sunday morning, but if ever God was guiding someone's hand, it was then.

I frowned at Mary's question, one I had never considered, probably partly because I was only eighteen and partly because I'd never really figured on having anyone care enough about me to want to know.

"I've had nightmares about fire since I was a little girl," I said finally. That will happen when you live next door to a meth lab, but I kept that part to myself. "So I'm going to be buried. Someday. Hopefully not soon." The giggle that followed the words was awkward and uncertain, and Mary nodded, pointing her finger at me.

"Have you ever wondered why we fear death? Like, especially so much that we don't talk about it, or it makes us uncomfortable to think about? It is the one inevitable thing we all have in common, after all."

I blinked slowly, not sure what to do with any of that. I supposed she was right in a way. "And when we die we go to heaven," I said.

"Exactly," Mary pounded one hand on the desk, making me flinch. "We shouldn't be mourning Lisa, but celebrating the fact that she's with Jesus this morning, toasting the good news of his resurrection at a most heavenly gathering. It's selfish of us to want her to still be here with us."

It was an interesting way to look at it. Unconventional, and maybe slightly unemotional, but somehow not wrong.

And it certainly wasn't my place to argue the rewards of the afterlife with the pastor's wife. I nodded. "I never really thought about it like that."

"I think it's time we start," Mary said. "With baby steps, of course. We don't want to offend anyone."

"I'm sure if anyone can do this, it's you." I returned Mary's warm smile and checked my watch. "I have to get back to the store. I pulled the stock boy over to cashier for the morning because it should've been pretty quiet, but I should be there for the afternoon crowds so he can restock the shelves. Do you think my car is done?" I'd clean forgotten that Mary had said her mechanic friend would look at my transmission until he'd shown up that morning.

"It should be, I would think. Is Sam still out of town?" Mary's eyebrows went up. "Ruthie was at service yesterday, was he?"

Seeing Ruthie alone at the Easter service had disappointed me in a way nothing in Whitney Falls had managed yet, but it felt unkind to think that, let alone say it out loud.

"I haven't seen him. I'm not sure where he went or when he'll be back." I looked away from Mary's gaze, which seemed unusually piercing right then.

She tapped one finger on her chin and stood, crossing the room to shut the door.

Had she not just heard me say I needed to go?

I furrowed my brow as she turned back to me, grabbing both my hands and squeezing tight.

"Here's the thing." Mary bit her lower lip like something was upsetting her and my stomach suddenly felt like it had been dropped into an ice bath. Was she about to tell me something about Sam that I didn't want to know?

I closed my eyes, every muscle tightening like I was bracing for a smack to the face.

"I really would love it if you'd consider leaving the Pick and Go to come work here as Tim's secretary."

It took a full ten count for the words to stop milling around the office and sink in, and even then I couldn't swear I'd heard her right.

A job?

Here?

Me—working at a church? It was all I could do to stay still, equal parts of me wanting to jump in the air whooping with joy and fall to the ground laughing at the irony.

"It would be better for you in so many ways—fewer hours, less time on your feet, and more money, too." Mary practically tripped over the words, her eyes wide and pleading and locked on mine. "We need you, Martha—the entire town, with Lisa gone, of course—but Tim and me, especially."

I staggered backward half a step as the weight of it hit me. She was afraid I would say no.

The only reason to do that was about money: this paid more, she said, but one of the nicest things about the Pick and Go was their insistence on paying me in cash. No tax forms, no ID necessary. I bit my lip. Turning down a chance like this would be crazy, but giving Pastor Tim and Mary cause to wonder about me might be crazier.

"I should tell you up front that we prefer to pay church employees in cash." Mary watched my face as she spoke, not blinking. "It simplifies accounting."

Well, if that wasn't a sign from the Lord, I didn't know what could be.

"Of course I will," I said. "I am... it means a lot to me that you'd ask."

Her face might have cracked with the width of the grin that blossomed across it, bringing a rosy shine to her cheeks. "I wouldn't have anyone else. I told Tim he couldn't do better than you." She squealed and yanked me into a hug. "This is just going to be so wonderful, Martha. I know you'll be brilliant in the job. Half of it is keeping the church accounts and counting offerings, and you're so gifted with numbers."

"And the other half?" I asked when she let me go.

"Between you and me? Watching people in town, knowing their needs and how we might be able to help them. And of course, keeping secrets."

If she saw the flash of panic on my face at that last, she didn't let on.

"You're observant, I've noticed. And for some odd reason I haven't been able to figure out, people don't seem to notice you despite how pretty you are. That is the kind of thing you can't train a church secretary to do, but it's a very useful trait," Mary went on, and I nodded automatically, not really hearing the rest of what she said.

More secrets. Oh boy.

But there was no way out of it, so I would just have to figure it out.

Me, Martha. The pastor's secretary.

## TWENTY-THREE
### MARTHA

*May*

Spring ushered the valley right into summer, cool nights giving way to thick air, long days, and warm winds blowing down the mountain. I was so caught up in learning how to be the best dang church secretary First Baptist had ever had that I didn't much notice, though. My brain didn't have space for anything but work for weeks on end.

Except a heavy dose of guilt over how terribly I had misjudged Lisa. That grew in my gut for weeks, gnawing away until I could barely eat—especially not when the woman's daughter was sitting across Mary's table from me, pushing peas around her plate.

"Can I get you something else, Charlotte?" Mary asked, nearly vibrating with nervous energy as she popped out of her chair. "It's really okay for you to tell me if you don't like the peas, or anything else—I'm happy to cook whatever you like."

"My mother always told us her kitchen wasn't a diner," Pastor Tim said, cutting a bite of chicken. "'You get what you get and you don't throw a fit,' was her favorite saying at mealtimes."

Mary glared at her husband like she had some words she might like to share about his mother—or maybe just his timing. I hadn't been able to figure out how he felt about having Charlotte in the house—one day, he was asking if she'd like him to fix up her old bike, and the next he seemed annoyed if she breathed too loud.

"I like to cook," Mary's voice was tight. "Your mother wasn't the best at it, if I recall."

Pastor Tim stabbed his chicken with a steak knife and Mary rounded the table and leaned over Charlotte. "We can also skip straight to the ice cream if you'd like. I got you strawberry like you asked."

Charlotte nodded, keeping her eyes on her plate. Mary's face lit up like the fourth of July night sky as she half ran to the kitchen, returning with a heaping bowl of strawberry ice cream topped with fresh strawberries and whipped cream.

Pastor Tim stared for three blinks before he stuffed the rest of his chicken into his mouth and left the table still chewing it.

Charlotte turned her head to watch him go, but I couldn't read the look on her face. Her once shiny hair and sparkling eyes grew duller by the day, and I wasn't sure she'd said five words to anyone but Mary since Easter.

I'd tried to avoid her for the first few weeks, the guilt too much for me to handle. But watching her shrink into a frail, silent shell of the girl I'd first met reminded me so much of my sister—of what they'd done to my sister—my heart hurt. I had to do something.

Without thinking very much at all, I reached my teaspoon across the table and scooped up a blob of whipped cream, then turned the spoon around and flung its contents at Charlotte's nose.

"Desserts fired!" I shouted playfully, hoping Mary wouldn't be too mad about the mess.

My aim with a spoon still rivaled my accuracy with a slingshot—the cream splatted across Charlotte's freckles, freezing everyone in the room for about five seconds. Charlotte broke the silence with a giggle, flipping her full spoon around and returning fire with a bonus strawberry.

Her aim wasn't as good as mine—the whipped cream landed in my hair, while the strawberry sailed into Mary's gray silk drapes behind me.

Before anyone could speak, I scooped mashed potatoes off my own plate and flung them at Mary, whose eyes widened until I could see the white all around the bluish purple. I wasn't sure if she was shocked or mad—or both—but then Charlotte cackled, Mary's whole face softened, and she disappeared to the kitchen and returned with the whipped cream can.

By the time she'd sprayed both our faces, Charlotte and I were laughing too hard to breathe, trying to see through the cream to flick potatoes and ice cream at Mary, who screeched and made a show of ducking under the table to surrender.

"That was fun." Charlotte sounded almost surprised as she wiped her face with a linen napkin and shoveled a big spoon of ice cream into her mouth.

I couldn't help but smile as I caught a bit of the old shine in her green eyes, skipping from me to Mary, who was crawling out from under the table. She watched Charlotte take two more bites before she moved behind the child's chair and wrapped her in a hug. "It was lovely to hear you laugh, sweetie."

Mary met my eyes over the top of Charlotte's head. *Thank you*, she mouthed.

It was the very least I could do.

---

Mary was right about the fact that my new job involved a lot of numbers, which suited me fine, but it seemed like every time I thought I had it all straight, a new thing popped up that I hadn't learned yet.

All the studying in addition to my daily responsibilities led to late evenings alone with Pastor Tim, who wore his cologne heavier and his suits a little more tailored on those days. I prayed the best I knew how for the Lord to absolve me from noticing that, and for Pastor Tim to be good and faithful to his wife—even if Lisa had tempted him, she had died not long after, so I figured maybe he'd learned his lesson about infidelity and secrets.

And boy, had Mary been right about the secrets—I never would've believed a town like Whitney Falls could have so many. But it turned out the biggest one was the one I had to keep locked up the tightest—I couldn't even tell my best friend. Because it concerned her husband.

A lingering touch to my shoulder or hand here, a look that seemed to devour me from the outside in there. I told myself I was making it up—daydreaming about my friend's stupidly attractive husband in the only way I would allow myself to, which was by making it his fault.

Pastor Tim waited until early June to cross the line from friendly to so touchy-feely I couldn't pretend it was a daydream anymore.

I was photocopying the Sunday bulletin on a Friday afternoon so warm I had pulled my hair up into a plastic claw clip to get it off my neck. I didn't want to take off the light sweater I wore over my sundress on account of it having a sweetheart neckline. I'd dealt with enough men being fascinated with my boobs in my life that it hadn't escaped my attention when Pastor Tim had started to talk to them instead of looking me in the face my second week working for him.

As the last of the 430 copies rolled out of the ancient Xerox machine, I felt a hand on my thigh, pushing my skirt up as it slid north.

"I like this dress on you, have I told you that?" Tim asked, his breath so warm on my neck I recoiled, smashing my torso into the copier such that the edge of the lid bit painfully into my ribs.

He entirely misinterpreted the gasp that slid between my teeth, bending his knees and pressing his hips into my backside. Dangit.

Trapped between the machine and his taller, broader, stronger body, my heart pounded, a fine sheen of sweat instantly coating every inch of me. I wasn't afraid he would assault me—I knew how to take care of myself and I wouldn't let it go that far. But I'd sure love it if I could manage to twist myself out of this without losing the brand new life I owed in part to the man whose tallywhacker was digging into my hip.

"Mary bought it for me." The words popped out of my mouth like someone else thought of them.

And they were exactly the right thing in that moment.

His hand dropped away from my skin just as it was venturing into really inappropriate territory, and he stepped aside without a word as I gathered the bulletins and hurried back to my desk to fold them.

"I'm headed out, Martha, have yourself a nice weekend," he called from the back door that led straight out of his office a few minutes later.

My hands shook so badly I got three paper cuts folding two bulletins. Putting the second one on top of the first, I pressed my hands into the blotter on top of my desk, counting the number of lines on the calendar as I tried to regulate my breathing and calm my quivering stomach and trembling hands.

What in the world was Pastor Tim thinking? Mary was my very best friend. The only real friend I'd ever had who wasn't my baby sister. Her husband was good looking, well spoken, and could charm... well, the panties off a Baptist church secretary, it seemed. But if he thought I was going to step in for Lisa in that respect, too, he was mistaken.

I would never betray Mary that way, even if he didn't seem to have a problem with the idea. That wasn't even a question for me—my body wasn't going haywire because of temptation or indecision. Not about whether or not I wanted to sleep with my boss, anyway.

I took three deep breaths.

Mary loved Tim to distraction—I had caught myself, more than once, with bitter, nasty jealousy bubbling at the back of my throat watching the way she looked at him with a soft, dreamy cast to her face. And just last weekend, I had walked into the kitchen when they were... you know... bent right over the big marble island.

I had a dream that night, that it was me in the big fancy house with my bare skin pressed against cold marble and Tim behind me, and I'd woken up crying, knowing just the thought was a gross betrayal of my friendship with Mary and wishing I could unsee the dream. Afraid to go back to sleep, I'd taken my Bible to the loveseat and made myself some cocoa in the microwave. My brain tried to reason my way out of guilt as I read. I loved Mary. I would never touch her husband. The dream wasn't about him, really, but about her—I mean, who wouldn't want to be Mary McClatchy? I'd nodded to myself at that thought. Nobody, that's who. So that couldn't mean I was a terrible person. It didn't make me a bad friend. Because it's not like I would ever actually betray her—or have the chance in the first place.

Ha.

Maybe Tim's long, unblinking looks and his brushing past me in spaces that didn't require it had registered with my dream-brain before I'd wanted to believe them in real life. But now I knew.

And the things I knew would crush Mary. I couldn't be responsible for that.

I raised my hands to my face, wiping away sweat—and tears I hadn't even felt falling.

How could something like this happen to Mary and Tim? Elias Lane and the houses there had been a holy place—the location of the church not even part of the equation—to me from the first day I'd rolled into Whitney Falls. Growing up, I'd only seen places like Elias Lane on my granny's old color box TV. It had rabbit ears I had to adjust every time the wind shifted and channel five didn't work because the knob wouldn't stay on it no matter what we tried, but it was good for keeping me out of the way and I had loved having a little window in our trailer that let me see what life was like for people who had more money and kinder, better hearts.

When I'd happened down Elias Lane that first night in the snow, I'd wanted to run up and press my cold nose against the glass in every front door. Over and over, in the months I'd spent living at the Dreamscape, I'd pictured the houses and imagined the families who lived inside each one as people from those old TV stories. The kind of families where no problem was so serious it took more than thirty minutes to solve, even with commercial breaks, and truly terrible things simply didn't happen. Because the kind of people who lived in houses like Mary's didn't do terrible things.

And here Pastor Tim had gone and done a terrible thing.

Maybe more than one terrible thing, truth be told, but I couldn't think about that right then.

My hands had stopped shaking, so I started folding the church bulletins, giving every shred of attention to lining them up straight and protecting my fingers from more cuts. I folded fifty, then seventy-five, and my brain wanted something else to think about.

I couldn't—wouldn't—tell my good and true friend Mary

McClatchy what her husband had been up to. I also wouldn't bed the pastor, no matter how many dreams—day or night—I'd had about how nice it would be to have Mary's life. The jealousy was my problem, and I would not make it hers.

But I worried: selfishly, that rejecting Tim would cost me this job. I couldn't go back to the Pick and Go, since Sam was still gone and the owners had hired Ruthie as the new manager. People all over town were whispering about him running out on her, and while I admired her ability to pretend she didn't know that when she had to see the whole town come though the store every week, she was meaner than ever and I wasn't interested in hiring myself out as her whipping post.

Unselfishly, I was afraid that Tim would find another willing mistress who would hurt Mary. Who might even try to steal Pastor Tim away from my friend.

I couldn't allow that.

I was pressing the crease into bulletin number 346 when I realized maybe there was a tightrope I could walk that would keep the pastor's attention on me without betraying Mary's trust.

It wouldn't be easy.

But it was the only way I could think of to both protect Mary's bright, happy life and my new safe, comfortable one at the same time.

So I would figure it out.

## TWENTY-FOUR
### MARY

*March*

Only four letters were still partially readable on the diamond-shaped brown plastic key fob: E, M, C, and P—but they were enough. The dull, burnished-brass key dangling from the plastic fob must've been for a room at the Dreamscape Motel, a decrepit cesspool on the edge of town where actual dreams probably went to die. I knew exactly what went on out there—the place was popular with vagrants, truckers, and the kind of women you'd expect to appeal to both.

So what in berry blazes was a key from that hellhole doing in my husband's desk?

I turned it over in the light, wondering if I could have figured out how to check it for fingerprints if I hadn't grabbed it so quickly when my fingers brushed it in the back of Tim's drawer.

I had tried everything to squelch my suspicious thoughts about Tim's behavior during the growing pile of hours he couldn't account for—and there seemed to be more of them every single week. I wanted desperately to be a good wife. The wife he deserved. A wife who deserved a child. So I rebuked the devil in my mind. I would not entertain thoughts of my husband being unfaithful, I told myself. He'd promised me it would never happen again, and I trusted him. I had prayed, I had started exercising, I had written in my journal for the first time since before we came to Whitney Falls—I had even written a letter to my husband, one I hoped would seal the past where it belonged once and for all. An official, written commitment to moving forward.

*Jesus said forgiveness is the most powerful grace,* it began. Because I wanted to believe in him. In us. So I forgave. I asked forgiveness for him.

And then I went to his study to get an envelope for the letter and found a key for a seedy motel room in his desk.

I held it at arm's length, like it might bite. Why would he have this?

What if he...?

Every inch of me went cold as a New Year's Day ice bath. Surely not.

There had to be a good explanation. Another one, anyway.

And I would find it.

I tucked the key right back where I found it, but I didn't bother with the envelope, taking the letter to the fireplace and watching the flames eat it. Two minutes, and only ash remained. It was a stupid idea anyway.

I hadn't moved two steps away from the fireplace when the doorbell rang.

Walking through the foyer, I straightened the painting of the Alamo on the wall and checked out the windows for a car, smoothing my hair and trying to keep the shock off my face when I saw who was on my porch holding a bakery box.

"Hi." I didn't say anything else when I swung the door wide, keeping one hand on it just in case I needed to close it.

"Is this a good time?" Ruthie Tomlinson asked, her fingertips white from the grip she had on the pink box in her hands. "I should've called, but I wasn't sure what you'd say."

"You've given yourself good reason for that," I said.

She closed her eyes for a beat and nodded. "I have. But I'd like to make peace." She held out the box almost like a shield. "I brought a gluten-free cinnamon coffee cake."

In that moment, I wanted to be the smaller person. I wanted to tell Ruthie that she'd gone out of her way to make me feel unwelcome here, to be spiteful when she could have been kind, to make sure I didn't have so much as an opportunity to be happy in Whitney Falls. I wanted to tell her I knew she wouldn't be here with her custom coffee cake if I hadn't finally figured out how to beat women like her at their own game, if the ladies of the auxiliary hadn't accepted me regardless of her slights and subterfuge.

But I also wanted to make a home for my family in this beautiful little place. Ruthie and her husband Sam were sixth-generation residents who weren't going anywhere. They were our neighbors. It would be easier on all of us if they were also our friends.

And Ruthie's husband ran the Pick and Go. The daggers she'd stared at the checkout girl in church last week loomed over everything else I thought about her as I stood in that doorway, so instead of shutting the door, I swung it wide, pasting a grin on my face as I reached for the pink box.

"That is so incredibly thoughtful of you, to remember that I can't eat gluten," I said through the smile. "I adore coffee cake, but I can't eat it alone, you must join me."

She let out a long breath, her shoulders dropping, as she returned the smile and stepped inside. "I have loved this house since I was a little girl. What you've done with this foyer is stunning."

Balancing the box on one hand, I closed the front door and stepped around Ruthie, leading her to the kitchen. I put on a pot of coffee and chatted about the beauty spring brought to the valley and the surrounding mountains as it brewed, then poured two cups and cut us each a generous piece of cake, waving her into a seat at the island.

"Thank you for giving me another chance," she said.

"Nonsense." I took a bite of the cake. It flat melted on my tongue. "Jesus said forgiveness is the most powerful grace. And I couldn't turn away anyone who brought me something this delicious."

She giggled. "I'm so glad you like it, but I can only take credit for knowing where to buy the best pastry in town—apparently no matter the kind of flour."

I sipped my coffee. "I think you know a lot more than that about this town, and I'm still trying to find my footing here in so many ways." I cast my eyes down at the counter exactly halfway through my remark.

"I'm more than happy to help with anything you need." Ruthie's words had been dunked and marinated in eagerness to please. I met her gaze and paused just long enough for her to lean toward me.

"I couldn't help but notice that you don't seem terribly fond of the checkout girl at the Pick and Go," I said. "I'm wondering what her story is, if you'd care to share."

---

Oh, dear.

It was worse than I'd thought.

The checkout girl was a tart who flirted shamelessly with Ruthie's husband and half the men in town.

And she lived at the Dreamscape Motel.

I showed Ruthie out after letting her rant for nearly an hour, ate the entire rest of the cake by myself, stuffed the box down in the garbage bin outside, and paced the house for five hours, thinking and talking to myself and trying to ignore my upset stomach—sugar and stress were a bad combination for the gut, it turned out.

But maybe not a terrible one for the brain.

By the time I started cooking Tim's favorite beef and broccoli for dinner, I had a plan.

Once everything was in a casserole dish in the oven, I got my phone and went to work.

"Hi, Sam, it's Mary McClatchy, how are you?" I said when he answered at the Pick and Go.

"Can't complain, ma'am," he said. "Can I help you with something today?"

"Thank you so much for asking. I can't stand to be a bother, but I'm feeling under the weather today, and tomorrow is my usual grocery day. Since you were so kind to bring our groceries during the heavy snows this winter, I was hoping I might bother you to do that one more time. It will save me some embarrassment trying to drag myself around the store." I crossed my fingers behind my back as I spoke.

"Sure thing, Mrs. McClatchy, happy to," he said. "Anything you want me to add to your regular order?"

"Tim just loves rum raisin ice cream, and we're due for a warm day next week," I said. "If you wouldn't mind adding that. And I can pay you for it when you get here?"

"We'll put it on account, you get it when you feel better."

"That's very kind of you," I said.

"Happy to help the pastor's family, ma'am. Anytime."

I thanked him again and hung up, then immediately opened a text to Ruthie.

*Thank you so much for coming by this afternoon and for the lovely, thoughtful gift! I enjoyed our chat so much.*

She replied immediately. *It was so kind of you to have me as a guest in your home!*

Darn right it was. I smiled at the screen as I started to type. *I was thinking about what you said earlier, about Sam being distracted lately. Have you ever thought about sending him away for a night, or even a weekend? Tim sometimes goes on spiritual retreats and it always does him a world of good. He comes back focused on what's important to him. I was just thinking that tomorrow is Thursday and I happened across an absolute steal on a cabin just over the mountain for tomorrow night. Maybe some reflection and prayer time will help Sam.*

I sent the message and then laughed at the long blue column that came up on the screen. Wordy for a text, but necessary.

The dot bubble that meant she was answering came up after a minute, her message popping up shortly. *What a great idea! Can you point me to the cabin?*

I pulled up the link and sent it to her, then typed out: *I bet he could sneak out of the store early so he'd be there in time for sunset. That's a rewarding prayer time if you've never tried it.*

My phone buzzed with a reply immediately: *I love that. Will make sure he heads out by noon, this says he can check in at three and we should get our money's worth.*

I smiled as I slid the phone back into my pocket and retrieved Tim's favorite beef and broccoli garnish from the pantry, crumbling the brick of dried ramen noodles into a pretty blue serving bowl and going to set the table.

---

Tim retired to his study after a quiet, uneventful dinner, leaving me alone with the TV and my gratitude that he hadn't had anything unkind to say about the food tonight.

But I hadn't missed his unusually chipper mood, either. I recognized it, having been the cause of it hundreds of times.

It was still there the next morning. He actually hummed to himself while he was fluffing up his thick hair and tying his tie.

He hadn't touched me since Valentine's Day.

"Are you going to be late tonight?" I asked. "I'm making lasagna for dinner."

"I shouldn't be. If anything changes, I'll let you know."

I nodded as he dropped a kiss on my cheek that probably felt more perfunctory than it actually was. He always had doughnuts for breakfast at the church on Thursdays, so I didn't have to go down early and cook for him. Snuggling under the covers, I slept another two hours, waking after a fitful dream about the checkout girl being pregnant with Tim's child. The child that should've been mine. Sitting straight up in a cold sweat, I wiped my face on the sheet and shook off the repulsive thoughts, springing up from the mattress like it was full of bees and washing up to start a big day where I needed everything to go my way.

Hours of scrubbing and shining the first floor into a showplace later, I fluffed the pillows on the porch swing, checking my watch as the sun retreated toward the mountaintop.

I had just opened the front door to go back inside when a hideous squeal from the other end of the street turned my head. A gunmetal gray Honda that somehow looked like it shouldn't be a Honda at all because it had to be older than these hills inched up the street, drawing stares every time the gears ground.

Showtime.

I slipped back into the house, pulled out my phone, and texted Ruthie. *What in the name of Heaven is making that noise? I was trying to sleep!*

She replied so fast I wondered how she had time to read

mine. *It's that checkout girl's junk bucket car! The nerve of some people.*

I had just put my phone back into my pocket when it buzzed again. Ruthie: *She's leaving oil spots all over the road!* She tacked on the little orange mad face.

Perfect. I smiled as I typed back: *You know our men will be stuck out there cleaning that up, too. Someone really should do something. She doesn't even live here.*

I put my phone on the table and went to the dining room window to watch the fireworks through the blinds and time my entrance.

The battered old car turned into our driveway just as Ruthie charged into the road.

The most useful thing mother ever taught me was that it's wise to keep your enemies close—and absolutely brilliant when you can pull their strings.

My jaw fell open when the checkout girl plowed into the back of my new car, and I watched her sort of stumble out of the rusty Honda, blood dripping from her head. Most of my grocery order crashed to the blacktop when the hatchback on the car fell, and then Ruthie ran up and said something to the girl and actually kicked her! I couldn't have scripted this better.

Hurrying out the door, I set my lips into a hard line and prepared to play the hero.

Was this kind? Absolutely not. But there was no such thing as "too far" when my family's very existence was at stake.

# PART TWO
SECRETS AND LIES

# TWENTY-FIVE
## MARTHA

*June*

For weeks, I showed folks in to talk to Pastor Tim with a polite half smile that wasn't too sad or too knowing—Mary said both were important as she helped me practice that smile in the mirror one rainy Saturday—and returned to my desk, filing papers or balancing the church accounts or whatever other task I had on my list. I tried to ignore the words that floated through walls so paper thin they made my room at the Dreamscape seem like a CIA bunker. I didn't want to know everyone's secrets and problems.

Until the day Ruthie Tomlinson showed up.

"What are you doing here?" She stood in the doorway of the church office staring at me with a look of such genuine shock I wondered if it was possible that she didn't know I worked there. "Get away from Lisa's desk."

"It's my desk now," I said slowly. "I've worked here for nearly three months."

"It will always be Lisa's desk to me, and it's lunchtime," she barked. "I'm here to see the pastor now because I hoped you wouldn't be."

Pastor Tim opened his office door for Ruthie and nodded to me. "Maybe you should eat lunch at home today, Martha?"

I opened my mouth to argue and then shut it again. As much as I wanted to know what she wanted, I couldn't think of a good reason to say no, and the look on his face said a bad one wouldn't cut it.

I pondered that as I crossed the street. I didn't like Ruthie, and Mary didn't either, though she never said it outright. But I supposed Pastor Tim kind of had to like everyone. Or at least, he had to be willing to help everyone.

I reached for the front door handle, trying to decide if I should tell Mary who was in her husband's office right then, but before I turned the knob fully it flew out of my hand, yanked inward as Charlotte stormed out of the house with a force that seemed too much for a tiny person who barely ate.

"I hate every one of those morons," she snapped at me as she flounced down the steps. "I hate school, I hate this house, and she. Is. Not. My. Mother." The last was spit through clenched teeth, the black sweater Charlotte wore hanging to her knees and making me itch just looking at it in the blazing sun. She disappeared around the side of the house, and I stepped into the foyer.

"How are things going in here?" I asked before I realized Mary was talking.

"So without water, what else can Mars not have?" Mary asked a table of eight children and teenagers who'd been coming in for weekly summer tutoring sessions since school got out.

To look into the room, no one would think the ninth child had just had an outburst: Mary's tone was nothing but patient. Three hands shot up, and Mary pointed to the oldest boy, who had a full beard, but was only seventeen.

I stepped into the foyer and waited, noting the flipped chair where I assumed Charlotte had been sitting. I wondered if something about Mars had set her off, or if it was just more of the "grief anger" Mary kept saying Charlotte was working through.

"Plants?" The boy asked, and Mary grinned and nodded. "Very good, what else?"

I ducked back out—they might be a while and it didn't seem like Mary needed an audience. But Charlotte sure needed a friend, and it was time for me to stop worrying more about myself than I was about that little girl.

I found her sitting astride a branch of the wide oak tree in the backyard, swinging her feet in the air and singing softly to herself. Raising one hand, I walked to the base of the tree.

"Hi there," I said. I hadn't talked to her much, for a lot of reasons I wasn't even sure I fully understood. Charlotte had grown quieter every week that she'd been here after the first few, which made her easy to overlook. Mary said she was withdrawing into her grief, and she'd tried different things—the tutoring group among them—to draw Charlotte out of her shell. Mary thought maybe having other kids from school over to the house for the tutoring sessions would help Charlotte feel better. Didn't seem like it was working.

I knew deep down in places most people don't like to talk about, that Charlotte's silence wasn't what I'd been avoiding, though, and looking up at her in the tree that day, I knew just as deep it was time for me to set that aside. This child was hurting something awful. She wasn't my sister, no matter how much the resemblance occasionally stole my breath. I'd been able to reach her with the food fight—it made her laugh, and got her talking for a couple of days. Maybe I could do it again.

She didn't answer me, but she stopped swinging the leg that dangled near my head.

I pulled a butterscotch disk from my pocket. They'd always

been Granny's favorite, so they were mine, too. "Candy?" I held it up.

Still staring at something in the distance I couldn't see, she put her hand down and I pressed the sweet into her palm.

I leaned against the base of the tree.

She looked down. "I thought you were at work."

"Pastor Tim is busy," I said. "He told me to go home for lunch."

"Then why aren't you eating? You like to eat."

I laughed. "That'll happen when you've gone a long stretch without enough food. But right now I have something more important to do."

"Looking at old trees?"

I grabbed a low branch and swung up onto it, picking my way through a few more before I settled on the one next to hers. "Climbing them's more fun. Don't you think?"

She raised both eyebrows and let out a low whistle. "Okay then."

"Do I get a gold star? It doesn't seem like much impresses you these days."

"Fair." She nodded, her hair swinging around her face and then blowing in the breeze. It was oily from lack of washing, but still gorgeous and thick.

"I wish my hair was as thick and pretty as yours," I said.

She rolled her eyes and gripped her branch with both hands. "You are not serious. You're so pretty, Martha. I think you're the only person who doesn't know it."

I waved one hand. "I'll tell you a secret, Charlotte—very few women actually know how beautiful they are. I've yet to meet one who can't tell you something she doesn't like about herself."

Charlotte's mouth twisted to one side. "Mary."

"Oh, I think if you watch you'll find plenty she wishes was different."

"Pastor Tim is mean to her," Charlotte said softly. "That's probably why."

My eyebrows shot straight to my hairline and when I tried to speak, my voice was way too high. I cleared my throat and tried again. "Mean to her, how?" I'd spent a good deal of time in the McClatchys' gorgeous home, and aside from that first dinner when Mary had seemed almost afraid of her husband because she burned the prosciutto, I'd never seen evidence of a temper from the pastor. But Charlotte was around them more than I was.

"He yells at her. Checks the furniture with gloves and tells her she's bad at housekeeping. Not to ask where he goes when he's not home." She ducked her head and mumbled into her chest. "I don't think he likes me. I'm too much in his way. My dad always said I was in the way. He didn't like me, either, and my mom was trying to get him out of our house but then he died."

I wanted to say I was sure her dad liked her just fine, but I knew better than anyone that wasn't always true.

"I think sometimes God knows when we need people in our lives," I said. "And when we don't."

She cut her eyes to the side, looking at me without raising her head, letting the silence stretch as she studied my face.

"He crashed his motorcycle into a tree out off Route 5," she said finally, not a trace of emotion in her voice. "My mom said the devil used drugs to make him mean. She told me I have to be careful to never touch them, because addiction is a demon he might have passed on to me."

"Your mom gave you good advice, then," I said. "Best if you never test that one."

Charlotte sighed, lifting her head. "I'm trying. I miss my mom. I made my mom happy, you know? It's nice, knowing you make someone happy. I'm not sure I can make Mary happy. Not the kind of happy she thought when she took me in, anyhow."

"I'm sure Mary and Pastor Tim are both very happy." A small lump formed in my throat at the thought of poor Charlotte sinking deeper into herself, missing her parents and her home and thinking she'd become a burden on people who'd taken her in. Mary couldn't possibly have any idea this was happening.

Charlotte shrugged. "I don't mean to cause trouble. I just can't help my temper sometimes. Mary says when we struggle is when we need Jesus the most, but I don't know how to pray any harder than I already do."

I knew that feeling. "I'm sure they would never ask you for anything other than the best effort you can give." At least, that's what the moms on the TV always said.

She shook her head and pointed at me. "You really mean you don't think you're pretty?"

"I'm not ugly," I said. "But do I think I'm special? No."

"I think you are." She ducked her head. "I like your lip gloss and your... the shiny stuff on your cheeks." Her face fell. "My mom was supposed to teach me about makeup this summer. She said I could wear a little in the fall. To school."

My heart hurt. I swallowed hard and blinked, staring at the top of her head as she touched her chin to her chest and sniffled. I hadn't come to Whitney Falls looking for friends. I had come here to disappear. Being tangled up with Mary had gotten complicated enough without adding a kid to the mix.

Maybe if Charlotte hadn't looked quite so much like my sister I could've hopped back to the ground and walked away. There was plenty of reason to do just that: Mary was her momma now. I was nobody, and would do well to remember it.

But it wasn't enough to make me leave her right then. I missed my sister every minute of every day, and only had one photo of her in a dinky plastic frame I kept hidden in my nightstand drawer. Hand to God, I could feel the hole losing her had left in my heart. And sitting there looking at a girl just a bit younger, with thick shiny brown hair and big green eyes, who needed a friend, I figured most of a lifetime being a big sister qualified me for the job.

And the hole didn't feel quite so big.

I tapped Charlotte's knee.

She looked up just as a tear fell, skating a bright line down her cheek, snot bubbling out of her nose. She shook her head and wiped her face with a too-long sweater sleeve, sniffling.

"I could show you," I said, catching her eye. "I'm not your momma, but I'd be happy to help if you want."

Her head tipped to one side the way it had when Mary spoke to her that first night, her teeth closing over her lower lip. "I don't want Mary to know."

I didn't see any harm in keeping this from Mary, especially not if it might make Charlotte a little happier—and maybe even a bit less volatile. "I'm good at keeping secrets. Turns out it's part of my actual job."

The thinnest ghost of a smile touched her face as another tear fell. "My mom always said that. That everybody has secrets and the church secretary knows them all."

We were halfway through Charlotte's first makeup lesson before it occurred to me that her mother—First Baptist's last church secretary, who joked about knowing all the town's secrets—had ended up at the bottom of a ravine. And as far as I knew, nobody really had any idea how she got there.

# TWENTY-SIX
## MARTHA

*July*

That quick thought about Lisa was all it took to convince me I had to work to dodge secrets—the big ones, at least. Sure, I knew who was generous with their money and who hadn't put more than a dollar in the offering plate in decades, and who had requested prayers for strength battling an addiction to one thing or another. But despite my best efforts—wearing earmuffs in the office in July got me some funny looks—I also knew which wives worried their husbands were cheating—it was a shockingly high percentage; which husbands actually were cheating—it wasn't near as many as people suspected; and most of the time, I knew who the guilty ones were cheating with, because it was usually the mistresses who came in motivated to confess their sins to the handsome pastor. Who was also married, but now knew exactly which female parishioners were willing to overlook that fact.

Protecting my friend Mary was going to be more work than I bargained for.

As the mercury soared, I started wearing shorts and fitted tops to work.

I noticed Pastor Tim noticing the wardrobe shift, and played right up to the line to keep his attention on me: I lingered in his doorway a second too long every other time I spoke to him; I dropped things and bent down to pick them up.

One particularly thermometer-melting afternoon, Pastor Tim brought his lunch out to eat at my desk.

"I'm going to melt in that office even with my jacket off," he said, flashing a smile that would've made women call for smelling salts back when everybody wore corsets all day. He put his lunch container and big gray water bottle on my desk and pulled the chair that faced the front side close. "The box fan is just blowing hot air at me today. It's like sitting in a sauna in front of a furnace vent."

"I wonder why you only have the one tiny window when there are three out here?" I asked.

"Poor planning?" There went the grin again. "You got the ceiling fan, too, which seems to blow cooler air than my box fan. I hope I'm not intruding."

"Don't be silly." I pulled my lunch container out of the bottom desk drawer and opened it.

I made it through two strawberries before the way his eyes stayed on my lips when I bit them made me uncomfortable enough to unwrap my sandwich. I had gained ten desperately needed pounds from having real food whenever I wanted it.

I couldn't tell you the exact day I stopped thinking of eating as a luxury and discovered it could be a pleasure, but it was one of the nicest days of my life. I'd crafted a sandwich that morning out of bread Mary baked fresh with no gluten, then added roasted turkey I'd cooked for dinner the night before, bacon, mayo, homegrown tomato, and avocado. I topped it with a sprinkle of salt and a dash of lime juice, and I had been looking forward to eating it at noon since I put it in my box at seven forty-five.

I bit into it just as the pastor decided to start playing twenty questions.

"Why don't you date?" He waved a cupcake in my direction.

"Bad prior experience." I popped a whole strawberry into my mouth to avoid him staring. It didn't work.

He dropped his fork into the glass container of chicken salad Mary had made for him. "Martha, do you know the problem with men?" I knew many. But... was that a slur in Pastor Tim's words?

"I can think of a few." I tipped my lips up into a small smile.

He pointed his finger up in the air in a swooping motion like the cartoon tiger on the cereal commercial. "No, no. The real problem."

He was definitely slurring. I eyed his water bottle, which I now suspected did not actually contain water. "What's that?" I asked.

He let his arm flop down on my desk and leaned forward, sighing.

Holy Jim Beam. It was all I could do to keep from coughing.

I couldn't be too surprised, though. Something had to go wrong sometime.

I hadn't seen that black truck in weeks, and no more nasty notes had arrived, either. I had pretty well decided the one I found must've come from Ruthie, just fishing to see if she could spook me. I mean, a young single woman up and appearing in a town nobody outside the county even knows exists... you wouldn't have to be Einstein to wonder about my past. Mary was too kind and trusting to ask questions, was all. These days I figured Ruthie was too busy running the Pick and Go and ignoring gossip about her estranged husband to bother with harassing me. People had said all sorts of nasty things about her and her inability to give Sam the children he wanted. She'd been back to see Pastor Tim every week, and every week hers was the only appointment he wanted me out of the office for—this week he'd sent me to the post office to mail one of his antique Bibles to a collector friend in Louisiana, and last week I'd gone to get his dry cleaning and then stopped for lunch at Sergio's. With her closest friend dead and the whole town whispering about her, Ruthie didn't talk to much of anyone but Pastor Tim, that I could tell. It would've been enough to make me feel sorry for anybody else.

Since our two-man police force hadn't asked more than five questions about Lisa's death before they declared it a hiking accident, I'd been practicing trying to think maybe things were, in fact, good. But I wasn't at all used to the concept, so I spent about half of my waking minutes trying to figure out how my life would turn to rot again, because surely this couldn't last.

Sitting there eating a sandwich I suddenly couldn't taste, all signs pointed to the pastor.

"The trouble with men is that we're liars, Martha. Every Godfearing one of us," he went on. "It's in the bones, in the blood, in the very nature that the Lord gave us. We crave the hunt, but are supposed to sit now in tiny rooms with one window all day and talk to people or look over documents. This unnatural life has turned many a good man into a lying heathen."

My daddy hunted plenty and still never stopped chasing skirts. But Pastor Tim didn't need to know about my family, so I just nodded.

"The lies, they start to eat you from the inside out after a while, like they're avenging the people you made them up for. Maybe? I don't know. But it's a miserable way to live."

I blinked slowly. I hadn't lied to Mary about my background, exactly. I'd just stayed quiet about it. It didn't really seem like he was talking to me anyway, his head flopping onto the arm that was already resting on my desk.

Whether he thought he knew something about me or not, I couldn't resist the opportunity.

"I never really stopped to think about how hard it must be to be you," I said. "I have my hands full with my one good friend and my work. Do you need someone you can visit with, you know, the way people come visit with you? I probably don't have life-changing advice to offer you, but I can listen."

He raised his head halfway, looked me dead in the face, and said, "Liars, everywhere. Nobody is who you think they are. Don't trust people and you'll be okay."

His eyes rolled back so far all the color vanished, his head landing back on his arm as he passed out.

I didn't want to wake him, and I didn't even want to touch the water bottle he was using as a flask, so I took my sandwich into his office and settled myself at the desk.

He was right, the room was an oven—I had sweat running into places nobody should sweat before I'd eaten half my food.

My eyes fell on Pastor Tim's calendar and the date jumped out at me in a way it hadn't from my own—three months. Today marked three months since Good Friday, when I'd moved into the McClatchy house.

When Lisa had last been seen alive.

I thought back over everything that had happened since as I gobbled up the rest of my strawberries.

At home, I cooked, I helped clean, I pulled weeds in the garden beds, and I taught Charlotte how to put on lip gloss and highlight powder.

At work, I kept the books, made sure our budget was on track, and greeted everyone who came in with a smile—even the women who'd been so nasty to me when I worked at the Pick and Go.

Most of all, though: everywhere, I kept the secrets. And I wouldn't let anyone find out that the pastor was passed out from a whiskey bender in the middle of the day. Going back to the front office, I tiptoed around picking up lunch trash and took the bins outside, locking the door as I came and went so no one would happen across Pastor Tim in his current condition.

I liked leaving the offices tidy on Friday afternoons, because Monday mornings were much nicer when everything was orderly.

Back inside with the door locked and the pastor still snoring, I went to clean his office, sweeping under the desk and around his chair.

I almost threw it away without looking.

A piece of paper, maybe five by seven inches, folded smaller, that had tumbled under the desk.

I plucked it out of the dustpan at the last second to make sure it wasn't important. Unfolding it, I spread it across the desk.

A list of names, with ages, heights and weights in different columns, marked April and May of this year.

I felt my forehead wrinkle as I read it again. Only first names were listed, and I didn't recognize them all, though I knew the Sunday School rosters backward and forward.

None of the ages were outside school-age range. Maybe it was kids who'd asked about having Mary tutor them. But why would he need their weight for that?

What required weight? Sports roster, maybe? Two months could be a sports season, and the church sponsored the local little league teams for baseball and softball, though this list was mostly girls' names—only two boys, Atlee and Brayden, both ones I didn't know.

I counted eleven names, my eyes pausing on the last one with every pass over the sheet, pulling my heart higher in my throat. Charlotte. Twelve, five foot four, a hundred and seven pounds.

It wasn't an uncommon name, but in Whitney Falls we only had one twelve-year-old Charlotte.

"She doesn't play any sports," I muttered.

Her name was at the bottom—maybe Pastor Tim had hoped getting her on a team would help with her grief.

I dropped it into the small trash bin next to his desk, figuring it ended up on the floor because he went to toss it and missed, then picked up the pile of mail in the pastor's inbox, opening the top middle desk drawer to get his letter opener and finding the biggest tangled mess I'd ever seen in my life. Paperclips looped through rubber bands, loose change, old Post-it notes. I saw the opal end of the letter opener's handle and reached for it, and a paper moved, revealing another note, this one scrawled in black ink, but not the pastor's handwriting.

*GF, 4:30, Bottleneck Cave.*

GF. Good Friday. Not that it couldn't be a hundred other things. It was just that I had just been thinking about Good Friday, that was all.

I pushed the other paper hastily back over the note and shut the drawer too hard for a desk that old. The wood creaked as it shuddered.

"Martha?" Pastor Tim called from the front office.

"I'm just straightening up in here," I called, putting the mail down and the letter opener in my pocket.

The chair by my desk groaned as he stood, and a minute later he appeared in the doorway. "I think it's stuffier in here than it was this morning." He rubbed at his eyes with both hands. "I can't believe I fell asleep out there."

"You've been busy lately," I said. "I won't tell anyone."

"You're the best, you know that?" He grinned. "Did you get to enjoy the sandwich you made this morning?"

"It was delicious."

"Why don't we call it an early day for today? There's not as much to do this time of year anyway, and it might be cooler outside than it is in here."

I nodded and followed him to the door, shutting off the lights on my way out.

My stomach knotted tighter around my lunch with every step.

Sure, GF could mean loads of things. But I was pretty sure I knew the right one.

Good Friday.

Bottleneck Cave.

Right above the spot where Lisa's body was found.

It was one of the most horrible things I'd ever seen—and that was saying something—and I'd replayed it in my head at least once a day since. Following Pastor Tim outside three months to the day later, I saw it all like I was back in the woods that chilly spring night.

———

*Branches swiped at my face as I felt my way through the trees in the pitch dark, my flashlight only giving me inches of sightline that I needed for my feet, so I didn't trip over something and die out here. Problem was, I was trying to find the cave from memory, which was difficult when I couldn't really see anything.*

*I'd stumbled through trees for half an hour and was about ready to pack it in when the clouds cracked, moonlight trickling through. It wasn't bright, but it was enough.*

*I wasn't far from the cave, if I was remembering right.*

*I stepped carefully over gnarled roots sticking out of the ground, clambering over a boulder I remembered from the last time I'd been out there. The cave should be right ahead.*

*I found the mouth of it, shining the flashlight inside but staying quiet. Only idiots go into dark, unknown caves in the late spring—a hungry bear coming out of hibernation isn't anything you want to see up close.*

*I didn't see a bear. I also didn't see Pastor Tim or Lisa.*

*I wasn't sure whether I should be thrilled or worried.*

*I turned away from the cave just as the clouds shifted apart, the ravine lighting up like someone flipped a switch on.*

*I peered over the edge—I wasn't looking for anything, really. The silvery wash of the moon had always fascinated me, and I was just... looking.*

*I saw her coat first.*

*It was red, with black buttons and a sash belt.*

*"No." I clapped my hand over my mouth, backing away from the edge. I couldn't tell if there was blood because of the color of her coat, but the dark hair and the face were unmistakable, her neck and limbs sticking out at such unnatural angles.*

*Charlotte's mother wasn't coming home.*

*I had no idea how Lisa ended up crumpled like a tissue at the bottom of that ravine, but I knew I couldn't be there, and nobody could help her, so I hightailed it back to my car and retreated to the warm safety of my soft new bed on Elias Lane. By the time I woke up Saturday morning and went to the kitchen for coffee, Mary was using the church phone tree to organize a search party.*

"Does Lisa like hiking?" I asked, sipping my coffee after she hung up the phone.

"I don't think I asked." Mary looked up from the eggs she was cooking for Charlotte. She had four pans going: scrambled, fried, sunny side up, and a bacon and cheese omelet.

"I was just thinking that there are plenty of places someone could get hurt up on the mountain and not be able to get back down," I said.

"That's a great point." Mary turned the stove burners off and slid all the eggs onto one plate. "Is this too much?"

"For a linebacker? No." I smiled and sipped my coffee.

"I always try too hard." Mary put the plate on the counter and I hopped off my stool.

"I was teasing," I said. "You are amazing, covering every base to make Charlotte a good breakfast. If a dozen people are coming here to go look for Lisa, the eggs will get eaten."

Mary looked up, squeezing my hand. "Thank you. For your kindness and for the idea of where to look."

"Sure thing. Let me change and I'll come help."

Half an hour later, I led the first and fourth deacons to the cave, though they didn't realize that's what I was doing, really.

"I haven't been up here since I was in school," one said, looking around the inside walls.

"I forgot it was even here." Four laughed, stepping to the edge of the ravine. "What a view, tho—"

The rest of his comment got swallowed by a shout when he saw the body.

We rushed back to the McClatchy house, where Mary took one look at my face and asked Charlotte to fetch her a glass of water from the kitchen.

"Please no," Mary said as soon as the child was gone, clapping a hand over her mouth.

I shook my head and squeezed her hand. "She fell into a ravine. She—hopefully it was quick."

Someone called the police, and a chunk of the morning blurred by as people came and went. Mary hovered over Charlotte, who sobbed for about twenty minutes before she retreated to stone silence.

Pastor Tim walked in about noon, his smile fading when he saw a dozen people milling around his house including two police officers, everyone subdued.

"What's going on?" he asked.

"Where've you been, Pastor?" the mustached cop asked.

"I was at a retreat." Tim looked at Mary. "I go every year."

"And where did you go this year?" The cop's tone was conversational, his expression curious.

"Up to the woods west of town. Uh. North of town. I'm not great at directions. I was in the woods." He gestured to his clothes: jeans, a sweater, and sneakers.

"You see anyone else while you were gone?"

Pastor Tim shook his head. "Being alone is kind of the point."

"You go anywhere near Bottleneck Cave, or the ravine that runs past it, by any chance?"

Mary stepped away from Charlotte for the first time in hours, putting her hand on Tim's arm.

"I wish I was the type who could help you, but I wouldn't be able to find a ravine in a dark mountain forest with two hands, a flashlight, and a bloodhound."

The cop laughed. "I understand that, sir." His walkie talkie beeped and he stepped away. I stood in the corner watching Pastor Tim's face, which seemed too flat for someone who'd just heard of a coworker's death, especially if my suspicions about his relationship with her had been right, and wondered why he went on annual retreats in the woods with little to no survival skills.

---

Three months later, under the blazing July sun, I walked next to the pastor as we crossed Elias Lane toward home, casting a sideways glance at his profile. I knew the police believed he didn't know what had happened to Lisa because I had believed him— and I was for sure better at spotting a lie than those two dorks.

But Pastor Tim had lied. He had been there. At Bottleneck Cave. The night Lisa died.

Liars, everywhere, he'd said earlier.

Today, a quarter of a year after Lisa's death, he'd been blitzed on whiskey by lunchtime. Pretty easy to assume there had been something between them, given Lisa's widow status and the way Pastor Tim had been with me.

He stared straight ahead, his steps sure for a man who'd downed a decent quantity of Jim Beam. But the lines around his eyes looked deeper today, and sadness seemed to cling to him like a heavy cloak.

It reminded me of Charlotte, but in reverse—Pastor Tim was usually charming and talkative, at least in public, not this booze-riddled sack of bones prattling about lies. In Charlotte we saw glimmers, here and there, of the bubbly girl she had been before Easter weekend, but on the whole, she slipped further into despair by the week. I wondered if maybe the pastor was right and talking her into trying a sport might be a good idea.

You don't know until you try, my granny always said. And if something didn't take a turn for Charlotte soon, I was flat afraid the gloom would eat her alive.

## TWENTY-SEVEN

### MARY

*July*

"Charlotte, sweetheart your lunch is ready," I called from the foot of the stairs, drying my hands on a dish towel and then using it to wipe a smudge off the shiny cherry wood bannister. I sighed when I didn't hear any movement from upstairs—who knew getting a twelve year old to eat would be such a chore? I would've at least been prepared for feeding issues with an infant. I waited ten seconds and then called again. "Charlotte, I'd like you to at least come down and see what I made."

I heard footsteps, light and quick, on the floorboards over my head before her door opened.

"I'm not hungry. You have it."

I swallowed a laugh. There was more food on her plate than I'd eaten in the past two days.

"I can't do that, Charlotte, you need it. You're a growing girl, and this is an important time in your life. Please come down, I haven't seen you at all today."

I heard her sigh so surely she could've been standing next to me, but then the door closed and she appeared at the top of the stairs. Today's oversized sweater was bright sapphire blue, hanging to her knees with a turtleneck that dangled forward under her sharp chin.

I remembered seeing Lisa wear that one to work last February. Charlotte's obsession with wearing her mother's clothes was sad and sweet, but I was beginning to worry it was holding her back from moving on.

"Good afternoon, sleepyhead." Smiling, I tried a one-armed hug. Charlotte shrugged me off and bolted for the kitchen. Well, then. I was still "not her mother," as she'd reminded me a thousand times since she'd come home with me. At least if she was going to dismiss any attempt at affection—again—I'd chased her in the direction of the food. My husband might not think there's any such thing as too thin, but the line does exist, and Charlotte was slipping further past it by the day. How would it look if social services took her from us because she was malnourished?

Sighing myself, I followed her to the kitchen, where I found her staring at the pile of fresh chicken salad I'd stacked on an open-faced croissant. "Even the mayonnaise is homemade," I said, nudging the plate toward her. "And I cut the fries myself."

"In crinkles?" She plucked one from the pile and inspected it for signs of being store-bought.

"I have a tool." I pulled it from the sink and held it up, laughing. "I didn't do it with a knife or anything."

She nodded, staring at the fry for several beats before she dipped it in the sauce on her plate and bit the end off. Her eyes widened and she took another bite. "What's in that?" she asked as she chewed the third one.

"I learned to make it from a woman in Texas," I said. "It's mayo and sour cream with garlic, paprika, and a little ranch seasoning—then I add a teaspoon of pickle juice and a dollop of ketchup." I felt my whole heart lift, watching her eat. In recent days even the ice cream she'd liked early on had been a challenge. I kept my eyes mostly on the counter, afraid watching her might scare her back to starvation.

"You could bottle that sauce," Charlotte said as she finished the last fry and picked up half of the croissant.

"That's very kind of you to say."

"My mom didn't like to cook." Her eyes widened as she chewed the chicken salad. "I only know how to make SpaghettiOs and cereal. And toast. I can make toast." She took a bigger bite and I willed my feet to stay still. I wanted to dance around my kitchen. She was eating, and she was talking to me with more than one word at a time. I wasn't sure what had happened but it felt like a page was turning right in front of me.

"I could teach you." I leaned on the edge of the counter, smiling. "Between Martha and me, we can cook just about anything, I've found."

Charlotte bit her lip and put the half-eaten croissant back on her plate.

"What's wrong?" I stood up straight. She needed to keep eating, but it was like storm shutters had closed over her face.

"I'm fine." There it was, the melancholy, monotone voice that had become normal for her.

I took a deep breath. I'd had her back for a minute. Maybe I could get her again.

"You know you can talk to me about anything," I kept my voice soft. "Food, life, makeup. Clothes, boys. Your mom. Whatever. I want to help you."

Charlotte fidgeted, hopping off the stool and twisting her long dark hair around her fingers.

"How well do you know Martha?" she finally asked. I was so shocked by the question I nearly staggered backward. Of all the things I'd thought might be about to come out of her mouth, I wouldn't have guessed that one.

"We're good friends, she lives over the garage and works for my husband. So, pretty well I think." My brow furrowed. "Why?"

"My mom didn't like her," Charlotte said finally. "Or maybe it's better to say she didn't trust her. She said she thought Martha watched us with a funny look sometimes, and nobody knew where she came from—not even my mom, and the church secretary is supposed to know everything. She said—"

"She said what?" I asked, a beat after she cut herself off. My breath was coming too fast, but I couldn't slow it down.

"She didn't like the way Pastor Tim looked at Martha," Charlotte said.

My face crumpled, just for a second before I got control over it, but it was enough.

"I'm sorry," she whispered. "I didn't mean to upset you. Martha is nice to me, and I shouldn't have said that." She pushed her plate away.

I pushed it back. "You didn't do any such thing. And I bet if you finish that other half of your sandwich I'll forget all about it." I kept the bright smile pasted on, glad my lunch today had consisted of part of the peach I'd chopped for the chicken salad and a couple of stalks of celery because my stomach was trying to turn itself inside out. But I couldn't let Charlotte see that.

She nodded and picked up the croissant, and I watched her eat, wondering what her mother had known that I didn't.

Charlotte took two more bites and I nodded encouragement, refilling my water from the refrigerator and holding up a cold bottle of apple juice. "Would you like some juice?"

Charlotte nodded, still chewing. I wasn't sure what had made a difference for her that day—maybe she was just plain tired of being hungry—but between the food and the conversation, I was hopeful for the first time in months. Maybe I could pull this off after all.

I poured her juice and went to set the glass down in front of her when the back door flew open, right into the wall. Charlotte jumped at the sudden noise, and I watched my husband stumble over the doorjamb, stomping his left foot on it and swearing.

"Light day today?" I asked, keeping one eye on Charlotte, who looked like a fawn in the path of a Mack truck—wide-eyed and ready to bolt.

"Friday in the summer," Tim said, pulling off his tie. "Nothing to do but roast in that little cracker box office. I got tired of sweating."

He dropped the tie on the island and glanced at Charlotte. "I guess all the chicken salad is gone, then."

She stood back up and moved toward the other end of the counter, her eyes on the floor.

"I'm sorry." The words were nearly too quiet for me to hear.

"Speak up, if you have something to say," Tim roared, his deep voice filling the kitchen.

Charlotte flinched, and I put myself between the two of them.

Tim nodded and threw up his hands. "Sure. Coddle her. That's worked so well for you so far, Mary."

I studied his face, taking in the red-rimmed eyes and the dry skin flakes on his cheekbones.

Dear baby Jesus, he was drunk. At one o'clock in the afternoon.

"Why don't you take a nap, Tim?" My voice was colder than I meant for it to be, but I couldn't help it. His resentment had been building for weeks—I'd been absorbed with getting Charlotte settled, trying to make her happy, and dealing with social services, not to mention running my tutoring group and the First Baptist Ladies' Auxiliary. All of which left little time for being an attentive wife to Tim, and he wasn't used to playing second fiddle.

But he was also a grown man who was inching across the

line between acting like a baby and bullying a grieving little girl. I would not stand for that.

He stared at me for what felt like a long time, his eyes narrowing before his face fell. "Yeah. My head hurts."

I turned back to Charlotte when I heard his footfalls on the stairs. "I'm sorry. He's not normally like this." That was increasingly a lie, but she didn't need to know that. I wanted her to feel safe here, it was the only way this was going to work out.

"I'll just go back to my room."

"I wish you wouldn't," I said. "We could play a game, or watch a movie."

"I don't need you to coddle me," she snapped before she took off up the stairs.

"Damn you, Tim McClatchy," I muttered as I picked up Charlotte's nearly empty plate and scrubbed the already-shiny-clean island, Charlotte's comment about Martha rattling around my swirling thoughts like a tree branch in a tornado.

Putting the rag on its hook under the sink, I looked around for something else that needed doing, the idea of sitting down making my skin feel too tight for my bones.

Everything in the house, from the baseboards to the light fixtures, sparkled like a museum. Not a single knickknack sat out of place. My eyes fell on the door Tim left open when he came in, and I wandered out back, the soft breeze rustling the fat green leaves on the old oak tree, birds yammering in the high branches. I lifted my face to the sun and the breeze, my eyes falling on Martha. She stood in her window, in front of the air conditioning unit, looking down at the house.

The unit was keeping her apartment decently cool—I had gone up to check a few days before. Or that's what I told myself, anyway. That I was checking the air conditioning because she wouldn't complain if it was too hot up there.

I'd found a few other things, too. New tops with plunging necklines, makeup in the tiny bathroom—and in her tampon box, a folded piece of paper with thick black letters scrawled across the middle:

*I know where you come from. I know what you did.*

*I'm not going away, so you should.*

Chilled in the slightly stuffy little room, I'd stuffed it back where I found it and clattered back down the stairs and across the lawn like someone could see right through me.

Looking up at her through the glare of the midday sun off the window, I wondered again who the note was for, and what Martha knew. She had a gift for fading into the background. What did she see when we didn't realize she was watching?

## TWENTY-EIGHT
### MARTHA

*July*

Reason number 579 that I loved Whitney Falls: summer twilight. For about ninety magical minutes after the blazing summer sun disappeared behind the mountain to the west and before the evening humidity set in, being outdoors was heavenly. As long as the mosquitoes didn't like you, anyhow. Some days I took walks, others I sat on the front porch with Mary and chatted over iced tea. This particular night, Mary wasn't home—she took what she called "wind down drives" most nights now, to clear her head before she tried to sleep, though it seemed like they were getting earlier as summer wore on—and I didn't feel like walking, so I'd carried her gardening bag out from the garage to tend to the flowerbeds. I was nearly wrist deep in heavy topsoil, hunting the root of some stubborn Johnson grass, when a scream split the still air, high and long, springing every hair on my arm straight up.

"Charlotte?" I ran up the kitchen porch steps, sprinting for the door to the house, my breath coming too fast for such a short run. Panic radiated from every part of my brain.

Good Friday. The cave. Lisa.

Pastor Tim.

Sweet Jesus, what now?

I skidded through the kitchen, my shoes tromping over Mary's shiny floors in my haste.

"Charlotte?" I called.

Another howl. Upstairs.

I took them two at a time, stopping short at the top of the staircase.

My brain didn't want to process the scene in front of me. Pastor Tim had Charlotte in a sort of wrestling-looking hold, a pair of gold scissors gleaming in one of his hands. The girl struggled against his grasp, alternately panting and screaming.

Even more disturbing was the condition of the bathroom they stood in—bright red smears splashed across the sink and floor. I stepped closer, sucking in a sharp breath when I saw the broken mirror over the sink.

"Let go!" Charlotte hollered, stomping on Tim's foot.

"Not until I'm sure you won't hurt yourself." His voice was calm—almost frighteningly so, given the circumstances.

"You can't tell me what to do!" Charlotte slung her head to one side. That was the first time I noticed her hair. Normally long and shining chestnut, it looked like someone had at it with a weed whacker, entire chunks missing right up to her scalp.

And it was red. Bright, blood red.

"Charlotte," I blurted with no plan for what to say next.

That may have been the first time either of them noticed me, really.

"I've got her, Martha," Tim said. "This is not your problem."

"That doesn't mean I'm not interested in helping." A ball of fear formed in my gut as I looked at him. Maybe the light in the bathroom was harsh, but his eyes seemed hollow and emotionless, like a snake's, and his stoic face betrayed no sympathy. If anything, he looked... angry.

I wasn't sure I'd ever seen the pastor angry. And I knew in my bones that whatever the heck was going on here, anger was the wrong reaction.

I ignored him, focusing on Charlotte. "What's going on?"

"I'm not pretty! I don't need to be pretty." The words came out almost as a growl, ripped out of her throat against her will. She looked straight at me, green eyes brimming with accusation and hatred, before she squeezed them shut and shook her head hard, bashing her temple into Pastor Tim's chin and going limp in his arms.

My jaw fell open as he stepped back and let her little body fall into a heap on the floor.

He put the scissors on the counter and turned to me. "I said I've got it."

"Clearly you're mistaken." My fingers flew to my mouth.

I hadn't really snapped at the pastor, had I? I took one step backward as a glare shrunk his flat, dark eyes.

*I'm sorry.* The reflex to say the words was automatic and strong, but somehow I couldn't force them up my throat.

"She's troubled. We're trying to help her."

"By shearing her head?" I blurted. In for a penny...

He stared. I didn't blink.

Neither of us heard the footfalls on the staircase's carpeted runner.

"What in the world?" Mary's voice made my head whip around.

I stepped hastily backward as she hit her knees next to Charlotte, who still wasn't moving.

"What have you done?" Mary's shriek swam in anguish, her eyes flashing accusingly between Tim and myself.

"N-nothing," I stammered.

"Martha," Pastor Tim barked.

I flinched. "Yes, sir?" Years of conditioning to a quick backhand for showing disrespect to an angry man had the words out of my mouth before I could think.

"Go home, if you'd like to keep a home to go to. Now."

I stumbled backward, lucky I didn't tumble right down the staircase. By the time I made it to the back door I couldn't see anything for the tears in my eyes.

"Mary's with her," I whispered to myself. Whatever was happening with the pastor, Mary wouldn't stand for him hurting that child. It was the only way I could have left.

The one thing my apartment lacked was a phone, and I was still afraid of being tracked somehow, carrying a cell phone. With my new job and the apartment, I had the money—but I didn't want anything bad enough to risk the wrong people being able to find me. Not until right then, anyway. Though having watched the police investigate Lisa's death, I wasn't sure who I'd have called, really.

"Mary will get it all straight," I whispered to my reflection in the mirror.

And hopefully, she'd come tell me what had gone wrong and how I could help.

I had seen a lot of terrible things, but I couldn't shake Charlotte's howls out of my head. I perched on the edge of my little sofa, my hands trembling. It had been nearly eight months since I'd wanted a drink as badly as I wanted one right then.

She didn't need to be pretty, she'd said. I'd seen her lose her temper a few times—turning over the chair and storming out of the tutoring group, snapping at Mary about how she'd eat when she wanted to, but whatever had happened in that bathroom seemed more serious. Mary insisted she was helping counsel the girl, and it wasn't like Whitney Falls had a shrink, anyway, so I had done the only thing I could think to and prayed for her every single night. Maybe I wasn't doing it right. I had only started praying daily because Mary did, and I wanted both to earn the approval she had so kindly offered me and to be more like her—but it wasn't like anyone had ever taught me how any of this worked. Well, except at AA. That one, I knew how to say.

And right then, I needed to pray for myself. I bowed my head and said the words right out loud. "God, grant me the serenity to accept the things I cannot change…"

A low tap came from the door just before it opened and Mary walked in.

I about jumped out of my skin, leaping to my feet like the sofa cushion was hiding a cattle prod.

"Are you okay?" she asked just as I said, "Is she all right?" The words seemed to collide in the air, and Mary dropped her chin to her chest and laughed, but it wasn't a happy sound. Low and choppy, it made the hairs on my arm stand up again.

"She's sleeping." Mary waved one hand when my eyes widened. "She came to, and I put her to bed. I'll watch her tonight for signs of concussion." She sighed and shook her head. "I know teenagers are supposed to rebel, and I suppose chopping off her hair isn't that bad in the grand scheme of things."

"You're…" I paused, chewing on the words I wanted to say next for a beat. They were bitter and rubbery, and I wasn't sure they'd come out as I intended, but I opened my mouth and out they tumbled anyway. "You're sure she's the one who cut her hair?"

"Who else would've done it, Martha?" Mary's voice was as quiet and melodic as ever, but her gaze had an edge of menace, I thought.

It vanished in half a blink, and I couldn't tell if I'd just imagined it.

"Charlotte is a troubled girl." Mary shook her head. "As much as I've been trying to convince myself she's not, it's true. I mentioned helping her with her hair the other day, teaching her about makeup, and something about that set her off. Probably simply that I'm not her mother, as she loves to remind me. Tim went upstairs and saw her with the scissors, mistook the hair dye for blood, and was afraid she was hurting herself. That's all you saw."

She stared at me until I nodded, then she turned back to the door. "I'm sure you understand I'll have to skip our girls' night tonight, I need to watch her."

"Of course." I stepped toward her, panic welling that I'd made her mad at me. I couldn't stand the thought. "I didn't mean anything, Mary. And well I... just, I think you're a good mom."

Eyes shining, she turned back to me. "That is the very nicest thing anyone's ever said to me."

She let herself out, and I forced down some Pop-Tarts and a glass of milk before I crawled into bed, but I couldn't quiet my mind no matter how many sheep I counted or halting prayers I tried to say.

I didn't want to think Mary would lie to me, but I wasn't sure I believed her story, whether she did or not. I couldn't shake the memory of Pastor Tim's flat, cold eyes in that bathroom—the hard look on his usually kind face had scared me. And we're all at our most vulnerable when we sleep.

I got up and dragged one of the kitchen chairs to the door, wedging it under the handle good and checking the lock again. Then I got a knife and slid it under my pillow.

It had been a while since I'd needed a knife in my bed, but until I knew what kind of bad things were indeed happening on Elias Lane, I'd do what it took to keep myself safe. I stared at the ceiling for a long time, another bathroom splashed with crimson streaks wavering in my thoughts. I closed my fingers around the knife as I dozed off, whispering a prayer that I wouldn't have to use it this time.

# TWENTY-NINE
## MARTHA

*July*

Mary got the owner of the beauty shop on Main Street to come to the house and clean up Charlotte's hair the best she could—between trimmers and three different kinds of scissors, it wound up center parted into a very thin chin-length bob with much of the underneath shaved close to her scalp. The color was a permanent gel, though, and since stripping such thin hair would make what remained brittle, the stylist recommended using the rest of the dye to make the candy apple red uniform, at least. Mary frowned, but shrugged and agreed there wasn't really another option.

Once the stylist had packed up her equipment, Mary reached to shake her hand, gripping the woman's fingers tightly. "Thank you so much for your help," she said. "And your discretion."

Reaching into the pocket of her white cotton shorts, Mary pulled out a hundred-dollar bill and held it out.

"Oh no, ma'am, I can't take your money. I'm happy to help the pastor out, of course."

"We appreciate that, but I can't let you come here on a Saturday and not pay you for your time," Mary said. "It wouldn't feel right."

"Just give it to the church food pantry, then." The stylist backed out of the kitchen, and a few seconds later the front door opened and closed.

Mary sighed and stuck the bill back in her pocket, turning to Charlotte. "Where did you get permanent gel hair dye?"

Charlotte folded her arms across her thin chest and clamped her lips shut.

"Charlotte, I'm never harsh with you, but I need to know where you got these chemicals you smeared all over your head." Mary's voice was tight. "Please answer my question."

Charlotte swung her foot above the floor and squeezed her eyes shut.

"Was it one of the boys from our science group? Did some boy put you up to this, get you the dye?" Mary's voice shook.

Charlotte stayed still, mouth and eyes shut, her arms folded tightly. She was coming up on thirteen and I couldn't help noticing the lack of development in her chest area, obvious even under the heavy violet sweater she had on.

I didn't really guess she ate enough for her body to do any growing.

"I know young girls like their secrets," Mary softened her tone, "I had plenty when I was your age. But the state has trusted us to care for you, and I'd really like to know where these chemicals came from so I know I'm keeping you safe."

Charlotte's eyes popped open, but she didn't get up. She stared at Mary instead, her eyes wide. Almost like she wanted to say something.

The silence stretched so long and deep you could've heard a flea sneeze. Just when I was about to start fidgeting, Charlotte's clear voice sliced through it. "May I go upstairs?"

"You may go to your room." Mary's tone was sad, matching

the defeated slump of her shoulders. If she wasn't an angel, she had the patience of one—even Granny would've popped me for refusing to answer a direct question. Charlotte didn't seem scared, though—she just sprinted out of the kitchen so fast we couldn't see anything but a purple streak.

"You okay?" I asked Mary when Charlotte's door slammed upstairs.

Stirring sugar into her coffee, Mary sighed. "She hates me."

"I think maybe she hates that her mother is gone," I said gently. "Nobody could hate you, Mary."

She glanced up, holding my gaze. "You really believe that, don't you?" She barked a short laugh.

"With all my heart. I'm sorry... about yesterday." That was the most gentle way I could think to say it.

"We were all entirely too upset." She sipped her coffee, staring past me out the window at the summer green interspersed with splashes of bright yellow cannas, pink and coral azaleas, and blue hydrangeas. I couldn't even decide yet which was my favorite season on Elias Lane because I hadn't seen fall yet, but so far summer had everything else beat. Growing up without air conditioning, I didn't mind the heat as much as most folks, and the beauty everywhere I looked, especially from my little apartment on the second floor, was breathtaking.

"Does the Pick and Go carry hair coloring like that? Fire engine red permanent gel?"

"Not that I ever saw anyone buy in my time there," I said. "I suppose it's possible that it's just not popular around here, though. It is an unnatural color—that's part of why I got scared yesterday—I heard her screaming from outside and ran up the stairs and the pastor had scissors and was holding her and the dye looked like..." I shuddered.

"Blood," Mary finished. "It looked like someone smeared the entire room down with blood. I spent an hour this morning trying to scrub it off the white marble and tile, and everything is still pink."

"Please let me help you," I leaned across the table and took her hand. "You have no business doing any of that in your... possible condition."

"I can't even hope today." She squeezed my hand as her eyes got too shiny and the tears started to fall, making small dark spots on her favorite blue blouse. "I don't know what I'd do without you, Martha. Thank you for understanding."

"Of course," I smiled. "Now—we need some bleach and some lye, and I'll get that bathroom looking good as new."

She gestured toward the staircase. "If you insist."

"I do. And I insist you settle on that couch with a book and let me take care of this."

I hauled the cleaning supplies up the staircase and opened the bathroom door, the smell of lemon oil soap strong in the small room.

Rolling up my sleeves, I got to work scrubbing. Hair dye is stubborn, but nothing is harder to clean than blood. Not that I ever expected to need that skill again.

Once the sink and counter gleamed snowy white again, I went after the tile floor and the side of the toilet tank, wondering what the devil had happened in here—was Charlotte trying to dye her hair or wreck this room? Coloring hair sometimes leaves drips on towels, but this was... like someone sprayed it. Or gave a tube of it to a toddler.

I was sweating by the time the mess was gone, and worried about what was happening with Charlotte. I knew this was her private bathroom. I dropped the last pink-stained cloth into the wastebasket and opened the cabinet under the sink. A pink plastic tackle box full of makeup and a stack of towels. I tried the drawers next. The top one held a brush and a pair of tweezers. The middle one had a curling iron and false eyelashes, and the bottom, a box of pregnancy tests.

I sighed and closed the drawers. Charlotte was a tomboy in just about every tree-climbing, outdoors-loving sense of the word. But with Mary still keeping her stuff in this bathroom, the girl wouldn't put anything she was trying to keep private in here—too much risk of discovery. And I had the feeling without asking that Mary wouldn't want to look in Charlotte's room without her permission.

It was just grief, I knew—losing a parent at all is hard, but losing a mother when you're young reshapes you. Rewrites your whole story. Charlotte was, sometimes messily, finding her way to dealing with emotions so big no kid should ever have to wrestle them. Finding who she was now, without her momma. I knew the feeling, but I was too afraid to share anything about my past with anyone here to try to relate to her that way.

Shutting off the lights, I picked up the bleach and the soap and headed back downstairs. Mary was curled under a fluffy blue blanket on the couch, fast asleep. Pastor Tim, thankfully, was at the men's Saturday breakfast, where he usually stayed until afternoon.

The back screen door swung wide and smacked into the siding when I opened it, the warm wind off the mountain gusty and strong. I pushed it shut until I heard the latch click, crossing the driveway. I'd made it up two steps when I spotted something on the ground in front of the garage door. Was that...

I knelt and picked it up carefully. A bouquet, of local summer flowers. Except they were all dead—shriveled and brown and so dry they scratched at my hands. I found a piece of twine tying them together, wrapped around a folded piece of white paper.

Looking over my shoulder, I took the whole mess up to my apartment, dropping the flowers in the sink and unfolding the note with hands I tried and failed to keep from trembling.

Same thick black scrawl as the other one.

*You think you've found a life here. Don't get comfortable.*

*I see you. I know you. And soon they will too.*

My eyes swam, my breathing harsh and ragged. I wanted to run water over it or burn it or shred it into confetti.

But I needed to know for sure where they were coming from. Who knew my secret. Who might upend my new life.

Ruthie, of course, would want that the most, and seemed to have time on her hands since her husband up and left, but how could she know anything about me really? I didn't miss Sam Tomlinson, exactly—he was often weird and moody, especially those last few weeks—but he had given me a job when nobody else would, so I hoped that wherever he'd gone off to he was happy there. I knew all about fresh starts, which was how I'd stayed out of the gossip about Sam. With so many little towns scattered all over the backwoods from here to California, if Sam didn't want to be found, he wouldn't be. It was just as simple as that.

The thing that had my heart pounding in my ears was the possibility that it wasn't Ruthie—or anyone else from Whitney Falls. I hadn't seen that black truck in a while, but what if this meant it was back? And that whoever was driving it had tracked me—all the way from Virginia? I knew plenty of folks sadistic enough to torture me a bit this way before swooping in to destroy my life here and haul me back home to answer for what I'd done.

Fingers trembling, I stuffed this note into the tampon box next to the other one and tucked the box back in the corner next to the toilet.

I'd all but dismissed the first note when things settled into such a comfortable routine after Easter. But a second one so many weeks later—someone was toying with me.

Their mistake.

I had worked too hard for this life to watch it crumble under the weight of a past that wasn't my fault.

# THIRTY

## MARY

*July*

Peeing on a plastic stick without getting a drop on my hands was a science that had taken me years to perfect. By that first summer in Whitney Falls, I had an entire ritual for testing day: always three days before my cycle was due, never the full six advertised on the test box, because six days felt greedy somehow. Like the punishment of waiting would lead to the reward of good news—someday, I hoped. It hadn't yet.

On a blistering morning in late July, I waited until Tim had left for work—I didn't remember when having the house to myself had become part of the routine. In Texas, maybe, or even as far back as Louisiana. Early on, he'd waited outside the bathroom praying every month, and somewhere along the way it had become too much, carrying his hopes and worry alongside my own.

Our lives changed: new responsibilities, new towns, new churches. We changed—the more difficulty Tim had getting excited, the more self-conscious I grew, until I thought the two things were feeding each other in a vicious cycle I didn't know how to break. I couldn't remember if I asked him to stop tracking along with me or if he did it on his own, not any more than I could remember how to trust him.

The past few months, I'd had the new responsibility of motherhood, such that it was, to fit in, too.

I made our bed, tucking the corners extra tight because Tim liked them that way, and then went to the kitchen to fix Charlotte breakfast. Overboard? Maybe: I cooked two scrambled eggs and one fried one, made stovetop grits with cream and honey and a tiny bit of salt, cooked three sausage patties and chopped a big pile of strawberries before I went to the bottom of the stairs.

"Charlotte," I called, keeping my voice light, but loud enough to be heard. "Breakfast is ready!"

"Not hungry," she called back. "You eat mine."

"What else is new?" I muttered under my breath, turning back for the kitchen.

I pulled a silver serving tray that had once belonged to Tim's grandmother from a skinny drawer under the base cabinets—I'd never seen one before we moved here, like a secret compartment. It was the perfect size for trays and serving platters, and impractical for much of anything else.

Loading her food onto the tray, I poured a glass of orange juice and wondered, for just a second, what the grits would feel like melting on my tongue.

I hadn't eaten grits in years, and I wasn't going to start by taking Charlotte's today.

I picked up the tray and carried it through the dining room to the stairs, my hands too full to wave at Martha when I glanced out the window and saw her turn the church van onto the street. She was taking the church's donations to the county food bank this morning, so she'd be gone for at least an hour. Hurrying upstairs, I tapped on Charlotte's door with my foot.

"I'm busy," she said.

"That's why I brought your food up," I said brightly. "You need to eat, but I don't want to bother you."

I heard footsteps on the hardwood, and the door cracked open, her fire engine red hair falling in front of the one eye I could see.

"You never let anyone eat upstairs," she said. "Not even Pastor Tim."

"Today, you get an exception." I smiled. "I trust you to pick up your mess."

She eyed the tray.

"I noticed you didn't eat much at dinner last night," I said, holding the tray out a bit more. "I know you like sausage and eggs, and the grits are my mother's recipe, you should try them." I widened my eyes and my smile—not enough to be scary, just enough to encourage her.

"I can eat in here?"

"If you're comfortable eating breakfast in here, I'll bring a tray every morning." Whatever it took to get her to eat. I could worry about family norms and discipline later.

She opened the door wider and took the tray, offering a half-smile before she ducked her head. "Thank you."

I nodded, not daring to hope too much just yet. "You can leave the tray out here when you're done."

She nodded and shut the door. I heard the lock click softly as I retreated to my own room and locked the door.

"I did it," I whispered, a slow smile spreading across my face. "She's eating breakfast today because I figured it out. I got through to her." I tipped my head back to the sky. "I can do this, Lord. I can be a good mother. Please."

I turned to my bathroom, where sunbeams shone straight through the window, dancing off the white tile like glittering snow. "Please," I whispered again.

I filled a glass from the cold water tap and downed it, my second in an hour. I wiped down the counter because I needed something to do, not because there was so much as a speck of dust on it, before I met my own eyes in the mirror. "Trust in the Lord," I said. "And in yourself."

Fingers trembling, I opened the high cabinet over the counter and pulled down the thick box of tests, retrieving one and unwrapping it.

I uncapped the test and pulled a necklace that once belonged to my great-grandmother—who had nine children—from my jewelry box, clutching it in my fingers as I assumed the position.

Not a stray drop of mess to contend with. I replaced the cap, set the test on the counter, and hit my knees on the cool tile, bowing my head and praying for this one to be different.

For this day, when Charlotte was eating breakfast and Tim had kissed me on his way out the door for the first time in weeks, to be the first day of the rest of my life.

The metal of the necklace bit into my fingers, but I only squeezed it tighter. Sometimes there is purpose in pain.

"Please God. Forgive my faults. Bless this house with new life."

Raising my head, I picked up the test.

I didn't believe my own eyes.

Two lines. Equally dark. Equally real.

I wanted to scream, but the sound stuck in my throat, warm tears welling fresh in my eyes and spilling down my cheeks.

A baby.

Forgiveness. Redemption. New life and new hope.

I crumpled into a ball on the floor and sobbed, my arms cradling my abdomen.

Later, there would be choices to make. News to share. Things to decide.

But right then, it was just my baby and me. And that was enough.

## THIRTY-ONE
### MARTHA

*July*

"Not every woman is cut out to be a momma."

My granny had said those words to me dozens of times—every time I asked why my mother took off on the back of some guy's Harley before I could walk, to be exact.

Growing up, I had learned there was truth in them, but so many layers of gray, too. Kind of like Granny: she was all I had, really, in the way of guidance or love, a shrewd, skinny little woman whose back was broken by hard work years before her only son broke her heart and his bad choices shattered her spirit.

But hearing them come out of the first deacon's wife's mouth on a rainy Saturday afternoon and watching Ruthie Tomlinson smirk and nod from the corner of my eye as I looked over the steaks at the Pick and Go made my cheeks flush hot, my armpits sweating right through the Secret deodorant I had put on after my shower.

"She's good with the kids, teaching them science," the deacon's wife conceded. She was just about the only member of the auxiliary Mary hadn't won completely over, though I was surprised to see her gossiping with Ruthie given the hateful things I'd heard her tell other women about Sam leaving. Not that Ruthie knew that—she was lapping up the attention like a starving kitten who'd stumbled right into a big bowl of cream. "And it's good of them to take Charlotte in. I hear she's not been easy to manage, and Mary has been very patient. It's not that she doesn't have the maternal instinct. But there's just something about her."

"There really is," Ruthie agreed quickly, her tone sharp. "But it's a real shame for Pastor Tim. He's the kind of man I bet would be a good father. Not that anyone here has thought about making a baby with the pastor."

The two of them dissolved into giggles.

I focused on the T-bones in the meat case, picking four and putting them into my cart. Right then I was too mad to remember to be thankful that I was buying steak at the grocery store for a cookout on a summer Saturday. Like someone from one of my TV stories.

What would one of those smart, sassy women I'd once wanted so badly to be—before everything went to hell and I had come to Whitney Falls to fade into the background of this safe, insulated little town—do if she were standing there in my three-dollar thrift store flip-flops?

Gripping the cart's handle so tight I couldn't feel my fingers, I stared at Ruthie, who had spotted me and leaned in to whisper something to the deacon's wife.

I wasn't a main character in Whitney Falls, I was a bit player. And bit players didn't march up and tell off the first deacon's wife and the grocery store manager.

Not on any show I'd ever watched, anyway. But if there was a more hurtful thing those vipers could've said about Mary, I couldn't think of it. I had pretty well figured Mary wasn't as perfect as I'd first thought—nobody could be, really—but she was a good person. And it turned out I didn't have it in me to walk away like I hadn't heard them being hateful.

I shoved the cart intending to march up to them, but I guess the fury made me go at it a little harder than normal. It sailed right out of my fingers, crashed into an ancient display for Chicken of the Sea Tuna, and took the cardboard mermaid's head clean off, sending cans everywhere. One landed on Ruthie's foot just as two more sprung leaks, spraying the deacon's wife with tuna water. I clapped both hands over my mouth as they sputtered and screeched.

"What in blazes is the matter with you?" the deacon's wife snapped, wiping her face on her sleeve as Ruthie rounded on me, her eyes hard as onyx stones glaring out of her pinched, sunken face, which had gotten thinner since Sam took off.

"She's an idiot," Ruthie said. "And a liar, too. Lord only knows what kind of state the accounts and files at the church have fallen into with her working alone in the office."

I straightened my shoulders and pulled my cart back out of the display. "I couldn't help but overhear your conversation," I said with a fake, overly sweet smile. "So I thought I'd come over here and remind y'all that Jesus taught folks not to judge others—and one of you is throwing some stones from inside a glass house, far as I can see." I stared at Ruthie as I said that last part, and her eyes narrowed until I almost couldn't see them anymore. "But the funniest thing happened, the cart slipped plum out of my hand. I guess the Lord does work in mysterious ways."

I turned the cart toward the produce section and forced myself to walk calmly away instead of hightailing it right out of the store—and maybe out of town—like I would've a few months ago. I wasn't the mousy cashier anymore. I was the church secretary. I belonged here at least almost as much as they did.

"Did you see that?" A voice came from behind me as I

stopped in front of the corn bin, and I turned my head just enough to see two women who lived on Elias Lane pushing carts side by side, looking at green cardboard boxes of strawberries. "I swear Ruthie Tomlinson must have done something to smite either Jesus or the devil himself."

The second woman giggled as she picked up strawberries, and heat crept up my neck as I examined corn, willing them to stay nearby. "True story." The second voice was high and nasal. "Remember when nothing happened around here without her blessing? Now she's just... sad. A grocery worker who couldn't keep her man."

"I heard he left her for a woman who could give him a baby." The first woman lowered her voice. "They ran away to Memphis so Sam wouldn't have to pay for a divorce."

"Can you blame him?"

I tucked a fourth ear of corn into a plastic produce bag. The story about Sam was plausible, certainly, but so were a hundred other ones that might not make Sam out as quite such a villain. I mean, I didn't even like Ruthie, but I couldn't help feeling a little sorry for her picturing that version of events.

I picked out four baking potatoes, and got through the checkout and all the way out of the store before my hands stopped shaking, thinking about Ruthie.

"Nothing wrong with telling off some hateful broads for gossiping about my kin," I muttered as I put the groceries in the back of my Honda, keeping one hand on the hatch so it didn't fall.

Kin. I paused before I closed the car up, wondering when I'd started to think of Mary as family.

And whether that was a good idea.

I was glad to have Mary as a friend and thankful for the apartment she was renting me and the job she'd provided, but I was getting in too deep and I knew it. The McClatchys were not perfect TV sitcom people—Pastor Tim's day drinking and flashes of temper had too many shades of my daddy for comfort, and as much as I hadn't wanted to think it, I couldn't stop wondering how much Mary knew—and overlooked. Or hid. That first dinner when she'd seemed afraid to tell him the casserole wasn't exactly what he wanted had flashed through my head half a dozen times in the past few weeks.

I knew just enough to know there were things I still didn't know. I just wasn't sure I wanted to know them.

---

"Now that was a wonderful dinner, ladies. Fattening, no doubt, but what a way to get fat." Pastor Tim leaned back in his deck chair and patted his flat stomach through a blue Polo shirt that showed off his muscular shoulders and arms in a way I shouldn't have been noticing. I jumped to my feet and started grabbing dishes.

"Charlotte, it's time you started helping out around here," Pastor Tim said, his tone sharper than I'd ever heard it. "Martha, put that down. You and Mary cooked. Let Charlotte take care of the dishes."

I didn't really think it wise to point out that he hadn't cooked anything either—Mary had grilled the steaks while I roasted the corn and prepared the "twice baked" potatoes she said were the pastor's favorite.

The potatoes had been delicious, but the stormy look on Pastor Tim's face as he stared at Charlotte, whose eyes were fixed firmly on her shoes, was flat the most unattractive I'd ever seen him look.

Probably because he'd never looked more like my daddy.

"I really don't mind," I said slowly.

"I mind," he snapped, locking eyes with me. The darkness in his sent a shiver down my spine in the summer night air that was so real I could've sworn someone dropped an ice cube down my tank top. "She sulks around here worrying Mary and being halfway rude to everyone at best, and she does nothing to earn her keep. Instead, we all tiptoe around her and somehow feel like it's an achievement if she bothers to eat food that's been prepared for her. No more. Spare the rod and spoil the child was good enough for me, and this child will not be spoiled on my watch, under my roof."

Charlotte sniffled, but didn't move, her chin still tucked into her collarbone.

I turned to Mary, who stared at Tim with the saddest, most confused look I'd ever seen on a face that didn't belong to a dog. She opened her mouth twice, but closed it silently both times before she stood and went into the house.

Pastor Tim shot out of his chair and around the table, yanking Charlotte's chair—with Charlotte in it—backward so violently I wasn't sure how he didn't dump her into a heap on the deck.

"I said, clear the dishes. Now." His voice was tight and controlled, but I knew the look on his face. If she didn't get up, he was going to hit her.

I couldn't watch that.

"Charlotte, please." I'd never forced so much begging into two small words.

She pulled in a hitching breath and stood, turning her face up so her nose was inches from his. "Yes. Sir."

I stared, holding my breath, but Pastor Tim just shook his head and stepped aside. Charlotte started picking up dishes, piling all the plates and three of the four salad bowls into a precarious tower of blue porcelain before she stomped toward the house.

Pastor Tim muttered something about not winning before he pulled his keys from his pocket and got into his car, squealing the tires as he backed out of the driveway.

I watched the car for a few seconds before I grabbed the

glasses and the straggling salad bowl and hurried to the kitchen. Mary was nowhere in sight, but Charlotte was loading the dishwasher, tears running down her cheeks.

"I'm sorry," I said. "I can do that if you want."

She shook her head, jamming plates into the slots with a fury that shook the whole island.

"I'm sure he didn't mean that—" I began, and Charlotte shoved the rack into the dishwasher so hard I was half surprised it didn't shoot straight out the back of the island onto the floor.

"Yes, he did. He meant it, Martha. I know you aren't stupid." She wiped her face on the sleeve of her long pink sweater. "He doesn't want me here. But I don't have anywhere else to go."

"Are you sure about that?" I asked.

"He..." She bit her lip, looking at me for a few seconds before her eyes went to the door, then to her shoes. "Yes. I'm sure. I'm very sure."

Her shoulders seemed to collapse in on themselves, and suddenly in place of the willful girl I'd gotten used to over the past few months, stood a defeated child.

"It can't be that bad here," I said, leaning across the countertop. "Can it?"

She looked up at me after she started the dishwasher. "Do you trust him? The pastor?"

"Trust is a funny thing," I said. "Trust him how?"

She stared at me for a minute, her teeth closing over her bottom lip.

"Nothing. Forget I asked." She spun on one bare heel and disappeared.

"But—" The rest of the sentence stuck in my throat in an empty room, and I sat heavily on one of Mary's soft barstools.

A couple of months back, I would've said I knew Pastor Tim—pretty well, really. Like most people in Whitney Falls, I'd imagine.

It got clearer every day lately that we mostly knew what he wanted us to know.

Seeing some of the cracks this summer made me wonder what else the McClatchys might be hiding about their not-so-perfect life.

# THIRTY-TWO
## MARTHA

*August*

All my life, I'd slept as fitfully as a long-tailed cat in a room full of rocking chairs—every whisper, creak, or sigh had me sitting straight up. In my world, it was a survival mechanism.

Between the dead flowers with the ribbon, the black pickup, Charlotte, Mary, and what I'd seen of the side of Pastor Tim he kept very carefully hidden from the rest of the town, sleep that summer in Whitney Falls went from elusive to nonexistent.

I tossed and turned, and when that didn't help, I paced. My brain fired questions like skeet clays, refusing to let me rest.

I couldn't figure out the real story behind Pastor Tim and Mary's perfect front, and I had no idea how to help Charlotte when she wouldn't talk to me. I got the feeling that was because she didn't trust me, but what was I supposed to do with that? If I was right, telling her she could trust me wouldn't help, since that's exactly what someone she shouldn't trust would say. And if I was wrong, I might make her worried about why I thought that in the first place.

So I kept my mouth shut except just plain trying to be nice when I saw her, and focused on the biggest threat looming in my own life: someone knew my secret, and I needed to know who—and how.

I started with the obvious: had someone in Whitney Falls come across a news story about me? I couldn't see it—especially since I wasn't even sure there'd ever been one. A suspicious death in a trailer park wasn't exactly rare or interesting in America, and the internet wasn't really a thing in Whitney Falls—we were too far out into the mountains to have high speed service, not much worked over our temperamental phone lines, and the cell signal wasn't strong enough for data.

I knew nearly every soul in town by that point, and as such could say for sure I hadn't ever seen one of them before I arrived here in December. Besides, if that were the case, why send me creepy notes and dead flowers? Why not just tell everyone I was a "person of interest" in a murder a thousand miles away?

So if the notes weren't from someone in town, had someone from back home tracked me down?

That was the question that haunted my sleep—I'd doze off some nights just long enough to dream that I walked out of the church onto Elias Lane, and there in the middle of the road, sometimes up on a cross, and sometimes laid out on the ground, was a body without a soul, a set of glassy green eyes staring at nothing. Forever.

Because of me. While I knew in my bones that the world was a better place for it, there were those who disagreed. But surely if one of them had found me here, I'd already be dead. And I knew that with the kind of certainty that quieted the fear that they had come for me.

I paused my pacing halfway back past my bed. They would've come for me.

Wouldn't they? Daddy was fond of sadistic games—he enjoyed watching people he hated squirm.

And the second I started thinking the notes might be from a past I wanted desperately to forget, I started to squirm. I wondered if anyone else had seen that black truck in the area the day I'd found the withered bouquet with the second note.

I'd been telling myself for weeks that whoever left the notes simply wanted me out of town.

I perched on the edge of the couch, turning that over in my head.

What if that wasn't the case? What if it was my past, reaching in to snatch away whatever contentment I'd managed to eke out here in Whitney Falls?

I swallowed hard. On one hand, nobody I had run from would care whether I died here or back in Virginia as long as the job was done.

On the other, what if I wasn't the only thing they wanted? Maybe they wanted to see where I'd go if they could run me out of Whitney Falls. If anyone else had been part of what I'd done. Before they killed me, of course.

The thing that made it hard to breathe in the darkest hours was that I truly had no idea which theory was right. If any of them were.

I'd thought it dozens of times since I'd found the first note: how many young women showed up with no money and no family in towns like Whitney Falls? Not many. Which might make it easy to assume I had a past I'd rather keep hidden. The notes had no names or dates, or even specifics about what I'd done.

But when you got right down to it, if they were intended to poke at me—a sort of test to see if I'd run, or do something stupid—did it really matter who sent them?

It mattered some, since one of my possibilities probably wanted me much more dead than the other. But either way, I figured at the core I could take the notes as a test. One I simply had to pass because there was no alternative.

The only way I could see to do that was to figure out who was sending them before they got bored of their game and started shooting—or talking, depending, I guess. Being the church secretary meant I had access to handwriting samples for nearly everyone in town right in my office filing cabinets. I only had two challenges: one, that we had thousands of prayer cards on file, and Lisa's system of keeping order was so lax it didn't count as a system at all. Two, I couldn't let anyone see me searching because I couldn't come up with a believable reason for it to save my life.

It turned out the latter issue solved itself, because Pastor Tim made himself scarce around the church office as the summer days stretched on, which was fine by me—working alone was far less awkward than wondering what might go sideways with him on a given day, and left me more time to try to figure out who my mystery pen pal might be.

I started with Ruthie Tomlinson, of course—in the eight months I had lived in Whitney Falls, Ruthie had gone from queen bee of the women's social scene and formidable enemy to a sad, whispered afterthought when people talked about what had happened to Sam. She went nowhere but to work at the Pick and Go and to church on Sundays, where she had taken to slouching in a back pew, alternately glaring and scribbling in a little purple notepad.

I wondered what she was writing down—and for a while, if the notepad would look similar to my mystery notes. After three days of hunting through church files, I began to think it might be easier to get a peek into that notebook than to find her prayer cards.

On a Friday morning in early August, I was just about ready to work on a plan for swiping the notebook that Sunday when I remembered Ruthie was once the ladies' auxiliary president. Bingo—her meeting agendas were handwritten and filed under the auxiliary, and her personal prayer requests were in the same file, in a folder marked "priority."

Her handwriting, though, was a neatly rounded, looping script—nothing like the faintly foreboding, spiky letters of the notes. So either she wasn't guilty, or she was a master at disguising her writing.

Pastor Tim popped in around noon—I hadn't seen him since Wednesday, and was glad he only caught me eating my lunch.

"I'm not here," he waved as he hustled past my desk, "I'm taking Charlotte out for a while this afternoon. She needs some sunshine and I think a little trip might do her good."

I choked so hard on the "What?" that tumbled through my lips it set off a coughing fit, the scene with the hair dye and the scissors jumping to mind as I hacked. Not that he so much as looked at me. He stayed less than five minutes, picking up papers in his office that he walked back out tucking inside his suit jacket.

I wondered if I should be worried about Charlotte, but decided since there was less than nothing I could do, I might as well hope that this would be a turning point for her and Pastor Tim, and things would get better between them. Maybe Mary had talked some sense into him. Or Jesus had.

Since he wouldn't be back, I pulled the ladies' auxiliary file out of my drawer and checked the sign-up sheets I'd found in it for years of past luncheons. Every one of the women had the bubbly penmanship of a third grader.

I had moved on to the deacons, rooting through the files in the pastor's office to check the ledgers and minutes from their meetings, when I heard the door open.

"Hey there, anyone here?" a man's voice called.

Jumping up from the pastor's chair, I slammed the men's benevolence fund ledger shut and hurried to the door to find the postman standing next to my desk.

"Can I help you?" I asked, smoothing my skirt where it was stuck to my legs thanks to the heat.

He waved a handful of envelopes. "Pastor asked me last month to bring these inside."

"Oh, well, then thank you so much." I stepped forward and took them. "He's out for the afternoon, but I'll leave them on his desk."

"Sure thing. Thank you." He said it to my chest, staring a little too long before he turned to leave.

I waited until I heard the outside door close and then locked the office door, just in case. He wasn't a small guy and something about that stare had creeped me right out.

Hurrying back to the pastor's office, I flipped through the envelopes, nodding. These same four came every month, sometimes a couple of times a month. I didn't know what was in them, Pastor Tim had told me on my first day that they were confidential and not to be opened by anyone but him, and I had respected the pastor's rules. Until now.

I toyed with the edge of the top envelope, wondering if I could get it open and then re-seal it, but it was stuck tight from one edge to the other.

I picked the second one up and held it to the lamp bulb, but all I could see was the outline of a piece of folded paper. Tapping the envelopes on the desk, I shook my head. It was weird. I wasn't even a real church secretary and I knew it was weird for the church to get mail nobody but the pastor could open. "Maybe they're prayer requests," I muttered, my gut pinching with the certainty that I was just wishful thinking.

"I don't need to know today," I said finally. And it was the truth. I put the sealed envelopes on the pastor's desk and checked the clock. Ten minutes to five. Surely he wouldn't care if I left just a little early—it was Friday and Mary was expecting me for girls' night. She'd taken her wind down drive early today, even—she turned her Grand Wagoneer into the driveway as I shut Pastor Tim's office door. I grabbed my bag, looking around outside for the leering postman before I hurried across the street to the safety of my new home.

# THIRTY-THREE
## MARY

*August*

"Mary? Funny or sappy?"

I blinked as Martha waved the TV control wand at me from the other end of the sofa. Pasting a smile in place, I waved one hand. "Funny, I think, if that's okay. I'm a mess lately, sappy will probably break my tear ducts. I cried yesterday because the vacuum canister got full before I finished the foyer and dining room."

I clamped my lips shut to keep myself from chattering any more. Mother had always said it was the worst thing about me: I talk too much when I'm nervous, mostly with no regard to what I should be saying and what I shouldn't.

Keep it together.

It had been nine weeks without so much as a twinge or red spot. I was so close to the end of the first trimester. I just needed to hold it together for three more weeks.

I could do anything for three more weeks.

Martha pointed the control at the TV and chose a movie,

and I reached for the bowl of popcorn on the table and settled back into the cushions. Or I tried to.

I really did.

Bouncing up off the couch, I put the bowl back on the table and hurried to the kitchen. Martha paused the credits on the screen and turned so she could see me. "Do you need me to get you something?"

"I just wanted water," I said.

Martha pointed at the table. "That water?"

I opened the cabinet in the corner and reached for a tall metal cup. "I wanted my purple cup." I flashed a smile and set about filling it with ice and water from the fridge.

Walking back to the couch, I plucked at a loose thread on my white linen top and sipped the water.

"Maybe a movie isn't the best idea tonight." Martha put the control wand on the coffee table and picked up the antique Bible from the center, carefully opening the cover. "I was surprised the pastor sold the white one with the blue pages. After what you told me about how important it was to him."

"Sold what?" I popped out of my chair again, staring at the shelves to the right of the fireplace. She was right. The white Cambridge Bible was gone. I turned to look at Martha, whose head was tipped just a bit to one side as she stared at me. Like she was waiting to see my reaction.

I smiled and returned to my seat on the sofa. "I remember now. He got an offer online and said he couldn't turn it down. But he was a little sad to let that one go."

Martha nodded, not looking away from my face.

I let the silence stretch for several seconds before I changed the subject. "So, you said Tim left with Charlotte at what time?"

"It was right at noon," Martha said, moving the TV wand to the arm of the sofa. "I was eating my lunch when he came through."

"And he didn't say where they were going?"

"He didn't say much of anything. Not even goodbye, or have a nice weekend. I figured he was in a hurry." Martha raised one eyebrow. "Are you okay?"

I laughed, aware that it sounded slightly too high, but unable to do anything except ignore it and hope she did the same. Martha noticed things. Little things, often, that made me wonder if I'd been stupid to set it up so that she was living here. Not like there'd been much choice.

"Of course I am. I'm excited about watching this movie with you." I pointed to the TV, completely clueless as to what we were about to look at. "Sorry."

I had only left Charlotte at home alone with Tim because I had to go to Malvern to the doctor. A strong heartbeat. A black and gray computer printout of a peanut that was starting to take the shape of a baby.

Security in the knowledge that I could juggle it all.

Charlotte was a test, and I had passed. Until I got home and she was gone.

"You don't need to apologize," Martha said. "I didn't mean to worry you when I said the pastor took Charlotte out. I thought it was a little strange." She ducked her head and then looked up at me with an uncertain furrow to her forehead. "I hope you don't mind me saying that. He's been maybe a little hard on her. But then I figured you wouldn't let him take her off so we could have our girls' night if you weren't sure she was safe, and I felt bad for worrying."

I nodded. "Of course. I would never."

Martha played the movie.

I made it through the opening music. "Did you see which way they went?"

She paused the TV and turned to me. "Mary, I'm starting to worry."

"About what?" I tried to widen my eyes to look like I didn't know what she was talking about. From the look on her face, I just managed to look disturbed.

"I try not to prod into things that don't concern me, but it's pretty clear it's bothering you that Pastor Tim took Charlotte out, and for reasons I don't like to talk about in polite company, that is making me afraid," Martha said. "Do we need to go look for them?"

I shook my head and pointed to the TV. "Of course not. I'm sure they're fine. Everything is just fine."

I knew she could tell I was trying to reassure myself as much as I wanted to reassure her.

I just wasn't sure there was anything to be done for it.

# THIRTY-FOUR
## MARTHA

*September*

Mary was pregnant.

Not that she told me—or anyone else, as far as I knew. I figured it out the day before school started. The bread gave her away.

We'd planned an end-of-summer cookout, just the four of us, and I walked back into the kitchen to get tongs for the grill just in time to see Mary stuff an entire Parker House roll into her mouth. I only knew I didn't imagine it because I saw butter running down her chin, too.

I had not ever, not once, seen Mary eat regular bread. And from my apartment window I could see a whole lot of what happened in Mary's house.

She didn't say anything, so neither did I, but as I stepped back out onto the deck, a whole slew of odd things I noticed lately piled up in my head, and they only had one thing in common: a baby.

Mary had been weepy and moody, she'd been extra tired—I knew because I made the pastor's lunch and left it in the fridge three days that week when she didn't get up before I left for work—and now she was swallowing buttered dinner rolls whole when she barely ate anything, least of all bread?

I was so shocked I almost dropped the tongs.

"Everything okay?" Pastor Tim looked up from his newspaper, his brow scrunching up.

It was all I could do not to hug him and tell him congratulations—which I couldn't, of course. I had to wait until they told me. I hurried to the grill and turned the steaks, thankful for the cooler evenings, the air drying from summer's humidity.

I found myself watching Mary and Tim closer than usual for the next few days, alternately feeling sure they were just keeping their good news to themselves and wondering if I was going crazy, assuming something that wasn't true.

Maybe Tim had been serious all along and the bread thing was about diet and not illness.

No, it had to be a baby.

But Mary's figure was as trim as the day I'd met her.

Though it would be early on for her to show, still.

And so it went, me arguing with myself and wondering, if I was right, was this a good thing or a very bad one?

---

The last Monday in September, I hunched over my desk opening mail from the weekend at the end of a long morning. Advertisements for the trash, letters to the pastor from the new kindergarten class at the primary school for the pastor's desk and then for the Sunday school classroom bulletin board, and three of the special "confidential" envelopes. Thankfully, the postman had just left them in the box this time—I had enough to do without worrying about fending off an unwanted advance.

Putting the mysterious mail pieces in a stack, I wondered about them for the dozenth time in the past four months.

Nearly every able-bodied person in Whitney Falls could walk to First Baptist from their home, and we didn't do any fancy live broadcasting on the internet on account of not having the ability or the desire to.

Which was fine by me—the feeling of being cut off from most of the modern world that the lack of twenty-first-century technology in Whitney Falls provided had been one of my favorite things about the town at first, making it easy to pretend I'd moved to a simpler time, like I was living in one of my old TV stories.

But the isolated feel I loved so much did make the regular arrival of these envelopes seem odd: were they letters? Prayer requests? I knew they weren't tithing checks because I balanced the books every month and Pastor Tim hadn't ever told me to add anything other than the regular Sunday offerings.

Whatever was in them, the envelopes were never more than a passing thought, gone as quickly as it came once I'd laid them on the pastor's desk.

I counted and deposited the weekly offerings every Monday, so I had the bank bag out, stamping checks to go alongside the cash I had already counted and wondering if I should start writing response cards to the kindergarteners. Pastor Tim had been out of the office more than he'd been in it lately, and things that were usually his job had started to pile up.

That Monday, the pile started to slide sideways right around noon, the first time the phone rang.

"Good morning, it's a blessed day at First Baptist, how may I help you?" I tucked the phone between my ear and my shoulder and flipped the page on my word of the day calendar to September 26th.

"I need to speak to Tim McClatchy." The voice was definitely male, and definitely agitated.

"I'm sorry, the pastor isn't in this morning," I said. "Can I take a message?"

"No, you may not take a message, you may get him on this phone. At once." The man's voice cracked.

I sat up straight in my chair, closing my fingers around the receiver. "Sir, I really wish I could, but I promise you, he isn't here."

"Where is he then?"

"I'm afraid I don't know." Not that I would've said at that point if I did. But he didn't need to know that. I kept my voice even, if cold. No one could have said I wasn't polite, though. "I'm happy to leave a message for him to call you as soon as he gets in."

The clatter as he slammed down his phone was so loud I pulled mine away from my head.

"What in the blue blazes?" I muttered, pulling the Sunday prayer cards out of my inbox and starting to sort them.

At 1:02 I had four piles of prayer requests ready to put in the appropriate cubbies and needed another glass of water when the phone rang again. I answered.

Heavy breathing came through into my ear, sending shivers rippling down my neck.

"Hello?" I said a second time after five breaths.

"Tim. McClatchy." It was the same voice from before, but this time the words sounded like they were forced through clenched teeth.

"I'm sorry, he's not in this afternoon, may I take a message?" I was impressed with how normal I sounded. The situation was downright unsettling.

"Please tell him to call his bank at once." Every word came through the speaker like a shot. "At. Once. It's the most important thing he will do today."

Another ear-rattling hang-up cut the call off before I could really process what the man had said.

Bank? The church, like everyone in town, kept their

accounts at Farmers National three blocks over. And I didn't recognize that voice as anyone who worked there.

I got up and went to get water, then locked the office door before I put the prayer cards in the slots for the deacons, the ladies' auxiliary, and the children's ministry. I took the ones marked as "private" to Pastor Tim's desk, pausing on my way out of his office.

There were six of those "nobody opens these but me" envelopes on the pastor's desk.

He hadn't just been less present at the church lately, either. I had barely seen him in weeks, even in his own home. His headlights came directly in my window when he turned into the driveway, so I knew that he'd taken to coming home very late at night—mostly near or even after midnight—but he was usually gone for the day by the time I made it to the kitchen in the mornings. The one upshot to that was that he made good coffee and there was always plenty. Mary slept in these days, and I wasn't sure she drank coffee when she got up, anyway. I had noticed a switch to decaffeinated iced tea on her grocery list toward the end of August. Right about when Pastor Tim made himself so scarce.

I didn't want to think the two of them were having trouble. I really didn't want to think that might be because of something to do with whether or not Mary was pregnant.

But that Monday, after weeks of trying to avoid that thought, it caught up to me in the form of six plain old white envelopes and one strange phone call from an upset banker I didn't know.

What if...?

"Lord forgive me, because I'm not sure the pastor will," I muttered, grabbing a letter opener and picking up the first envelope.

I slit the top and reached inside to find a sheet of copy paper.

Wrapped around a check made out to First Baptist Church. For fourteen thousand six hundred and thirty-one dollars.

I sat down in the pastor's chair so heavily it groaned.

Fourteen thousand dollars.

Even with nearly a thousand people packed into the pews, we barely took in eight thousand in weekly offerings. Whitney Falls wasn't a wealthy town.

I looked at the name on the check. A trucking company in Biloxi.

Why was a trucking company in Mississippi sending this much money to our church? Money I had never seen or deposited into a church account? I stuffed the check back into the envelope, then bit my lip. Pastor Tim had been adamant that he didn't want me opening these. Right then I had a lot of guesses about why.

I retrieved a plain white envelope from my desk and went back to the pastor's. Perching on the edge of his chair, I flipped the open envelope over and copied the address on the front, in crisp, all capital block letters.

Was it perfect? No. Was it good enough if he didn't have a reason to be suspicious? Highly likely. I wrapped the check back in the sheet of paper and tucked it inside, sealed the envelope, and added a stamp from the book tucked into the corner of his blotter, then slid the finished product into the middle of the stack of "confidential" mail, my hands shaking so much they upset the pile and I had to re-stack them.

There had to be a good explanation for what I'd just seen. One that didn't have anything to do with criminal activity—I was just wired to suspicion because of Daddy and the way I was raised, that was all.

Maybe he was planning a project for the church—and the McClatchys had moved from Mississippi, hadn't they? So perhaps he knew someone there who could afford to help with whatever he was trying to do.

I nodded, reassuring myself—until I thought about Mary again. Something wasn't right between them, and now I had another possible reason why.

What would happen to the church if the McClatchys' marriage was in trouble? To the town?

To me?

It was still just a bit warm in the pastor's office, but I trembled from head to foot like I was standing in a freezer.

Maybe they just needed some help. Didn't most married people on TV need help from time to time? Lord knew I'd seen Pastor Tim help enough of the married couples in Whitney Falls. But maybe he didn't understand how to help himself.

I swallowed a laugh at the idea that I was in any way qualified to offer help to the First Family of Whitney Falls.

A scrawny nobody from nowhere who'd made my share of terrible choices. Sure. I was exactly the kind of person they ought to listen to.

"Maybe not, but I might be their only choice," I muttered, grabbing my pocketbook and digging my car keys out of the bottom before I let myself out and locked the church up behind me.

I knew way more about drunks than most people did, and the core truth was that they're predictable at least to a point. Taken together, everything I'd seen the past few weeks meant Pastor Tim wasn't simply retreating from a troubled marriage— he was hiding in a bottle. Which meant I could probably find him if I looked hard enough, and nothing else I had to do right then was more important.

# THIRTY-FIVE
## MARTHA

*September*

I'd been in and out of four bars on the north side of Malvern in two hours with no luck, and thought I might be on the verge of giving up when a middle-aged, middle-sized bartender with kind blue eyes and an inexplicably delightful smile decided to hit on me.

I used the opening to ask about Pastor Tim in a roundabout way. He said nobody he'd seen matched the description, but that folks who liked to drink on the quiet maybe wouldn't risk being seen, even in a little beer joint like his, with its peeling pink paint outside and boarded-up windows. The ancient sign above the door had probably seen better days when Carter was President, duct tape both holding it together and blocking out most of the "Girls! Girls! Girls!" in block letters across the bottom.

Looking around, I was sure I was the only woman who'd set foot in this place in at least a decade.

"Where would he go if he didn't want to be seen?" I asked,

picturing myself knocking on motel room doors and maybe winding up in a dumpster.

"Folks who don't like questions or eyeballs go to the VFW out off 617," he said, putting a club soda on the bar.

I sipped it. "I don't think he's a veteran."

"Don't matter out there. You got cash, they got booze. Handful of regulars too drunk by noon to notice or care who comes in, and a bartender who hasn't spoken an unnecessary word since God was a boy."

That did sound promising. "How would he know that, though?" I wasn't even sure I meant to say it out loud.

Eyeing me up and down and nodding to the club soda, the bartender winked. "How would you know, sugar? Drunks got a sixth sense about such things, don't you?"

A short laugh escaped my throat as I finished the cold soda in one gulp. "That we do." I reached into my pocket for cash and he waved me off.

"I'll take your phone number in trade." He leaned on his elbows on the scarred wood bar top. The air seemed to crackle around him, and I leaned closer like a magnet tugged me forward.

"You're really not going to believe me, but I don't have one," I said, feeling just a tinge sorry that was the truth. Which was insane. The guy was easily twice my age, decent enough looking for it to be evident that he'd had his pick of women back in the day, but certainly not appealing enough for me to consider upsetting my very carefully constructed life. Or, he shouldn't have been, anyway.

"You got a name?" he asked as I blinked and stood up straight.

"Martha." I wasn't sure why I told him. It wasn't looks. But that electricity snapping around him in the air almost reminded me of Pastor Tim. Was this what my granny had meant when she said my daddy had once had charisma? I wanted to stay and talk to the bartender more, to be closer to him. Maybe to go to bed with him. The thought made me flinch. I had only ever slept with one guy—on purpose, anyhow—and it had been nothing like a movie, or even like Mary and Pastor Tim on the kitchen island, from what I'd seen and heard that night. My lone experience was messy and awkward, and not at all fun. In the nearly two years since, I hadn't really figured on ever doing it again, until now. I had nothing logical for that except to say from the second the bartender opened his mouth I'd felt calmer, and by the time he asked my name I felt downright safe.

Me.

I'd so seldom actually been safe that I recognized the feeling because it was odd.

"So, Miss Martha, tell me the truth: you looking for your old man?"

I shook my head so hard my ponytail slipped askew, letting curls fall around my face. "No, no, I'm not married. My..." I let that trail. Boss? Friend's husband? All of the above? It was reflex for me to keep information close, but for the first time since Granny died, I didn't want to. "He's a friend. I'm worried." That was true. And didn't give away anything I might come to regret sharing.

"I'd say that makes you a friend worth having." He winked. "I'm here every day of the week from two to midnight if you make it back this way." He tipped his hat and turned to the door as it opened, waving at the old bikers who strolled in.

"Thank you," I called as I hurried back to my car, shaking off the weirdness of the encounter even as I fought the urge to turn and run right back to the barstool.

What was with this day?

---

Smoke hung thick in the air when I stepped into the small, dark barroom at the VFW post, and it had been so long since I lived in a cloud of it I choked, coughing hard enough to make my eyes water as I looked around, every cell in my body recoiling from the heavy despair pressing out against the cinderblock walls.

I almost left. This was clearly a fifth strike, and the afternoon was wearing on. The air inside the little room was like a concentrated hit of the hopelessness that had prickled my skin on long nights at the Dreamscape when the walls proved a little too thin to fully muffle the sounds of what was happening in the other rooms. There, I had pulled musty pillows over my head and shut my eyes. But here it was too thick to ignore.

Scanning the space through tears, I shook my head.

"I'll be damned." My fingers flew to my lips as the words slid out—I hadn't said even a baby swear word in months now, and it tasted bitter, even if I was sure it might be about to prove true as my eyes locked on Pastor Tim, slouched in a rounded wood pub chair in the far corner of the little room.

He was nearly alone—one barstool was occupied by a skinny man with a long gray ponytail in faded cargo shorts and a Bruce Springsteen T-shirt, a cane leaning on the wall next to his seat. I wasn't sure if the Springsteen fan was the bartender, or if there was someone else on the other side of the swinging door with the porthole window behind the bar.

Or maybe there just wasn't one. I knew the actual meaning of desperation, and I wasn't sure anyone could pay me enough to work there.

I had gone to the American Legion post near Granny's with my daddy once—she'd threatened to brain him with a cast iron skillet for taking me to a bar, but it was the very best memory I had of time passed with him. That place had been loud, fun, and bright. He'd let me drink three Shirley Temples that night, and the lady behind the bar put extra cherries in every one.

Thinking about it now, I realized she was probably being

nice to me hoping that he'd be nice to her. Not that women ever had to try that hard with him.

I shook off the memory as I crossed the room to Pastor Tim, the footfalls echoing in the quiet room, but neither man looking up.

"Go 'way, Martha," Tim slurred when I paused behind his chair. "I'm not hurting anyone."

I froze with the hand I'd intended to put on his shoulder in midair. "How did you see me?"

He barked out a laugh. "Would you believe God told me you were coming?"

"I believe God has more important things to concern himself with."

He thumped his hand down onto the table. "Your perfume. It always smells like strawberries when you come into my office."

If he could smell a single thing but cigarettes and cheap booze, he needed to pursue a career as a bloodhound. But I had no other explanation for how he knew I was there. I rounded the table and took the chair across from him.

"I think you know who you're hurting," I said.

"My liver is made of cast iron," he said, spinning a short, cloudy glass of amber liquid on the wood. "It's in my DNA."

"I wasn't talking about you." I reached for his hand and then thought better of it. Even here, he was the kind of handsome that would've made people notice him—had there been anyone here who cared to.

Even knowing how much he might be hurting Mary, I was still, sitting there looking at him in all his day drinking, rumpled splendor, the tiniest drop jealous of my friend.

I waited for him to say something. He bent his head so far forward his chin smashed into his collarbone, rolling his eyes up to glare at me as he pushed the glass around the table in front of him.

Just like that, the jealousy dried right up. He looked like a spoiled child—a mean one—and for the first time, I wondered how much of his godly image, good reputation and success had been Mary's doing.

Fine. I sighed, speaking first.

"Pastor, Mary needs you."

He shook his head.

"You don't think she needs you?" Was I missing something? Surely he couldn't really believe his pregnant wife didn't need him to get his act together. "Look, I understand the demons you're fighting in that glass there in a way I never wanted you to know. I can help you. Twelve steps. You can be the man she needs—the man the whole town already thinks you are. I have faith."

My glance slid to the occupied barstool, but the skinny guy showed no sign of interest in anything but his own sad little glass. It should've been a victory for me, to be in a place like that and not feel a lick of the fire in my throat that demanded whiskey or tequila to soothe it. I was so focused on getting what I'd gone there for that the personal win didn't register until later.

Pastor Tim laughed, but it was a dark, grating sound. "Faith. Sure."

Maybe it was the overwhelming sadness of the space, but the despair he packed into those words hit me like a fist to the throat.

I wasn't going to say it, and then it just popped out, the words almost floating in front of my eyes like I could grab them and stuff them back down my throat.

"You're going to be a father. It's time to grow up."

His head snapped back like I'd hit him, and he just let it rest there, Adam's apple sticking out like a thorn on a rose stem, chin wobbling side to side in disagreement.

"I have prayed for your family every day for months, twice

as hard since I figured out Mary's secret," I said. "And before I came to Whitney Falls I had never said a prayer in my life, because I didn't figure it was possible anyone was listening. You changed that for me. 'Sometimes the Good Lord's answer to a prayer is giving us the gift of opportunity, to make the reality we want for ourselves.' Remember when you told the congregation that?"

He gave no indication that he was listening, but I kept talking anyway.

"Well, here I am, taking the opportunity to help your family." I pushed the chair back and stood. "Get up. We're going home, and you're going to sober up. Pastor. Sir." I fidgeted, twisting my fingers together as I realized I'd raised my voice.

He raised his head and met my eyes, and the deepest, bone-frozen chill I'd ever felt started in my gut and roiled to every hair follicle and fingernail. My teeth might have chattered in the stuffy little room, which was still smoky even though no one was smoking.

"You think you know... anything?" He raised his voice right back, waving his arms like he was conducting the choir. "Nobody knows. Nobody knows me. I had a vasectomy five years ago." Both of his arms landed on the table, shaking it all the way to the floor. "Whatever Mary has been up to, I will never be a father." He pointed one index finger at me, but I couldn't look away from his face, twisting into a purple-red, furious nightmare. "If you like your current situation, you'd do well to stop sticking your nose into things you can't understand."

He didn't blink as he downed the rest of the whiskey, reached under the table and produced a bottle, and poured another.

I had never seen eyes so cold. This couldn't be the same man I'd heard talk almost like a poet about the grace of God. The same man I'd heard through the thin office walls counseling dozens of people about how to have a closer relationship with Jesus by being better wives, husbands, brothers, and parents.

Booze truly was a demon, and on a sunny Monday in September, it had possessed Pastor Tim McClatchy, body and soul.

## THIRTY-SIX
### MARY

*October*

"Of course, we're more than happy to help out," I said, pinching the phone between my ear and my shoulder while I chopped vegetables for lunch, a lovely early October breeze blowing through the kitchen from the back screen door. I took a deep breath, the chilled air laced with woodsmoke. Someone was having a campfire. "Feed the animals morning and night, right? Do they usually eat before sunup?"

Martha came into the kitchen and plucked an apple from the bowl on the counter, moving to wash it as I finished the call and hung up.

"What was all that?" she asked, biting off a chunk with a loud crunch.

"The third deacon's wife is having hip replacement surgery in Malvern on the twenty-ninth." I scooped bits of tomatoes, carrots, and red bell peppers from the cutting board and dumped them over my lettuce before I turned to the fridge. Adding cheese and bottled dressing to a salad still felt so decadent, but I told myself the baby needed the calories.

I pulled a little pink bag clamp from a drawer and gathered the carrot bag closed, snapping the clamp around it. Martha leaned over for a better look. "I've never seen a clip like that. My granny always closed everything with clothespins."

"I found these in an Ikea store in Dallas years ago and I love them." I dropped the carrots back into the crisper drawer. "I swear they keep everything fresher. I just wish I'd bought the bigger ones, too, these little guys don't work on bigger bags, and I've never found them anywhere else."

"So anyway—someone's having a hip replaced?" Martha bit her apple again.

I nodded. "They live out off Route 4 and they need help with their livestock for a few days. I told them I would take care of it. They'll be home on the fourth, he said, if everything goes according to plan."

"I will help with the livestock." Martha gave me a once over with a furrowed brow. "You have enough to do," she said finally.

I was pretty sure she knew I was pregnant, but still enjoying keeping my little one all to myself—I wouldn't be able to hide it soon enough, and what a wonderful day that would be.

"What kind of animals?" she asked.

"Hogs, he said. And they eat early."

Martha shuddered. "Gross. On both counts. But anything for the deacon." She smiled, biting her apple again.

"Might be a good idea to add it to the prayer list in next week's bulletin, too." I stirred my salad and stabbed a big bite, pausing to chew. "They do so much for the rest of the community."

"Consider it done. Could we have people take meals after they come home?"

The oven timer sounded, and I grabbed potholders from a drawer and pulled a pizza stone from the center rack, the cheese bubbling ever so slightly in the middle. Holding one finger up in Martha's direction, I turned toward the doorway. "Charlotte!

Your pizza is ready!" It smelled like Heaven: bread and cheese and the spicy bite of pepperoni. Maybe she wouldn't eat the whole thing and I could gobble the leftovers after everyone went to bed.

I turned back to Martha, who was staring at the pizza. "That smells fantastic."

"There's another in the freezer," I said, though I knew Martha would eat the whole pizza if she made one. She had the metabolism of a teenager. It was irritating.

I swallowed another big bite of salad and changed the subject. "That's a wonderful idea, about sending meals for the deacon's family. I'll activate the ladies' auxiliary phone tree this afternoon." I pulled the pizza cutter out of the drawer by the stove and cut eight slices as Charlotte walked into the kitchen. She stopped short when she saw us, like we weren't supposed to be there.

"Hey there, Charlotte," Martha said. "How is school going?"

Charlotte shrugged without a word and piled six slices of pizza on a plate.

"I got a call that you weren't in science today," I said.

Her head snapped up. "Oh my God, are you kidding me?" She rolled her eyes.

"Please don't take the Lord's name in vain," I said. "I've told you it's not appropriate. Certainly not to defend yourself when you're skipping class."

"Is that what they told you?" Charlotte blinked. "That I skipped?"

I glanced at Martha, whose eyebrows were hovering near her hairline.

"You didn't?" I asked.

"The police came to talk to me."

I caught a sharp breath.

"Why?" Martha blurted, her eyes wide.

"I don't have to tell you that," Charlotte said, looking between us. "I don't have to tell you anything, and you can't make me."

She snatched the plate of pizza off the counter and bolted up the stairs.

"What in the wide world?" I closed my eyes for a long blink and shook my head at Martha.

She bit her lip. "What would the police want with Charlotte?"

I waved one hand and stabbed another bite of salad. "I'm sure she's making it up. She didn't want to admit she skipped science." I leaned forward as I chewed and caught her eye. "Really. I haven't wanted to say anything because I feel like I'm failing her, but she's struggling at school. A group of boys has been teasing her about her 'dead mom,' and it has her rattled. She doesn't want to be in class. That's all it is. Now... do you know anything about hogs?"

"I've been around a few," Martha said. "It's not hard work, really, except that the feed buckets are heavy and you shouldn't lift them. Just in case," she said hastily when I lifted an eyebrow.

"Of course," I said. Knowing she suspected but wasn't completely sure was kind of fun. "It's kind of you to offer to help."

Martha laughed. "I don't think I could ever feel like I'm helping you enough, Mary."

"You're such a good friend." I forced brightness into the words I didn't feel right then. Those books aren't kidding when they say pregnancy makes you irritable. I hadn't thought about Martha and Tim that way in weeks, but once the idea was in my head, it was nearly impossible to shake, and I could've cheerfully strangled her with a kitchen towel in that moment.

I said a quick, silent prayer for forgiveness.

Surely they wouldn't. I mean, he would. But this woman I had welcomed into our home, given a place of her own that was clean and warm and safe—albeit with a child-sized bed... she wouldn't look me in the face and smile while she was sleeping with my husband behind my back. Would she?

I studied her face. She looked nervous, but maybe that was about having me watch her cook. Or maybe I was an idiot and fooling myself. Tim hadn't touched me since I'd told him about the baby, and even with his little problem, he'd never abstained this long.

There was someone. I could feel it in my bones, stronger every day.

Maybe it was the hormones, but as Martha went out the back door to weed her flower garden and I reached for the phone tree list, the need to know for sure if it was really my one true friend who was betraying me burned so hot in my chest I thought for a minute I might be having a heart attack.

I'd never wanted to have Tim followed—partly because it felt low and wrong to me, but mostly the issue was that the other towns we'd lived in weren't that different from Whitney Falls, and I was afraid if I tried, people would know, and gossip would start. A church gossip mill is more reliable than a Japanese car—it starts on the first try, and runs at peak efficiency until the whole town knows your business. I put one hand on my belly, just swollen enough for me to tell when I touched it that there was life growing in there. The stakes were higher today than they'd ever been, and I couldn't stop what I didn't know for sure was happening.

Maybe it was time to think about looking for a detective.

# THIRTY-SEVEN
## MARTHA

*October*

"Can you take this by the post office on your way home?" Pastor Tim dropped a thick envelope on my desk with a *thud* two Fridays before Halloween. "I have an appointment today, I don't have time to do it myself."

"Of course, Pastor." My words said yes, but my tone said he knew good and well the post office was across town and home was across the street.

He didn't acknowledge it, though, waving and muttering about the weekend on his way out.

I sighed. "No, I don't have enough to do organizing the fall festival. I can run your personal errands, too," I said to the empty office once I heard him go out the door.

Kneeling, I counted orange pencils with "Jesus saves" stamped on them in black letters into prize buckets for games, then dumped a bag of fifty plastic spider rings into each bucket, too.

Standing, I arranged the prize buckets in big cardboard boxes so I could carry six at a time, loaded the apples for the bobbing contest into Mary's giant igloo cooler, and dragged it all out back to load it into the church van so I could deliver it to the football stadium, where the festival would be, since apparently I was headed that way to go to the post office anyhow.

Shutting the cargo doors, I went back inside to retrieve the pastor's outgoing mail and spotted a stray Halloween pencil on the floor under my desk.

"We'll need every last one," I muttered, crawling to get it.

I reached up and grabbed the corner of the envelope the pastor had left on my desk and pulled as I stood, but it was heavier than I thought. The whole envelope ripped as soon as the far corner came off the desk, spilling a worn white leather-covered Bible to the floor.

"Dammit." I covered my mouth with my free hand, feeling like the word was especially bad given where I was, and plucked the book from the mottled brown carpet, stepping closer to my desk.

"Lord forgive me," I muttered, wondering if the accident was a sort of penance for my annoyance with Pastor Tim. "Though I'm honestly not sure why you'd protect that man anymore."

I pulled a thick padded envelope that was much sturdier than his yellow paper one from my bottom drawer, wiggling the Bible back and forth to slide it in because my envelope was a bit smaller than the pastor's. When it hung up on one side, I flipped the package over and saw the corner of a piece of paper sticking out of the middle of the book. Sighing, I pulled the whole thing back out of the envelope, opening the Bible to the marker and looking over it.

Adam, 15, L, T, G

Evie, 13, S, P, I

Grace, 14, M, A, A

And so on. There were seven lines in all, but not a single name I recognized.

"Probably an old note he made himself about a group at a different church." I said it out loud like speaking the words would make them true. The actual truth was that I had no idea what the list was, but I did know it was the second one I'd seen in the past few months, and the last one had Charlotte's name. I remembered tossing it into the trash thinking it was a sports roster. Maybe this was, too—I didn't know enough about sports to be sure. But something about it was unsettling. I started to put it in the trash bin, too, but my hand paused halfway there and I put it in the bottom of my top desk drawer instead.

Whatever it was, it wasn't part of the book, and I was sure the pastor hadn't intended to leave it stuck inside. But for a reason I couldn't have put words to for anything right then, I didn't want to throw it away, either.

I wiggled the Bible into the envelope and sealed it up good, copying the address from the ripped one. Mississippi again.

I couldn't swear it was the same address as the trucking company the large check came from, but it was familiar. I took a Post-it note from my drawer and copied it down there, too. Just in case I had reason to wonder again.

---

"Isn't strawberry your favorite?" I held a milkshake cup out to Charlotte as she paused on the front walk when she saw me sitting on the porch steps. I'd thought about the two lists and the Mississippi addresses the whole way to the post office, and by the time the Bible was in the mail and I was back outside in front of the diner, I had a plan.

"Yeah." Her eyes were hooded as she reached for the cup, stepping back down onto the walk as soon as it was in her hand and putting her book bag on the bottom step. "Why'd you get me this?"

"I was by the diner and I thought it might be a nice surprise on a Friday."

She took a long sip, swishing the ice cream around her mouth before she swallowed. "Why are you being nice to me?"

"Aren't I always nice to you?" I furrowed my brow, touching my lower lip. "I have noticed you haven't been a people person lately, but I haven't ever meant to be anything other than nice."

She tipped her head to one side and took another big swallow of shake, not blinking, and not taking her eyes off my face. "I can't figure you out."

"Me? You're the moody one around here, kid," I blurted. Oops. "Not that you don't have reason to be moody." I muttered hastily, looking up at her. This wasn't going the way I'd planned.

Forcing a casual note into my tone, I swirled my milkshake. "Has Pastor Tim ever tried to get you to play a sport?"

She blinked at me.

"I know it's out of the blue," I said. "I'm just curious."

"No." She pulled another drink of her shake. "I'm not a sports kind of person, I trip over my own feet too much."

"I understand that." I fiddled with the hem of my shirt. "Charlotte. Do you want to talk to me about anything? School, homework, boys, friends? I used to be a good listener."

"Used to be?" She still looked guarded, but maybe a bit less so.

"Seems like a long time ago now that I had people to listen to." I couldn't keep a tinge of sadness out of my voice.

She drank the rest of the shake before she spoke again, tracing the outline of a stone on the step with the toe of her sneaker.

"Do you think there's such a place as Hell, Martha?"

Didn't see that one coming—I would've fallen right down if I hadn't been sitting. "I... I don't guess I've thought too hard about that. But I suppose if I want to believe in Heaven, then I kind of have to, don't I?"

She stared for another twenty or so seconds before she nodded, grabbed her bag, and went inside. Two minutes later I heard her bedroom door close.

I knew plenty of people I'd condemn to Hell given the chance, though at least most of them were hundreds of miles away, and I hadn't seen that black truck in weeks. But Charlotte asking about that with such a serious face—who was a seventh grader worried about damning to eternal fire?

---

The garbage cans clattered to the pavement at two thirty-four in the morning the day before Halloween. That's how I knew what time Pastor Tim rolled himself in—he'd hit them with his silver Toyota Camry again.

I flipped over in the bed and squeezed my eyes shut the way I once had when Daddy's friends had too much to drink or one too many pills and wandered into my room at the back end of Granny's trailer. I wasn't allowed to have a lock on the door after she died, and he threw parties a handful of times a month. Those nights were a mixed bag for me, because he usually drank until he passed out, which meant he left me alone. But it was even odds on whether anyone else would bother me. I figured out that while pretending to sleep didn't work on Daddy, it was effective with a lot of them.

Years later, I pressed the heels of my palms into my eyeballs in my perfectly warm, perfectly soft bed behind the McClatchys' perfectly enviable home and wondered if Charlotte pretended to sleep. If I was sacrificing her safety for my comfort.

It had started that day in the kitchen with Mary, when the third deacon called about his hogs: something about the anger in

Charlotte's eyes as she shouted at Mary and me had me feeling guilty, though I didn't really know for what. Not for a while, anyway.

What could the police be talking to Charlotte about that would have her angry with us? Not anything to do with her mother—if they had new reason to suspect Lisa's death hadn't been an accident, I'd know it by now.

Staring at my ceiling, the look on the child's face flashing on the backs of my eyelids every time I closed them, I heard Pastor Tim in my head. "I had a vasectomy five years ago."

Why would a man who had no children—and a wife who desperately wanted a baby—go off and get himself snipped? To make sure a terrible secret stayed safe?

A man who drank his days away after a young girl came to live in his home. Who'd moved from small town to small town quite a bit in a handful of years and didn't ever talk much about where he'd been. Who counseled sinners about temptation and preached about restraint and grace with words that could hypnotize an entire community.

They all thought he was a saint.

I was pretty sure he was the worst kind of sinner.

Just not sure enough yet to force myself to do anything about it.

*Coward.* The word danced around my head in shining green neon.

Damn my daddy to the deepest ring of Hell, somehow he was still causing me trouble. I wanted to help, but I had to know if I was righteous in my suspicion, or if I should be ashamed of myself for projecting my father and his evil friends onto Tim McClatchy. That was the thing that kept me quiet: the what if. I had been wrong about so many things in my life. If I said something and I was wrong here, I wasn't just ruining the comfortable, food-in-the-fridge, warm-and-friendly, full-belly life I'd found for myself here. I was ruining Tim's life. Mary's life. Whispers like that can't be undone once they begin to spread. I'd seen it happen right here in Whitney Falls, to Ruthie.

The thing about people is, most would rather believe the most terrible story about even a neighbor or a friend, because it makes them feel just a bit better about their own selves.

So what would people be eager to believe about the handsome young pastor—and by extension, his beautiful wife?

Exactly. There was no way a scandal like this could take down Pastor Tim and not ensnare Mary. And my friend Mary deserved the very best of everything. Certainly at minimum, she deserved for me to be darned sure I knew what I was talking about before I breathed a word of suspicion to anyone.

So I laid in my bed, wrestling guilt and covering my eyes, trying to figure out how to prove my theory one way or another.

Maybe I could leave a note for Charlotte explaining that I just wanted to help her.

But what if she wasn't the first person to find it? Mary cleaned in Charlotte's room almost every day. I couldn't even think about what it would do to Mary to know I suspected Tim of such a thing.

Thinking back to my own past, I wondered if there was a way for me to see if he was going to her room without him noticing me. I sat up, considering the layout of the second floor —Mary had taken to going to bed before it even got dark out. Which probably meant she slept pretty soundly, too. If I slipped into the guest room across from Charlotte's tomorrow night, I could stay awake and watch Charlotte's door until the pastor came home and see for myself if I was right about him.

And then what?

"Figure that out when you get there," I muttered out loud, disgusted with my brain's very real resistance to disturbing the life I had found here. Me, of all people. I should not even be capable of entertaining the idea of keeping my own comfort above that child's safety. Maybe everyone has a little more selfishness and hardness in their heart than they want to think.

I had a little money stashed under my mattress in an empty breath mint box. And if it turned out I was right, well... I was still the church secretary. Maybe the new pastor would keep me on like Pastor Tim had kept Lisa around. I'd been there and been paying attention long enough to know I'd be valuable to whoever took the job next.

I nodded slowly, kicking the covers off my legs and standing to go look out the window. Had he made it inside tonight? There had been a Thursday morning in late September when I found him slumped over the steering wheel passed out when I went to make coffee in the kitchen at six in the morning. I'd ushered him inside quick and quiet, so none of the neighbors would notice or gossip.

The moon glared bright off the windshield of the Camry, the seats empty.

The windows of the house were dark, the air peaceful to anyone who didn't know what I knew.

Who didn't think what I thought. What I couldn't prove.

The house in the moonlight was as gorgeous as ever. If I'd had a camera, I would've taken a picture—just so that if this all went to hell I wouldn't forget.

A picture. I closed my eyes, a memory leaking in that I had managed to tamp down for nearly a decade. One long ago night when I'd pretended to sleep on a bare mattress on the floor in a room with a door that didn't lock, I'd felt my clothes being moved, and heard the click and whir of a camera. Somehow I'd kept my eyes still, my breath even. Whoever it was took half a dozen pictures and left.

Was there evidence that would damn the pastor without me waiting any longer, just sitting in the house a few yards away?

I leaned my head against the cool glass of the window, the notes I'd found outside popping into my thoughts for the first time in weeks. No others had arrived, and my fears about Pastor Tim and what evil might be hiding behind the mask of his perfect life had completely eclipsed my worries about my own secret. The skeleton in my past was nothing up against what I thought of the pastor. I had never found any handwriting on anything at the church that matched the notes—but standing there staring out into the moonlight I wondered if I would've been better off had I heeded them and left Whitney Falls months ago.

Maybe.

Charlotte wasn't my sister. And nothing I did here could atone for the mistakes I'd made in the past. But who would help Charlotte if I wasn't here?

There in my little garage apartment in Whitney Falls, I lifted my head from the glass and went to my door slowly, feeling for the first time in my life like Granny had been right, and the reason for every bit of what I'd been through—from learning to pretend to sleep to learning to stand up for myself to losing my sister and winding up here because of something as simple as a wrong turn on a snowy night—was because my life was leading to this: I was put here to take care of Charlotte.

I didn't want to hurt anyone. But I knew I could if I had to, and if he was hurting that girl, I would make sure it stopped.

No matter what.

# THIRTY-EIGHT
## MARTHA

*October*

The first skill a child learns in a chaotic environment is how to disappear.

Fading into the background was second nature to me before I could read. Moving through a space without making a single sound was a skill I'd perfected while other kids learned the alphabet. "My baby ninja," Granny had said, her way of acknowledging a terrible part of my life and letting me know she was proud of me for adapting without saying that many sad words.

Creeping through the McClatchy house in the small hours of a late October morning, I felt her with me, and I knew what she meant.

The big house was unusually silent that night, none of even the usual creaks and groans as the wind blew or the old wood shrank and settled with a change in humidity. And definitely no footsteps. Or any other movement, on furniture or otherwise.

I still didn't want to believe anything so disgustingly imperfect could happen in the McClatchys' perfect house on Elias

Lane. I wanted, for just a minute, to go back to late January, when I'd rolled slowly down the street to see the beautiful homes in the snow and stopped for a long while in front of number eighteen, watching flakes fall from the darkness and smoke curl into the indigo sky from the chimney, imagining a bright, inviting living room like the one from *Full House*, and a kitchen that always smelled like cookies, the handsome pastor reading by the fire while his beautiful wife tended to dinner.

The idea that people with money and status could do terrible things was so opposed to everything I'd ever believed I had to force myself to move deeper into the house, because wasn't that exactly the point? No one would believe Pastor Tim was capable of such a thing. No one who hadn't been in their house, lived above the driveway his car lurched into entirely too late at night, found him in the VFW post in Malvern, and been groped from behind at the copy machine, anyway. I had seen too much with my all-access pass to the pastor and his wife. So if I didn't help Charlotte, who would?

Exactly.

I checked the Bibles in the living room first. They were the only thing in the house I'd ever been told not to touch, so my first thought when I decided to go snooping was that there might be a reason besides them being old.

If there was, I didn't find it. Nor did I find anything in either of the downstairs closets, or the cabinets beneath the bookcases in the living room.

But the study—that was Tim's domain. I remembered as I reached for the doorknob that Mary barely even dusted in this room. She'd told me Tim said he liked his privacy more than he minded the dust. We had laughed about how cute it was that long-ago spring afternoon when I still thought her husband and life were perfect and I was the luckiest sinner this side of the Mississippi that she'd chosen me as her good and true friend.

It didn't seem cute anymore.

The air in the room thrummed with an energy that could've just been my nerves, but it made me move faster as I hunted for something... anything that would let me know if I was right or wrong.

I found ledgers with long lists of numbers I didn't have time to decipher, envelopes with lists of names and addresses, bank statements, and tax records.

But none of the things people investigating hunches in the movies seem to find: no photos. No ID cards from other states with other names. No journal with a written confession. No police record.

I pulled out the skinny top drawer of the desk more out of habit than hope.

And there in the back corner, I felt a familiar shape.

Closing my fingers around the worn plastic, I pulled out a key to a room at the Dreamscape Motel.

I stood in front of the desk like my socks had put roots into the rug.

Pastor Tim, who had sounded so disgusted that I lived at the Dreamscape the first night his wife had invited me into their home that I wanted to melt into the shiny hardwood floor under his dinner table, had a key to a room there.

I opened the drawer with the ledgers again, wondering if the weekly cost of the room was in one of them. I shut it again because I wouldn't know how to find that in dozens of pages of numbers with a map and a flashlight, and I wanted to get out of the house before anyone woke up. Better to not even give them reason to think about me being there in the middle of the night, I reasoned.

If there was one thing I knew inside and out, it was secrets and how to keep them. My gut screamed that whatever Tim was hiding was at the motel—far from any prying eyes, including his wife's. I slid the key into my pocket. As long as I got it back into his desk before he knew it was gone, I was safe.

And maybe if I could figure out what was going on here I could make sure Charlotte was, too.

While the key fob didn't have a room number on it, it was blue, and I knew that the ones for the side of the building where I had lived were brown. So this room had to be the building across the parking lot, and that building only had five rooms.

If he showed up for work that day at all, it wouldn't be until after he'd slept off yesterday's boozing, so I should be able to run out to the motel early.

No chance I was getting a wink of sleep now, so I scrubbed my bathroom and got ready for the day, pulling on soft jeans and my new First Baptist Fall Festival hooded sweatshirt. I wolfed down cherry Pop-Tarts, and at five after seven, I crossed the driveway again, letting myself into the house at normal volume and pausing in the doorway when I saw Charlotte at the bar eating a bowl of cereal.

Her hair had started to grow back out, and Mary had kept up with a close pixie cut that showed off Charlotte's beautiful eyes, but somehow made her look older. She wore a pair of skintight jeans and yet another sweater of Lisa's that swallowed Charlotte right up, but at least the sweater was in season now and she wasn't roasting in them.

"Morning," I said.

She drank the milk from the bottom of her bowl and stood, putting it in the sink and hurrying up the stairs.

"But not a good one, I guess," I muttered, turning on the coffee maker.

Her attitude fit with what I suspected, I just didn't understand why she wouldn't talk to me. I wasn't Tim.

Easy to think that in my shoes. Harder for a scared kid who was tired of being hurt—without my granny, I hadn't had the first clue who to trust. Teachers, neighbors, police: I had tried every one and nobody helped. The cop was the worst—he showed up asking about my story and left with two grams of meth and an "unsubstantiated report."

I'd lost two fingernails entirely that night, and Daddy swore he'd kill me if I told another soul.

I knew he meant it. When I could think straight again, I knew what I had to do.

And if I had to do it again in Whitney Falls, well... I wouldn't make as many mistakes this time.

I touched the room key in my pocket on the way to my car, pointing it toward the Dreamscape.

# THIRTY-NINE

## MARTHA

*October*

I woke to the phone ringing.

I sat up when I realized that, shaking my head as I reached for my nightstand in the dark.

When did it get dark?

When did I go to bed?

What phone was ringing? I didn't have a phone.

So then why wasn't I in my bedroom?

The question idled in a foggy brain that didn't want to work as fast as I was asking it to.

I groped in the dark, realizing by the third ring that I was cold, and by the fourth that I was on the sofa in Pastor Tim's office.

What in the world? I vaulted to my feet, everything seeming to happen in slow motion, and grabbed the phone. I would've traded my left arm for a clock right then.

"'Lo?" I mumbled, putting the phone to my ear.

"Martha? Oh, thank you, Jesus," Mary sobbed.

Mary was crying.

The heartbreak seeping into her words cleared a layer of the fog from my head. I clenched the phone in my fist, patting myself down with my other hand when I shivered and gasping—somehow, I had curled up and passed right out in Pastor Tim's office in my underwear.

What in the wide world was going on? If I didn't know better, I'd swear... no. I hadn't. I wouldn't. Never again.

Right?

Hands shaking so hard the heavy brown receiver was beating me in the side of the head, I tried to focus on Mary.

Because focusing on me was certain to pretty quickly render me completely useless to either of us.

"Mary, what's wrong? Is the baby okay?" I asked. They'd gone public with her pregnancy at church last Sunday, and her sobs had my foggy brain worried that now something was wrong. I flipped on the light, looking around for my clothes as Mary caught her breath.

"I think so," she said, sniffling. "I... Martha, are you alone?"

I put her on speaker, setting the phone back in its cradle. "I think so."

"I need you to make sure," Mary said, her breath coming in ragged gasps.

Where the blue hell were my clothes? I put my free hand to my forehead. A fragment—pulling on my dark jeans and my new First Baptist Fall Festival hoodie.

I looked behind the pastor's desk, in the closet, behind the couch, and under it—nothing.

Cracking the door, I checked the office where my desk sat. No one out there.

"I'm alone," I called to Mary, slipping out and snatching a fall festival hoodie out of the lone box of leftovers and yanking it over my head. It swallowed me all the way to my knees, which helped me feel less exposed, though I still wanted pants.

Turning back to the door of Pastor Tim's office when I

heard the soft, panicked cadence of Mary's voice but couldn't make out her words, I spotted the bottle.

My stomach flipped clean over and turned itself inside out. I clamped my hand over my mouth.

I couldn't deny I knew this feeling, but I wanted to unsee it with everything in me.

Bulleit Rye Bourbon. It was a decent size, probably a full fifth of whiskey.

And it was empty on the floor next to the end of the sofa where I'd woken up.

Dammit. Martha didn't drink—Martha didn't even really know anyone who drank.

Two hundred and forty-three days, I'd lasted. I could practically taste that one-year chip.

And somehow I had blown it.

Brain fog, sluggish muscles, missing hours. I'd been here before. I'd just never expected to be again.

"Martha?" Mary's shriek yanked my attention away from worrying about how I had tossed away my hard-won sobriety—she needed me, and clearly I had already screwed up badly enough without adding letting her down to the mix.

"Sorry, sorry," I said quickly, hurrying to the desk. "Can you repeat the last thing you said? I think the connection cut out."

"We're real friends, me and you, aren't we? The kind of friends who can count on each other for help no matter what?"

"Of course, Mary. You know that. You can always trust me with anything."

I leaned over the desk, my fingers curling so tight around the edges of the wood it hurt.

Something was wrong. I could hear it in her voice.

It wasn't the baby, she'd said.

Pastor Tim—my head whipped back and forth in a panic. We hadn't—he hadn't—I hadn't... surely I wouldn't do that even with the bourbon.

I had just woken up mostly naked in my boss's office with a large, empty bottle of bourbon—somehow Daddy's favorite had become my drink of choice after he was gone—nearby. But I couldn't bring myself to believe I'd slept with Mary's husband. I wanted to laugh at the absurdity of that—I knew better than anybody what I was capable of with enough booze in my system—but I couldn't laugh. Mary was downright distraught.

"What's wrong, Mary?" It came out too high. I cleared my throat and tried again. "Just tell me how to help." That was better. "I'm so thankful to have you as a friend, of course I will do whatever you need me to do."

"Really?" She sniffled.

"Cross my heart."

"I'm... I just can't even... Martha, I can't stop shaking." She dissolved into more sobs.

"Stress is bad for the baby," I said thickly. My skin prickled in a wave that started at the nape of my neck and spread until I felt like every nerve ending was hovering just above a live wire.

I knew something.

Something the bourbon had hidden. Something I didn't know I knew anymore. Something that would help me make sense of what was going on here.

It danced around the edges of my brain like a cheap beer joint stripper, teasing awkwardly, trying too hard. But I couldn't make out what I was missing.

Waking up after you've had so much to drink that the booze steals your memory makes whole days feel like a bad dream—no matter what else I ever tried to focus on, my brain would revert to trying to fill in the missing time. And I didn't even know, right then, how many hours I was missing. It's like trying to solve a puzzle when you don't have all the pieces.

My heart thumped against my ribs entirely too fast.

"Mary, listen to me. You have to breathe." Talk about preaching to the choir. "Your first priority has to be to take care of your baby right now. You're too upset. Breathe with me. In for three, hold for two, out for four." I'd seen that on TV—a random moment from a sitcom, I could recall just fine. How I ended up in this room in my underwear with an empty bourbon bottle, I had nothing for. I hate my brain sometimes.

The phone spurted what sounded like static as Mary blew into her microphone. I closed my eyes and focused on my own breath, my pounding heart and blood rushing in my ears the only sounds.

"Martha?" Mary's voice was small, but calm.

"Feeling any better?" I let a last breath out before her next words sucked all the air out of the room. "What can I do to help you?"

"Do you know how to hide a body?"

# PART THREE
## THE TRUTH WILL OUT

# FORTY

## MARTHA

*November*

Bodies. Plural, it turned out.

"Two is going to be harder," I said, feeling the same electric prickle in my skin I'd gotten in the pastor's office, looking around room twenty-three at the Dreamscape Motel. All at once, it felt like half a lifetime and just a few minutes since I'd checked out of the motel for good.

I tried to avoid looking them in the eyes as Mary hid in the bathroom, sitting on the edge of the bathtub and occasionally retching quietly into the toilet.

Mary had opened the flimsy motel room door staring out of the biggest, most bloodshot and swollen eyes I'd ever seen, and locked every lock on the door behind me. She backed up all the way to the bodies, then turned away from them and ducked into the bathroom. A bruise blooming on her cheekbone, blood smeared on her upper lip, and her wild hair and torn dress backed up her story about being attacked, but I was having trouble understanding how she was still alive and they... were not.

"You'll still help me, won't you, Martha?" She hiccupped from the other side of the wall. "I can't let my baby be born in prison. Can't let someone else raise my child. This wasn't my fault. I..." The words were swallowed by deep, wracking sobs for at least the fifth time since I walked in. Right on time for the kind of drinking I'd done, my head started to pound, keeping time with her sobs, so that each one lanced into my brain like an icepick.

A dull one.

"Of course I'll help you." I had thought all the way through what would happen to my friend and her baby in the seven minutes it had taken me to speed over here and hide my car behind the building. Mary had prayed for this baby for actual decades, I couldn't let it grow up without her.

Turned out there wasn't a faster path to sobriety than trying to figure out how to destroy corpses sufficiently to keep your bestie out of the hoosegow: my head might well split right open over the threadbare brown carpet, but I was as stone sober as I'd been last Sunday morning as I examined the scene. The biggest, most immediate problem was getting them out of there without anyone seeing us.

There wasn't much blood and the place was a hole, so cleaning the room well enough that nobody here would notice shouldn't be a problem.

"I'm going to need bleach, and some strong lye soap. Borax too, maybe," I said, studying the carpet as I walked to the bathroom door. She'd slid down the edge of the tub to the floor and was curled in a ball, hugging her knees. She'd just started to show the tiniest baby bump, and she'd been so proud of it, beaming like an angel as she and Pastor Tim told the congregation just a week ago how thrilled they were that God had finally blessed them with a baby they were going to get to raise among the good people of Whitney Falls, at First Baptist.

I'd watched him closely as he spoke and been unable to

detect a lie, but if he'd had a vasectomy, who was the baby's father? It wasn't like I could ask Mary—I felt bad even wondering it myself.

Pastor Tim had to be lying about something, but I didn't guess I really knew which thing, exactly. The realization that he could lie straight to my face and I couldn't tell was unsettling, but I couldn't deny it was true, and that made me feel awful for Mary.

She had done so much for me: invited me into her home and her life, trusted me with her keys and her husband, given me a job and a home—and now her life and happiness hung on my ability to fix this.

"And rubber gloves, a few pair if you have them," I added.

Mary nodded. "I have all that at home." She sobbed again. "Can I even go home?"

"You should, now while no one is awake to see you and think anything is strange. Put those clothes in the fireplace and clean up, try not to touch much of anything until you've gotten a good shower." I took a deep, steadying breath and closed my eyes when a wave of nausea tried to make my knees buckle. "It's Sunday, right? Yesterday was Halloween, so tomorrow morning is Sunday."

She blinked. "Saturday was Halloween, Martha. Yesterday was Sunday. We're coming up on Monday morning."

I had lost a whole day?

I felt my hands start to shake.

"Right, sorry," I said. "Not really thinking straight here. What time is it?"

She looked at her watch, fresh tears falling. Her eyes were in real danger of swelling shut. "Two thirty-five."

"Good," I said. "Be back here in an hour. We'll have three hours before sunrise, and we shouldn't need that long."

"What about, um..." She waved her hand in the general direction of the room.

"I'll work on that while you're gone." I couldn't think of a single thing I wanted to do less, but Mary needed me. I might not know everything that had happened between Saturday and now, but I knew I wouldn't let her down.

She nodded and I put out a hand to help her stand. She grabbed my fingers and floated up almost effortlessly. I forgot sometimes, because of the way she looked, just how strong she was.

"They attacked you," I said, not quite a question, but not really a statement.

She turned her huge blue-violet eyes up at me, fresh tears springing into them. "It hurts, to think about any of it, you know?"

I bet it did. "Of course. I need to know where the weapon went, Mary."

"Weapon?" Her forehead scrunched up.

"What did you hit them with?" I asked.

"Oh." She pointed to the bathtub, where a crowbar rested in an orangey-red puddle. "It was on the table. I just grabbed it and swung when he hit me." Her hands started shaking again. "Caught him right in the throat. I didn't even realize what I was doing until he hit the ground, and then I didn't have any choice but to... well. You know. I couldn't let anyone hurt my baby."

I stared at the bar, the tugging, teasing feeling floating around the edges of my thoughts again. Shaking it off, I patted her shoulder. "I'm so sorry this happened to you, Mary. But you'll be okay."

She squeezed my hands, staring me straight in the eye. "With your help, I think I might be. I can't even—there just aren't words to thank you, Martha. Should I bring back anything else?"

"A tarp." I could stack them face-to-feet and roll the whole thing up like a plastic man burrito.

And then what? Haul a body roll out of the local motel into

the pastor's wife's very expensive, very recognizable car in front of God and everybody? This place was always crawling with truckers, and that's not a crowd known for healthy sleep habits.

This wasn't a trailer park in southwest Virginia. I couldn't forget that, or Mary wouldn't be alone in prison, and I hadn't managed to escape facing a judge over Daddy's disappearance just to get sent up for aiding and abetting my good friend.

I had flown over here in a hungover haze because my friend called me crying, but I was in this ass-deep now—if she got caught, I did too. Every move had to be calibrated to our current surroundings and community standing.

I swallowed hard. "Don't come back here in your car, everyone knows who drives that thing. Get the work van from behind the church, the keys are in the First Baptist coffee cup on my desk. I'm going to need a butcher knife, and the hedge-trimming shears. A hand saw. A hammer. Pliers, duct tape, and a straight razor."

She hurried out of the bathroom, repeating the list under her breath as she rushed past them, staring straight ahead.

"He really said he was going to kill your baby?" I blurted.

"First." She choked out. "He said he would kill the baby first, and then I could go join it."

Jesus.

He really was a monster.

"Mary," I called as she unlatched the door.

She paused.

"Get the really big Igloo cooler from the garage. The one we use for church potlucks and cookouts. Is it too much for you to lift if it's empty?"

"I'll figure it out." She slipped out the door. I didn't even count to five before I heard her car start.

I went to the bathroom and retrieved towels and washrags, and walked back to the bodies. I knew exactly how to make them disappear, I just had to beat the daylight.

Bowing my head and shutting my eyes, I prayed with everything I had, considering I had so little practice. For Mary and her baby. For forgiveness. For the luck and strength of the righteous.

Opening my eyes and looking at what I was about to do, I prayed for their souls, wondering if there was even any point in that. Was there such a thing as redemption for true evil?

It wasn't for me to say, and standing there over the naked corpses, I realized I had no one to ask.

What I had was simply two objects that had to be gone from Whitney Falls without a trace by sunup. That's all they were. Not people. Just things.

Empty, staring shells that used to be Pastor Tim and Sam Tomlinson.

## FORTY-ONE

### MARY

*November*

He didn't say he'd kill our baby. Not exactly.

*"I'll cut that little bastard right out of you, and then send you after it."* Tim's words burned my ears from inside my brain, repeating on a loop as I drove out of the parking lot at that godforsaken motel, toward the home we were supposed to raise our family in. I would carry the secret to my grave, but that's what he'd said, his eyes glassy from liquor, his bare skin shiny with sweat and his hair mussed more than usual, lying on top of...

"Lord save me, this has to be a bad dream," I whispered.

Sam Tomlinson. The missing deacon had returned to Whitney Falls, holed up in the mystery room at the Dreamscape Motel doing unspeakable things with my husband. All those nights I'd lain awake, all the days I'd stared at myself in the mirror wondering who he was cheating with now, trying to figure out why I wasn't good enough... and he had taken up with a man. How stupid and blind could I have possibly been? And who else knew? Did Ruthie? My heart hammered my ribs so hard I felt sure something would break. It was too much to think about all at once.

And what came next—I hadn't gone there to hurt anyone. At least, I didn't want to think I had.

The whole day played in my head for the hundredth time, no matter how hard I tried to shut it out.

———

*I walked into a silent house, fall sunlight trickling through the stained-glass windows in gorgeous bursts of color on the white marble floors.*

*"Hello?" I called, stepping up to the third riser on the stairs and pausing to listen for a reply that didn't come. "Charlotte, is that you? Time to get ready for church."*

*"Mary, it's me." Martha's voice floated down the stairs. "Pastor Tim and Charlotte aren't here." Something about her tone was just enough off, anguish she was trying to hold back seeping into the words. Every part of me except my belly went numb, like I could sense I was about to learn something I didn't want to know.*

*Martha came down, her face flushed and her eyes a little too bright.*

*"Are you feeling okay?" I put a hand on her forehead, my thoughts racing with worry about where Charlotte had gone.*

*"I'm actually not, I shouldn't have come over here." She backed toward the door and I watched her for two steps before I sighed. I couldn't leave her. Not now, like this.*

*I ordered her to the sofa and went upstairs to fetch things to make her comfortable before I made her some soup, my skin tight and itchy I was so desperate to find Charlotte.*

*As Martha dozed off, I patted her arm. "You rest, now. I have to find Charlotte before it gets any later."*

"I saw her." Martha bit her lip, her eyes big and sad. "I think Pastor Tim took—"

I didn't wait for the rest of the sentence, my feet barely touching the marble as I sprinted out to my Grand Wagoneer. No. He hadn't taken Charlotte. I put up with a lot out of Tim McClatchy, but I wouldn't abide that.

I drove straight to the Dreamscape Motel, that blasted key I'd found in his desk dancing through my thoughts. I should've thrown it away. Or demanded to know why he had it.

Maybe I didn't because deep down I knew why. In places I didn't recognize, because I didn't want to know. But maybe it wasn't too late.

I spotted his car from the road, and a wave of nausea hit me so hard and fast I had to stop the car behind the motel to open the door and vomit into the weeds in the field.

Stepping carefully, I checked the number on the door nearest Tim's car and hurried across the gravel parking lot and into the office. The pimply-faced kid behind the counter dropped his magazine and stood up straight, his eyes big. "What are you doing here?"

I smiled my most patient smile. Everyone in Whitney Falls knew the pastor's wife. "I don't believe that's a proper way to greet a customer."

"I just meant... I mean, you don't really... what can I do for you, ma'am?"

"That's better. I need a key to room twenty-three. My husband has ours and I need something from the room."

I watched his face carefully for a reaction to the news that the pastor had a room in this place. Not even a hint of surprise disturbed his bumpy red forehead.

"Yes, ma'am." He reached into a box and pulled out a key. "This one is a master, all the keys to that room are out right this minute. So if you could just please bring it back."

"Thank you so much." I took the key and sprinted to the

*room, not pausing to catch my breath before I threw the door open, lips already moving to tell him to stop whatever he was doing with Charlotte.*

*I didn't even see Charlotte, but I sure saw my husband—Tim didn't seem to have any performance difficulty in that dim little room, tangled up with someone entirely too big and hairy to be Charlotte.*

*They didn't see me until I was standing next to the bed with the crowbar in my hand. Why there was a crowbar on the table inside the door I had no idea, but then somehow I had picked it up and I was by the bed—not sure why even in the moment, mind you. I didn't feel a thing but rage at the multiple layers of betrayal writhing around in front of me. It really did burn, the anger—I'd always thought that was hyperbole, but my cheeks felt like somebody had a flame thrower cooking my face right off as my eyes locked on the tube of KY Jelly on the nightstand.*

*"Why?" The word ripped out of my throat on a howl, and Tim's head whipped around, his eyes the kind of shiny and bloodshot they got when he drank too much.*

*For some stupid reason I looked down at his hips, which were still moving. It was all I could do to keep from vomiting again.*

*"Why do you think?" He pushed himself up with both arms. "You think it's easy, living with you, watching your belly grow with something I never wanted? Something you found a way to get anyway? Get out."*

*I couldn't have moved if I'd wanted to.*

*"Go find whoever you've been screwing, you're not wanted here." His eyes narrowed. "So help me, I'll cut that little bastard right out of you and then send you after it."*

*I swung the bar without thinking, the words still hanging in the air, hateful and thick, when Tim's hands went to his throat and he tumbled over on top of...*

*"What have you done?" Sam Tomlinson roared, shoving with one arm at Tim's weight and struggling to get up.*

*Tim clearly couldn't breathe, the eyes I'd once found so mesmerizing bugging out of his head as he tried, his fingers clawing at his neck like that would fix anything.*

*And Sam had seen... well, everything. He knew far too much. And he might hurt me or the baby if I waited for him to get to his feet.*

*So I didn't.*

*Three good swings, and he didn't move anymore, either.*

*The silence in that motel room was the loudest thing I'd ever heard. Blood rushed in my ears with a noise-canceling roar, the crowbar falling to the carpet with a thud I felt through my shoes, because I couldn't hear anything.*

*And all I could see were Tim's eyes, frozen wide, the last thing he'd said whirling through my brain like a tornado, uprooting and destroying my good memories of the man I'd pledged to love until death.*

*"Vasectomies fail, you asshole," I said, right before I ran to the toilet to vomit again.*

*Not that I knew that until the doctor told me.*

*I had broken right down in the obstetrician's office and cried telling the kindly, balding doctor that when I shared what I thought would be the happiest news of our lives, my husband claimed he'd had a vasectomy he never told me about and accused me of cheating. I kept the part about how hypocritical that was to myself, of course.*

*The doctor had just laughed. "If I had a nickel for every vasectomy baby I've delivered... well, Miss Mary, I could buy you a fancy coffee. It's rare, but more common than folks think, especially if it's been more than a few years. That procedure counts on scar tissue to close up the tube, but scar tissue changes over time, and now and again, a couple of swimmers slip through if that's happened." He patted my shoulder. "You tell your husband I said the good Lord means for you two to have a family, and he shouldn't question that—or your honor. His pride is just wounded. You go on home and make sure he knows he's your one and only, and it'll right itself. The truth always outs."*

---

Out, the truth sure had, right there in a seedy motel room, naked and ugly.

And still, when it came down to it, I hadn't been able to repeat Tim's cruel last words to Martha. Twice I'd told her a version of the story, and twice I'd lied right to her face. Again.

Martha, who I'd never noticed until I suspected her of betraying my marriage—had turned out to be the only real friend I'd ever had.

Just another guilty cross for me to carry.

Not that I was alone there. Tim had betrayed me in every sense of the word.

Breaking his wedding vows. Sharing our deepest secrets with outsiders.

I parked my Grand Wagoneer in my driveway, wondering what would've happened to us if we'd never come here. Or if we'd told each other the whole truth about why we did.

What would be happening to me right that second, I wondered, if I hadn't thought Tim was interested in Martha all those months ago?

Taking off my shoes and carrying them inside to the fireplace, the time before Martha was my friend seemed like another lifetime. A thousand years ago. And in a way it was. Mary McClatchy had come into her own here in Whitney Falls.

The biggest thing on my mind as I stripped off my clothes carefully and lit a long match was how to keep the life I'd built here without Tim to lead this church.

First Baptist couldn't have a woman as the minister, not even a pastor's wife could be called to that job.

Flames crackled and consumed, eating my clothes and whatever evidence they might have held. Not that I was truly worried about evidence, after seeing our police department in action when Lisa passed on. But Martha was right, it was better to make sure there was nothing that could be traced back to me—or to her, really.

My face fell as I considered that. I wasn't sorry for what had happened to Tim and his... Sam Tomlinson. It was them or me, and since me also meant my baby, I couldn't feel anything but proud of the choice I'd made in that split second.

I mean, the bar was right there. I couldn't—or didn't want to, maybe—imagine why they'd had it, so I chose to believe the Good Lord left it there for me to find. To save my baby, by saving myself.

I went up to the shower, running again through the list of things Martha had said she needed me to bring. I couldn't let Martha down. I had to do everything just as she'd asked. Her former life was going to save my current one. My mother would be able to see the poetry in that, but I only saw salvation and relief. Black and white, that had always been me.

I wasn't even sure when I'd figured out that Martha had hurt people in her past.

I'd idly wondered one day what she'd do if she knew who I used to be, and somewhere in wondering, I realized that she was my best friend—even if I did feel a bit of guilt over how that had come about—and she lived in my house and worked in our church, and I didn't know her last name.

At first, I'd panicked, wondering just what I had invited into my home. A bit of time to think had calmed my nerves. And helped me solve a problem I wasn't even sure I had yet that day.

I mean, who doesn't have a last name?

People who aren't who they say they are.

Who up and moves, all alone, to a tiny, remote mountain

town with one church and one grocery store and two police officers who couldn't run a traffic light in a big city?

A woman running from a secret.

The kind of secret that could put a young woman in prison, wasting the best years of her life.

The kind of past that might come in handy if I found myself in a jam.

# FORTY-TWO

## MARTHA

*November*

A day lost to a fifth of bourbon meant the hogs would be extra hungry.

It was like my granny was standing in the corner of the room at the Dreamscape, stepping out of the faded blue and cream wallpaper and leaning in to whisper "Everything happens for a reason. We do the best we can with the cards we're dealt."

I had used the motel towels to move the bodies so they were easy to pull onto the tarp when Mary got back with it. She'd backed into the room tugging the giant cooler with both hands, having packed the other things I asked for inside it before unloading it from the work van.

Looking at me like she wanted my approval, Mary tipped her lips up into the slightest ghost of a smile I'd ever seen. "I got everything you asked for."

I squeezed her hand, having made up my mind about this next part while she was gone.

No matter what had happened this summer, or over the

past few hours in this room, my friend Mary had been Mrs. Tim McClatchy for more than half as long as I had been alive.

She couldn't do this. She couldn't see this.

I pressed the keys to my Honda into her hand. "Go. I got this, and I will not have you under this kind of stress. Park my car in the driveway and go inside and lie down. I will come get you as soon as I can because I'll need your help getting rid of their vehicles."

She started shaking her head before I stopped talking. "I would never ask—"

"You didn't ask," I cut her off. "I offered. This won't be good for the baby and I'll work faster on my own. Go on."

She swallowed hard and patted my arm, keeping her eyes locked with mine—and off the rest of the room—before she turned and hurried back out into the dark.

I locked the doors and checked the shades and said another prayer or five before I got to it.

A pen of a dozen or so grown hogs can eat a two-hundred-pound man in less than ten minutes. I knew that because my granny had a neighbor, a nice young guy who was a decent mechanic, who'd been killed by his sister's hogs—she went out of town and he was supposed to take care of them, but he'd stepped into the pen one day to look at one hog that was acting sickly, and the others swarmed and knocked him down.

A neighbor who'd seen him drive up walked over about ten minutes later to ask a question about his transmission, and there weren't many pieces left for him to find.

I'd been terrified of hogs for years, until the night my daddy died.

I didn't know about the hair and the teeth then, though. That's how I nearly got caught—turns out of all the things, hogs can't digest human teeth and hair. They tend to leave the teeth, but will eat the hair anyway, and it makes them sick. It also gets found and can still be DNA-tested after the hog in question is slaughtered, which is how I ended up in Whitney Falls.

I wouldn't make that mistake again.

I picked up the razor and shaved them first, closing their eyes before I started, working head to feet, and carefully collecting every last hair into the plastic bag from the wastebasket in the bathroom. When both men were hairless and the bag was full, I tied it shut with the precision of a boy scout knotting a cord on a rock-climbing harness.

No traces.

The teeth were harder than I thought, and I had to put the pliers down and go vomit in the bathroom more than once as I worked, but in forty minutes, I had a box of sixty-four next to the bag of hair, and two things that needed to be creatively folded into the cooler. I wasn't too worried about getting them into the back of the van on my own—Sam wasn't a big guy, the loading deck on the van was low, and corpse-hauling muscles got a long memory. There was, of course, a chance that someone would see me, but I hauled odd items around town for the church all the time. I had a better than even chance of being dismissed.

I worked fast, singing Granny's nursery rhymes to myself to give my thoughts someplace less grisly and nightmarish to focus and keep my breathing from being too loud in the silent room.

When the cooler was stuffed full and shut tight, I looked around. Everything that might even have a little blood on it and wasn't stuck down—the bedspread, my tools, the crowbar, and a tube of KY Jelly I'd found on the nightstand, I piled carefully in the center of the tarp before I used the borax and lye to remove every trace that anyone had been there. Phone, lamps, light switches, faucets, doorknobs, shower curtain, toilet, tub, carpet—thank God for the ugly mottled brown that was more forgiving with spots than anything I'd ever seen. I wasn't just removing Mary and me from this room, I was removing Pastor Tim and Sam and anyone else they might have brought here.

The cleaning required focus, because I couldn't forget so much as an eyelash and be able to sleep at night from here on out, but about a million questions swirled in my head. "Later," I muttered under my breath.

When I was satisfied I'd done all I could, I dropped the towels onto the tarp and rolled it all up tight, wrapping the whole thing in the entire roll of thick tape.

As soon as the cooler, the tarp roll, the bag, and the box were closed up in the back of the van and I had the engine running, questions started falling right out of my mouth, aloud to the empty van. "Where the heck has Sam been? And what could Pastor Tim and Sam possibly have thought their sneaking around was going to lead to?"

Right behind those, two others lurked, too dark for me to give voice to, which was saying something given what I'd spent the past ninety minutes doing.

Why had my friend Mary McClatchy murdered these two men, really? I'd heard her say Pastor Tim threatened her, but Pastor Tim had been stark naked and... probably occupied, from what I'd seen. Mary could've run, surely.

Which led to my next question: Who was the father of Mary's baby?

I pulled onto the highway, keeping the headlights low to avoid standing out, and hunching over the steering wheel to peer into the dark.

No moon tonight—another thing that would help.

My brain kept returning to that awful question. I didn't want to doubt my friend, and suspecting her of breaking a commandment sure seemed like doubt to me. But the things I'd seen, fitting Pastor Tim and Sam into the cooler—well, they changed my view of the sermons I'd heard the pastor give about Paul's Letters to the Corinthians and the gays and sin, that's for sure. I never could hold with it anyhow—I think sometimes folks plain forget the Good Book was mostly written by mortal men, and to my mind, old Paul clearly had some issues of his own. If you read the whole book, he didn't think anybody ought to ever have relations unless they were trying to reproduce, and I for sure didn't agree with that. I didn't know many people who did, except maybe Mary. And it sure seemed now like Pastor Tim had maybe been preaching more to himself than anyone else, anyhow.

How could Mary not know?

What if she had?

I gripped the steering wheel a little tighter. "Did she know Tim betrayed her? Somehow, did she know he'd had the vasectomy?" I sounded a little breathless even to my own ears asking the question. "Or did she know something else, even?"

I hadn't breathed a word of the pastor's drunken VFW hall confession about his secret snip surgery to anyone. But that didn't mean Mary hadn't found out and decided to double cross him by finding another way to get the baby she wanted.

I didn't suppose I could really blame her for that. Besides, I was in this up to my neck. Wondering too hard about Mary's reasoning or her story wouldn't do anything for me, not when the last memory I had before I woke up in the pastor's office was of looking out my window at Mary's beautiful house, thinking to myself that if Tim McClatchy was living his life the way my daddy had, abusing a little girl in his care, then he could damn well die like my daddy had, too.

As it had turned out, that's exactly what happened—I just hadn't had to kill Pastor Tim myself.

Like Granny said, everything happens for a reason.

# FORTY-THREE
## MARTHA

*November*

It was still so dark when I turned into the driveway at the farm where I'd been tending the hogs all week for the third deacon that I could barely see five yards in front of the van. I flinched when I thought I saw a curtain move as the headlights flooded the front of the ramshackle old farmhouse, but I leaned forward and blinked, looking closer, and everything was still. The house, sided with faded green clapboard shingles, was as dark and silent as it had been all week. The deacon and his wife weren't due back from the hospital until Wednesday.

I backed the van up until the rear doors were as close as I could get to the hog pen without allowing the tires to leave the gravel. Driving over dirt leaves tread marks, which I learned when I was thirteen and driving my drunk father to deliver a warning to a drug dealer who had dared to skim cash from his sales. I turned too wide and let a tire slip off the narrow driveway into the weeds, and caught a backhand to the eye. "Tread marks are evidence," Daddy barked, slurring the longest word. "Stay on the concrete."

The dealer got a lot worse than I did. I stayed in the car, but nothing I stuffed in or over my ears kept out the screams. On the one hand, stealing from the Dixie Mafia wasn't smart. On the other, I'd always found Daddy's surprise at discovering that criminals stole money when handling large amounts of it funny.

I didn't let a tire touch dirt after that. Ever. And I wasn't about to start now.

Clean out of breath by the time I lugged the cooler to the edge of the pen, I opened it and avoided looking at their faces while I hefted pieces into the trough. It took me seven minutes to empty the cooler.

It took the hogs twelve to finish off the soft tissue and twenty-one to get through the bones—even the long ones. I had shoved Daddy in and run—this time I stayed to make sure the entire job was finished.

Gone. Without a trace.

As the animals staggered about with full bellies, I closed the cooler, grabbed the hose and filled their water, and hurried back to the van just as the sun's first baby rays crept over the edge of the mountains to the east.

I'd taken too long. Their cars were still at the Dreamscape.

Speeding back to Elias Lane, I prayed awkwardly for forgiveness and protection, for myself, for Charlotte, and for Mary and her baby. I parked the van behind the church, stuffing the tarp ball into the cooler and slamming it shut, double timing it across the road without looking around like I was guilty of something. "I had early church business," I repeated to myself.

I had a plan for the cooler, but right then I stashed it in Mary's garage and hurried to the back door of the house, reaching into my pocket for keys before I remembered these pants had come from the lost and found at church. Before I could panic, the door swung open and Mary peered through the screen door at me in the fading darkness.

Her face asked the question without any words, so I just

nodded once and reached for the door, waving her out and holding up their car keys. "We have to hurry," I said, looking at the corner bedroom window upstairs. "Will Charlotte be asleep for a while yet?"

Her turn to nod. "It's a teacher workday for the end of the term so she doesn't have school. I don't imagine I'll see her before noon."

She handed me the keys to my Honda and went to the passenger door as I unlocked it and slid behind the wheel.

We rode in silence, both of us seeming to understand that the other wasn't up for chatting without anyone having to say it.

I parked in my old spot at the Dreamscape because my Honda still fit in with the general vibe there, and parking behind the building in the growing daylight could invite more questions than it was worth. In the lot were three semis, the desk clerk's Datsun—by some miracle still held together with rust and tape—Pastor Tim's Camry, and a Nissan I didn't recognize.

The trucks hadn't been there before, which meant the drivers should be asleep a while; the clerk never cared more about what was happening at the motel than he did about whatever comic he was reading, which was probably a self-defense mechanism in a place like this; and the keys I'd taken from Sam's pocket were for a Nissan. I blew out a long slow breath.

"Almost done."

The words ricocheted like bullets in the small space. Mary yelped. I myself flinched.

"Sorry." I whispered that one as I took Tim's keys and handed her the others.

Mary turned in the seat, her voice uncharacteristically fierce. "Don't you dare apologize to me. This... you... Thank you for being my friend, Martha. I will never know what I did to deserve you. And I'll never be able to repay you."

"This isn't the kind of thing you do expecting to be repaid."

The words came out thick with emotion that sprang up out of nowhere. "You pay it forward." I barked out a laugh when Mary's eyes popped so wide I could see white all around the blue. "Hopefully not like this. But any other way you can. Someday a friend will need something that might cause you real trouble. I hope you think of me when that happens to you."

She sniffled, brushing at fresh tears with the back of her hand. "I keep wondering where we'll go. What we'll do." She laid a hand on her belly.

"That's a question for tomorrow."

We started to get out of the car and the door in front of us, the one that led to my old room, opened. A skinny girl wearing shorts and a T-shirt stepped out, froze when she saw us, and darted back in, slamming the door.

Mary took a step toward the door, glanced at me, and stopped.

"It's fine," I said quietly, hoping I was right. "I lived here for months and saw dozens of people come and go, and I couldn't point one of them out to you today for love or money. Let's go."

Mary's shoulders rose with a deep breath and she nodded, following me across the gravel lot to their cars.

"Where are we going?"

"Up the mountain," I said, opening the door and sliding into Pastor Tim's car. "To the lake."

---

"She's going to sleep all day." Mary stood up from her kitchen stool four hours later, pushing her empty water glass across the counter toward the sink. "Which I wouldn't mind for once, but I need to change her sheets today."

She stretched before she turned for the stairs, and I watched her go, wondering what she planned to tell Charlotte and trying to ignore the voice in my head that whispered questions about why she seemed... fine. I was the one who'd told her she had to act normal. I was just disturbed at what a good job she was doing of following the direction.

I didn't get any deeper down that rabbit hole before Mary's voice came from the top of the stairs, high and clear and not at all fine. "Martha, do you see a note from Charlotte anywhere? Check the living room and the front porch, please."

"I thought there was no school today." I hurried to the living room and checked every table, then went to the front door and the porch, walking to the foot of the stairs and looking up at Mary. "I don't see anything."

Mary's face crumpled like a soggy napkin, tears pouring down her cheeks as she whispered something I couldn't make out. I took the stairs two at a time, pausing next to her and looking toward Charlotte's open bathroom door. So she wasn't in there either.

"There's no reason to jump to conclusions," I put one arm around Mary, "I'm sure she went to the library, or out with a friend."

Mary shrugged me off and strode back into Charlotte's room, waving for me to follow and pointing at the closet with a shaking hand. "With half her clothes?"

I pressed my fingers to my lips. My brain conjured an image of Charlotte's face, and her mint green backpack stuffed full of clothes. I turned, spotting her schoolbooks on the white wood desk in the corner.

But I hadn't seen her book bag packed with clothes, not really. Not that I could remember.

Mary sobbed quietly into a blanket that lay across the foot of Charlotte's bed.

I swallowed hard. I had suspected Pastor Tim of doing awful things to Charlotte, and now it sure looked like she had taken off, right as Mary had... well. Pastor Tim wasn't coming back.

"We just have to find her," I said. "She probably doesn't know it's safe here."

Mary looked up from the blanket and sniffled. "Why would she not be safe here?"

"I... I don't know." I clapped my hands with a loud crack and changed the subject. "We'll get her back, Mary, don't worry. We need to go drive around and look ourselves, because how far could she have really gotten? But if we don't have her home in a couple of hours, we have to call the police."

Mary's eyes popped wide, the bright red blood vessels creepier the more of them I could see. "Are you crazy, Martha?" She stared like she wasn't sure.

That was okay. I wasn't sure either, given how I'd spent the morning.

"We cannot call the police, we... we did a terrible thing." She dropped her voice to a whisper on the last words.

"That's exactly why we have to," I said. "If we don't find her, people will notice that she's missing, Mary. It's a small town. You know, who wouldn't call the police if their foster kid took off? Someone with something to hide." I put my hands on her shoulders and looked her straight in her puffy, red-rimmed eyes. "As of right now, we have nothing to hide. Say it with me."

"We have nothing to hide," we said in unison.

Mary wiped her nose with the back of her hand. I patted her shoulder.

"Get your jacket and your keys," I said, taking a last look around the room. Everything seemed to be in its place except Charlotte's clothes, and the framed photo of her mother that she kept by her bed. "She can't have gone far."

# FORTY-FOUR
## MARY

*December*

"I'm so sorry, Tim isn't available right now," I said, laying a hand on my impossibly distended belly and smiling when I was rewarded with a swift kick.

"I tried the church office and the secretary said he wasn't in." The man sounded frustrated, but I didn't recognize his voice.

"I'm not sure when he'll be back, truthfully." I straightened a glittery red bow on the Christmas garland lining the dining room doorway, keeping my voice even and bright and my comments deliberately vague. Don't share more than absolutely necessary—that was the rule. Everything had gone according to Martha's brilliant plan for nearly seven weeks now, and it got a little easier to beat back the nerves with every call or visit.

"I've been trying to reach him for weeks." The man still hadn't identified himself, but he sounded annoyed. "It's always the same, no matter what time I call or who I talk to."

"I'm happy to pass him a message." I pasted a smile on my

face as I spoke to keep my voice upbeat, a trick my mother had taught me from her pageant queen days.

"No thank you," the words sounded tight, the kind that come forced through clenched teeth. "I'll try him another time."

"Of course. Have a merry Christmas!" I hung up, wondering why this guy didn't want to say who he was.

The oven timer rang before I got very far with that—it wasn't terribly unusual in our line of work, anyway, and I was starving. I'd been starving for weeks, ever since my nausea up and disappeared overnight. I couldn't get enough meat or bread, and my stomach had stopped reacting badly to the latter nearly as soon as the pink line appeared on the test. I had a fresh loaf of honey wheat in the bread machine and bacon-topped chicken cordon bleu in the oven.

The baby did a somersault and I laughed, patting my belly. "Easy there, tiger. We have to wait for Auntie Martha."

I'd have started calling her the messiah by Thanksgiving if I wasn't such a devout Christian. My friend had truly saved the day... saved my life... in every living sense of the word. I'd left the Dreamscape Motel that cold, dark November morning knowing Whitney Falls was finished. Another town, another church—another disaster. I'd finally gotten in the Lord's good graces enough to have new life growing in my belly, but my baby would have no home, no family. Tim had ruined everything. I had depended on him. Trusted him. And he'd let me down in every way he could.

By the time those cars disappeared beneath the flat, cold surface of the lake, my fear of the fires of eternal hell was the only thing keeping me from walking right in after them. I wouldn't get another chance after Whitney Falls. We'd arrived here knowing this one had to work out, and God knew I had tried everything, only to find myself disposing of my dead husband's car. I wanted to cry, but there weren't any more tears left for that day.

As the last bubbles popped and the lake went still as a sheet of glass, reflections of gnarled tree branches reaching across it like long, confining arms, Martha turned her back to the water and told me she had everything figured out.

"Here's how this is going to work," she'd said, steel in her tone I'd never heard from her before, every bit of the uncertain girl who tried to fade into the wall gone for the moment. "You're not going anywhere. We're not going anywhere."

"I can't go to prison."

She patted my arm as she turned for the trail that would lead us back down to the Dreamscape. "Definitely nobody is doing that. They can't charge anyone with a murder that never happened, Mary."

I blinked, following her as she stepped onto the old hiking trail. We were about four miles from the motel, which would be a good bit of exercise on such a cool, beautiful morning. Thankfully every step of it was downhill, and I had so much nervous energy to burn, I could've walked three times that far.

"But—"

Martha's head shook, hard. "Nope. We saw nothing. I still have the note Sam Tomlinson left me at the Pick and Go when he took off months ago. Can you fake Tim's handwriting well?"

"Very few people know what Tim's actual handwriting looks like," I replied slowly, trying to wrap my brain around what she was suggesting. "I've been writing his notes and signing things for him for years."

"Perfect." She'd thrown a smile over her shoulder. "We'll need a note. Not yet, but when the time comes."

"Martha, I understand what you're saying, I think, but I can't stay here if I can't take care of myself. The house is owned by the church and will go to the new pastor and his family. I'm afraid you've put a lot of thought into this for my benefit, but I'm going to have to leave Whitney Falls, as much as I really don't want to."

"No you're not," Martha said firmly. "And neither am I. From this minute forward, we have to believe, and make everyone else believe, that Pastor Tim and Sam are alive and well."

I stopped walking and stared at her. I might've been less shocked if she'd sprouted a second head.

"What?" I sputtered.

"Mary, I'm sorry if it hurts to hear this, but your husband clearly wasn't who you thought he was," she said. "And that wasn't even all of it. Not a single deacon at First Baptist would've voted to call an alcoholic, homosexual pastor to lead their church. Pastor Tim didn't just lie to you—he lied and pretended to be something he wasn't to the people here, and it didn't end well. But what's done is done, and losing our home isn't going to undo any of it. So we're going to lie, too, and make you something you totally are."

I was having trouble keeping up with her, both physically and mentally.

"And what's that?"

Martha stopped and leaned on a tree about thirty yards down the side of the hill from me.

"You're not giving up your home—your baby's home—to the next pastor of First Baptist Church," she said, her eyes bright for the first time all night. "You are going to be the next pastor of First Baptist Church."

## FORTY-FIVE
### MARTHA

*December*

The one wrinkle in an otherwise perfect holiday season was Charlotte's continued absence. There were still posters all over town, of course, getting beaten and torn by the swift winter winds that blasted through the valley almost nightly now, and faded by ice and snow. Fat lot of good they were: if she were in Whitney Falls, we'd know it. But I think it helped some folks feel better to leave them up, so we did. And every Sunday, we prayed together.

On my own, I prayed every night for two solid months that she was safe and warm and happy, wherever she was, and then selfishly that someday we'd know where she ended up. But on New Year's Eve, pouring two glasses of sparkling cider for Mary and me—fifty-nine days sober again and counting—as the cameras in New York City went to the lighted crystal ball, I prayed for the first time for her to come home.

Mary had broken down and told me that morning that she had walked in on Tim and Sam doing unspeakable things to each other and to poor Charlotte that night at the Dreamscape, and Charlotte had bolted through the open door while Mary did what had to be done in the room. By the time they were dead and Mary's shock had worn off, Charlotte had just vanished.

Ever concerned about Mary's unborn baby, I didn't want her to be upset about even small things, so I patted her back and told her I understood everything, she did nothing wrong, and then we prayed about Charlotte.

I took the empty cider bottle out to the recycling and rushed back inside to get the glasses to Mary, freezing when I stepped into the kitchen and could practically see Charlotte sitting at the counter with a bowl of cereal.

I knew instantly it was a memory, but it felt unfamiliar in a way that made me recoil mentally, like I wanted to crawl out of my own skin because my brain was showing me things that didn't belong to me.

It was the third time since Halloween that I'd had that feeling, and every time I'd managed to banish it with a few deep breaths.

I'd lived through memories from times I'd lost to a bottle coming back before, and never once had chasing them been anything but painful. I didn't want to know what I'd forgotten. Things were good here. We'd celebrated a quiet Christmas together in our home, where I lived in the guest room and we were turning the fourth small bedroom next to Mary's into a zoo-themed nursery.

And phase one of The Plan was nearly complete.

The entire town believed the whispers about Pastor Tim having fallen asleep at the wheel on the way back from a meeting in Malvern just after the Fall Festival—we told the congregation the following Sunday that he'd run his speeding car into a tree and been taken to the hospital clear down in Little Rock, which explained both his absence and the disappearance of his car. Of course, his face had been terribly injured and though he was recovering—we'd just announced that the power of First Baptist prayer had enabled him to take three steps last week—he didn't yet want to be seen by anyone but Mary and me. "Not too much longer now," we'd say when anyone asked when the pastor would be home.

Selling the lie was easy—folks gobble up stories about terrible things happening to perfect people, like God exacts a tax on those who have too many blessings. The whole town—even the women who'd spent the past few months hitting on the handsome pastor—had developed a morbid fascination with his vanity, and the idea that a good-looking guy like him being disfigured in a car crash was a punishment for the sin was widely accepted. Add in his beautiful, pregnant wife standing by her man when the rumor mill had practically turned Pastor Tim into the elephant man, and Mary had every last soul's sympathy and admiration. What a dedicated, loving woman with a kind heart.

The perfect sort of woman to shatter the concrete ceiling in a church that wouldn't hear of women in the clergy.

I was almost jealous of the popularity my story had brought Mary—she'd be elected mayor in a walk if she wanted to run, but we had our sights set higher. The real seat of power in Whitney Falls, like most small southern towns, was the one behind the pulpit. And I was more sure every day we'd get her there.

"Martha, they're starting the countdown!" Mary called from the living room.

I grabbed the glasses and rushed in as she said "Seven," her eyes on the TV.

"Six," I joined in.

"Five, four, three, two, one... Happy New Year!" We clinked the glasses together and drank our cider, and Mary laughed when the sugar got the baby dancing around her belly at midnight.

"You can't complain now if she comes out with her days and night mixed, up, Mom." I laughed and put my glass on the table.

Mary clapped a hand over her mouth. "Say it again," she whispered, her eyes bright with tears.

"Mom." I grabbed both of her hands in mine. "Get used to it."

She nodded, blinking hard. "Thank you so much, Martha."

She bowed her head. "Lord, as we begin this new year we ask that it be full of blessings for Whitney Falls, for our church, and for our children. Please Lord, watch over Charlotte and help bring her home safely. In Jesus's holy name."

"Amen," I said. "I hope Charlotte is safe and happy, wherever she is."

"I wish she knew—" Mary hiccupped. "I wonder sometimes if she knows that I wasn't part of what they were doing. I want to tell her I'm sorry, explain that I didn't know." She sighed. "I wish I'd left them to face justice for what they did."

"Sometimes justice is served in different ways," I said.

My sister would be proud.

"When are we going to tell everyone?" Mary asked.

"In just a couple more weeks," I said. "Do you have Sunday's sermon on empathy ready?"

Mary nodded.

"It will work," I said, taking a moment to think through any possible pitfalls with phase two of our plan. "It will actually work quite nicely. Almost everybody loves to believe the worst about people they admire. We create heroes and idols so we can rip them down all the time."

"Everyone has been so kind to me," Mary said. "I think between Charlotte running away and Tim's 'accident,' people really do feel sorry for me. Ruthie even smiled at me when I was at the Pick and Go last week."

"They're almost ready." I put my glass down and clapped my hands. "It's about time we confess the truth: that Pastor Tim ran off with Sam Tomlinson and left you to raise this baby on your own."

"And you really think the deacons will hire me as the pastor?"

"I think by the time we're through with them, they'll do anything we ask."

# FORTY-SIX
## MARTHA

*January—Saturday*

Two small paintbrushes, a tarp, and a quart of black enamel in my hand, I was almost to the cash register at the hardware store on the last Saturday in January when I dropped the whole shebang to the tile floor, my eyes on the black pickup parked at the curb across Main Street in front of the hair salon.

The paint can busted open, the lid flying four tiles away as the contents seeped out onto the floor in a kidney-shaped puddle.

"Oh my gracious, are you alright, honey?" The older woman who'd run the store since her husband passed on was one of the only people in town who didn't go to church, so I didn't know her name. She hefted herself off the metal stool behind the counter and shuffled over with a handful of blue shop towels, dropping two of them on top of the paint.

"I am so sorry." Shaking my head, I crouched and righted the can before I flattened my hand over the towels and began corralling the mess. "Please, drop those here and let me get this, it's the least I can do." I laughed.

I used the towels to clean up the paint and looked back up at the big front window just as a tall, lanky man with longish, tousled black hair swung down out of the driver's seat of the pickup and started across the street.

Panic closing around my chest like a vise, I tried to place his face without staring. I had seen him somewhere, I thought—but maybe not? There was glare on the window and he had sunglasses on, and I had seen a hundred people come and go from Granny's trailer in the seventeen years, ten months, and six days I'd lived there. My daddy hadn't been near as important to the Dixie Mafia in the end as he had liked to think, but as a low-end middleman who brought dealers to the suppliers in a part of Appalachia where the organization knew they needed a local to keep things running smoothly no matter how many bribes they paid to state and local officials, he knew a whole lot of people. Most of them drove pickups.

And one of them had found me.

I didn't know how, or even really why, I just knew I had to go.

I scooped up the brushes and the tarp and stood, whirling for the back of the shop. I could drop them and apologize again and duck out the back door before he made it past the spray insulation display inside the front door.

Where I'd go, I didn't even have the head space to consider, but I'd figure it out, just like I had every time before.

"Oh good." The old woman came around a corner smiling, pushing a mop bucket and holding out another small can of the paint Mary wanted to outline the animals we were painting on the baby's walls. Well, she was painting the animals—I was in charge of the sky, but we had two more cans of blue. "I mixed another can. You don't worry a bit about the spill, sweetie, everyone drops things now and again."

"I have to go, I'm so sorry," I shoved the things in my arms at her. "Is there a door back here?"

"Are you all right?" She dropped the mop handle with a clatter to catch the paint supplies, managing to grab everything and hang onto the paint can she'd tucked quickly under her arm. "Should I call someone?"

"No, I just have to go." I ran past her when I heard boots clicking on the linoleum, approaching fast.

I ran straight through the door to the storeroom in the back, past a desk covered with papers and folders, the sharp stench of turpentine strong enough to knock a person over. She must've put it in the mop water for the paint on the floor.

Spotting the red exit sign hanging from the ceiling, I veered left around a storage shelf full of bins.

And stopped dead.

The door was blocked entirely from sight, frame and all, by a stack of boxes three times as wide as me and nearly twice as tall.

I whirled back, listening.

"... ran to the back before I could tell her my nephew hasn't come in to unpack yesterday's delivery," the old woman said.

"So the door is blocked?"

"Can't even see it," she said. "That new delivery guy is plum lazy, he steps about half a foot in the door and puts everything down wherever he can reach. I had to get a ladder last night to stack the lighter ones on top so I could even move around back there."

"Thank you," he called, the boots already hurrying my way.

My skin burned like I'd walked into a furnace, every nerve ending crackling with an almost painful electricity as I looked around for anything I could use as a weapon. I hadn't made it this far—almost home—for this joker to ruin everything in the bottom of the ninth inning.

No baseball bats in sight, but I spotted a stack of garden borders that looked like railroad ties. Grabbing one, I ignored the splinters stabbing into my fingers and hefted it to my shoulder with some effort—the thing was three times as big as a bat and somehow ten times as heavy.

"Leave me alone," I said as soon as Black Pickup stepped into view.

"Whoa now," he raised both hands. "There's no need for all that."

"I just want to go," I said. "Just get on out of here and keep driving when you hit the eastern road out of town."

"I'm afraid that's not possible, but I'm not here looking for trouble."

"Then what do you want with me?"

"I've been watching things here in Whitney Falls for a while." He raised his eyebrows and moved one hand slowly toward his back. I tried to jiggle the railroad tie and got three more splinters and nearly fell over. Probably not the level of menacing I was going for.

Flipping open a wallet, he held up a badge. "I'm thinking now I might be wrong. But I walked in here thinking we could help each other. Can you put that down so we can talk?"

In all the people my daddy had known, not a one followed the law, much less worked for it.

"Who are you?" I asked slowly, twisting my arms and lowering the wood to the floor, my muscles protesting the entire time.

"Arkansas state police," he said, waving the badge. "I'm looking for Pastor Tim McClatchy."

# FORTY-SEVEN
## MARY

*January—Saturday*

"The giraffe has seven eyelashes on one eye and five on the other," Martha said, standing in the middle of the rug with her hands on her hips and squinting at my safari mural.

"That is a level of art critic I didn't expect from you," I laughed, picking up my smallest brush and reaching for the black paint tray.

"Numbers," she said. "I've always been good with numbers. But the painting is fantastic, truly. What a lucky little one."

I smiled as I feathered in the lashes, laying my free hand on my belly. "Not much longer now." I stepped back and Martha yelped. I turned my head to make sure I hadn't landed on her foot. I was about as graceful as a hippo and twice as big, and loving every milkshake-and-French-toast-sprinkled day of it.

Though I could do with less back pain.

"I didn't step on you, did I?"

"No, but I have to run out for a little while." She looked at her watch.

"Where to?" I lumbered around to face her, putting the paintbrush in a glass of gray water with the others.

She waggled her eyebrows. "That's for me to know and you to find out, my friend."

"A surprise for litt— well, make that great big—old me?" I fluttered my lashes and grinned.

"I'll be back in an hour or so," she said over her shoulder, already halfway down the stairs. "You should put your feet up and read or watch TV for a while."

"Don't mind if I do," I said, mostly to myself as I wandered out of the nearly finished nursery to my room. The room I used to share with Tim. I swallowed a lump in my throat as I glanced at the boxes of his clothes stacked neatly in the corner. Martha had packed them all up silently, and she was going to take them to a goodwill in Little Rock this week.

The room I couldn't bear to look at was Charlotte's. I'd kept the door shut since she disappeared—I didn't even want to know what kind of dusting nightmare was in there after weeks of sitting untouched, but it just hurt too much to even think about her. I tried to believe the Lord always knew best, but I hadn't been able to work out how that worked with Charlotte disappearing just when things here were going so well. So much better than I ever could've imagined when I'd called Martha from the motel that awful night.

As much as I wondered where Charlotte had gone, and wished I could ask her why she left, I thanked God for Martha daily. Sometimes more than once. She was the kind of smart you can't learn in school, that girl, and it wasn't an exaggeration to say she'd well and truly saved my life.

And now, it was finally time for phase two, she said. I had given the last eight sermons at First Baptist while Tim was "recovering" from his fictional accident.

Of course, Martha and I had led everyone to believe I was simply serving as the conduit for my husband's words on

Sunday mornings. But I had written every one of them myself, start to finish. Turned out, I didn't need to go to seminary. Being married to the pastor and a scholar of the Bible was enough. The past two Sundays in a row, more than a dozen people had asked me to tell Tim that was his best sermon ever.

Best sermon ever.

Me. Mary McClatchy of Ponchatoula, Louisiana. I gave the best sermons some folks had heard at First Baptist in over a year —one lady said last week's message on perseverance was the best she'd ever heard, and to look at her, she'd lived through thousands of Sundays.

I had never said it right out loud, but I did grow up southern and all, and that first day when Martha said we could stay here because I was going to be the pastor, I'd thought she had lost her mind.

Maybe she had, a little. Could you pull all the teeth out of two dead men and feed their bodies to hogs without being a little bit crazy? I wasn't entirely sure I'd have been able to get through it. All the more reason to be thankful to the Lord for sending Martha to me in my season of need. Even when I had no clue what I needed, the Lord provided.

Women weren't supposed to preach, to lead men, to teach others about God. Our role was to support. Caregivers, cooks, sounding boards—I had spent years listening to different drafts of Tim's sermons every week, bringing him food while he worked, rubbing his shoulders when he was tired and brainstorming impactful Bible verses with him.

The first Sunday, I had read one of his old sermons. He kept a file of them by topic in his study. But tomorrow, and last week, and even the six weeks before that, the words and ideas had been all mine.

And the people had responded. I sucked in a deep breath. Because God wanted me here. For this. Everything had worked out the way it did, good and bad, for a whole year now to lead to this weekend. Phase two.

I knew Whitney Falls was different when we first got here. Knew this house was my home, where I was supposed to raise my children.

My phone rang, the shrill sound in the quiet house nearly sending me out of my skin. I grabbed it from the dresser.

"Mrs. McClatchy, this is Wayne over at the police department," a deep voice that was growing familiar said when I picked up.

I tried to control my breathing. One thing I had learned while our local police investigated Charlotte's disappearance was that I wouldn't want to have to rely on those guys to help me out of a shallow ditch, let alone solve an actual crime.

"Why hello there, Wayne," I kept my voice even and bright, "I hope your holidays were good."

"Yes, ma'am. My favorite kind, they were quiet."

"What can I help you with?"

"I just wanted to follow up with you about Charlotte," he said. "I'm guessing you haven't heard from her?"

"I wish," I said, almost too soft for him to hear.

"We finally got through to the guy at the TV station in Little Rock, and he's going to have Charlotte as their missing persons story this week," he said. "They want to interview you, and they need a recent picture of her. I was thinking the one on the flyers y'all put up, but they want the original for TV."

"Sure thing." My voice sounded low and agreeable, but inside I was panicking. I could not go on TV in Little Rock, to talk about Charlotte or anything else. I couldn't say that, of course, but I was already planning to talk Martha into going in my place. I could fake being sick at the last minute.

"I will get all their details to you," he said. "Mrs. McClatchy, I'm awful sorry. About the girl taking off and then

Pastor Tim getting hurt. I hope you know the whole town is pulling for you."

I thanked him and hung up, thinking about his last comment. I just needed four deacons to be pulling for me now. And to make sure the vote went my way, I needed a little help.

I pulled the tie out of my hair and fluffed it around my face, pulling on stretchy jeans—surely one of the best things about pregnancy was jeans that weren't binding—and a blue sweater with red cardinals on it.

Grabbing a bag of cookies out of the pantry, I stepped out into the frigid January mountain air, pulling in a deep breath.

We had a plan. It had worked so far, and I was determined to see it through. I stepped carefully down the steps, always mindful of ice these days, and crossed Elias Lane at an angle, ringing Ruthie Tomlinson's doorbell. She took Saturday evenings off from the Pick and Go, and it was time I mended this fence for good and grace.

I pasted on a smile as I listened to the shuffling footsteps on the back side of the thick solid wood door. It didn't falter even when she opened the door and frowned.

"What d'you want?"

If the slight slur in her speech hadn't tipped her hand, the smell of wine on her breath definitely gave her away. I ignored it and spoke through the smile. "I need to speak with you, Ruthie. And I can't consider myself a good Christian and put it off any longer. I owe you an apology."

Those last five words will open a lot of doors. Even people who don't like you—maybe especially people who don't like you—will hear you out if they think you're apologizing.

She stared at me, her eyes flicking to the cookies, then blinked twice before she shrugged and pushed the door open. "I'm not doing anything anyway."

Southern hospitality at its finest, right there. I managed to avoid rolling my eyes as I slipped past her into the house. It smelled musty and stale, with a faint odor of... I wondered if the litterbox needed cleaning just as a gray cat leaped off a table to the right of the door and curled itself around my leg. I flinched and Ruthie frowned again. "She hates everyone. Even me."

I smiled and bit down on the end of my tongue to keep it from getting me in trouble.

"I don't have no engraved invitations," she said after a few beats. "Come on in. I can make some coffee to go with those cookies."

The house was still beautiful—with antique detailing on the door moldings and burnished cherry flat paneled walls with picture frame moldings lining the foyer—but it looked sad. Neglect was all around us, from tufts of cat hair blowing around in the draft from the door shutting, to dust built up on most every flat surface. I wondered if the store wasn't paying her what they had paid Sam for doing the same job.

Or if maybe she just didn't feel up to cleaning when she was off work, and didn't have a housewife the way Sam had to keep the place shining.

Following her to her kitchen, I found them equally plausible. Passing Ruthie and Sam's wedding portrait in the hallway, I pulled in a deep breath and directed my gaze at the carpet, trying to shake out of my head the image of Sam's glassy, dead staring eyes. I had made my peace with Tim's ending, but Sam still haunted my dreams some nights after weeks of thought and rationalization. I might not have known what I was looking for when I went to the motel that day, but I hadn't gone there looking to kill Sam Tomlinson.

Not that I could apologize, exactly. But maybe I could make things right with Ruthie. Or more right, anyway.

She pointed to a scroll back chair at the kitchen table and filled the coffeemaker with water, getting two mugs out of a cabinet and turning on the machine. In thirty seconds, the delicious smell of brewing coffee filled the space. I had mostly avoided caffeine for weeks, but given that tequila was out of the question in my condition, perhaps a couple of sips of coffee would serve as liquid courage today. Once I opened my mouth in here, there was no going back.

I busied myself opening the cookies and stuffing one in my mouth as she filled the cups and delivered them to the table, her quilted pink housecoat dragging the floor under her feather-adorned slippers.

She came back with milk and sugar and put both down in front of me. I added three big spoonfuls of sugar and a splash of milk to my cup and took a quick sip. Ruthie took the chair opposite mine and fixed me with a shrewd stare. "Now then, you said something about an apology?"

"I'm so sorry, Ruthie," I said, widening my eyes for effect. "I'm sorry I misjudged you when we moved here, and that I misunderstood so many things about your situation. I think we could have been friends." I looked down. "I hope maybe we still can. But I have something that's been heavy on my heart, and I feel compelled to share it with you. I cannot keep it from you any longer."

"If you're talking about how your husband ran off with mine, save your breath—and your sympathy. I know. Good riddance. They deserve each other. I hope they get the plague and rot, the both of them."

I sat up straighter in the chair, trying not to recoil too much from the flat, cold darkness in her eyes.

She was mad at them, not at me. Good. A common enemy would make this easier.

"I was so shocked when I found out," I said, laying one hand over my heart. "And I was angry for a while, too. How long have you known?"

"Since last spring—well, I guess I should say I suspected. I found a note your husband left for mine when I was looking for stamps in Sam's desk at the Pick and Go. They were planning to meet, off in the woods at a cave, both of them lying to both of us, I imagine. Wasn't hard to figure out what they meant, thinking how long it had been since Sam so much as looked at me, let alone touched me." She nodded to my belly. "Tim swinging both ways, I guess? Maybe he couldn't help himself, looking at you."

Oh boy. I swallowed hard, real tears leaking into my eyes as she talked. I hadn't counted on actually feeling sorry for her when I came here.

"Ruthie, I am so very sorry," I said.

She waved one hand. "My momma told me Sam would break my heart someday. Thinking about it like this I wonder if she couldn't tell, even way back then. I wish she'd have just said he was queer straight out if that was true. He was always so over the top about noticing women—any pretty woman, particularly if they had a big rack, you know? Called himself a breast man at every cookout we ever went to. He even got in a fight once with a man who took exception to Sam staring at his wife. It took me way too long to figure out on my own that it was all for show. Like from *Hamlet*—instead of protesting too much, Sam acted too much like a letch. To cover up what he was really interested in."

Wow.

"Would you have believed your mother if she'd tried to tell you?" I asked.

Ruthie sipped her coffee and ate two cookies before she answered. "I wouldn't have wanted to believe her. But if I was being honest with myself, I let a whole lot of things go in the name of what I didn't want to believe."

I sipped my coffee. "I know that feeling."

"I was going to get mine done, you see." Ruthie glanced down at her chest. "That's when I started to have to admit to myself it wasn't about the boobs I didn't have or how lousy he always said I was in bed. Because he flat told me I couldn't have the surgery. I begged him, told him I was willing to go through the pain if it would make him want me, look at me the way he looked at other women. He got real quiet and sad and said I shouldn't take that personal, and he left and didn't come home for three days."

She glanced at the sadly horrified expression on my face and grunted.

"You know, I still didn't even want to believe it when I found that note? I stuffed it back where it came from and drove home and nearly scalded my skin off in the shower. Then Sam just up and took off, no boo, bye, kiss my behind, nothing. After I gave him my best years. Even then, I wondered. I don't guess I was completely sure until Tim disappeared too." She twisted her mouth to one side, a gleam in her eye for the first time since I got there. "You've had a good little game running with this story about an accident." She sipped her coffee. "Did Tim have others? Men, I mean? Before you came here?"

"That's one of those things I don't want to admit to myself," I said slowly, pushing away memories that suggested she was right on the money.

"I'm pretty sure Sam had to go to Malvern or Little Rock, and it wasn't that often. We've lived right here in Whitney Falls all our lives. He didn't have any options in town for such things until you all came here." Her voice was flat. Dejected, not angry.

"I'm sorry."

"Better I guess that I don't have a kid to explain this to." She pointed to my belly. "What are you going to do about that?"

"I haven't considered it," I said. "Until this moment. But I'll think of something. I have time."

She put her coffee mug down. "So you know what I know,

and I know what you know. But none of this really needed to be said for us to know it. Why'd you really come here?"

I dropped the cookie I had just picked up. I wasn't sure if the past few months had made her jaded, or if working at the store had given her some kind of newfound power of observation, but to have been so easily manipulated just less than a year ago, Ruthie was smart today.

"I need your help. We have to let people in town know the truth. In particular, I want the deacons to know the truth."

"Why them in particular?"

"Because I've been watching you, and I admire you, Ruthie." I got it out with a straight face and everything. "Like you took over the store, I want to be the new pastor. I know you have pull with the deacons at First Baptist, and I'd like you to use it to help me, because I need a majority vote of the board to be hired."

"Can you do the job?"

"I've been doing it for the past eight weeks. All me."

She nodded, but she didn't say anything.

"I know it's different, and I was raised on the idea that women didn't belong in leadership in the church, but every time I think about the fact that Tim was doing the things he was doing and serving as the spiritual leader of this wonderful town, I feel sick. I can do better than that, I know for certain." I pointed at her. "Look how much better the produce has gotten at the Pick and Go."

"I changed the supplier," she said. "Sam was using this awful trucking company that was twice again slower than the guys I'm using."

I clenched my jaw and nodded. "But I bet a lot of folks didn't think you'd be as good as he was."

"It's two different things, running a store and running a church." She drummed her fingers on the arm of her chair. "But you say you've been writing and giving the sermons for weeks now?"

"I get nothing but compliments."

"Times are changing," she mused, propping her chin on one hand. "Most other places they done changed, if we're telling the truth." She smiled at me. "You've got my vote. And I can pull at least three of the board members, so you just pray on a fourth to show up for an emergency vote and start calling yourself Pastor Mary."

Ruthie tapped her finger on the side of the table. "Will you keep Martha as your secretary?"

"I... I was planning to."

"There's something about that girl." Ruthie shrugged. "I think she thought I suspected her of sleeping with Sam, but I knew better by the time she got here. He only hired her because of her boobs, but it was to fit his cover story, nothing more. She irritates me, though."

"I didn't like her when we first moved here either," I confided. "Lucky for me," so, so very lucky, "Martha is one of the kindest, most forgiving people I've ever known. You ought to get to know her."

"I'm not sure I could face her. I was downright awful to her. The things I said... the things I assumed." Ruthie covered her face. "I don't even know how to apologize. It's sad, how an attractive woman brings out the worst in so many of us, isn't it?"

I just nodded.

"Good that she found herself a fella. She's too pretty to be without a man. And other ladies in the auxiliary will see her as less competition if she's attached, too."

"What makes you say that?" I asked, trying to strike the right balance of informed and interested.

"I saw her climb into his pickup outside the church, just a while ago. I haven't seen him before, though," Ruthie said.

"Kinda long hair, tall, driving a big black pickup. Doesn't she talk about him?"

"Of course. I was just trying to make sure you hadn't gotten the wrong impression," I said. "She knows a lot of people. But that's him."

Big black pickup. I knew the truck.

What in the world was Martha doing with the guy driving it?

# FORTY-EIGHT
## MARTHA

*January—Saturday*

"If you're Arkansas state police, why does your truck have Virginia plates?" I asked, buckling my seatbelt and wondering if this was the dumbest thing I'd ever done. I wasn't exactly raised to trust cops.

"Because this is my personal vehicle and I bought it off a guy in Virginia last year, and I haven't changed them out yet," he said, tugging on his hair. "I'm lazy like that. I don't remember to get my hair cut, either—this isn't a fashion statement."

"What do you want with Pastor Tim?" No sense beating around this particular bush.

"That's complicated." He turned onto Route 5 headed west out of town. Toward the Dreamscape.

"Make it simple."

"I was good friends with Lisa Solomon many years ago," he said. "She called me last spring, said she thought her new boss was into something bad and the local cops here would be no help. I took her to dinner in Malvern one night, we had a nice time, she told me she had seen something on Dateline about the

Dixie Mafia and she thought she had this McClatchy guy figured as one of them, and she would get me evidence if I agreed to put the guy away. She was worried that no police here would be interested in investigating a minister. I told her I didn't care that he was a preacher. If he was breaking the law, as far as I'm concerned God and the United States of America judge criminals, it's just my job to bring them in. She called me on Good Friday and said she needed to see me and it couldn't wait. The next morning, she was dead."

My jaw loosened. "You think Pastor Tim killed Lisa?"

His jaw flexed. "I can't see any other possibility for how she wound up at the bottom of that ravine."

Lord knew I had spent enough time wondering about that myself, but to hear it from a cop made it more... official, somehow.

"What did Lisa think he was doing?" I clenched my hands into fists so tight my nails bit into my palms.

His eyes went to my hands. "What do *you* think he's doing?"

Is doing. Present tense. He didn't think the pastor was dead, and I needed to remember that. I relaxed my fists and closed my fingers over my kneecaps instead. "I asked you first."

"From what Lisa told me, it started with questions about some checks the church started getting, donations that came in the mail. Big checks. Every month. All from companies in Mississippi and Louisiana. Lisa tried to reach out to the donors to see if they wanted to have their names on an event, like the summer ice cream contest or the fall festival, but the listed phone numbers for the companies on the checks were disconnected. When I dug deeper, the addresses were all for warehouses across the gulf coast."

"Shell companies?" My forehead scrunched.

"Very good." He shot me a sideways glance. "You do her job now, have you seen any checks like that?"

"One, on accident." Kind of, anyway. "Pastor Tim insists on handling certain pieces of mail himself, though. I haven't looked at those." Every word of that was true. The checks had come in November and December, but I didn't know what to do with them—putting them in the regular account I had access to seemed like a good way to draw attention, so I left the unopened envelopes on Pastor Tim's desk. I figured once Mary became the pastor, we could figure it out together.

"Could you look at them?"

"Maybe?" I pinched my lips together, choosing words carefully so I didn't reveal too much about myself. "What you were saying a minute ago sounds like something I saw on TV once, too. Lisa called you because she thought he was like... laundering money? Through the church accounts?"

"That is exactly what she thought. And it's interesting, I did a little checking in Texas, Mississippi, and Louisiana. The local police in the last three towns where McClatchy worked got concerned calls about sloppy bookkeeping after the new pastors came in behind him. In every case, McClatchy took over the books and the mail from the church secretary shortly after he arrived, and in every case, he left abruptly."

Interesting, indeed. I chewed the inside of my lip like it would help me digest all that information, but I stayed quiet.

"I've been building a case for months, but it's hard in a town like this. Nobody likes outsiders." He chuckled. "I even resorted to leaving a vague note, tied to some dead flowers on that big expensive SUV McClatchy just bought. Thought it might spook him into doing something stupid."

"That was you?" The words busted out of my face far too loud, with an accusatory edge I needed to walk back right quick. "I mean, that's his wife's car. She's expecting, and you scared her." I paused. "There were two notes, though."

"Lisa told me she planned to leave one for him the night before she died. It's where I got the idea—I figured maybe he'd think she hadn't deserved to die and feel guilty, or get scared she was haunting him and confess." He flashed a smile when I laughed right out loud at the last part. "I wasn't trying to scare the lady, though."

I was so busy being relieved the notes had nothing to do with me I barely heard him. He waited a beat and asked the question he'd probably wanted to lead with.

"I got wrapped up in another case the end of the year and am just now getting back into this—just when I thought I had enough to go by the church and chat with him, McClatchy seems to have left Whitney Falls. What do you know about that?"

"Not much," I lied, but thought it best to steer clear of the accident story since he could catch me in that one just by looking for a report. "Just that he wrote sermons that his wife is giving until he gets back."

I kept my eyes steady on his temple as I spoke, since he was watching the road. He nodded.

"But you don't know where he is or how to get ahold of him?"

"I don't." That was the God's honest truth.

He sighed. "While I'm talking with you... The social services file says the McClatchys took in Lisa's daughter after Lisa passed. I don't want to upset the kid, but I wonder if her mother told her anything about McClatchy—the stuff she suspected. I figure Lisa was a single mom, she might have talked to the kid."

"She doesn't live there anymore." Jesus, this guy was going to trick me into saying something I shouldn't if I didn't get myself out of this truck.

He turned into the parking lot at the Dreamscape and shut off the engine, turning in the seat to face me. "Where did she go?"

"She ran away. I think." Should I tell him that? I mean, the posters were still all over town, so no harm, right?

"Was there a police report filed?"

"Yes. And posters put up. The church even raised five thousand dollars for a reward."

"I need you to think about this very carefully, and tell me the truth: did the girl disappear when McClatchy did? I know you've been helping his wife make it look like he's coming back, and I understand that she's expecting and will lose her home and his salary, so I know why, but this is important."

I gave it a five count, screwing my face up like I was thinking hard. "She did, yeah. That was a very stressful time." I glanced around at the parking lot, the usual scattered crowd of semis mixed with a handful of cars.

A door opened—the door to my old room, actually—and a girl maybe a little older than Charlotte stepped out looking dazed, peering into the sunlight. Same as when I'd seen other girls in my days living at the motel, I wondered how she ended up in a place like this. Like always, I looked away, not worrying over it for long.

Outside the building where Pastor Tim's room still was— we'd faithfully sent the weekly rent since that night—there was a gray sedan that reminded me of his Camry. It was a Mazda, but my heart still skipped a beat or two.

"You're sure? Reasonably?" The cop's voice was tight.

"Pretty sure."

"Jesus," he muttered.

Something in the single word, or maybe the way he said it, or seeing the other girl, or all of it together, made me realize what he was really after. Why he'd brought me here. Why he was asking me about Charlotte. Jesus had nothing to do with the thoughts firing through my head. I turned in the seat.

"Officer, you don't think Pastor Tim—"

"Is trafficking young women through this hellhole motel in

the middle of nowhere because money laundering wasn't enough? I don't just think it, I'm pretty sure of it. What I need to know now is if you're willing to help me prove it."

My stomach rolled as his words landed, and I barely got his door open before I puked into the gravel parking lot.

"I... uh... you okay?" He fumbled in the glovebox and handed me a couple of fast food napkins.

"I don't think I am." I leaned my head on my arm, gulping deep breaths of the cold mountain winter air, memories I hadn't wanted back flying at me faster than I could process them.

Human trafficking. Charlotte. The Dreamscape. Pastor Tim's car outside that room.

I had tried so hard to just let the whiskey erase that day, because the truth was so much worse than what I'd imagined.

I closed my eyes, the whole terrible morning flooding back like a movie I'd forgotten I had seen.

———

*I sat in my car, outside the motel, for a good five minutes after I parked, afraid to get out and go snoop but knowing I'd never be able to live with myself if I didn't. Pastor Tim was hiding something—I was sure of that in a bone-deep way it's hard to put words to.*

*"What if he figures out I was here?" I asked myself right out loud. "What if he does? Am I really going to let Charlotte be hurt because I don't want to be poor again?"*

*I stared into my eyes in the rearview mirror.*

*"No. No, ma'am, I am not."*

*I got out of the car, my eyes falling on the crowbar, just lying there in the back floorboard. My daddy had taught me a lot of questionable things, but one of the more useful ones was never go anywhere near a fight empty-handed. Was I looking for a fight? No. But I knew if Pastor Tim turned up I might find one* anyway, and he was a lot bigger than me. The crowbar could help even the field if it came down to it. I grabbed it and went to the first door before I lost my nerve.

I paused to listen. The TV was on, so I moved to the next room, figuring I could always go back if the key didn't fit any of the others.

I tried the second door with no luck.

The third one, room twenty-three, was the one. The lock turned and I opened the door slowly, not sure what I would find.

It was empty. Quiet. And very lived in.

I didn't want to turn on the lights, so I cracked the faded orange drapes open to let in enough light to see. Takeout containers littered the round, Formica-topped table inside the door, and a half-empty bottle of Scotch sat on the dresser next to the old box TV set. I went to the closet and found men's clothing in different sizes and styles—everything from beach town T-shirts and flannels with cargo shorts and jeans to a suit and a couple of button-down shirts.

I heard a key in the lock just in time to squeeze myself to the back wall of the closet and slide the door shut. Standing in the clothes, I noticed they smelled of two different kinds of cologne—and one of them was the pastor's favorite.

The door opened and my heart jumped into my throat when I heard Pastor Tim's voice, low and tense.

"I know what you said."

What had I said? Oh Lord, he'd seen my car and he was looking for me. The air in the shoebox of a closet felt too thick for my lungs. Was it better to step out of the closet, or stay put?

"I got everything under control," Pastor Tim said. "She didn't know anything, not really."

He was on the phone. I almost laughed when I realized it, but thought better of it. He'd still hear me.

"Yes. The accounts are current. What do you mean?" He paused again.

*"I don't know. I'll look into it. At some point today."*

*I heard the phone hit a table and a drawer open—probably the nightstand, but maybe the dresser, I couldn't tell.*

*Two more drawers opened and closed, and Pastor Tim muttered a swear word under his breath. And not just a regular one, either, but one my granny would've washed my mouth out with soap for using.*

*I concentrated on not breathing too loud and begged God to keep him away from the closet.*

*His footsteps were headed my way when I heard the door rattle in its frame like someone was banging on it.*

"I'm coming," Pastor Tim barked.

*I heard whimpering before the door opened, and once it opened the whimpers were replaced by sobs—deep, guttural sobs —and words I couldn't make out. I leaned closer to the door.*

"What?" *Pastor Tim sounded shocked, and his footsteps stumbled backward.* "How did you—?"

"I— I— I—" *Each attempt had a hitching breath in between, but I would've known Charlotte's voice anywhere. I put one hand on the door, waiting.*

"I can't do i—" *The words exploded out of Charlotte, cutting off so abruptly I was as sure as I could be without looking that the pastor had slammed a hand over the little girl's mouth.*

"Just wait," he said. "Quietly."

*There was a pause before he said,* "Come now."

*I started to open the door and then stopped. Her sobs quieted with every breath.*

*What the heck was happening out there?*

*I cracked the door the slightest bit and pressed my eyeball to it. If he saw it move, or came to get something from the closet, I was fired—at minimum—but I didn't care. She mattered more. She wasn't my sister, yet somehow she was—another scared, crying little girl with no one else to help her.*

*It took a second for my eye to adjust to the light in the room and when it did, I nearly gave myself away with a gasp.*

*Charlotte was wearing a short purple T-shirt and a pair of lacy panties. That's it.*

*Both were torn, her eyes were swollen half shut, and she had a bruise on her left cheek.*

*I stuck my fingers in the opening, preparing to throw the door open and... well, I didn't exactly know, but it involved tackling Pastor Tim and getting Charlotte out of there. We could just drive until we figured out where to go. And then we'd call some kind of real police department who could arrest Pastor Tim and keep him from hurting anyone else.*

*Before I could move, Pastor Tim glanced at his phone and grabbed Charlotte's hand. "Come on," he barked, his voice low and rough.*

*I opened the door, and a scream stuck in my throat. Their backs were to me.*

*He scuttled her out the door without bothering to close it, shoving her and her bulging-at-the-seams school backpack into the back of a black sedan and shutting the door. Pastor Tim watched the car drive away, and I slid the closet door mostly closed, my thoughts racing.*

*Who was that?*

*Where were they taking Charlotte?*

*Where were her clothes?*

*Pastor Tim strode back into the motel room with both hands buried in his hair.*

*He paced the room for a few minutes, muttering things I didn't understand, though I caught a stray word here and there: money, Lisa, dead, and girls among them.*

*Girls.*

*I had seen so many girls come through this place in the weeks I'd lived here. Had heard some truly terrible things through the walls despite my best efforts. Beatings. Rapes. Begging, crying, and plenty of shouting were nightly features at the Dreamscape. Could the pastor be responsible for all that, too?*

*He turned his back to the closet and stood, hunched over his phone.*

*I stared, my breath coming faster.*

*The crowbar was right there by my foot.*

*Whatever he'd done, it was monstrous. One look at Charlotte's bruised, terrified face and skimpy clothes before he pushed her into a car I'd never seen before was enough to know that.*

*It wasn't bad if I saved more people than I hurt.*

*I picked up the bar. Stepped out of the closet.*

*It only took one swing for him to fold onto the carpet like a squished paper doll.*

———

The cop touched my arm with one finger, pulling me back to the cab of his truck twelve weeks later, the faint smell of vomit wafting in the open door. I opened my eyes and sat up, but I still couldn't speak. Holding up one hand, I felt tears burning their way down my cheeks, the sting of anger and regret tracing a hundred paths to my collarbone.

I didn't find Charlotte. By the time I left the motel the car was long gone and I'd looked as far as I dared to go, but I wasn't even sure what model of car I was looking for, and black sedans aren't exactly rare.

Now weeks had passed, Charlotte was gone, Pastor Tim was dead, and I hadn't really been responsible for any of it but there was no way I'd convince this guy that was true.

"I'm sorry," I choked out finally. "I just—I work with him every day, you know? I thought I knew him. I guess you can never be sure."

"It's the first thing I learned from being a cop. It's difficult to ever truly know another person."

"How sure are you about this?" I asked, mopping at my face with my sleeve.

"I'd bet my badge I'm right about this guy. He's the worst kind of scum."

I shook my head, covering my eyes. "I didn't know." And it was true, kind of. I had seen it, but then I had lost it. Maybe on purpose—the memories certainly explained the empty bottle of bourbon. Whatever might be true about that, I had never been so glad Pastor Tim was dead as I was right then.

"He should pay for what he did to Lisa," the cop said. "For what he's doing here."

I couldn't say that he already had.

"Why don't you just raid the motel?"

"I wish it was that easy. It's like what I told you Lisa said about trying to find the people who wrote those checks: operations like this are dozens of layers deep. McClatchy is sort of middle management. But if I can pull him in and make a deal with him, flip him, we might be able to get the bosses who run trafficking syndicates all over the south. Really bring it down and help a lot of victims instead of just a few. I need a better case against McClatchy, and then I'll make him an offer."

Not so much, but there was no way to say that. "I can try to help. How do I get ahold of you?"

He handed me a card, plain white paper stock, with a ten-digit phone number and nothing else: no name, no rank.

I furrowed my brow. "Can I see that badge up close please? What kind of cop are you?"

"The kind who doesn't trust people he just met who work for Dixie Mafia consorts." He handed me the badge. State police. It looked real enough. And I couldn't say his argument was illogical.

"I understand trust issues." I pocketed the card. "Drop me off two blocks down from where you picked me up, I'll walk."

He started the truck. "You sure?"

"It helps clear my head."

He drove back to town and let me out two blocks from Elias Lane, at the opposite end of the street from the church. And from home.

"I look forward to hearing from you," he said as I hopped to the ground.

"I kind of hope you're wrong and I never see you again. No offense."

He laughed as I slammed the door. The truck pulled away and disappeared into the closing darkness, and I shoved my hands in my pockets and started walking.

He wasn't wrong.

But as my stomach turned itself inside out again, I sure hoped I was.

# FORTY-NINE

## MARTHA

*January—Saturday*

By the time I got to the church, I had to run to get to the bathroom before I puked again. Like a good little recovering blackout drunk, I had shoved down the memories of that terrible day any time they'd tried to float up in the weeks since. I thought I was protecting myself. Turned out I was lying to myself to protect someone else.

It had been a year and six days since the McClatchys came to Whitney Falls. I turned off the bathroom light and went to my desk, sitting heavily in the chair in the dark and remembering their first Sunday. The young, handsome pastor and his gorgeous, angel-voiced wife were so different from the balding little man with three front silver teeth who'd led this congregation since right after World War Two. I wanted to be there every Sunday in a new way that had very little to do with Jesus. I'd wanted to be close to the McClatchys, to see inside their perfect house. To know what it was like to be them.

But then I'd gotten to know them—or so I thought. I leaned one elbow on the desk and cradled my head in that hand. The thing about remembering a blackout is that once the pieces start to fall into place, you can't keep them out. At least, I had never been able to. A fleeting fragment here and there could skate by, maybe, but once I had a chunk of my missing time, it was always only a matter of minutes—maybe hours—before I had it all.

I had hit Pastor Tim that day, and looked all around the rest of the room trying to find some kind of evidence that would prove him guilty of abusing Charlotte, or selling her, maybe—or any clue about who was driving the black sedan he'd shoved her into. The sedan. My thoughts kept returning to it, and it took a few minutes for me to catch up to why.

Mary had told me that Charlotte was in the motel room with Pastor Tim and Sam later, after she got there. She had cried and said Charlotte was what broke her; the reason she'd killed the men. I suppose I couldn't swear the black sedan hadn't brought Charlotte back after I left. I wasn't sure how likely that could be, but I didn't want to consider an alternative right then, either. My brain was still busy vomiting memories, and my stomach was trying to vomit lunch as a result.

Regaining lost time is often disorienting—it feels like the events are happening again in real time, whether they were twelve weeks or twenty years ago. I could feel Pastor Tim's breath on my hand, sitting there in the office weeks later. I knew I'd checked on him before I left—he was still breathing, and there was no blood. I didn't kill anyone.

I had decided I needed to know more about what was happening. I had to find Charlotte and get her to talk to me. It was early, nobody had seen me. I'd hurried out, leaving the damn crowbar because I was already thinking about what was next instead of worrying about the here and now—there and then. Whatever. When I realized I wasn't going to find that black sedan, I went to my apartment, burned the clothes I'd had on at the motel just in case, and put on a blue skirt and a button-down blouse for church before I went into the house.

I could see it all so clearly, sitting there in the office.

———

*I opened the back door and poked my head inside.*

*"Mary?" I called, softly at first.*

*I crept through the kitchen.*

*"Mary?"*

*No answer.*

*In bare feet, I went to the living room. It was quiet, a blanket draped over the arm of the sofa and a coaster on the end table.*

*I checked the dining room and the pastor's study, putting the motel room key back in his desk where I'd found it.*

*Upstairs, I looked in the master bedroom first. The bed was made, corners pulled so tight and smooth you could bounce a quarter off the duvet. The bathroom and closet were empty.*

*Mary wasn't home. I knew Tim wasn't home, and neither was Charlotte.*

*And I was on a mission, after what I'd seen at the motel. I wanted evidence that I was right, and I thought I might know where to find it because I remembered what Daddy and his friends had done to me. Back in Granny's trailer, two nights after she died, Daddy had come into my room drunk or high or both, plopped onto the floor next to my mattress, and handed me pictures. There were six in all, of kids doing things no kid should ever do. He made me look closely at every one, and asked me what I thought. I said it was weird. He told me I had to look at them for five minutes before I went to sleep. Then five became ten, and ten became twenty, and a few weeks later when he had explained it all in bits and pieces and I could answer every question about what was happening, he said it was time for me to graduate from looking to doing.*

*I put one hand on the knob on Charlotte's door and paused, pulling in a deep breath before I opened the door and stepped inside.*

*Her room was entirely too neat for a girl her age—not a single garment was on the floor or draped over a chair, not a book or paper was out of place. Her bed was made, too, almost as neatly as Mary's, lilac flowers on the white bedspread that matched the curtains and the walls.*

*I crossed to the nightstand in five long strides, yanking the drawer out before I could lose my nerve. I'd missed something that should have been obvious to me of all people—there were so many clues. Charlotte's descent into depression, her volatile outbursts, and her hair. That was the first thing I should've really paid attention to. Why does a twelve-year-old girl who's just lost her mother hack her gorgeous hair down to her scalp?*

*Because she's trying to make herself ugly. Because she's been taken in by a monster. She'd even said it that day: "I don't need to be pretty." But I didn't get it.*

*A single beam of sunlight shone through the window over Charlotte's nightstand, right onto the photos. They were just there, sitting on top of a red leather-bound Bible. Not even hidden.*

*I pulled them out and made myself look at what she'd had to endure here.*

*Color photos of girls her age or a bit older, doing shocking, sometimes violent things with a variety of clearly grown men. Peering closer at the backgrounds, I realized every one had been taken at the Dreamscape Motel.*

*When I recognized Mr. Zip Code from the night I moved my things out of the motel and realized the thumping on the bathroom wall after he'd collapsed had probably been a plea for help from whoever was trapped in there, I tried to get to the trash bin by the desk but didn't make it—I puked all over Charlotte's white, flowered bedspread, the retching deafening in the silent house.*

*Catching my breath and wiping my lips with the back of one hand, I turned the photos over and found names and definitions, all in small, neat cursive.*

*That handwriting, I knew. I stared at it until tears blurred my vision, baffled by how similar Charlotte's situation here, in this gorgeous, perfect home, was to the things I'd endured in my dirty, decrepit childhood trailer park.*

*Was there some kind of playbook for this brand of evil?*

*Right there under my nose, they had—what did the TV news people say?—groomed, that was it, they had groomed that girl for horrible things. And I didn't see it.*

*Because they were good at hiding it?*

*Or because I liked being in the perfect pastor and his perfect wife's inner circle, even after I started to suspect it wasn't quite so perfect?*

*I barely made it to the toilet before I started retching again, but burning yellow acid was all that was left to come up.*

*They were monsters, both of them. But had I helped?*

*I shoved the photos into the pocket on my skirt and looked around the room, wondering if there was more evidence.*

*"Hello?" The word drifted up the stairs, Mary's voice like bells. "Charlotte? Are you up, sweetie?"*

*She couldn't see this. Not until I had time to figure out what to do here. I snatched a sweater from the closet, my brow furrowing at a line of empty hangers, and tossed it over the puddle of vomit on the comforter.*

*"No Mary, it's me," I called back, trying to keep the desperation out of my voice. If she would just stay downstairs, I could buy time.*

*I hurried out of Charlotte's room and slammed the door behind me, smoothing my skirt and fixing a smile on my face before I bounced down the stairs. "Morning. Pastor Tim and Charlotte aren't here."*

Mary tipped her head to one side and blinked, studying my face.

"Are you feeling okay, Martha?" she asked, her flawless forehead wrinkling as she laid the back of one cool hand on my face.

"I'm actually not feeling the best this morning." I took a step backward. "Sorry for coming over here, I shouldn't make you sick. I just thought maybe you had some medicine I could borrow. I don't want to miss church."

"We only have the 11 a.m. today, remember?" she asked. "It's the remembrance service."

I smacked my forehead, waving a hand over my outfit. "I forgot all about that. Pretty silly when I'm the one who types the bulletin." I tried to keep my voice normal, but it seemed like the more effort I used, the less normal it got. Mary's right eyebrow went up. "I know it's early, but why don't you let me make you some soup."

"I really don't want to make you sick."

I turned for the door and Mary laughed. "I was a nursing student, I have a cast-iron immune system. Go on in and lie down on the couch, and I'll get you some soup."

"Oh, please don't go to any trouble, I'm not hungry." I had to get out of there, but I couldn't let her see that something was bothering me.

"Which is why you need to eat. Your body needs nutrition to fight germs." She shoved my shoulder gently. "Go on now."

I went to the couch. I heard her go up the stairs. Doors opened and closed, and she came down with a pillow and a clean white blanket.

"I'll get your soup." She handed me the TV remote and disappeared, returning with soup and hot tea. I drank about half of both before I passed out.

I woke up for just a moment in Pastor Tim's office—I could see his desk sideways from the couch, bleary and blurred, and my head felt like it was splitting open over and over again, axe blows *coming from every side. I gripped my hair and screamed, and behind me liquid stopped pouring.*

*"Oh no you don't," Mary's voice was clear, with a menacing edge I had never heard from her. Something pinched my arm.*

*And then the phone was ringing.*

*I didn't fall off the wagon with a fifth of bourbon.*

*Mary drugged me.*

---

And now here I was, sitting at my desk nearly three months later, trying to figure out how to right all the wrongs I'd been party to since then. I went to Pastor Tim's office and found the green checkbook I'd seen in his drawer, looking closer this time to confirm what I already knew: that this First Baptist account wasn't at Farmers National, but a bank in Little Rock.

I looked out the window at the house across the street, sliding the checkbook into my back pocket.

Mary's house was pitch dark, and had been empty for a while, because the light over the cooktop wasn't even giving the kitchen doorway its usual faint glow. Going to the bigger window near my desk, I saw that the Grand Wagoneer was gone. Another of her "wind down drives," I bet. She'd told me they helped her sleep better, but another wave of nausea from my gut said that had been another lie.

She'd gone upstairs before she made my food that day. I had never seen anything stronger than an Advil in the McClatchy house, but somewhere, Mary had a stash of sedatives.

Sedatives she was good at dosing women with. I mean, she had studied nursing.

That cop, he'd said he needed something that would hold up in court.

I locked up the church and crossed Elias Lane, the perfect

Victorian at number eighteen downright ominous in the full moon's glow.

Evil seemed to pulse in the air around the grand old house, and the moon was so bright the church cast a long shadow, just like that first Friday. The steeple lanced across the porch and into the front door.

My friend Mary McClatchy was nobody's friend at all. Her handwriting on the back of those unspeakable photos she'd left in a child's bedroom—a child she'd been revered as a saint by the town for taking in, mind you—combined with the knowledge that she not only knew how to drug people, she'd done it to me, told me everything I needed to know about how deep she was into this disgusting scheme.

But if she was up to her neck in trafficking these kids, why had she killed Tim? And where did Sam fit into any of it?

My head throbbed, an unfamiliar voice floating through my thoughts: *"I really have to talk to Sam."*

I sighed, my chin dropping to my chest as I unlatched the McClatchys' front gate. Way back before Good Friday, I'd dismissed the aggravated blond delivery guy who wouldn't leave anything at the Pick and Go without seeing Sam as a nut job and gone on about my day. But standing outside the biggest house on Elias Lane months later, I realized the only place in Whitney Falls that really big trucks went on a regular basis was to the Pick and Go.

Sam's sudden schedule change to early arrivals for deliveries after the McClatchys came to town wasn't because the stock boy was slow. He was helping the McClatchys use the trucks and the store to trade in humans. Humans who were being abused.

"Monsters," I said it right out loud, my face turned up to the sky, my empty, quivering stomach twisting. Mary had murdered her husband and his... I wasn't sure I could believe her about anything right then, but it would make sense that they got Sam's access to the big trucks by way of some flirting, and somehow they must have figured out Sam was more interested in Pastor Tim than in Mary. I was pretty convinced from what I'd seen and heard at the VFW hall in Malvern that day in September that Pastor Tim downright hated Mary, so I could see where he would have taken up with someone else. Even Sam.

Had she really been so mad that they were messing around that she'd killed her own partners in crime?

Hell hath no fury, they said.

I heard the hogs screeching in my head, but I didn't regret helping rid this town of that kind of evil. Helping Mary hide their bodies was only the first thing I'd done, though.

I had also helped her craft an elaborate lie that was just hours away from letting her take over the church, and the town along with it.

I couldn't allow that. Not now.

I had helped Mary get exactly what she wanted. I was her best friend. She trusted me.

I could bring her down.

# FIFTY
MARTHA

*January—Saturday*

My granny cleaned houses for rich people when she was young, to make money to feed my daddy and pay for the trailer after her husband left her. She always told me that rich people were a strange bunch, hiding secrets in plain sight and trusting other folks entirely too much.

Standing in Mary McClatchy's beautiful master bathroom, the house empty and quiet, I had to agree.

Right under the sink, I'd found a bottle of peroxide, a box of unused ovulation test sticks, and a large wood box with a latch on the side that had the kind of teeny padlock people put on diaries.

In Mary's nightstand drawer, I found the key.

I opened the box and let my eyes fall shut.

Mary had a selection of drugs that would've impressed my daddy: two gallon-sized Ziploc bags of pills: one full of red and blue capsules and one of small white tablets stamped with "OC" on one side and "15" on the other. Underneath, I found several vials of something labeled "Versed" and a couple dozen hypodermic needles. And under that, a stack of twelve copies of dosing instructions by body weight.

Evil had rooted itself in Whitney Falls, wearing beautiful faces and hiding behind the cross. From a criminal point of view it was brilliant: Whitney Falls was about as far as you could get off the beaten path, and Mary and Tim were the perfect couple —I had grown up in the low rent fringe of the Dixie Mafia and I never would have so much as suspected them of knowing what that was, let alone being part of it.

I fished the cop's phone number out of my pocket and went to Mary's bed, perching on the edge of her snow-white duvet as I dialed.

All those young girls I'd seen at the Dreamscape—girls younger than me, younger than my sister had been when she'd run in after Daddy screamed that night because I'd stabbed him. Before he'd grabbed the pistol on his nightstand and fired at me, but hit her right square in the head. Those girls were victims.

I was not—not anymore.

"Hello?" The cop's voice was thick with sleep.

"Hi there, this is Martha... I uh... well, I'm the secretary at First Baptist in Whitney Falls." I shook my head, frustrated at my inability to get the words out.

"Sure, Martha, I got you." He woke up right quick. "What can I do for you?"

"I found some stuff," I said. "Things you might need for what you're doing. I have to help you."

"Do you know where I can find Tim McClatchy?"

"I do not." Not exactly a lie. I sucked in a deep breath. "But what you said, about the motel—you were right. Except it's not just Pastor Tim who's doing it, it's his wife too—and I do know where you can find her. I have drugs she's been using to sedate the girls at the motel, and I have some pictures I found, that she gave Lisa's daughter. Bad pictures."

"What kind of bad?"

"You should just see for yourself. I can give them to you. The handwriting on the back is Mary's."

I heard water running and drawers closing in the background. "Where are you?" he asked. "I'll come to you."

"No. Not tonight. I need you to come to the church tomorrow morning, about 11:40. This has to happen in front of the congregation. Can you arrest her?"

"Very possibly. What kind of drugs did you find and how much?"

"Sedatives and pain meds, I think. I know the white pills in this big bag are Oxy, they even have the stamp. I think she's keeping the girls asleep during the day, and I bet she's got most or all of them hooked on Oxy, and she's their supplier so they do what she says. Probably paying off that sleaze ball who works the desk at night to keep an eye on them, too. Maybe even to dose them with this stuff when she can't get out there? I wonder if you'd find more at the motel?"

"I have no doubt there's Oxycodone in abundance at that place," he said. "How many pills would you guess you have there?"

"Hundreds," I said. "A thousand maybe? It's a really big bag full."

"And you found this in McClatchy's home?"

"I did."

He blew out a slow breath. "Can you put it back where you got it without her realizing you saw it?"

"I can."

"Do that, then."

I opened the box and looked at the papers in the bottom again. "There are several copies here of a little sheet that says how much to give people based on their weight." I clapped one hand over my mouth, looking at the letters and numbers on the little slips as he muttered a string of cuss words that would've made my daddy blush.

"Oh my God," I whispered. "I saw an order form."

"For what?" Boards creaked like he was pacing.

"The night we moved my stuff to the McClatchys' garage apartment, I saw a piece of paper on the dresser in a room near mine at the Dreamscape. I'd seen a teenage girl around there a few times, but she always looked a bit out of it and she never spoke to anyone. Anyway, that night this big dude, he OD'd and Mary and me saw him and called an ambulance. The fire department will have a record of that, right?"

"They should, yep. Who was he?"

"No idea, but maybe they have that too. The important thing I saw was the paper—we went into the room the big guy came out of, and I saw this paper on the dresser. I thought it was a receipt, I remember because I wondered who was staying at the Dreamscape who could afford a two-hundred-dollar shirt."

"Now you don't think it was a shirt?" the cop's voice was tense.

"It was an order form. I'd bet my car, which is basically all I own, on that. He paid two hundred dollars for two hours with a medium, petite girl." I paused. "I wonder... did he overdose on something he brought in, or did the girl dose him with a hypodermic full of this Versed stuff, like Mary did me?"

Not that it really mattered, except I kind of hoped the girl had gotten him just for the element of justice.

"Wait. Mrs. McClatchy drugged you?" His voice went up a full octave. "You really shouldn't stay there."

"She has no reason to think she needs to do it again, and she's not here right now." I shut the box holding the drugs and laid it next to me on the bed. "Is what I just told you enough for you to be able to arrest her?"

"As long as the pills are there when I search the house, I can pick her up on the drug charge and get warrants to keep digging."

"Come in the front doors of the church tomorrow morning with your badge out. Be loud. I'll meet you out front with the photos and tell you where to find the drugs. I didn't touch the vials of the sedative she gives as shots, you should be able to get prints from the glass."

"I'll be there by 11:30," he said. "Please take care of yourself tonight."

I hung up the phone and went back to Mary's bathroom, sitting down on the rolled edge of the huge claw-foot tub and staring at the box until I realized she could walk in the door any second and find me just hanging out in there like an idiot.

Dropping a handful of the capsules in my pocket, I took one of the papers and folded it, then put everything back the way I'd found it and went to the kitchen to start dinner.

I wasn't sure I'd need them, because I didn't really have a whole plan yet, but if the first rule of battle is to know your enemy, the second is to match their weapons.

I had fourteen hours to stop Mary from taking over the church, and hand that cop enough evidence to not just lock her up, but hopefully get the higher ups that would really put a dent in this syndicate's reach, and save who knew how many more kids.

I could do math in my head that most people needed a computer to figure out. I had survived a childhood in hell, homelessness, alcoholism, near starvation, and creepy bosses, and I wasn't even twenty yet.

Surely I could manage to find an answer to this problem before time ran out.

# FIFTY-ONE
## MARY

*January—Sunday*

"And all God's people said together," I said, my head bowed and my eyes closed, a smile touching my face at the chorus of "Amen."

Everything was going just as I'd rehearsed it in my head.

I opened my eyes and raised my head, setting my lips in a solemn line and nodding to Ruthie.

"Church family, before we all go home to the football game today, I need to tell you something that's weighing heavy on my heart." I swallowed hard and dug my nails into my palm, until tears sprang to my eyes. On cue. Every time.

Gasps and murmurs swept the sanctuary, a couple of "the baby"s floating loud enough for me to hear.

Perfect.

"Ruthie, could you join me up here, please?"

I waited for her to mount the stairs. She wore a simple black suit with black gloves and a black hat. I couldn't have chosen her outfit more perfectly myself.

A woman in mourning will get sympathy every time, and

death isn't the only thing we mourn. I stepped down from the pulpit to the lower stage and took Ruthie's hand. It was cold through her glove.

"Church family, I can't tell you how much I appreciate in my heart all of you waiting for Pastor Tim to recover from his accident." They all nodded, murmuring about how kind they thought I'd been—because being kind makes people like you. I'd learned a lot of ways to make people like me, growing from a scared little girl into a full-fledged student of human interactions. I studied people around me and figured out what they needed, and then became that for them. Trophy wife? Done. Out-of-practice nurse and best friend? Check. Local crime boss with a squeamish husband? I aced that. First Baptist's first female pastor? On deck.

Because these people all loved me.

I stood on the stage through a dramatic pause and soaked up the concern like flowers soak up sun and water. It fed me.

"But I'm afraid I have to tell you today that Pastor Tim has left Whitney Falls, and he's not coming back." A roar rippled through the crowd, quickly from one side to the other, six hundred pairs of wide eyes on me.

I laid one hand on my belly.

"As much as it pains me—physically and emotionally—to share this with anyone, I know I owe it to y'all." I paused for a deep breath, and more than half the crowd took one, too, leaning forward as a unit in their seats. "Ruthie and I discovered yesterday that Pastor Tim and her husband Sam have been carrying on an illicit affair. I know we have all prayed for Sam's safe return home, but it seems he was establishing a home in another state, and Tim left Whitney Falls—left our baby, and left me—yesterday to join Sam and begin a new life."

"A life of sin!" a deep voice called from the back.

That set off a chorus of jeers and shouted epithets. I stayed quiet, casting my eyes down and rubbing my swollen middle.

Sliding my eyes to one side, I watched Ruthie.

This was the thing that fed her. Their hatred, their anger—her eyes jumped around the sanctuary as they worked each other up, a slow smile spreading across her face.

Good to know.

I gave them two full minutes before I raised my free hand. "I understand the feelings of anger and betrayal, but we must not lose sight of the word and work of God, especially in trying times. It is for him to judge, not for us. Our mission is to move forward in love and kindness as the wonderful church family we are. To lead First Baptist to be the best little church in the south. And that is what we need to discuss today, now that it's clear Pastor Tim has moved on from us." I patted my belly on "us."

The entire room erupted into chaos. Several men roared "That's outrageous!" loud enough to rattle the stained glass in the windows. Of those, about half of their wives scrunched up their faces and joined in the complaints, and about half of them thwacked their men with a pocketbook or a backhand and shot Ruthie a thumbs up.

Problem with that was, the deacons were all men.

"Brothers and sisters, ladies and gentlemen." Ruthie turned loose of my hand and raised both of hers. "I believe the Lord Jesus on high sent Mary to this church, to our town, to conceive and raise this miracle child she's carrying. I believe her baby will be a boy, and I believe he will have the holy spirit within his heart from his first breath. Her child is special. She is special. And God wants her here."

"It's... no one does this, Ruthie," a man called from the back, the anger gone from his voice.

"Sure they do. Methodists do this. Episcopalians, too," someone else said, the other denominations coming out like slurs.

"And the Lord has not smited any of them yet," Ruthie said.

"Aren't all y'all happier with the Pick and Go's organization now? The produce? The cleanliness?"

Nods and murmurs.

"Ladies, how many of you have commented about Mary's work with the auxiliary—her teachings about the scripture, her knowledge of the Bible, her ability to listen to and counsel you?"

I watched almost every woman nod. "She knows more about the Bible than my daddy did, and if you knew my father, you know that's saying something," a tall woman in the back said.

"Deacons, I move for discussion and vote," Ruthie cried. "I nominate Mary McClatchy to be the next pastor of this church body."

I closed my eyes and sat in the moment.

Pastor Mary. It was happening. I was about to reach the top of a very long hill.

"This isn't a board meeting," one of the deacons called.

My eyes snapped open.

Ruthie jabbed one finger in the air. "Five out of seven, you have a quorum here," she said, looking at each of them in turn and poking me to follow suit. "Who wants to tell her no, gentlemen?"

I went down the line again, looking each man in the eyes.

"We have always kind of done our own thing out here," someone said.

"The conference forgets about us when it's time to pass out money. I say we forget them and their ban this morning."

A slow round of applause started on the second "aye" vote. By the fifth, the whole room was in an uproar. "Motion carries," Ruthie cried, turning to me. "Welcome to First Baptist, Pastor Mary."

"Is she even ordained?" someone hollered from the middle of the crowd that was now pressing forward to try to congratulate me.

"I can do that on the computer at the library," Ruthie said into my ear before she leaned into the crowd and hollered, "Yes, sir!"

I soaked it in for almost an hour before people started talking about chickens needing to go in to roast and football games that were approaching halftime.

By then my back was killing me, spasms coming every few minutes that made me want to hit my knees. I needed a heating pad and a handful of Tylenol.

Ruthie ushered me home, where I hugged her on the porch and thanked her for her faith and her friendship. She beamed, rubbing my stomach like a genie might pop out.

"I meant what I said. This child is special. He makes you special."

Or maybe I made him special. But I wasn't about to say that to her or anybody else. And I wanted a daughter, anyway.

I thanked her again and let myself inside, kicking my shoes into the basket by the door and waddling to the kitchen. I poured a big glass of water and took four Tylenol before I retrieved the heating pad from the front closet and plugged it in next to the sofa, lying down and reaching for the TV wand.

I should go out to the Dreamscape Motel and check on my girls—the meds from last night would wear entirely off before dinnertime, and I had been so careful to keep them at least moderately loopy pretty much around the clock.

The drugs had been my idea, a way to both keep girls from running and make them more compliant, no matter how wicked or violent a given customer's proclivities. The operation chief liked the results so much he'd given us twice as many girls in just a few months' time.

That, I was pretty sure, was where we'd started to lose Tim.

I shook my head and turned to lay on my side like the doctor had told me. I didn't need to think about that now. I needed these cramps to stop so I could go to the motel and handle my business—business I needed this town, and this job, to be able to continue.

The pain dulled, but the spasms came faster, and the ligament stretching pain I'd battled in my hips for the past three weeks decided to join in the fun.

"How anyone thinks men are the stronger sex when women have to endure all this to be mothers, I will never comprehend," I said as a swift kick to the ribs from my little miracle stole my breath. "Four more weeks, bitsy," I said, patting what I thought was a tiny bottom through my belly. "Four more weeks."

I was through four episodes of *Friends* and was singing along with the theme song for a fifth when it occurred to me that I hadn't seen Martha since yesterday afternoon.

# FIFTY-TWO

## MARTHA

*January—Sunday*

"You were incredible this morning, Pastor," I said, striding into the living room in my favorite Sunday dress, grinning like I'd won the lottery though my gut was twisting in revulsion and worry—while the plan I'd spent weeks carefully crafting for Mary had gone off without a hitch, the monkey wrench I'd engineered for it the night before hadn't.

I paused when I saw Mary lying on the couch watching TV. Even lately, with the baby due in just four weeks, it was hard to get her to rest in the middle of the day, and coming off the high of getting everything she'd—we'd—been working for? Something was off.

She smiled, tipping her head to one side and wriggling her legs with a grimace. "I didn't even see you, I was just thinking that."

"You think I would have missed it?" I shook my head. "Ruthie was a shock to me, but she was pitch perfect, and you were the absolute most incredible mix of demure and strong I could have imagined. You had the whole congregation eating out of your hand." I plopped into a chair. "I couldn't even get to you to hug you before Ruthie hustled you out though, so I stayed to get everyone on their way and lock up." And fume about the fact that the cop hadn't shown up. Not that I could tell Mary that.

She smiled again. "Thank you."

"What's all this?" I waved my hand at her. "You feeling okay?"

"I think I have finally found my limit." Mary laughed. "Overdid it. My back hurts and my hips are doing the shock thing that caused the Braxton Hicks contractions before."

"Did you take something?" I asked.

"Tylenol," Mary pointed one index finger up and waved it in a circle. "Barely touching it."

"I'm sorry, friend. Can I bring you some of that tea you like?"

"What would I do without you?"

I patted her foot and went to the kitchen, pulling one of the red and blue capsules from upstairs out of my pocket. After some reading on sedatives, I figured she'd probably put this one in my tea or my soup that awful day. If it could steal my memories as effectively as bourbon, maybe it could loosen her lips the same way, too.

I sprinkled about half the flakes into the tea, leery though everything I'd read said a full capsule wouldn't hurt the baby. Even massively pregnant, Mary wasn't a big person, and almost never took anything stronger than a vitamin. The effect I wanted shouldn't take much.

Carrying the tea back to her, I helped her sit up enough to drink it, put the cup in her hands, and returned to my chair to wait, glancing at the antique tape recorder on the bookcase. Nobody would notice that the red record button was pressed down slightly because it was running—I'd found a six-hour tape in the cabinet and turned it on after she left for church—I figured having a recording of whatever was going to happen in this house today couldn't be bad for me, and then when the cop didn't show I decided to try to coax a confession out of Mary myself instead of waiting for him.

"You know something I realized the other day?" I asked after a whole episode of her sitcom had run. "I don't know your maiden name. How is it possible that we've been friends all this time and I don't know that?"

"Dayton." She slurred it just a little, waving one hand. But it was enough.

Showtime.

"Like the town?"

"Silly, isn't it?" She turned her head. "Why do you care?"

"You're my boss lady now," I said. "It may come up on a form for something at work when you're not around to ask. Or on paperwork for... you know... a divorce."

"Divorce." She blew a raspberry. "He's dead! Dead and gone, without a trace." She dissolved into a fit of giggles.

Full steam ahead.

"You killed him good," I said.

"Him and his boyfriend." She put a hand to her throat and made gagging sounds. "Sam."

"What about Lisa?" I figured that was worth putting a toe in.

Mary shook her head, mussing her hair on the pillow. "Lisa knew about Tim. She opened a check, a big check from Mississippi she wasn't supposed to see. Tim didn't ever mind the money, not even washing it. Stupid Lisa, she shouldn't have ever said anything—she was so big on keeping the church business to the church, she had to go be nosy about things that weren't her business. Tim wanted to pay her to help us out, but then Sam said she wouldn't take money, and he was right. She told Tim no. Said we better stop using her church—her church!—for illegal money, and so he told her to meet him in the woods and..." Mary put one hand up and scrunched her fingers in and out. "Bye bye. And then you were the secretary. You're so much better, Martha. We trust you. I trust you, that's what it is. Me. This is all mine now. And the baby's. Thanks to you."

Her eyes started to close.

"What about the Dreamscape, Mary?" I asked. "I've seen the girls there. Is that all yours, too?"

"Tim didn't have the stomach," she muttered. "Moving up from laundering, finally getting into real money instead of piddly cuts, and he couldn't do it. Wanted to let them all go, starting with Charlotte. Charlotte, who was the only one we didn't have to buy. We just had to train her and I was getting so close. I had her..." Mary looked around and laid one finger across her lips. "I was dosing her food with Oxy, and she was finally getting hooked. Doing anything I asked her as long as I gave her the meds."

I had to lock my jaw to keep my mouth shut. Charlotte hadn't been starving herself out of some sort of wicked stubbornness. No, she was trying to avoid the demons she'd told me her father had battled—but Mary wore her down. My chest felt heavy, sorrow settling there as I fully realized that Charlotte hadn't been sure she could trust me. She'd kept all this to herself because she thought I might be helping the McClatchys with more than church paperwork.

Mary pounded one fist on the sofa cushion. "Have to do every dang thing I want done right. All by myself. More money. More security. For my baby and me."

I folded my hands in my lap to keep them from flying up to cover my face, not that I thought she would've noticed. Breathe. Don't shout. "Mary, where is Charlotte?"

"Tim thought he was so smart," Mary sneered, her speech more halting, her eyelids heavy. "Taking her out of a customer's room and sending her to the police station in Little Rock. I didn't get there in time to stop it, but I got a cop in

Little Rock to take a bribe to give her back. Had to trade her, she couldn't come here, not after all that. She had to go be taught better."

I couldn't stand to listen to any more. If that wasn't enough, the cop was on his own.

I blew out a breath and sagged back into the chair. Mary's eyes rolled back in her head and she snored. I crept to the kitchen and picked up the phone, fishing the cop's card out of my pocket again.

Voicemail.

"This is your pickup friend from the hardware shop," I said, keeping my voice low. "I missed you this morning, but I do have what you wanted—I even got a confession on tape—and Mary is asleep. Come to number eighteen Elias Lane and get it."

I wasn't sure how long I'd been staring out the window, not sure what to do next, when Mary let out a scream that could've turned cream into yogurt.

Heart pounding, I raced back to the living room, where I found her writhing on the white couch, clawing at her belly and howling. I stepped closer and saw that the couch was soaked amber and pink under her hips, her pants dripping.

"Help me," she screamed. "It's going to break me in half."

"Your water broke." I put my hands to my head. What did people do in movies? "Boil water. I'll boil water. Get towels. I can do that."

She bolted upright, her breath coming ragged. "I have to push," she said.

"No, no, wait," I said. "You're still dressed, and I have to get the towels and the water."

"Now!" she screamed.

I jumped, turning to the cabinet where she kept art supplies and getting the sewing scissors. It took me a minute to cut her sweatpants off, but I got them, and then sliced horizontally through her underwear.

"Dear God, that's a head," I dropped the scissors. "I'm supposed to boil water."

"I have to push!" Mary grabbed her legs behind her thighs and roared, the baby's whole forehead coming out before part of it retracted when she sagged back into the sofa's arm panting a minute later.

"This is amazing," I breathed. "You can do this, Mary. Come on. Push."

"It hurts so much, Martha," she whined.

"The baby needs you to be strong now." I patted her knee and waited for her to look at me. "Come on, Momma. You got this."

She pulled herself back up and screamed her way through another one.

"I see his eyes," I yelped. "They're not open, but he has two!" I didn't know why I felt so sure that Ruthie was right about the baby being a boy, maybe she'd just sounded that confident, but I was all in until I could see different because I didn't feel right saying "it."

And so it went, for thirty-three minutes, until Mary McClatchy pushed her firstborn son out into the world on a ruined white designer sofa in her living room.

"Why isn't he crying?" she panted, pushing out the placenta and collapsing backward, exhausted and now bleeding all over the couch.

"How the heck should I know?" I could barely hear anything over the pounding of my own heart. The baby was blue and seemed to be getting bluer, and I dang sure wasn't a doctor.

"Run your finger inside his mouth," Mary said. "Scoop out the goop, then turn him over and smack his bottom. I've been watching reality shows about birth for half my life. Now, Martha!"

Blinking back tears, I did as she said. He was so cold.

"Come on, little man," I muttered through gritted teeth. "You can't do this."

It took three smacks—two on the butt and one on the back, before he filled his lungs and screwed up his little face and howled. Like magic, he turned from blue to pink all over, screaming a high pitched, raspy wail that made me want to poke my eardrums with a nail.

"My baby," Mary sobbed, holding out her arms.

"Here." I laid him on her chest and covered them both with a thick throw blanket, looking down and getting worried about how much blood I saw on the couch. "I'll get towels and blankets and boil water. I'll be right back."

I ran and gathered everything, put the pasta pot on to boil, and ran back to find Mary counting fingers and toes.

"He's perfect."

"Does he have a name?"

"David." She whispered it with a kind of reverence I had never heard, stroking his tiny forehead with one finger.

"Strong. I love it." I leaned over them. "Hello, David."

She coughed, and blood gushed onto the sofa.

"Mary!" Both hands flew to my face.

"What?" Her eyes looked glassy, one arm going limp.

"I think you're losing too much blood," I said. "I'm going to call the rescue now."

I ran back to the phone and dialed the fire department. The only ambulance was on a run, but they told me to press on her abdomen right near her belly button and put towels between her legs until they could get there.

By then the water was at a full boil, so I turned it off and dipped the kitchen shears in it, holding the blades under to sterilize them good.

Grabbing two of Mary's little pink carrot bag clamps from the drawer, I clipped and cut the umbilical cord and rubbed Baby David, who was warming up, down with towels before I wrapped him in two blankets and laid him on the rug while I turned to Mary. "They're coming, but they told me to apply pressure until they get here."

I leaned both hands on her belly, holding even though she whined. The blood flow slowed. "It's working."

"You're hurting me."

"I'm helping you." I couldn't believe I was, truly—she was the worst kind of monster and I knew it, but she'd been right that morning when she said judgement is reserved for God. And, you know, maybe the courts. I refused to be responsible for another corpse, so if she didn't make it, it wouldn't be because I stood back and let her die.

I glanced up at her face. Her eyes looked more normal, and she was moving her arm again.

"Give me my son," she said.

"Just a minute, I have to make sure the bleeding is better."

I relaxed the pressure, and the blood continued at a trickle. Sighing, I grinned at Mary. "You did it. Mom." I turned and picked the baby up, putting him in her arms.

"He's perfect," she breathed.

"He has Pastor Tim's nose," I said, because it was true—I hadn't been sure what to make of her story about the doctor saying vasectomies could fail, but that baby had Tim McClatchy's nose as sure as grass is green. I looked closer. "And maybe his chin, too."

Mary grunted, shifting. "I told you, I never cheated on Tim. Not that he could say the same."

Her face crumpled, just for a second before she sniffled and smiled at baby David, and it hit me—she might have thought her husband weak, and she had even murdered him in what I was pretty sure now was cold blood—but she was also truly hurt that he'd been having an affair. Whether that was because she'd been thrown over for a man, simply because he'd wanted someone besides her, or because she actually loved him, I didn't know. But the anguish on her face when I mentioned him was real.

Humans are messy creatures.

Standing over a woman I'd thought of as a friend—even as family—watching her hold the baby she'd prayed for every day for over a decade, I felt that with my whole self.

Because once I knew she was going to be okay, I still had to turn her in to the police.

# FIFTY-THREE
## MARTHA

*January—Sunday*

"Pastor, ma'am, he is perfect," the town's lone trained EMT said, pulling one of the small blankets I'd brought down from the nursery tight around baby David and winking at me. "Nice work with the cord. I'm so sorry Pastor Tim wasn't here to see him."

"God will judge Tim McClatchy for his sins," Mary said, reclined in a chair with a clean nightgown on and a soft pillow under her backside. The medic had helped her get up and I had brought her fresh clothes. The last of something the ambulance crew called a banana bag was running through an IV into Mary's arm, and sitting there with the baby, I swear she actually glowed.

My eyes flicked to the door for the hundredth time since the rescue squad had come in, willing the cop to show up now, while there were other people here.

No such luck.

I turned back to Mary, smiling at the medic and his fireman driver while a voice in the back of my head asked how she could show this face to the world and do the horrible things she had done behind closed doors.

I didn't have an answer, but right then what I needed was to get through the next... however many hours until the cop showed up. Surely, he'd gotten called away on another case and he'd be here soon.

I wanted to believe that, at any rate.

"Do they need to go to the hospital?" I asked as the medic removed the IV from Mary's hand and started packing up.

"Not unless you want to," he said to her. "Your bleeding has slowed to normal, your vitals are fine, and the hospital is an hour away on bumpy roads. Women have babies at home all the time."

"You're not worried about all the blood she lost earlier?" I asked.

"It always looks like more than it is," he said. "Her pressure is normal. She's fine, and so is her little man."

"I'd rather stay home," Mary said. "Martha takes good care of me."

The men waved as they left, and I perched on the far arm of the ruined sofa, pointing to baby David. "Did he actually eat earlier?"

Mary's bright eyes lit up. "I think so. It feels so strange, but what a blessing to be able to make food for him, isn't it?"

"It's pretty cool," I agreed. "Do you want anything to eat?"

"I'd kill for a couple of slices of pizza," she said, wiggling her eyebrows and flashing a smile that made me cold in places that should never be cold.

"Coming up," was all I said, standing. "You'll be okay here alone? And you won't try to get up while I'm gone?"

She held up two fingers. "Swear to Heaven."

That sounded serious enough.

I got to Sergio's just as they were closing and sweet talked them into a large pepperoni by letting the staff be among the first to know the pastor's baby had arrived. They refused to take payment, which made Mary tear up when I got home.

"God bless that sweet family," she said, laughing through her tears. "My hormones are a wreck, Martha. Consider yourself warned."

"I think I can handle you."

I ate two slices myself and went upstairs to put the baby's basinet next to Mary's bed. I was more tired than I'd been in months, I couldn't imagine Mary wasn't exhausted.

When I had them both tucked in, I waved and crossed to the door. "Just holler if you need me."

"Martha," she called as I put my fingers on the light switch.

"What?" I turned back.

"Thank you for being my very best friend."

I smiled, swallowing hard. "It's my pleasure," I lied.

---

I'm still not sure what woke me up. Had I heard the baby fuss? Was the wind kicking up outside?

Did Mary make a noise as she crept into my room?

I opened my eyes at two fifty-six with the hair on my arms prickling. It took a couple of seconds for my sight to adjust to the darkness, but once I did, I bolted upright and screamed.

Mary stood at the foot of my bed, staring at me with a vacant smile—and a butcher knife in her hand.

In the next room, the baby started crying, probably because my scream startled him. Mary's eyes went to the bedroom door, and I pushed back with my legs, flinging myself into the headboard and flattening my back against it. "Mary? Are you okay?"

"I'm more than okay, Martha." She held the knife up in the moonlight. "I'm a mother."

"I'm so happy for you, truly." I tried to keep my voice calm, but the knife was awfully big, and her smile was anything but happy. "Do you need me to get you anything? Food? Water? Was the baby hungry?"

"My baby is perfect. He is my greatest gift from God." She flicked the tip of the knife with one fingernail, taking half a step around the edge of the bed with every word. I scooted myself into the high corner. "Which is why I have to make sure I protect him. Always."

I had just gotten one foot on the ground when she shrieked and launched herself at me, the knife high above her head.

It ripped through my sheets and into the mattress with a metal-on-metal squeal when it hit the springs as I landed in a heap on the floor, my ankle giving way with a gut-twisting crack.

"That didn't sound good," Mary said, sitting up on the bed and yanking her knife free.

"Have you lost your mind?" I choked out.

"I think you should ask," she huffed, crawling out of the covers as I scrambled backward on the floor, tears in my eyes from the pain in my ankle, "yourself that. I was blitzed, not out, you idiot. All those questions. Do you think I'm stupid? I didn't get here by being stupid, Martha. And you're not going to go run to the police with your story and cost me my son."

"I don't know what you're talking about," I shrieked.

"Liar!" She dove with the knife again as I shoved backward with my injured leg, screaming. The knife got stuck between floorboards.

"You know." Bent forward with her hair hanging in her face, Mary struggled to pull the knife free. "About all of it. The Dreamscape, the money, Lisa, Tim, and Sam. You aren't my friend. You're trying to take my son's mother from him." She got the knife loose and whirled on me. "So now you have to die. I've already promised God you'll be the last one."

I flipped to my hands and knees, crawling toward the door with my broken ankle dragging behind me.

"You're crazy," I blurted. Probably didn't help anything.

Her breathing grew more ragged with every step. I'd almost made it to the hallway before I realized I was crawling faster than she was walking.

"I am," she panted, "perfectly sane. I'm just practical. You're a threat to my freedom, and therefore a threat to my son. So was Tim. So was Sam. So were Charlotte and her nosy mother."

She bent at the waist, both hands, including the one holding the knife, going to her chest. "A good mother doesn't abide threats. I really liked you, Martha. But if I have to choose between your life and watching my David grow up, I choose us."

I had stopped crawling when she bent forward, but I grabbed the edge of the door and flung it wide, scrambling out into the hall. Her feet shuffled faster behind me, the knife bouncing off the wood doorframe with a clang.

"You'll never make it out of here," she said. "And who would believe you if you did? I'm the pastor, you hear me? I own this town! There's nothing you can do to me."

I felt the draft from her nightgown swishing behind my leg and panicked. I didn't see her raise the knife, but somehow I knew she had, all the same. Grabbing the top step with both hands and pushing with everything my legs had left to give, I flung myself down Mary McClatchy's grand staircase.

Breaking my neck would at least be quicker than getting stabbed to death.

Every bone I had hurt by the time I bounced to a stop at the bottom, cracking my skull on the baluster, my limbs twisted up like Granny's Gumby doll.

But I wasn't dead.

I looked back, spotting Mary halfway up the stairs, taking one at a time, all the color gone from her face, the knife hanging at her side.

Time to go.

Pulling in a deep breath and screaming over the baby's wails from upstairs, I turned over and crawled through pain that stole my breath, dragging myself toward the front door.

"I command you to stop in the name of God!" Mary screamed, the words fading like she ran out of air before the end.

I turned my head just in time to see her go completely still for a moment, her face slack, the knife dropping from her hand and bouncing down the steps, landing with its wide handle wedged against the thick rug, one side of the upturned blade resting against the bottom step.

She pitched forward in slow-motion, tumbling head over heels down the remaining stairs. Turning, I used the table in the foyer to pull myself to my feet, swallowing a scream when I put my right foot on the floor, but slightly amazed I could move everything else, given the situation.

I moved slowly to Mary, gasping when I saw the bright red puddle ebbing from underneath her torso.

She'd landed on the upturned knife. I wondered about the concept of divine intervention as I stood there, my eyes stuck on the tip, poking through her nightgown just below her shoulder. I probably could've dropped that exact knife down that staircase ten thousand times and maybe never had it land that way again, but I also couldn't say for sure she wasn't dead before she fell. Some medical issue after the baby, maybe? She'd looked awfully pale and out of it on the staircase, and something had to have made her fall. Might not have happened if she hadn't been trying to kill me.

One look at her empty, staring eyes and I was pretty sure she was dead.

With a knife in her back and me and a newborn in the house.

I couldn't be here. But I couldn't leave a helpless baby here alone, either.

I dragged myself up the stairs one at a time, grabbing an ace bandage out of the hall closet and sitting on Mary's bed to wrap my ankle tight.

In the closet, I found a sneaker of Pastor Tim's that fit over the bandage and put one of my own on my left foot before I went to the bassinet. I couldn't walk normally, exactly, but I'd live.

Which was more than I could say for most everyone else who'd spent more than a night in this house the past year.

I made shushing noises, but baby David had worked his arms out of the blanket and was cold, probably hungry, and downright furious.

"It's okay, little buddy. We're going to be okay."

I carried him downstairs one step at a time and laid him on the living room rug while I grabbed the car seat from the closet and a bottle and can of formula from the pantry where Mary had put everything after she'd sterilized the bottles twice last week. I made up a bottle of formula and hobbled back to the living room. It took a minute to figure out how to buckle the baby into the car seat—it didn't work with him wrapped up in the blanket, so I took that off, which was very offensive by the howl it earned me, and settled him and his giraffe pajamas into the seat, making sure I didn't pull the buckles too snug. Tucking the blankets around him before I lifted the carrier carefully, I snagged the diaper bag Mary had packed for the hospital and hurried to my car, juggling the baby and his stuff and the key, but not dropping anything.

The silence outside was flat and comforting, not so much as a hooting owl breaking the cold, still night.

I set the seat in the back and looped the belt through quick, then shoved everything else in the passenger seat and slid myself behind the wheel, starting the engine and backing out of the drive. My transmission locked up for the first time in months, shrieking one last time on Elias Lane. I paused for a final glance at number eighteen, and saw nothing perfect about it in the silver moonlight.

Pointing the vents to the back, I cranked the heat, turned in front of the church, and aimed the headlights west.

Baby David screamed again as I spotted the black pickup coming at us from the opposite direction. No idea what had taken so long, but it wasn't my business now. I'd done my part—everything was there for him to find, and Mary wasn't my problem anymore. I passed the truck and kept going until I made it to north Malvern, parking behind a lonely VFW hall and getting out to feed and diaper a baby who hadn't stopped screaming for seventy-nine miles.

David sucked the bottle down in four minutes and settled comfortably into his dry diaper, pressing his face against my chest, his tiny mouth falling open as he slept. I stroked his hair and cooed at him, then bundled him back into the car.

As I pulled out of the lot, I turned the radio on low and pressed on the gas. "I got you, little man. I'll make sure you're safe and warm and nobody ever hurts you. No monsters in this family—just you and me."

My hands shook as I said the words out loud. I didn't know what to do with a baby. But I'd done all right so far, hadn't I? I couldn't take him back—he'd come into the world with a hand lousier than even the one I'd been dealt. As far as I knew, both of his parents were dead, and even if I was wrong and Mary came to like the monster at the end of a horror movie back there, she was going to prison for a long time once that state policeman found the tape I'd made of her confession and the drugs under her sink.

With Pastor Tim's secret green checkbook and a stack of the Mississippi checks worth nearly thirty grand in my glovebox, I had real money—enough to get us fake papers and set up a life somewhere else, since I could fake his signature as well as Mary did. I'd stop and get cash at the first open banks we passed after sunup. With an ID for me and a birth certificate for the baby, I could take him to the doctor, and someday, register him for school. But not as David. I couldn't make us that easy to find. Just in case.

"This is my son." I tested the words out, glancing in the rearview. "Cory, after his great-grandmother—and the girl his momma used to be." Well. I was Corianna, like Granny, and her momma before her, who'd grown up in a little town in the Arkansas mountains that might have even been Whitney Falls, for all I knew. Her story was why I'd headed for the Ozarks in the first place. Who was I to say her spirit hadn't led me right where I needed to be to find my own little family?

I would miss so much about Whitney Falls, but we could make our own life anywhere we wanted. Together. Even if Mary survived and tried to find us, where would she look? Who would she look for?

I mean, the truth was, Martha didn't even exist outside Whitney Falls.

# A LETTER FROM LYNDEE

Dear Reader,

Thank you so much for coming along with me to Whitney Falls in reading *The Pastor's Wife*! I am so thankful every day that I get to go to my computer and create stories and characters, and readers like you make that possible. If you'd like to be the first to hear about my new releases, you can sign up using the link below:

*www.bookouture.com/lyndee-walker*

Martha and Mary lived in my head for nearly a decade before they found their way into a novel, and to me, these characters and this story are a testament to the powers of having friends who believe in you even when you don't, and of perseverance even when you're not sure where you're headed.

It started one January day when I had a novel on submission to publishers, and I was nervous and stressed and tired of checking my email every few minutes to see if my agent had heard from anyone. Chatting online with my friend Art Taylor, I said I was thinking of throwing in the towel. "What was so wrong with being a stay-at-home mom?" I typed. After all, I was still doing that, I had just added writing novels to the mix. And I had six published books—that was pretty good, wasn't it? My friend pointed out that there was certainly nothing wrong with being a full-time mom, but also (he's an English professor as well as a talented writer) that he thought I had let the stress rob me of the joy I'd always found in writing. "You just need to remember why it's fun," he wrote.

As I was mulling over that, my friend Shawn Cosby messaged me to ask if I wanted to join him and some of our other friends for a Noir at the Bar event (if you've never been to one, it's a crime fiction event where writers read their work live, usually held at a bar or pub). The caveat was that they wanted Valentine's Day themed material, and I had nothing that would work. I went upstairs to fold laundry and Martha popped into my head as I was working. I got my laptop, and a couple of hours later I had a 2,500-word short story that was the darkest, most twisted thing I'd ever written—and a giant smile on my face because it was so much fun. (No one ever believes this, they say I'm too nice to write such dark things. I say I get all the not-nice out on the page.) I messaged Shawn to say I was in for the event, and then messaged Art and said I'd found the fun in writing again. In the years since, I've read that story at events all over the U.S., from Seattle to Dallas to Raleigh, and I'm amazed every time at how the audience reacts. When I was approached about writing a psychological suspense novel—a new genre for me as a writer, though I love to read it—for Bookouture, I had just read the story at an event in Washington D.C., and started to wonder if the characters could carry a novel.

Over the next few months, my editor and I brainstormed about how to take the characters and their town and build a good psychological suspense story—one deeper and different than the short story, but preserving the voice and spots of dark humor.

I had more fun writing *The Pastor's Wife* than I've had with a book in many years—maybe ever, it's hard to say for sure—and I'm so thankful to my writer friends for encouraging me at the right moments, for every audience member who loved the short story, and for everyone who's read this book. I hope you enjoyed reading it as much as I enjoyed writing it, and I hope you'll enjoy the one I'm working to bring you next, as well.

With much affection,

LynDee

instagram.com/lyndeewalkerbooks
facebook.com/lyndeewalkerbooks

# ACKNOWLEDGMENTS

So much work from so many brilliant people goes into every novel, and I am so thankful for everyone who had a hand in bringing this one to readers.

My fabulous editor, Lydia Vassar-Smith, thank you so much for reaching out to me in the first place, for your kindness and patience, and for helping build Martha and Mary's story out into something so big and sinister. I loved working with you on this book and I learned so much, too!

My wonderful agent, John Talbot, my goodness this past year has been a rollercoaster. Thank you so much for always making yourself available to give advice—or to talk me down when I get stressed and overwhelmed—and for your calm, steady focus on what's best for my career.

I'm lucky to have intelligent experts in so many fields among my friends, and want to thank two of them for lending their expertise to this story: Dr. Monica Powers, I am so thankful being sports moms brought us together and made us friends, and very much appreciate your advice on this one! And Bruce Robert Coffin, my partner in crime on our least crime-driven books, many thanks again for lending your law enforcement experience to help me out here.

I also want to thank the entire editorial and publicity staff at Bookouture for being so kind and welcoming, and for your lovely words early on about this story and these women.

I would never get a book out the door if it weren't for my amazing family, y'all, so all my thanks as always to Justin and the littles for picking up slack around the house and making sure my deadlines get met, and especially on this one, to Justin and Avery for asking to read and giving me some confidence by loving what you read.

Last but never least, thank you readers, especially those who've followed my stories for years and kept buying books and leaving reviews and encouraging me to keep going. As always, any mistakes you may find are mine alone.

## PUBLISHING TEAM

**Turning a manuscript into a book requires the efforts of many people. The publishing team at Bookouture would like to acknowledge everyone who contributed to this publication.**

### Audio
Alba Proko
Melissa Tran
Sinead O'Connor

### Commercial
Lauren Morrissette
Hannah Richmond
Imogen Allport

### Cover design
Eileen Carey

### Data and analysis
Mark Alder
Mohamed Bussuri

### Editorial
Lydia Vassar-Smith
Imogen Allport

**Copyeditor**
Laura Gerrard

**Proofreader**
Jon Appleton

**Marketing**
Alex Crow
Melanie Price
Occy Carr
Cíara Rosney
Martyna Młynarska

**Operations and distribution**
Marina Valles
Stephanie Straub
Joe Morris

**Production**
Hannah Snetsinger
Mandy Kullar
Ria Clare
Nadia Michael

**Publicity**
Kim Nash
Noelle Holten
Jess Readett
Sarah Hardy

**Rights and contracts**
Peta Nightingale
Richard King
Saidah Graham